CELTIC CIRCLE

Forever

a novel by
Sherry Schubert

Published by Sunway Press
P.O. Box 5825
Twin Falls, Idaho 83303-5825
mcallistersh@yahoo.com

Cover design by Sherry Schubert McAllister

ISBN 978-0-9829563-8-0   (pbk)
ISBN 978-0-9829563-9-7 (ebook)

Dedicated
to
Mark & Molly

Embrace the uniqueness of your personal history.

I wish to acknowledge travel companion Sondra Ingalls
whose sharp eye for detail and discerning ear for dialect
helped shape this story's adventure abroad.

Books by Sherry Schubert
Puffin Island
Celtic Compass, Part I
Celtic Compass, Part II
Celtic Circle~for Better, for Worse
Celtic Circle~Forever

Celtic Circle
Forever

"...to have and to hold from this day forward..."

*Is it possible that vows are forever
with no time limit on them?*

Dearest Kirin,

This Celtic Circle is as ancient as my ancestors. The Celtic world turned on circles, from the shape of the earth, sun and moon, to time measuring seasons in a continuous cycle of days following on days, to natural rhythms like the tides or human breath moving in and out only to move in and out again. The three intersection points on the circle represent many triads.

First, the three worlds in the Celtic belief system: The underworld beneath the surface of the landscape where the fairy people dwell; the human world; and the supersensual world of the heavens where a warrior might walk again fully clad and pass through the thin space that separates his domain to spend time in either of the others.

Second, the phases of our existence through time—our states of being which cannot be imagined until one arrives there: the unknown, in the womb; the known, on earth; and the unknown, beyond our life on earth.

Third, the Celtic Trinity knot, so named by Christians to represent Father, Son, and Holy Spirit in their religion.

Fourth, the connection of one generation to the next from grandmother to mother to daughter. Pick your point on the circle. Another for your mother and the last for our daughter. Trace your path to Paula. That was your life as a sentient being in her belly. Trace the other path to our daughter. Your essence flows from your mother, through you to her and then to her daughter—our granddaughter who will then inhabit the space of her great-grandmother, and so on, until generation layered on generation continues around the circle. A father may pass his name to his descendants, but mothers provide a seamless passage to complete and continue a circle.

Finally, a Celtic Circle can represent the promises of a man to his wife: to love, honor, and protect her eternally as she weaves their thread through a complex knotwork of experience to connect them through all time. I promise to protect and guide you on your journey from this phase of your life to the next. Listen to the good fairies whispering from their world. Reach toward the heavenly world when you birth and baptize our children, assured that our souls entwined to shelter you now and will bring us together again.

Grá anois agus go deo, mo anam ċara.
Michael

Chapter 1

Depending on one's point of view, Michael Thomas O'Connell began life fifteen months after his father's violent death in Syria. The little baby inhaled his first breath nine months later, right on schedule, the day after his mother and father would have celebrated their fifth secret wedding anniversary with pledges to one another. His mother Kirin finally fulfilled hers—made shortly before their fated mission together two years earlier—to bear her husband Michael's children.

His father—as fathers do at important transitions in their sons' lives—warned the wee one that he would spend a period of time alone in a warm, secure world before passing into the next to be held and loved by his mother. After more time she, and then he and other family, would pass into his father's hands again to be sheltered beneath his wing eternally.

The adoring father advised his namesake that two conflicting forces would dominate the child's earthly life: the rigid traditional conservatism of his grandfather who bowed to the sacred word and his mother's ancient Celtic sensibility. Like the simple folk of old, she embraced the sacredness of all things in creation, the importance of community and hospitality, and the magic in signs and fairy whispers. *Listen with both ears*, the spirit cautioned, *and be guided by both influences, but do not feel compelled to follow either. Dedicate your life on earth to shepherding and protecting your mother and others you love in my stead. Remember that you are the product of the lives and loves of generations… of millennia… of ancestors whose choices through eons made your conception possible.*

The minuscule creature understood nothing of time, worlds, love or mother, of course, but as a sentient being, he detected change through feeling. He was content in the dark, watery world where he developed form and sensed stirrings in his soul like the vibrations of a harp—the instrument that would become central to his family's life. He learned to recognize beings outside his compact world not by their voices but by the quavers they created. One such was soft and soothing; another, less frequent, was slow and steady. On two occasions, harsh tremors intruded and his environment tightened around him, threatening his very survival—the first, when he was about the size of a plump little pea pod.

*   *   *

"Pregnant!" a plum-faced Thomas shouted. "Who is the rake? I'll strangle him with my bare hands!"

"I thought you looked a little… full, stepping out of your new swimming pool just now." Paula threw her arms around her daughter. "If you're happy, I'm happy. When?"

"Early October. A little girl."

Paula raised her eyebrows to match her smile. "Confirmed already?"

Kiri nodded shyly. "I can sense it, and I'm thrilled!"

Her stepfather/father-in-law was not. The stubborn seventy-year-old paced back and forth in the long, narrow garden at the rear of Kiri and Michael's modest house on Quincy Street. With his hands locked behind his back and his nose pointed to the ground, he was oblivious of the explosion of honeyed scents and vivid hues of scarlet tulips, yellow daffodils and blue bells surrounding him. He finally interrupted the women's shared delight. "I assume you know who the father is. Will he marry you before the baby arrives?"

Free-spirited Paula was aghast. "Thomas! How can you ask such a thing!"

Kiri laughed at his gruffness. "That won't be necessary. The baby is Michael's. Your son is the father. He's sending us a daughter." She opened her arms wide, expecting one of the family patriarch's signature bear hugs at the great news.

Eyes afire, he stepped back and raised a finger to her. "Don't toy with me! Michael is dead and in the ground. I mourn him everyday. His fathering your child is impossible!"

"Not in this day and age. It is 2014, you know." Kiri tucked wet strands of hair behind her ears. "He left me explicit wishes and the means to follow through. I thought you would be pleased knowing that Michael's line—and yours—will be perpetuated."

Torn between his desires and his teachings, Thomas tried to explain. "The Church opposes all technological interventions as mechanical adultery."

"Call it what you will." Kiri straightened her shoulders and set her jaw. "I can't believe you would reject a child born out of wedlock to someone dear in your family, so why do you have a problem with a married couple?"

Thomas did not like where this conversation was headed. Did Paula share their secret with her daughter? "Your choice deprives this child of its right to be born of a father and mother bound by marriage and the covenant of love."

Strong-willed Kiri defied her unyielding stepfather. "It will be. Michael and I were married twice, you might remember. What greater manifestation could there be of our 'covenant of love' than to have this child? You're talking in circles."

Thomas leaned in close enough for Kiri to feel the heat of his breath. "You don't understand. The child will be the result of a process in which others have intervened."

"Will the life that results be less human or deserving of love? Will her cousins treat her differently? Will her grandfather?"

Thomas' bushy eyebrows kept time with his words. "What you have done is morally unacceptable. It dissociates the procreative act from the sexual act—the spiritual from the biological."

"I truly believe Michael's spirit was present at the conception of this child and continues to infuse this house. Can you refute that?" She did not wait for a response. "I know *my* God will not forsake this child. Will yours?"

The determined man blustered. "But the burden of single motherhood...."

Her intense blue eyes squinted hard at him. "You're grasping, Thomas. I *will* have Michael's child... his daughter... whether you approve or not. He taught his nieces and nephews that if one cannot bear a burden alone, to call for help. You don't have to answer if you are so repulsed. I did what I had to do to keep my promise... to honor the commitments we made to one another. What do you want your grandchildren to learn from you—never to color outside the lines? Have you never in your life broken the rules?"

Flooded with guilt twice over—from conceiving a child with Paula that summer so long ago and from disguising his first wife's suicide as a natural death—the confused and battered man pulled out his handkerchief to wipe his furrowed forehead. "I'm sorry, Kirin. I cannot get past the fact that the child you carry was conceived contrary to natural and divine law."

"What do you expect me to do? Get rid of it!" The thirty-five-year-old widow flung her towel to the ground, darted through the gate and dove back into the pool, denying her mother an affectionate goodbye and Thomas, another opportunity to challenge her.

Her snappy retort pierced him like an ice pick to the heart and he grabbed for his chest. Paula clapped one hand over her mouth to stop a shriek. The other gripped her stomach. Neither could look the other in the eyes.

All of the calls Paula made to her daughter throughout the afternoon went unanswered. *Kiri closed the door on us again*, she thought as she drove her husband around the city and outlying areas.

Thomas, uncharacteristically quiet after such a row, did not trust himself behind the wheel when his mind was everywhere but on the route. He sat with his eyes closed and his fingers steepled under his chin, shaking his head. He finally directed her to St. Mary's for a visit with his favorite father.

Paula waited for him for what seemed hours and cemented her argument for her own position while she watched the minutes tick by. Nearly fifty years earlier, Thomas fathered a child out of wedlock—hers—during a summer romance on Puffin Island off the western coast. He never knew until they met again a few years ago and learned of its passing before its first breath. He mourned the loss of that first son as much as he did his last—Michael, her own daughter's legitimate husband for a mere three years. Sometimes the gracefully maturing woman felt that their unborn child bound them stronger than the prospect of a happy future together.

Thomas' balding head appeared at her window. "I'll drive now," he mouthed and opened the car door to step in, forcing his wife of four years to shift to the left. The rest of his words fell into his white beard in mumbles.

Paula broke the sudden, heavy silence. "Kiri is carrying my flesh and blood. I will not be alienated from my daughter again when she needs my love and encouragement. I ache every time I remember turning my back on her to support you after Michael was killed. This time I choose my daughter... and my first grandchild."

The man behind the wheel stared straight ahead through Dublin traffic.

Paula's fingers pulled at the fringed ends of her scarf. "I bite my tongue when I disagree with you on matters of doctrine, but I will not be silent this time. I don't know what Bishop Byrne told you, but I'm telling you. Doctrine has its place in our lives, but a mother has a place in her children's lives, too. This time, my place is with Kiri."

Thomas' scowl nearly cracked the rear view mirror as he tightened his white-knuckled grip on the steering wheel.

"You have a choice," Paula attempted to reason. "You can disavow this grandchild... alone... and never have influence on its life, or you can welcome it and guide it toward those beliefs you hold dear—*if* Kiri will ever allow you near her or her child after your shameful outburst today."

Thomas lurched to a stop in their drive and hurried to the front door without waiting for his wife.

Paula caught up to him as he entered. "I'm going back to Quincy Street now to try to undo the damage you've done. Please come with me. An apology from you may save us from heartache this time."

"Leave me alone!" was all he said as he climbed the stairs to their second-floor suite and, for the first time since he was a child in this Georgian family home, he slammed a door.

Paula answered with a slam of her own as she ran back to their car and sped away.

* * *

Henry Callaghan, Michael's closest friend and current team leader, arrived that early May afternoon for his regular Monday tea date at four. The tall, slim man sporting Darcy good looks and impeccable grooming worthy of a champion show dog looked forward to the weekly informal sessions Kiri called her personal therapist's house visit. He used them for a different purpose—to reel her in slowly to return to work for the network's extraction team. He was not alone.

The remnants of Michael's team took the grieving young woman under their wing to comfort and nurse in the days and weeks following their comrade's death. The quick and on the sly guys—Doyle, the congenial one with dark skin, thick black hair and an aggressive nature; Frank, the active one with darting eyes; Devin, the nondescript and contemplative one; and gorilla-man Gus, whose kind heart exceeded the span of his outstretched arms—resumed their companionable surveillance when she returned to Dublin after her year's mourning in Colorado. They enjoyed the brief minutes they shared with her, but an ulterior motive lay beneath every contact—to compel Kiri to remain in Ireland. The survival of their team and its funding depended on her loyal silence.

Today, the patient and supportive forty-three-year-old bachelor came to tea with a new idea—one that would keep Kiri on the payroll indefinitely. If she agreed, he would have good news for the guys when they gathered later at Ryan's Pub nearby to debrief following their return from the Ukraine. When Kiri did not answer by his third knock, Henry went looking. He discovered her towel on the ground beneath the wounded fir tree and was only slightly concerned until he heard frenzied splashing in her aquatic center's pool next door. Recalling her multiple suicide attempts over the last several months, he sprinted through the gate and found her swimming laps with Olympic ferocity. He grabbed her wrist when she reached out for the wall.

Her glazed eyes searched his face. "Henry, what are you doing here?" she asked between pants.

"This is our regular tea time. Remember? It's near four. How long have you been battering the water?"

"I started about two," she hollered over her shoulder as she pushed off for another lap.

Henry's brooding gray eyes tracked her progress as his feet followed alongside the pool to the opposite end. "Get out now. You're exhausted."

"Can't." She struggled to inhale deeply and started back.

Henry beat her to the shallow end and caught her again. "What triggered this marathon?"

She wrenched her arm away and shouted "Thomas!" before her hazelnut brown curls disappeared and her svelte body followed.

He jogged to the deep end and pulled her up. "What's the old boar done now?"

"He condemned me for being pregnant!" She whirled and shoved off, leaving an astounded Henry wiping chlorinated spray from his face.

"You? Pregnant?" the normally unflappable man shouted when she came up for air in the shallow end.

She rolled to her back to float the next length. "Yes, me. I'm carrying Michael's baby." She noted Henry's shock as he walked briskly along beside her. "Thomas is as angry as a wet rooster that I've breached conception etiquette since the baby's father was physically absent at the pinnacle moment. I thought the 'grandfather' would be overjoyed. Are you going to scold me too?" She flipped and disappeared underwater before she heard Henry's answer.

He grabbed her above the elbows and pulled her shoulders out of the water when she arrived at the near end. "Never, for choosing to have Michael's baby, but I'm scolding you good and hard now for jeopardizing it. Get out of the water!" She wrestled to break away from him. "I said, get out now or I'll pull the plug! Your lips are turning blue. You're shivering and breathing so hard because your body is screaming for oxygen. That little pea pod inside you is screeching for his mother to stop and be calm, but you can't hear its cry when you are so stressed yourself."

She blinked at him, disbelieving her ears when she heard the endearing term Michael frequently used for the child he hoped to father one day. "Why did you say 'pea pod' just now?"

Her handsome friend shrugged. "I don't know. It just popped into my head." He pulled Kiri's limp body from the water and helped her into the house. He swaddled her in a blanket as he often had during the past year and ordered her to lie on the floor and rest while he brewed tea with lemon and honey. "Let your mind focus on the grand adventure ahead of you." After forced silence in an atmosphere infused with the sweetness of herbal tea and compassion, she received a second command. "Throw on something decent. Four burly guys are waiting just up the road to shower you with heartfelt joy."

When Henry arrived at Ryan's Pub with Kiri, the rest of the guys were waiting with pints on the table, including her two-fingers glass. Gus led the hearty welcomes with an affectionate hug and signaled for a toast. Everyone raised a glass, but Kiri's did not touch her lips. "What's the matter, little lady? Don't you wish us good health?" Gus asked, with one arm still around her shoulders.

"I can't. I'm on lemon water only for the next few months." She lowered her eyes to study deep scratches on the polished oak table. "I'm expecting a baby."

He toppled his glass and spun her around until their nose tips nearly touched. "You're having a wee one?"

A delicate smile crossed her face when she nodded.

Gus's brows shot up to his hairline and his mouth dropped to his chest. "We're having a baby!" he shouted, nearly squeezing the life out of her. "We're having a baby!" The rest of the team, equally as shocked, joined in the gaiety and chanted "We're having a baby!" while pounding their glasses on the table. Any notion Kiri had of keeping her condition secret evaporated as the guys' wide-eyed joy infected the rest of the patrons in the pub who joined in the chant and added a jig-step until a voice in the back hollered, "Who's the father?"

All cheering ceased as the guys eyed one another. To their knowledge none of them were alone with Kiri for more than a few minutes each week since her return the previous October except when she favored each one with a birthday drive in Michael's custom sports car at the Raceleigh track. No baby-making was possible during those couple of hours each one struggled to keep the speedster on the road. All eyes turned on Henry as the only possible culprit.

He threw up his hands in defense and appealed to Kiri to save him.

"Michael. I'm carrying Michael's baby."

Wide eyes bulged into saucers and mouths plunked nearly to their waists when the men grasped the implication. Gus found his voice first. "Michael's having a baby! We're going to be uncles!" he shouted. Their merriment resumed as they alternated a swig of brew with a plan to "uncle" the little one. "I'll teach him to finesse a football." "I'll coach him in chess." "I'll carry him on my shoulders for trips to the zoo." "I'll advise him to dress smartly." "I'll help with schoolwork." "We'll take the little tyke camping… boating… driving… flying…" "Flying?" "Why not. One of us could learn how by the time he's old enough!"

Kiri hated to interrupt their fantasies, but she raised her hand to cut in. "He's not a boy. He's a girl. When Michael left me the Celtic circle, he wrote that we would have a daughter."

Stunned silence. Gus finally broke it. "Well, I guess I'll have to take charge since I know how to handle little girls because I have…."

"Eight sisters!" they shouted in unison, then continued their chatter.

"Bring the little mother some stew," Doyle waved to the barman. "Hold the shot of alcohol." He studied Kiri's face. "You're looking a little peaked this afternoon. What have you been up to?"

"I went for a swim in the new pool. I guess I overdid it," she admitted sheepishly.

"I'll say!" Henry's exclamation brought the group to attention. "She swam laps for two hours and nearly drowned from exhaustion."

Four pairs of eyes scowled at her and four pointed fingers wagged. "There will be no more of that," Frank said. "You will not compromise the health of *our* little niece! Now, eat up. Build your strength."

Henry commanded their attention again. "Kiri's near catastrophe this afternoon docs suggest an interesting proposition." All eyes turned his way. "We've talked about survival training for prospective hires and annual requalifying for you old guard. With a working pool next door to Kiri's house now, perhaps we could contract with her for time there. Save us begging from the private clubs around the city who ask why a news service needs to train in the water."

Devin picked up on his hint. "Actually, Kiri could run the training for us. Michael was our water expert, but she's not far behind, particularly in endurance. She's well qualified… and certified for the job. Doyle could handle the open water tests. A perfect solution." He leaned back in his chair, satisfied.

"I like it," Doyle added. "No one will question what we do at your place. Our vehicles are in and out all the time." He looked at Kiri who was baffled by how quickly the conversation got out of hand. "Will you do this for us?"

"I'll think about it," she replied nervously.

"Of course you'll take the job," Frank smirked. "You need the paycheck. You'll have two mouths to feed!"

At a nod from Henry, Doyle and Frank excused themselves before the others gathered to leave. "I say we make a quick pass by Kiri's now," Gus suggested. "We should check out what she has in mind for a nursery so we can fix it up just right before the little tyke... our dainty little girl... arrives. I have a sister who is a midwife," he added. "She'll tell us exactly what we need."

Devin rolled his eyes at the mere mention of Gus's sisters. "We can take another look at the pool, too. Make sure there's room for what we have in mind." He winked at the others as they walked out the door.

* * *

Thomas went straight to his safe to retrieve the report of Michael's fatal mission the instant he heard their car round the corner with more acceleration than necessary. Henry entrusted that file to him over a year ago with instructions that he open it only in case of emergency. Within minutes of receiving it, however, the anxious father had broken its seal and glanced through the written reports quickly. He discovered that his son's wife was an active member of Michael's team and witnessed his tragic death—a secret Thomas did not share with her mother. Somewhere in that file was another clue to Kirin's aberrant behavior now, he knew. No young woman... no person... could make the series of self-assured decisions she did—and hold fast to them—from the moment she brought her husband's body home.

With trembling hands, he read her report again and noticed how carefully she chose her words, giving up nothing specific. Initially, he had bypassed the videos, but now he plugged in the first USB drive and watched bits of news footage from a variety of sources. The second contained blurred images taken from moving vehicles, some with Michael and Kirin in them. The third revealed what, in a movie, would be the climactic death scene taken with Doyle's phone.

Over and over again, Thomas stared at his computer screen and strained to hear the litany of death wishes and promises traded by Michael and his wife until he knew them by heart. He looked past the gruesome scene into the implication of each one and recognized Kirin's relentless pursuit of their fulfillment. The words *everything you need* and *bear my children* rang in his ears when he realized Michael's hand guided her every decision. Tears rolled down the aging man's cheeks and pooled on his arthritic fingers. If Thomas charged Kirin with transgressions against nature and divine law, he must find his son guilty of the same... and he could not bear that.

His mind caromed from the spiritual to the biological, from religion to science, from past sins to present desires, like metal spheres in a pinball machine. *No mortal man is perfect. Children make mistakes and are forgiven. Parents are fallible. Some priests are proven fallible. The Pope, preeminent to my faith, stepped away from his flock.* His decision made, Thomas had second thoughts only for Paula. He absolutely could not share his discovery. He was double... no, triple honor-bound now to keep the mission's secrets. He replaced the classified items in the file and locked them away again. Satisfied that all were secure, he shuffled quietly to the bathroom, turned on the water, and barred the door.

Paula returned to the 19th century Georgian mansion feeling as old and dispirited as the building looked, her disappointment obvious from the tousled graying curls above her forehead to the trembling bare toes in her sandals. She dragged herself up the stairs longing to sink into the calming, lavender-scented suds of a soothing bath in her oversized tub but found the door locked and no sound coming from within. A wave of dread supplanted her disappointment as she twisted the knob frantically. "Thomas! Thomas!" she shouted, banging on the door. When it gave way, her gaping mouth replaced her fretful wrinkles. "My word, what have you done!"

He pulled her into the dim room lit only by a profusion of fragrant candles surrounding the bubbling soak she had imagined. "If a Pope can resign, a simple man can change his mind!"

He swamped Paula in a hug still robust for his advancing age. "You were wrong when you said this grandchild was *your* flesh and blood," he whispered in her ear. "He... she... is *our* flesh and blood. The only human being in *this* world created from both of us. Truly yours and mine." He pleaded with the smile that never failed to melt her. "Forgive me?"

"It's Kiri's forgiveness you need, not mine."

"Then, my peace offering can wait. Let's go to her now. I'll fall down on my rusty knees and ask her to forgive this rigid old man who wants nothing more at this moment than to welcome her child with an open heart and mind."

Paula gripped the collar of his bathrobe as a tear escaped her eye and dropped onto his bare chest. "We can't. The house is empty. She's gone. You drove Kiri away again."

*   *   *

Kiri's mind whirled on the drive back to Quincy Street. Only hours ago she was in the watery depths of despair and now her life seemed alive with new possibilities... a new purpose. She invited the men in to have a look upstairs—all of them since Frank and Doyle unexpectedly met up with the rest. She pointed them up the staircase that divided a common area on the west from the private area on the east and the upper family-only floor from the lower all-friends-welcome one. She led them to the empty room she and Michael called the stable, the one that once held the rocking horse, Dreamer, awaiting its tiny riders. A pang of remorse struck her when she realized how empty it was without the wooden steed she hurled out the window after Michael's death, carrying their dreams for a family with him.

The guys scratched their chins and pretended to make notes as if they were experts on children's nurseries. "Good morning light." "Needs fresh paint." "Some shelves and such to hold all the little... stuff."

Kiri chuckled to herself as she then led the way to the pool, unaware that Doyle and Frank lagged behind. Gus and Devin kept her engrossed in details about the facility whose construction they had monitored almost daily. The whole group reunited under the tree Aurora to say their farewells and repeat how ecstatic they were with her good news. On a count of three, they scooped her up in a chair and five manly faces crowded around her middle and five manly hands patted her tummy as one of them snapped a shot. "The best 'proof of life,' yet," they laughed. Henry winked at her and mouthed, "overjoyed."

She waved goodbye and returned to the house, all giddy inside. Michael had remodeled the turn-of-the-century, two-story plus attic home especially for her. He protected the north-facing front from standing out among others along their cobbled street, but he customized the interior by removing long hall walls both upstairs and down to allow natural light to splash in from the banks of windows along the entire south face. A fireplace in the living area down, and the sitting area up, commanded the center of each west wall in the two large, open and airy rooms. Her portrait of her husband hung above the fireplace in the living room painted in muted tones of the Irish landscape's greens. An empty space above the sitting room's fireplace awaited another moment of her creative inspiration. Furnishings were formal on the main floor and comfy in the family rooms. Her only concession to the modern was the video complex mounted below the sloping banister on the open staircase.

The home's unique features were two octagonal rooms reminiscent of Paula's Colorado house. The kitchen's bay windows jutted out to form a breakfast nook with a three-sided work area opposite. In her bedroom immediately above, three tall windows surrounded a small fireplace and were set perfectly to gather the sun's beams throughout the day and project them across the room onto the three walls opposite, muraled in mountains at the head of her bed quilted in wild flowers. Passageways formed the remaining two sides of each room. An octagonal skylight above her bed allowed Kiri to gaze upward, day or night, in the hope of a glimpse of Michael's soul hovering nearby. When disappointed by its absence, she took refuge in her large, custom-designed bathtub—the place where their daughter would enter this world.

On her way to her bedroom, she peeked into the stable to imagine what would soon take place there. She gasped when her eyes met Dreamer's soft, brown ones shining out from beneath his real horsehair forelock. She examined the antique toy closely and found well-glued fractures in his arched neck, sturdy legs and jaunty tail cleverly camouflaged with a new paint job. A note was attached to his mane: *We prayed you might want him to come home someday.* When she fell to her knees to hug him around the neck, she spied a single black feather resting on the saddle.

CHAPTER 2

Harsh vibrations interrupted the wee babe's tranquil world again some three months later, although he had no means of marking time. In the intervening period, he added new quavers to his memory bank, but his mother's remained relatively calm and steady… until this moment.

"Home birth! You are *not* having *my* grandchild in *this house.* Forget that silly notion!"

"It's not silly. It's what I want. It's what Michael would want—for his child to be born upstairs where his spirit still lingers. Our tub is perfect with temperature and motion controls. The baby will hardly know it has passed from one world to another."

"You're talking nonsense. You need doctors… nurses."

"I have a midwife. Gus's sister comes once a week to make sure I'm on track. She's very knowledgeable and…."

"A midwife! No grandchild of *mine* will be delivered by a *common* woman. Who is your doctor? I'll speak to him about this!" Thomas' arms flapped like an angry goose.

"Don't bother." Kiri plopped into a lawn chair like an obstinate adolescent. "I'll *have* this child my way and *raise* it my way without any interference from you! I can't believe your daughters allowed you to meddle when they were expecting."

"I didn't have to. They had husbands to steer them away from any foolishness. I'm assuming that role for you. Here." He handed her some clippers. "Come cut a few flowers with us. We're taking them to the graveyard in remembrance of Michael's birthday."

"No thank you. I have other plans."

"Like what? Sitting beneath this ridiculously disfigured fir tree twiddling your fingers? Come with us. You'll feel better."

No, Kiri thought. *I will not. I know what visiting that gravesite will do to me, and I'm trying hard not to fall into a dark place today.* "Sorry. I'm staying home."

"You dishonor Michael by pretending that his soul is beyond the need of prayer." He stomped to the flower garden and began to cut.

"Humor him, Kiri," Paula said, putting her arm around her daughter's shoulder. "He's upset today, as I know you are. Being with family will do you both good."

"You don't understand, Mom." Kiri's lower lip began to quiver.

"Come." She guided her daughter with a firm hand toward the car. Thomas followed with an armful of flowers.

Standing over Michael's gravesite with her head bowed did not do Kiri any good at all. She tried to remain positive and remember the happy times but when Thomas began a litany of sorrows, she felt herself lose control. He insisted they drive to the church to attend Mass together. She watched the older couple climb the steps arm in arm until they disappeared through the door. Then she bolted in the opposite direction and did not stop running until she was out of breath and had no idea where she was.

*   *   *

Henry wove in and out of slow-moving traffic, anxious to return to his office after putting Devin and Frank on a flight to Ukraine and Doyle and Gus on one to Iraq. Syrian chatter about grisly, barbarous actions contemplated by ISIS concerned him. As he pondered the dangers that journalists faced, especially independents with no company safety net, he welcomed the interruption of a phone call... until he recognized Kiri's blubbering. "I need help!"

He noted his location and glanced at his watch. "I'm on my way. Can you hold on for about twenty minutes?"

"I'll try," she wailed. "I can't make it stop! You told me not to get into the pool again when I'm upset. I can barely get a blanket around me, let alone roll up in one... and I shouldn't flop around on the floor trying. And I can't stop crying!"

"Cry all you want, but don't go near the pool or your cars. Unlock your door so I can get in. Then go upstairs and put on warm clothes."

She shouted into his ear. "I don't *fit* into any of my warm clothes! I don't *fit* in this house... in this dreary city... in this depressing life!"

"Yes, you do. Now go upstairs and layer your clothing. Keep your phone on and talk to me until I arrive. Do you understand?"

"I'll try," she sniffled.

Henry did not attempt to make sense of the jumble of words that followed as long as he could hear her voice. He exited the motorway to take a side route—less direct, but also less crowded. Despite the urgency in her voice, he felt a thrill. For the last few weeks since her return from July's camping trip to Colorado, she seemed distant—always pleasant but less willing to involve him in her daily ups and downs in favor of family. But today, when she desperately needed someone, Kiri called *him*.

Her attitude toward Henry and the rest of the guys changed the day he came for Monday tea as usual to discuss expectations for training security advisors for the network's cadre of foreign correspondents. Perhaps she could offer independent journalists a similar service on the side. He planned to introduce another idea—for her to take on trauma counseling and substitute communications assignments. A call from Meggie interrupted their conversation. The little niece wanted to know what to pack to go see the buffalo. Kiri tried to explain that there would be no trip to Colorado this summer... or any summer in the near future.

"But Uncle Michael *promised* he would take me! I'm eight now, so I'm the right age to go," she squealed loud enough for Henry to hear.

"I'm sorry your uncle cannot keep his promise. Some events are out of our control. You'll have to wait until your own family can take you."

"*You* are my family!" Meggie cried as she hung up.

Kiri, obviously flustered by the exchange, resumed her chat with Henry by filling his already full cup to overflowing. They both laughed; she, nervously.

Within minutes, Brendan raced up on his bike as if chased by a tornado. He screeched to a stop, dropped his two-wheeler in the drive, and removed his cap to spruce up his hair in the glare of the window. He noticed his aunt and Henry sitting under the tree, so he let himself in through the gate, strode up to them and sat very straight in a lawn chair to join the adult conversation.

"Aunt Kiri, can you help me explain to Meggie what I can't understand myself? Last summer, none of the cousins got to go to Yellowstone because Grandfather said you lived in a different town and could not get off work to take us. This summer, you are home and unemployed, so there should be no problem. Fíonna and Meggie are both eight and above and have never been, so they should get their turns. You need two helpers, of course, to hold their hands at the mud pots and keep them on the trails. Grace and I will volunteer for that job so you won't have to worry about the youngsters."

Kiri expected that suggestion the minute Brendan mentioned Yellowstone.

"Grace can also help with the camp cooking, and I can help with the tents. I think Uncle Michael would approve of your hiring Uncle Kurt to take his place this trip for the camping bit. Aunt Tanya would be good company for you if you don't feel up to the longer hikes. In fact, you might want to stay in a cabin while we kids camp. Fíonna and Meggie can't miss the barbecue and fireworks from Paula's deck either. That is a great tradition!"

Kiri and Henry could barely hide their laughter from the serious young man of fourteen trying so hard to lead his band of cousins responsibly. She pretended to blow her nose before she said, "You make some very good points, Brendan. I'll give your proposition some thought. What do you think, Henry?"

Henry remembered exactly what he thought that day under the tree. He thought Kiri was as lovely as he had seen her in months wearing the flush of impending motherhood on her face and her rich brown curls finding their way over her ears to frame it. He thought she should spend every Monday afternoon with him... and maybe some Tuesdays and Thursdays, also. Whole Saturdays would be wonderful. He thought that devoting more time to O'Connells would pull her further away from him. He thought that Kiri valued his opinion and that one word from him would scuttle the young man's scheme... or save it. "I think," he said slowly "that you should honor an important *Koyle* tradition."

He was right. Kiri agreed to the expedition, and when she returned she was less dependent on him, less sure of herself and more involved with the O'Connells. Meggie called almost daily to ask if she felt the baby kicking. Brendan biked over frequently to check on her, and Thomas visited every morning. Henry barely found uninterrupted time with her, except Monday afternoons and her unexpected call today.

During one of their now rare times alone together, she let slip that her brother scolded her for knowingly—intentionally—bringing a child into a single parent family. "What kind of selfishness is that? We know better than most what growing up with an absent father is like. Your child deserves a good male role model."

Kiri lowered her eyes as if embarrassed when she told Henry that she had assured her brother there were plenty of good men in her life eager to mentor her child. The implication of her statement warmed him, but Kurt's reaction upset him.

"You've got to cut the guys loose. They are good men, but they are still single adult males who put their lives on hold to support you for almost two years because they feel guilty. They deserve to be released to get on with their own lives."

Kiri had countered her brother. "The stepfamily is no help. Pious Thomas has such high standards, I'll never measure up. Tommy is so focused on his career that he can't see what he's doing to his eternally pregnant wife. Charles worries about his reputation and pleasing his wife, and Stephen has anger management issues. He dominates Emily. I can see in her eyes that she's afraid of him. Even with their own shortcomings, I'm an embarrassment to all of them. I can't count on their support. What other alternative do I have?"

"Me!" her brother had answered. "Move back to Denver. I'd love to play the role of favorite uncle to the little tykess. But what if you are wrong and you have a bouncing baby boy. Wouldn't that throw the family into chaos? Thomas would go berserk, and the stepsibs would string you up by your toes to shove the little guy back in for threatening to ruin their inheritance! Do it, Kiri. Come back to Denver."

Kiri laughed as she recounted this story to Henry. "I can't go back. Not yet. I believed my decision was well thought out, but after talking to Kurt I'm not so sure. I made my choice, and I have to live with it... for now."

Henry tried to find the humor in her brother's remarks, but he could not. He was appalled that Kiri would consider turning him and the rest of the team away or returning to Colorado, but he did not show his hurt... or his concern for her growing distance from the team's influence. He managed a fake smile and promised himself to tread carefully. And he did... until now when she called *him* for help.

He still heard Kiri whimpering into the phone when he pulled into her drive. He let himself in the kitchen door and followed her feeble cries upstairs, grabbing sofa blankets on the way. The outrageous sight that met him would have been laughable were it not so pitiful.

Kiri followed his directions and layered her clothing. She wore short socks over long socks, none of which matched. A full-length skirt, now reaching only to her knees in front, covered plaid, flannel pajama pants. She wore three layers on top: a sweatshirt, flannel shirt and T-shirt in that order, with the tight T on top, squeezing the others beneath it. A dismal attempt at a stunted ponytail poked from the side of her head as if she forced it while gripping her phone between her ear and shoulder. Every rejected clothing option littered the floor.

Without a word, Henry tenderly wrapped the pathetic clown in blankets and helped her to his car. He struggled to snap her into the seatbelt, unsure how to arrange it. He tilted her seat back slightly and stuffed her hands with tissues. Then he headed south along a coastal road. "A change of environment will do you good. I'll find us a safe place." South of Kilcoole he turned toward the sea and drove carefully onto an old fishing pier that jutted far beyond the shore. He opened all the windows to the invigorating salty air and grinding sounds of surf surrounding them. He cozied the blankets around her head before he asked, "What triggered this flood?"

Kiri's hand trembled as she wiped her nose. "Thomas. He forbade a home birth and forced me to stand over Michael's grave." She wiped her eyes and choked back a sob. "I could have handled one or the other today. I know I could. But not both... not on Michael's birthday. I did what you advised for anniversaries—anticipate them by scheduling positive acts to honor the event without dwelling on the sorrows. I did. I planned this one perfectly: sleep in so the day would seem short, eat a hearty breakfast, and walk to the teashop for a treat to celebrate the happiness it once held. I got fairy cake. The tea lady said it was a very old recipe that few could make anymore, but of course my cake ladies could."

She gazed wistfully out the window. "Michael would have enjoyed that—fairy cake. It would make him laugh. I brought some home to have with supper before an early to bed. I planned to spend the afternoon reading about home delivery under the fir tree and repeating the directions aloud in case Michael was listening. Thomas showed up to cut flowers for his son's grave and ordered me to go with. I knew I shouldn't. I tried to think positive. Bring the baby into the world with joy, not sorrow. But when Thomas got so gloomy, I did too. I started thinking about all the events Michael would miss—birthdays, smiles, steps, graduations—and couldn't hold my sorrow in, so I ran. Typical. I ran until I was so exhausted that I couldn't catch my breath."

"The baby? Should I take you to the doctor?"

She shook her head and rubbed her tummy. "She's fine, but I became disoriented—couldn't find my way. I wandered forever it seemed, and kept asking the way to Quincy Street, but not a soul knew where it was. It's like I live in an imaginary world. Finally, I asked for directions to the teashop. 'The only place in town to find good cakes anymore,' a kind man said."

She turned toward Henry with a puzzled look. "The strangest thing happened. One of the cake ladies stood outside the teashop waiting for me. She took me by the arm, led me home and fixed a huge pot of tea. When I turned to thank her, she was gone. I suddenly felt like a single grain of sand on the lip of a volcano, so tiny and insignificant that a mere wisp of wind controlled my fate... so alone... and confused... and incompetent. I didn't know where to turn, so I called you. Oh, Henry. I'm so afraid to be a mother. I can't even find my own way home!"

The floodgates opened again, and Henry was beside himself with worry over how to help her. She sobbed so hard and loud, she shrieked. The waves of tears surging down her contorted face tore him apart. Her sobs turned to gasps for air, and he feared for the baby's health. What to do? Her piercing cries grew more violent and her choking, more desperate. He reached across her to unlock the belt and tilt her seat all the way back when she nearly convulsed.

Stop the airflow long enough to return her breathing to normal. Instinctively, he pressed his lips hard against hers and held them there until the shock stopped her struggle. She jerked away, inhaled deeply and slapped him across the face so hard his head snapped back and he landed in his seat. Her wild animal eyes glazed over, she passed out and fell into a deep sleep.

His first thoughts were for mother and child. When her breathing became less labored, he smoothed her matted hair from her forehead and face and felt the pulse in her neck and wrist—racing but regular. He pulled the blankets away from her tummy and placed his hands there to gauge the baby's vitals—frequent but sporadic hard kicks, nothing so regular as contractions. He checked again. Mother—pulse slowing; baby—less active. He re-covered her but kept hold of her hand, ostensibly to track her pulse, and shuddered with the realization that he crossed a line with her—unintentionally—and she would never trust him again.

His second thoughts were of the kiss itself. He had no memory of how it felt or how she looked—if she looked—at him. Throughout his young adult years, and the women who shared them, he found intimacy elusive. Frequently, in the throes of passion, if he opened his eyes, he saw only the priest's frenzied caterpillar eyebrows gamboling in front of him, leaving him too disturbed—even sickened—to continue.

From the moment he first met Kiri at the castle some five years before, he imagined how divine she would feel in his arms, bodies and lips pressing against one another, but the threat of his mind conjuring a revolting illusion from beauty prevented him from envisioning further. The closest he came with Kiri was the dance they shared barely a year ago at the brewery. They were comfortable together, he was sure. They moved as one. The Presley song that played then urged him to offer his hand... his entire life to her without waiting for one perfect moment. Then it happened... tonight... and he had no memory of it. "Forgive me," he muttered. "I couldn't help myself."

"Couldn't help what, Henry?" Kiri smiled weakly and squeezed his hand.

CHAPTER 3

Little Michael Thomas, fully formed with all systems operational, listened to final words from his father. *Time for you to meet your mother, little pea pod. Love her enough for both of us.* Then the wee babe felt a soft push and passed joyously into his brand new life.

*   *   *

Startled by the birth of an unexpected boy child, Kiri lifted her newborn onto her chest, bent her head to touch his lips with her own, and blew gently to fill his lungs with his father's last breath. When she heard his soft coo, she smiled and sprinkled him with his father's spirit water, massaging each precious drop into his delicate skin and saving the last one for his tongue. After a tiny cough and another coo, she slid the two of them further into the body-temperature water of her tub until only their heads remained above its light undulations. "Thank you, Michael," she choked in a teary whisper, "for this beautiful son."

Midwife Maeve poked her head through the doorway. "You wouldn't be allowed to do that in a hospital now, would you, dear?"

Kiri shook her head and smiled her appreciation for those first moments alone with her baby.

"Made of fairy dust and angel wings, that one is," the kindly woman smiled back. "I'll go let the others know there's a new babe to fold into the family. You can have him for two more minutes. Then I'll come carry out all the necessaries that'll make him a healthy, official little Irishman."

She moved swiftly to the upstairs sitting room where the family awaited: Thomas, Paula and Brendan. After dealing with the grandfather who demanded to see his new grand*son now* and was refused, she moved to the landing to sprinkle a handful of blue confetti over the railing to the team waiting below. A stern finger to her lips signaled there would be no hoopla allowed until she said so, but that did not stop Devin from dashing out the door to the off-duty emergency response unit Thomas hired to stand by—Kiri's only concession to his list of demands for her home birth.

No one dared disobey the midwife's orders—not even Thomas. Gus's sister was a carbon copy of her brother—a gorilla of a woman with a head of thick curly black hair, prominent brow ridges, a broad chest and massive arms, and a bosom so generous even a grown man would smother in it. Her wide hips swung precariously near every knick and knack with each purposeful step she took, but she never toppled a one. Her bark caused even the fireplace stones to tremble, and her demeanor shouted, "*I am in charge!*" But when she presented a newborn, she had the gentlest touch, the lightest step, the sweetest voice, and more just-right places to cradle and tuck an infant than any mortal woman could imagine.

Kiri pointed to the blanket Paddy gave her just before she helped him settle his wife in a care center. "As soon as we got home from your wedding, my Maureen hunted up all the leftover scraps from your quilt and stitched them together for your first wee one. This is the last thing she ever put her hands to making," he had said sadly.

"A fine piece of work this is," Maeve said as she wrapped the bare baby up tight. "He looks just like a pup rolling in a flower garden, he does. Lay him down on your bed and you won't find him for a week." She glanced at Kiri lolling back in the warm water. "You're next. Don't fall asleep before I get back, and don't set one foot outside that tub. New mothers need as much tender care as their babes." She lifted the treasured package to her breast and carried him away to meet the vibrations that excited his fetal life.

Thomas waited at the door of the sitting room, face aglow and arms outstretched. "Put your flippers down, sir," Maeve whispered. "This little one is going to meet the guys down below. By ones and twos they've been here 'round the clock for the last week, and they deserve a gander. You'll have your turn."

She stopped Thomas' puffed-chest bluster. "Let me put it to you this way. You can hold him for one minute now or ten minutes later. Which will it be?" He stepped back and glared at the intimidating woman. "I thought so. Come with me, son." She nodded at Brendan. "You're here for a reason, I expect. Let's find out what that is."

The fourteen-year-old youngster followed the formidable figure down the stairs to the living room where she seated him in a chair beneath the portrait of his uncle. Five additional manly pairs of eyes stared down in awe as he cradled his arms to hold the precious bundle.

"There you go, lad. Now, what do you think of that?"

His adolescent face beamed. "I think he'll make a *fine* leader of our cousins."

Maeve surveyed the proud faces surrounding him. "No hard pokes, no loud noises, no bright lights," she whispered. She stood off and watched the men discover their gentle sides as they stroked the baby's cheeks, cupped a hand to rub his small head and held his tiny fingers. Even her burly brother kneeled to squeeze closer to the little guy. Frank brought a round of Irish whiskies so each could offer a proper blessing to the newborn and a toast to his father.

"Off with you, now, and take the lad too," she said, retrieving the bundle of baby. She pointed at Henry. "Except you. Sit. Stay." She shook a finger at them. "Remember. No visitors for three days. This little boy and his mother need time to get used to each other." She waved the guys out the door and turned to find Thomas peering over the railing at the top of the stairs... and his son staring at them all from his place on the wall.

When she reached the anxious grandfather, she placed the baby in Paula's arms and winked at her. "Men are so proud to pass along their names, but we women know it's the mothers and grandmothers who make that possible." She jerked her head toward Thomas. "You can let him have a turn, if you've a mind. I'll give you two until I've finished with Kiri." She bustled off, leaving Thomas dumbfounded.

Paula hugged the newborn to her chest and inhaled the sweet scent of her first grandchild. Then she laid him in her lap, unwrapped him and proceeded to count fingers and toes and to examine him for any imperfections like all mothers—and grandmothers—do. She found none. She bent to rub noses and listen for a coo, but Thomas grew impatient so she reswaddled the baby and handed him over.

Thomas' hands trembled as he took the child from her. For a moment he was unsure what to do. "I'm grandfather to sixteen... or is it seventeen now. I can't remember. And this is the first time I've held one so new— within minutes of his first breath. Usually, as you know, we wave to them through the glass in the hospital. I'm embarrassed to admit that Kirin was right about taking control of her own situation. This moment is priceless."

He sat on the sofa with his wife beside him and positioned the baby's head on his shoulder while he told the little one all about his father. Soon tears streamed down his cheeks, onto the baby's soft ones and then to his tiny lips. The wee one mouthed at the salty drops with a suckling motion.

"You promised Kiri, only joy today. No sorrow," Paula reminded him.

"Oh, my love. These are tears of the greatest joy. Despite Kirin's expectation of a daughter, I knew she would bring us a son—*our* grandson, Paula. The son of *our* son—yours and mine. I know it!"

"You are delirious!"

"Delirious with joy. When I opposed Michael and Kirin's marriage, I didn't realize that their children would bear pieces of us both in every cell of their bodies. This little one carries *our* genes in the same proportions as if our son were his father. No other individual in this world carries *our* DNA. Our hillside of sons is flourishing. Don't you see?"

"I see that you are crazy and have grasped at science now when you need it to support your absurd illusion. Don't you dare mention this ridiculous idea to Kiri, or she won't let you touch him again."

"God's hand is in the creation of this child. Our son was taken from us before a doctor's action would condemn his soul to eternal Hell. He returns to us now that we are able and prepared to accept him. My faith told me that our child was not lost to us forever. God *did* sanction our union, and I hold the embodiment in my hands."

"You hold Michael and Kiri's newborn in your hands, and best you loosen your grip on him before you squeeze him to death. I need to get you home and put some food in your stomach before your mind conjures up an entire village of Koyle-O'Connells. Heaven help us all if this innocent little boy should inherit your irrationality."

"If there is any question in your mind, just wait. His eyes will be the color of the sea."

"Shush, Thomas. Calm yourself or you'll disturb the baby."

"I know I'm right, Paula. These are not the ravings of a desperate, silly old man. This child is ours... the one I longed for... the first-born son of *our* son."

Midwife Maeve bustled into the room and addressed Paula. "Kiri needs her baby now, so will you take the little one in, ma'am? Spend a few minutes with your daughter if you'd like, but then it's time for you two to leave. Time for everyone to get some rest. You'll be allowed one visit per day for the next week, no more than an hour, and not before eleven."

Paula lifted her grandson gently from Thomas' arms and disappeared. Before he could open his mouth to protest that the last half-hour was not near enough time for him, the midwife thrust a sealed, official envelope into his hands.

"Kiri asked me to deliver this—proof positive that this baby is yours. She didn't examine this DNA profile or give it to you sooner because she didn't want *you* to be disappointed by the sex of the baby. Something to do with not fulfilling your expectations... but that won't be a problem now, will it?" She patted his arm in her first act of kindness toward the family patriarch. "A true son of a son you have there, sir. Given the circumstance, the good Lord has truly blessed you with this one. Love him well."

She hurried down to the kitchen to portion and label foods appropriate for the new mother and to brew a pot of tea. Henry watched her hustle past, afraid to move from his spot lest she tear into him for disobeying an order. He chuckled at the thought of Gus growing up as the only boy in a household of eight similar sisters. No wonder he was quick to act and could be counted on to follow directions to the letter. He would not have survived otherwise.

Henry's thoughts turned to the whispered conversation the guys had exchanged while waiting to meet the newborn. The team agreed that independent journalists were hard hit over recent months once the elusive snake ISIS reared its poisonous head. To a one, they had volunteered to go in—to try to reach their own contacts and gain intel on hostages—but were strictly forbidden. "We can't verify the reports we get, and building a picture by pieces takes too long. We must find a better way to place our own eyes and ears where they have a chance to stop this savagery on our brothers. Maybe Michael's little guy carries a secret from his dad." They sighed wishfully at one another.

"Damn social media!" Henry shouted and pounded his fist on the armchair.

"What's that you say, love?" Maeve hurried in and noted Henry's agitation. She patted his shoulder. "Nothing to worry about. Mother and baby are fine—or will be, once that grandfather takes his leave. Come in here and lend a hand, if you're in need of a stretch."

He jumped at the chance.

"In the absence of a man of the house," she said as she handed him bread to butter, "I've chosen *you* to watch through the night. You seem the most level-headed of the lot. Will that be a problem? Is there someone you need to call?"

Even if there had been, no man could refuse the glare of her eyes boring into his. For Henry, she proposed the best of all worlds—time alone with Kiri and her baby as they began a new life together... and he would be part of it. "Happy to oblige," he said.

"She wants her little one on her chest in the water in a quiet, dark room—to ease his transition, she says. I say that she needs two hours of sleep between times to keep from sinking to the bottom and to mind his skin and hers. She says she doesn't want him alone in a cradle just yet. I say she'll lose him in that big bed of hers, so you may have to hold and rock him while she sleeps. Think you can listen carefully when that baby is out of your sight and take care of him when he is in your hands?"

Henry thrilled at the proposition but replied with a very controlled, "I'll do my best."

"Good. Babies need closeness and warmth. That grandfather of his doesn't count on either score, so I leave that next-of-kin's job to you." She gave his arm a squeeze. "As soon as the grandparents depart, go above and turn the fire up and the lights down. Take the pot of tea and anything else you'd like. Settle yourself in the rocking chair and wait. Here's my number in case of emergency, but there won't be one. I'll return first thing in the morning. You seem a patient man, so I leave them in your hands." Maeve checked upstairs and down one more time before she followed Thomas and Paula out the door.

He ascended the stairs immediately but did *not* follow the midwife's directions to the letter. He called to Kiri to let her know he was available as needed. When he heard the hum of the tub in the background of her reply, he retrieved Michael's earwig from its hiding place of nearly two years and threw it into the fire. Kiri had earned her privacy.

Henry had no idea how long he waited before Kiri walked into the room with her baby wrapped first in an old flannel shirt of Michael's—a cuddle cloth, she called it, infused with his father's scent—and then in the wildflower blanket. "Do you mind?" she asked, handing him the bundle. "I didn't realize how tired I would be. A nap sounds really good right now." At his smile and nod, she flopped onto the sofa nearby. "I've waited months to sleep on my stomach again." Exhausted, she inched a blanket up to the middle of her back, turned her face toward the fire and let her left arm dangle to the floor. Before she could thank him, she fell asleep.

As a single man, Henry had never held a baby before. He laid the tiny boy in his lap and loosened his wrappings just enough to examine what a newborn looked like. He marveled at the fluttering eyelashes, the chest moving up and down evenly, fingernails fully grown and slight dents in his arms that defined where muscles would form. He tucked the covers back around the sleeping infant and shifted the babe gently to his shoulder until its head lay in the crook of his neck above his collarbone and the shoulders and trunk nestled in the hollow beneath it. He felt its warm breath against his neck and the tickle of its fuzzy head on his cheek and ear.

A perfect, innocent being with no shame or guilt yet on him. He leaned back, contented, and began to rock when he noticed Michael sitting on the floor beside Kiri with his hand near her head, but not touching it.

"She's lovely, isn't she, Henry?"

At first Henry thought he must be in the living room with Michael's face staring at him, but the portrait was not on the wall and Michael's form was across the room. "Yes," he answered. "She is."

"When I returned from Yemen such a mess, 'tis like this she lay every night with her arm dangling toward me on the floor. I took her hand, placed it over my heart, and literally felt strength flow from her body into mine—the best therapy for me at the time."

Certain he must be hallucinating, Henry thought to reach for his handkerchief to wipe his eyes, but he could not quite manage it without disturbing the baby.

"She'll be a good mother to our son… watch over him as she did me. He's beautiful too, isn't he?"

"Yes, he's a treasure." Henry thought to challenge the apparition. "Aren't you going to touch Kiri? To kiss her?"

"I mustn't. 'Twould confuse her. She doesn't understand the thin space between us yet. She would spend the rest of her life looking over her shoulder for me, and she can't do that now. She has our boy to raise. She pledged to me yesterday on our fifth anniversary that she would bring this child into the world with joy and not sorrow. I see by the serenity on her face that she has kept her pledge. Now I must allow her to move forward and keep herself mentally healthy."

Michael shifted slightly, permitting fire flickers to play on Kiri's face. "This next stretch will be a challenging one. I hate to see her go it alone. She needs friends nearby to keep her on track."

Henry blinked, but the vision was still there. "Any man would be honored."

"You put your life on hold for the last two years out of loyalty to me. Your kindness to my family will be rewarded in time."

Henry clutched the baby tighter. "I will watch over them as much... and as often as they allow. I rather like being a part of this little melodrama."

Michael crouched near the rocking chair. "You're a good man, Henry." Then he tilted his head near the tiny baby's. "A beautiful, beautiful son. I couldn't be more blessed." He blew a gentle puff into the wee one's nose that caused him to twitch and open his delicate mouth. Then the father blew a long soul-breath into his son.

Henry flinched and opened his eyes. Michael was gone... *if* he had ever been there. The baby had slipped almost to his waist, and Henry chided himself for dozing off. What would Kiri say? Best not to mention the incident at all, he decided. No point in confusing her when he was not sure what happened. He moved the baby to his shoulder again and began to rock. He glanced over at Kiri and noticed that she clutched an old circular ornament in her right hand and a black feather in her left. A tear in the corner of her eye dallied between joy and sorrow.

CHAPTER 4

Little Michael Thomas entered into the family certifiably O'Connell as evidenced by his DNA profile. Grandfather Thomas proudly displayed the proof to his assembled children and announced that all talk of little Michael's parentage, legitimacy and rights to inheritance should cease immediately. End of discussion.

Michael's siblings were aghast. Their brother's son would replace Brendan as head of his generation if Tommy did not have a son of his own. Eventually the half-Irish boy would become the patriarch O'Connell! After the shock wore off of what the baby's lineage meant to the family order, talk turned to circumventing age-old tradition. "I still say he's Henry's," Anne complained, "despite this report. Any lab assistant can make a mistake."

The little one's sixteen cousins had no problem adjusting to the change. Brendan announced that he would mentor the recent addition to the family and that the rest had a responsibility to see that the new baby was raised in a way their favorite uncle would want. "That includes love and support," he said, "just like he did for all of us."

The cousins were in and out of the house on Quincy Street on a regular basis to check up on the little boy's progress, play with him and join mother and child for walks around the neighborhood to inspect the enterprises she spawned. Meggie was especially taken with the little guy. "I have two younger brothers now, so I'm an expert on baby boys," she said.

When the question of baptism and godfathers came up, Kiri proposed a cadre of five of Michael's closest friends. Thomas objected vehemently. "They aren't family. We know nothing about them. We don't even know if they are believers in the faith." He countered with his oldest son Tommy. Kiri quashed that idea since he had a vested interest in supplanting her son with one of his own someday. They compromised with Brendan who was thrilled with the honor.

Publicly, the stepsiblings disregarded the little boy. Kiri rarely attended family occasions. When she did, they avoided uncomfortable interaction with her baby. They decided that the single mother was best left to her own little world on Quincy Street—the north side of the river. Privately, however, they, their children and the grandparents secretly hoped that since he was an O'Connell, he would be a replica of his father.

Michael Thomas disappointed everyone on that score. By the end of his first year when he did not sport his father's bulky frame, ginger curls and mischievous ways, they all had to admit that the little boy would become his own brand of O'Connell. His deep-set eyes, strong jaw line and hint of a cleft in his chin were Thomas.' His prominent cheekbones

26

and broad smile, dark wavy hair, long, lean body and mellow disposition were Paula's. And his eyes… his eyes were the color of the sea.

*   *   *

"One… two… three… blow!" five manly voices encouraged the boy. Little MT—as everyone except his grandfather now called him— mimicked them so well, the flame on the fat candle of his first birthday cake disappeared without a sputter. His eyes grew to paper plate size at the mighty effect he had on a natural force. When the men around him began to laugh, he waved his arms and chose from his limited vocabulary—ma, gampa, no and mo—the word "mo."

Devin looked at the others and humored the little boy by lighting the candle again. The men sang another "Happy Birthday" and shouted "one, two, three, blow!" MT puffed up his cheeks, spit out another burst of air and, much to his delight it happened again. He giggled, waved his arms and shouted, "mo!" After six repeats, the men were exhausted. "That little guy doesn't give up, does he?" Frank asked.

Doyle glanced at the portrait above the fireplace. "Did his father?"

"I'm starved. I say we eat this crazy thing you call a cake. Barely an appetizer, if you ask me," Gus said, reaching for a knife.

The crazy thing in the middle of the table was Kiri's concession to a birthday celebration she did not really condone—a single, plate-sized, whole-wheat blueberry pancake with a fat candle stub smooshed in its center. She had planned a quiet day with kisses and hugs, a few sips of Michael's spirit water and a three-way conversation under the fir tree between father and son with Kiri as the intermediary.

The nominal uncles disapproved. "A boy has got to have a proper cake and presents!" Frank suggested a compromise—a wholesome pancake, one for each year, stacked. "At sixteen, it will rise so tall, he'll need his first pint of black brew to hold the candle in the middle!" Kiri's eyebrows shot up until she realized the game would not last that long.

Over her objection, Devin proposed the same for presents—one appropriate boy toy for each year of age. "And at sixteen, that will make sixteen bottles!" After lengthy discussion, they showed up with a pint-sized, nerf-type soccer ball. Four of them took turns working MT's little feet, batting the ball in a game of keep-away from the others, while Frank created the first flat cake.

After paltry servings of pancake topped with fruit, Devin took the little guy for a wash-up and ride on the rocking horse Dreamer to calm him down. Kiri set out a manly meal for the five men, then relieved Devin to put her son down for a nap. On her return to the party, she walked in on a conversation that tightened every muscle in her body.

"That little guy is so much fun. It's a pity there's not more of him to go around."

"I agree. MT needs a brother… or a sister… or two or three."

"A family is barely a family with only one child. And with no father, it's hardly a family at all."

No one noticed Henry stare at his hands.

"Siblings should be born close together. They're better friends that way."

"When will Kiri get busy and grow us another? She looks so sexy when she's pregnant."

"I'll be first to camp out here whenever she needs help. I love this old place. Imagine tucking in a tyke or two like MT every night."

"I say she has one with each of us... I mean, *for* each of us." Doyle flushed at his slip of the tongue.

"I say the party's over," Kiri interrupted. "I thank you all for coming and making this day a happy one for my son, but I'm really tired now and would like to nap along with him. Do you mind?"

The guys were surprised at her polite, but abrupt, dismissal. She usually let them linger as long as they liked, even as she went about her business. "Did we do something...."

"No," she said with barely a smile. "You've been great today with MT. He loved playing with his 'uncles.' But I would like you all to go now." Frank headed for the kitchen to clean up, but she waved him off. "Please, just go."

The bewildered group made its way quietly out the door—all but Henry. "Kiri, if there is something we've said... done... please tell us so we can apologize. The guys didn't mean anything by...."

She gritted her teeth, then blurted out, "Who are you men to tell me when, how often and with whom to reproduce? Single motherhood is a hard lot, and I did not make that choice lightly. You all have been a great help, and I thank you for it. But I feel like you are living your lives vicariously through me... and especially my son. If you want comfortable homes, make them. If you want companionship, find it. If you want children, produce them. Find the courage to make a commitment. For men who would walk through fire for one another, you haven't the guts to fight for yourselves!"

Henry was astounded. "We had no idea you felt so..."

"My brother Kurt was right. You've put your lives on hold for me long enough. It's time to cut you loose to make plans of your own."

Henry stammered. "What can we do?"

"Show me that you can pursue your own desires, and I'll welcome you again with open arms. Now, go. Please."

Kiri shut the door firmly behind Henry and went straight to her room to gaze at the kaleidoscope of chalky clouds and golden leaves in the octagonal skylight above her head. She was hurt and angry, but she did not cry. She tried to think rationally. The guys were just overgrown boys themselves, having a good time after a little too much to drink. They probably talked like that frequently, but she did not want to hear it. Give everyone time to cool down; then she would apologize.

She glanced at her watch. Thomas and Paula were due to arrive in a couple of hours—another birthday concession. As the grandfather, he wanted to take his grandson out for an unaccompanied excursion—something simple, like feeding the ducks. "Surely you trust me with him by now," he had said.

Kiri did not like the idea. She was never separate from her son. Everywhere she went, she toted him along in his ergonomically designed frontal baby carrier. "His body next to mine is so comforting," she said to herself.

"Please, Kiri," Paula had said. "It would mean so much to Thomas. I'll go along to make sure he sticks to the plan, and I'll decorate MT's first cupcake like a duck. He'll be no trouble at all for an hour or so. After all, he is one year old. Time to start loosening the ties a bit."

At the appointed hour, MT was ready to go on his first solo expedition with the grandparents. Thomas stood patiently while Kiri adjusted the baby carrier to his bulky frame and explained how to secure the little boy once they arrived at the lake. She strapped her son and his car seat into the back of Thomas' vehicle and waved goodbye, surprised at how empty she felt.

After cleaning up the mess from the first party, Kiri went outside to sit under the tree Aurora. She stole a few minutes the previous evening to burn her sixth anniversary pledge to Michael once she heard his son sleeping soundly, but she did not have time for a real conversation then. The guys scuttled her plans for that chat earlier with their own agenda, so this was her first chance to try to communicate with him. She told him about all the little boy's quirks, how delightful he was, and how blessed she felt to have him in her life. When she looked up at the tree, she noticed a one-inch needled sprig sprouting from an old scar… with a black feather clinging to it.

Thomas returned triumphant. The outing was a huge success. "I think we two should make the duck pond a weekly date. Give you some time on your own. Michael Thomas didn't fuss a bit for the first time away from his mother. In fact, he seemed to enjoy it. He is such a precious little man, I can't wait until you have another just like him—a flock of little boys to feed a flock of ducks," he laughed.

Kiri hurriedly collected her equipment from the car, waved goodbye and put her tired little boy to bed. A cold, queasy feeling rumbled around in her stomach and started moving upward. She ran downstairs to the mudroom, opened the safe, and retrieved their passports. Luckily she obtained one for MT when she chaperoned another trip to Yellowstone in July for the latest crop of eight-year-old cousins. She grabbed a handful of cash, then relocked, replaced, and returned upstairs to pack their bags.

Neighbor Paddy scratched his chin and tipped his cap back. Seeing a taxi across the road at this time of night was unusual. If Kiri had someplace to go, there were plenty of cars around that day. Surely one of them could take her. He picked up Michael's binoculars from the windowsill to examine the doings more closely. When he saw the driver put two large bags and the baby's car seat in the boot of the taxi and all the lights go out in the house, he knew what was up. He would tell his Maureen when he visited her the next day at the care center—not that she would understand a word he said. Then he would hurry back to keep watch… for Kiri was on the run again.

Henry: Home to CO to reestablish priorities free from family, friends and work. No worries. Not running away from self; just searching for same. Will return when head once again on straight.

Kiri: Msg. rec'd. I'll be here when you need a lift home.

Mom: Do not attempt to contact me unless there's an emergency. MT and I are taking a time-out in CO. If Thomas needs something to do, he could run my cars once a week. Keys are in workbench in garage—third drawer down on right. Will contact you when I have something to report.

Kiri: Msg. rec'd. Thanks for giving Thomas a job. He's at wits' end without his favorite grandson to tote around. Not another word from me.

Henry: Please come to tea Monday, Oct. 19 at 4 as usual. Of course, that will necessitate a lift from the airport at 10. MT misses his Uncle Henry, as do I.

Kiri: Msg. rec'd. Car and uncle at the ready. Bring head, even if slightly atilt.

Mom: Please come to brunch after Mass on Sunday, Oct. 25.

Kiri: Msg. rec'd!

After her return to Dublin in mid October, Kiri considered how to approach the guys who were currently on a mission in central Africa. She left a message waiting for them. *Please come for a family Thanksgiving. Nov 26, 5 p.m. Feel free to bring a friend.* Devin did—a slip of a thing, bookish but pretty, who obviously adored him.

CHAPTER 5

Aurora Kathryn's journey from conception—some thirty-seven months after her father's death—to the moment she burst into life—the day after what would have been his thirty-eighth birthday—was the flip-side of her brother's. Michael Thomas spent his time developing in the womb content and relaxed in his small, dark world with only a couple of hiccups along the way. Aurora Kathryn was *not* content and *not* relaxed in her cramped, dark world and fought against its strictures almost daily. She was a little girl in a hurry to get on with life and tried to somersault, back-flip and karate her way to freedom.

*   *   *

Kiri hosted an informal holiday gathering for her friends just before Christmas. Devin brought his young woman, and Gus brought his sister Maeve the midwife. "She made me," he said with a roll of his eyeballs. The three who came solo trembled at the sight of her, but she proved to be quite spirited at a party. MT provided the entertainment, tippling and tottering his way from one to the next across the floor on his own two feet. His mother stumbled from appetizers to dinner to dessert in the same fashion, barely able to stay afoot and keep the few bites she consumed where she wanted them to stay.

Maeve met her in the kitchen while the others lounged in the living room. "Do you have an announcement to make, dear? What a Christmas delight that would be!"

Kiri shook her head. "Not for a couple more months. I'm not sure I can hang onto this one. I'm sick almost all day, every day."

The kindly midwife rubbed Kiri's back. "You'll be just fine. The first three months are the hardest. Tell you what. I'll bring you a special tea. Drink a quart a day with soda bread to settle you some. It's hard to find in these parts anymore, but I will and I'll bring it 'round when I do." When she arrived a few days later with the coveted blend, Kiri gave her a reference to the grocer at the top of the road. "Marvelous idea," Maeve said. "I'll see him on my way home."

In mid February, the team held an after-debriefing debriefing at Kiri's. To a one, they noticed how drawn and fatigued she was. "Is she sick?" "Working too hard?"

"She has a full schedule of clients at the aquatic center," Frank said. "The security training we heaped on her could be one straw too many. Maybe we should reduce her load for a while."

"We could try to find someone else to help us with communications. Our next mission to Africa is short and uncomplicated—a good opportunity to train. Anybody know anybody?" Doyle asked.

"How about your friend, Devin?" Henry suggested. "Is she any good with a computer?"

"I'm embarrassed to admit that she can work circles around me," Devin replied. "With you and Kiri to teach her the rest, I'm sure she could handle the job. Maybe work out of here evenings for that trip so the two women could keep an eye on each other."

"Sounds like a possibility," Henry said. "But would it become an uncomfortable situation for you... mixing work with after work? Would she even be interested?"

Devin flushed and lowered his eyes. "She'd jump at the chance."

"We should probably ask Kiri how she feels about sharing the job before we make a decision. Where is she anyway?" Henry asked.

"We'll find her, won't we MT?" Gus raised the little boy over his head to ride on his shoulders on a search for the missing mother. They returned moments later. "She's fast asleep upstairs in the rocker—worn out, with worry creases fluttering across her face. I'll put this little guy to bed. They'll be fine if we let ourselves out when we're finished."

*   *   *

Brendan and Grace, the oldest of the cousins, approached Kiri in early April about hosting a party on the upper floor of her aquacenter to celebrate their sixteenth birthdays with friends—not cousins. She was reluctant to make a long-term commitment because she felt so lousy, but every problem she posed, they countered—parental approval, chaperones, clean up before and after, refreshments, music and all the "no's"—no smoking, alcohol, drugs, electronics or videos inside the party itself and the most important, no permission = no admission for all guests.

"Aunt Kiri," they complained. "You have to be kidding."

"Those are my conditions. You come up with a plan, and you can stage your party."

The teenagers presented a proposal. Kiri approved. Party night arrived along with thirty guests, and chaperones took their stations—Doyle and Gus on the doors to check for contraband, Devin and his friend to mingle with guys and gals and monitor the lighting, Frank to keep his eye on the food and the alcoholic content tester in the punch, and Henry to oversee all. After the final departure and wave goodbye, Henry reported to Kiri.

"The kids loved it. They were great. No problems, but it was an eye-opener to how teens conduct themselves these days. So different from when I was their age some thirty years ago."

Kiri chuckled. "We are getting older, aren't we? MT is closer in age to them than we are. I wish I could have watched like a fly on the wall."

"Next year we'll hook up a video feed so you can."

"Next year!"

"Oh, yes. They plan to make this springtime frolic an annual event. I can't say much for their music, but they did throw in a few oldies, to humor us I suppose." He smiled at Kiri and took her hand. "Let's go have a dance."

She hesitated. "MT…."

"We'll bundle him up and take him with us. The oldies I have in mind won't bother him a bit. The clean up crew doesn't come in until tomorrow after Mass, so you can enjoy the decorations and leftovers as well." He winked at her. "Come on. You deserve some fun."

They wrapped the little boy in some blankets and cozied him in a corner of the large room with polished wood floor where Paula attended a yoga group. That night, decorated with flowering plants and twinkle lights reminiscent of Kiri's own school days, it was perfect for dancing. While he programmed a series of slow tunes suitable for the two of them, she soaked in the ambience and sipped some punch.

Henry pulled her into a dance hold and then closer. She settled against him, happy to be in a man's arms again. "I haven't danced in almost two years," she said, "since the brewery. This is very nice. Thank you for suggesting it."

"My pleasure," he said. *You challenged us to find the guts to make a commitment and I'm trying.* "My pleasure." They danced through another and then another. Her arms reached around his neck; his arms, around her back. She snuggled against his chest. He rested his head on top of hers, afraid to close his eyes… afraid to open them. *I'm trying.* A familiar song came up… the Presley song… causing him to ask if they were meant for each other. He placed one hand on her lower back and clutched her as tightly as he dared.

"Oh!" he cried softly and jerked away when he felt a jab near the part of a guy where it really hurts. For an instant he thought that Kiri punched him for being so bold, but both of her arms were still clasped around his neck. "Sorry," he said, noting her startled look. "I must have stepped wrong." He pulled her close again and felt her ease in against him.

Two quick jabs caught him off guard. "Oh! I'm sorry." He pushed her to arm's length and looked her up and down. "That's you, isn't it? You're…."

She smiled coyly. "Yes, Henry. I am… and you're the first to know. The wee one inside me wants to dance with you too, I guess."

"I… I had no idea," he stammered. "I… I'm thrilled." The refrain in his head hinted that it was sinful to stay and charm a woman who carried another man's baby. Henry danced two steps forward and one step back on the long road to commitment.

*   *   *

Stepsisters Anne, Meghan and Emily and their sister-in-law Margaret gathered at Kiri's pool for the last day of swimming lessons—test day.

Meghan had no reason to be there because Michael taught her boys a few years earlier, but the chance to see Kiri for the first time since Thomas announced her pregnancy was too good to pass up. The recently remarried forty-two-year-old woman had plenty to chat about with her sisters, particularly the aquacenter which none of them had visited. The others were happy to be there without their little ones, for Paula agreed to entertain them during this important afternoon.

Kiri was uncomfortable with the whole situation. She did not want to give swimming lessons in her condition, but Brendan and Grace made a good case for the cousins.

"There are six of them now who are old enough but haven't been taught. Since Grandfather stopped sailing, our parents think lessons aren't necessary. You said that everyone should know how to swim in case of emergency, and for fun and exercise." The two of them also agreed to help. Kiri considered their proposition and decided that a two-week session met two of Michael's criteria for mentoring O'Connell offspring: keeping them safe and bringing them joy.

For the most part, the daily sessions went well. The children behaved, and MT splashed around in a shallow area she converted especially for little people. Brendan and Grace swam lengths with the younger ones as they practiced their strokes, while Kiri sat on the edge to rest. With barely six weeks to go before the birth, she took breaks often. The highlight of every session was the end when the children treaded water. Kiri lay back to float in the center of their circle with her whale of a baby bump above the surface. As the swimmers kept their arms and legs in constant motion, they counted her baby's kicks made noticeable by the sun glistening on her wet suit. Time passed so quickly, they were surprised when she called an end to the exercise.

Kiri particularly did not want to be on parade for the stepsisters who had not been to her house since the day of the funeral. They would watch her and talk behind their hands about her, for sure, while she tried to keep her attention on their children. They might even invite themselves into the house to snoop, and she would not be free to follow to prevent Anne from swiping another keepsake that caught her eye. She sent notes home about testing day and hoped they would not come, but there they were—four of them—lounging in deck chairs with their feet up and their faces turned to the sun.

Testing began with Brendan and Grace noticeably absent. They were not allowed to coach the students; that would not be fair. They planned to show up for the party after. The swimmers waved to their mothers, deep in conversation, and then they jumped in all smiles.

"Did you notice how this neighborhood is improving? The gardens seem neater and the houses have fresh coats of paint," Meghan said.

"That's not saying much for an old section of town north of the river." Anne inspected her nails.

"I noticed some new shops up at the top of the road as we turned down," Emily said.

"Tommy says that Kiri has her hands in some of them. Apparently, Thomas comes twice a week when Paula has yoga. He takes MT for a stroll and chats with the folks up and down the road to make sure the neighborhood is safe and friendly for his grandson. They often stop at one of the shops to pick up a treat and never have to pay for it because 'MT is a favorite around here.'" Margaret mimicked the grocer.

"You don't suppose Father supports her enterprises. That isn't right," Emily said.

Meghan, the only one without children there and the only one who glanced periodically at their progress, disagreed. "Kiri wouldn't allow him to, even if he offered. She is determined to support herself and her family."

"Family? What is she thinking—having another baby without a husband?" Anne asked.

"Probably that she wants another baby before she gets too much older." If the sisters had taken notice, they would have seen the yearning in Meghan's eyes.

"But still, no husband. Why hasn't she married Henry? It's not like he wouldn't be willing to make their relationship 'honest,'" Emily said.

Anne raised her eyebrows and smiled slyly. "That brings up an interesting question. Who do you think the father is this time? Could this be a Colorado accident?"

Meghan disagreed again. She did not display contempt for Kiri like the others. She liked her. So did Emily and Margaret but with Anne present, they dared not show it. "Believe me, Kiri's pregnancy is no accident. She wouldn't let that happen. She knows exactly what she's doing—even if it seems crazy to the rest of us. I think she's brave."

"Another baby is probably just a ploy to get more of Father's money. She's no fool. She'll get twice as much with two children as with one." Anne sat further back in her chair, self-satisfied.

"Look at MT, splashing around in the water as if he knows how to swim. Can you imagine him as head of our family?" Three of the four women tittered at the little boy.

"So, who do you think the father is? My bet's on Henry."

"Henry."

"Henry."

"Michael, absolutely… and I'm sure she'll prove it." Meghan ended that discussion.

Meanwhile, the young swimmers completed their stroke testing and circled up in deep water for endurance treading—ten minutes. Kiri refused to float in the center. "In an emergency, you won't have me to laugh at," she joked. She stood on the edge of the pool to keep time.

About halfway through, Meggie, chunkier than the rest, began to flounder and gulped in a mouthful of water. Her eyes covered her entire face and she panicked, sinking beneath the surface. Instantly, Kiri dove into the water and came up beneath the little girl, holding her aloft in a float with the tip of her finger at the balance point. She treaded water with the others until Meggie righted herself, and she stayed beside to poke her with reminders to straighten her spine for the duration of the test. When she called time and announced that they all passed, the kiddies cheered, high-fived one another and raced to the end of the pool.

Exhausted, Kiri floated behind and pulled herself from the water while the mothers threw towels around their children to hurry them home despite protests that they earned a party. Not one "good job" or "you did great" issued from the stepsisters' mouths, and not one word of appreciation or thanks was directed at Kiri who stood dripping as she waved goodbye. The only comment she overheard was Anne's. "I can't believe how gigantic Kiri is. None of us allowed ourselves to grow so big!"

Brendan and Grace pulled up on their bikes only moments later and found Kiri on her hands and knees near MT, still splashing happily in his section of the pool. "Aunt Kiri! What happened?" Grace tried to help her aunt up.

"I'm fine. Call Paula and tell her to have ice cream and cookies ready when your mothers stop to pick up the little ones. The swimmers didn't have time to stay, but they deserve a party." She stopped for a deep breath. "As do you two. You did a great job helping them. Thank you so much. Now hurry. If you pedal fast enough, you might get in on some treats too." She tried to smile.

They departed immediately, unsure if they should be worried.

Henry arrived about fifteen minutes later and found her in the same spot. "My God, Kiri! What happened? Brendan called to say I should look in on you because you were so tired. When he said you were by the pool, I thought.... Well, you know what I thought." He tried to roll her onto her side, but she resisted.

"Don't worry. I couldn't run away if I wanted to. And I can't swim another stroke. This is the most comfortable position I've found. I've considered floating on my stomach with a snorkel, but I have to watch MT."

"Can I help you inside to lie down?"

"Lying on my back is a killer. I can't breathe. Ditto for on my side. I wish someone would cut a belly-sized hole in a hammock and rock me in the breeze face down."

"I can't very well do that. How about sitting in a lounge chair?"

She shook her head. "Too far away from MT."

Henry coaxed the little boy out of the water, wrapped him in a towel and walked him over to the lounger. Then he did the same for the mother.

He scrounged in the cooler for a couple of juices and found the plate of party biscuits. He pulled up a deck chair to face her and lifted MT onto his lap. When he turned back to Kiri, he noticed a few tears—not the huge blobby kind but the tiny trickly kind.

"I don't understand what's wrong. The doctor says the baby is healthy, just really big and really active." She took Henry's hand and placed it on her tummy. "Who can get any rest with that going on?" She took a deep breath. *...more than you can bear... call for help.* "I need help. I'm so tired... so tired." She closed her eyes and fell asleep.

Henry looked down at the little boy curled in his lap. He did not move for fear of waking him or his mother, so he counted kicks. Since Kiri's episode with MT, he made it his business to research the acceptable range for activity and knew that a jolt every couple of minutes was normal. This little tyke was overdoing it, dancing on all fours. He rubbed gently and spoke softly, encouraging it to calm down and let its mother rest.

He marveled at how connected he felt to the three people around him. Kiri's hand was still on top of his, and together they massaged the new baby. His other arm supported MT whose foot tucked itself into his mother's free hand. He realized what he was searching for—a connection. He yearned to belong, to have someone to share his story with. As MT and Kiri slept, Henry opened his heart to the little being inside her tummy. Secrets hidden deep within him spilled out, and each one he whispered brought calm to him and the new baby whose jerks and jabs subsided.

He recounted the night that his papa did not return to play with him. "I still feel the pain of abandonment," he admitted. He and his mother were spirited away by three men who drove them to a heavily Catholic town in the Midlands and placed them in a small house near the church where she began work as a cook. He spent hours in and around that church—first helping his mother in the kitchen and later cleaning up and running errands for the staff. He heard constantly that he was "a good lad, a beautiful boy" and was proud that he did not disappoint his mother.

Then "it" happened—once, twice, he lost count—until his mother walked in on the priest toying with her pride and joy. She stood up to threats of the church fathers and exacted promises for her silence and that of her son. She demanded modest housing in a safe Dublin neighborhood where they could fade into the crowds, a guaranteed job to support their health and well being, and a decent education through college graduation for her son—the only pathway to respectability for him, she thought.

He and his mother kept to themselves in Dublin. He grew to a lanky adolescent, all arms and legs, and took up sports—not because he liked them, but for an identity as part of a team. His tall, slender build gave him an advantage in some positions over heftier fellows, so his classmates sought him out. He enjoyed the camaraderie but was careful to guard the story of his young life—a shame he still could not shake off.

Learning became his other passion. He dove into studies of history, government and later, law. Many destined for managerial positions in a family business or government coveted his analytical mind, but they were too lazy for the grindstone dedication required to achieve one. He received numerous job offers at the culmination of his schooling, but the bright young man surprised everyone by choosing journalism—a legitimate channel for seeking the truth and exposing it... for finding a connection, a personal history.

Henry basked in the serenity of the present moment, marveling at how his torment subsided just like the new baby's when he was in this place with Kiri. *I am not worthy of such bliss, I know, but if the sun set on my life this instant, I would die a happy man.*

*   *   *

Kiri watched her almost two-year-old son playing at her feet under the fir tree in her back garden. She promised herself to feel only joy and no sorrow on this, her husband's thirty-eighth birthday. She picked at the slice of fairy cake one of the neighbor ladies brought and reminded herself how truly blessed she was.

Once she admitted that she needed help, aid miraculously descended on her from all corners. Paddy trekked up and down the road, binoculars around his neck as if he were on a mission. Kiri found a bag at her back door every morning containing small portions of fresh baked bread, milk, eggs, fresh fruits and vegetables, a thick slice of cheese and a treat for MT. Maeve checked her daily and canvassed her therapy clients to determine whose sessions could be reduced to once a week. She knew someone who could help with the adaptive aquatics patients... a sister.

The guys called off security training indefinitely. Thomas and Paula spent more time with MT while Kiri rested or floated on her stomach with a snorkel, allowing the new baby to hang suspended rather than push against her organs. A light supper always awaited her when they left. The five nieces and nephews who were teens rotated overnights preparing MT for bed, sleeping in a bag on the floor of his room and fixing his breakfast—8 p.m. to 8 a.m.

"It will be fun," they said. "Just like camping. School is out, so we can text our friends and watch movies as late as we want, and since we know how to cook pancakes over a campfire, we can manage pancakes in a kitchen."

"Who gave you this crazy idea?" Kiri asked. "Your grandfather?"

"No," they giggled. "The fairies did."

Henry visited every evening and set her up in a recliner upstairs where she slept now. He readjusted it frequently for maximum comfort given the baby's constant shifting. He stocked tea and biscuits nearby and chatted with her until she fell asleep. Then he stayed a while longer to speak in calm, even tones to the little person who caused all this turmoil in their lives.

The doctor tried to convince Kiri to rethink a home birth for this broad-shouldered brick of a baby, but she convinced him that she and Maeve were well prepared, she was being pampered to death, and that Thomas already had the emergency medics lined up.

Yes, she was very fortunate and thankful for the support. Kiri marked the days off on her calendar—ten to go. She reached down to tousle MT's fine, dark-chocolate hair and felt a sudden stabbing pain.

Brendan arrived for his overnight shift to find the road lined with cars and an emergency vehicle. Paddy came out from his house shaking his head. "Grave doings… grave doings," he said. "Folks have been in and out all afternoon and evening. You let me know if there's anything I can do, will you, son?" Brendan nodded and ran into the house.

He waved to the five guys in the living room, worry playing all over their faces, then he took the stairs by twos to find Thomas and Paula in the sitting room with MT clinging to his grandmother. He picked up the little lad. "What's happening?"

"Nothing!" Thomas shouted gruffly. "Absolutely nothing. Your poor aunt has been at it since noon, and she's no closer to having that baby than I am!"

Brendan listened to the agonizing sounds that made MT so fretful and decided the best plan was to get them both out from underfoot. A little boy should not hear his mother in pain. He carried MT to his room, rolled a couple of toys into the sleeping bag, grabbed some snacks from the kitchen on his way out and announced, "We're going camping in the aquacenter. Call me when there's news." Some four hours later he still had not heard a word.

Thomas was worn out by the ordeal. Fatigue and perspiration marked his face. While he tramped up and down the long room impatiently waiting for the birth of his nineteenth grandchild, Paula remained very still and very silent, her nails biting into the flesh of her hands. Uncharacteristically, the guys downstairs exchanged very little banter. Maeve's large frame scurried from room to room, but the woman's face did not reveal the seriousness of the situation. The medics outside the house waited for her call.

"This torment has gone on long enough. Where is a doctor? I'm calling in the medics!" Thomas shouted as Maeve bustled through.

"*You* will not do anything, sir, other than lower your voice and soften your tone. Your ranting will frighten that baby right back to where he comes from. Patience is what's called for tonight… and quiet."

That quiet was interrupted by a piercing cry. "Miii…chael!"

Maeve ran to her instantly. "What is it, dear? What can I get for you?"

39

"Get me Michael! Now!"

The kindly midwife tried to put her arm around the shoulders of the exhausted mother, but they were too deep into the warm water of her tub. "You know that's impossible." She wiped Kiri's face with a damp cloth. "Let me have another listen and feel of the baby. See if he's shifted any." She shook her head. "No change, but he's still strong."

Kiri cried out again. "I need Michael! I need to talk to Michael! Bring him to me!"

Maeve darted from the room to report to the grandparents. "She's nearly worn out, poor thing, but the baby's vitals are fine. He's just lodged in so tight, he can't make much progress." Before Thomas could fuss further, she hurried downstairs to relay the same message to the guys below. "She keeps calling for Michael. I can ease a lot of the pain of childbirth, but never the sorrow of an absent husband. I need help from somewhere for this one." She searched the men's faces for any hints of a suggestion.

Henry longed to go to Kiri. He calmed her frequently during stressful times. He yearned to help her now, but before he spoke up, Frank pointed to Michael's portrait. "This might work. Worth a try," he said, lifting it from the wall. Maeve hustled up the stairs with the painting in her hands.

Relief flooded the distressed mother's face. "Thank you so much," she whispered. "Prop it on the counter where I can see. Then leave, please."

Maeve placed the portrait as directed and tiptoed out, closing the door behind her.

Kiri gripped the sides of her tub, pulled to a sit, and summoned enough fire to challenge Michael directly. "Look at me with those crafty eyes and hear what I say. This boxcar of a baby you sent fought me every day of its fetal life and sapped all my strength. I can't fight back anymore. I've tried to do what you asked, to live by my vows to you, but I can't bring this baby into the world alone." Her tears began to flow.

"Are you so vain that you can't bear to share your birthday with your own child? Or have you changed your mind and want this baby back? Well, you can't have it!" She splashed water toward him. "We're a package deal! In some strange way this baby and I are connected by the strongest of threads, and you can't reclaim one without the other. So, if you've changed your mind, take me too. Just know that your darling boy will grow up without a father *or* a mother, and you wouldn't wish that on him, would you? To be raised by your brother and sisters?"

She writhed with another contraction. "I love MT dearly and I'm trying to raise him as you would. I thought you wanted him to have siblings, and I've done everything I can to make that happen. Now it's up to you." She wiped wildly at the tears on her cheeks. "Let this night end in *joy*, not sorrow. Take us both… or let us stay… together. I'm giving up at one minute past midnight!" She fell back against the end of the tub, physically and emotionally drained.

At one minute past midnight, husky Aurora Kathryn, fully formed with all systems operational and all appendages in motion, was locked in a violent struggle between her mother's body and her father's spirit twining around her like tentacles refusing to release their hold. *You are my most precious. I'm grieved to part from you... But your mother needs you. Go now... and find your family.* The spirit set his wee babe free to muscle her way into a new world and her mother's arms.

CHAPTER 6

Kiri lifted her newborn onto her chest, bent her head to touch her lips with her own, and blew gently to fill her lungs with her father's breath. She heard no soft coo with this one, but a loud squawk. She smiled and sprinkled her with her father's spirit water, barely able to massage the precious drops into the baby's delicate skin as she wriggled in her mother's hands. The last one meant for her tongue scarcely made it, so fluttery were her lips. Kiri placed one hand on the little head to calm her baby and noticed her most telling feature—a tiny whorl above the right eye in her copper fuzz of hair where an unmanageable curl would sprout.

She laughed and caught Michael's gaze from his portrait. "You fooled me with this one. I was sure the hulk of a thing I carried was a boy just like his father, all action. This baby will be just like her father, all right... her father in skirts! Thank you, Michael, for this beautiful baby girl... the daughter you promised."

Thomas expressed similar amazement. "He looks just like Michael did when he was born," he said when the new baby was placed in his arms, wrapped in the wildflower blanket.

"Better have another look, sir," Maeve said slyly. "And here's your proof." She handed him a sealed envelope.

"And Kiri?" Paula asked.

"Worn out. Recovery won't be so quick as last time, but she will bounce back. I need to return to her straightaway, so if you would kindly show off this wee one to the men below, I'd be grateful. Ask Henry to stay," she called over her shoulder as she hurried away without waiting for an answer.

Thomas compared the little one in his hands to the one in his memory. "Same jaw line and flat chin. Same deep-set eyes. Square face and chunky build. And... this one's a girl!" he said, folding the cover back.

After several mirthful minutes, Paula wrenched the squirrelly newborn from him to meet her father's dear friends. Their reactions were comparable. "She looks just like her father." "That energy, and after a day such as she's had." "Ten mothers won't be able to hang onto this one." They crowded around the tiny bundle for blessings followed by Irish whiskey and a "proof of life" photo sent to Brendan next door.

As kindly as she could, Paula suggested that they leave. "The day has been long and harrowing for everyone. We all need rest, but thank you. The family really appreciates your moral support."

"We *are* Kiri's family," Gus said as they walked out the door.

Henry stayed behind, happy that he was singled out again for first-night duty. Soon after the grandparents left, he climbed the stairs to the sitting room and waited in the recliner. He stared at the disconcerting portrait of Michael, propped against a chair to rescue it from the bathroom's moisture.

Maeve appeared with the treasured bundle wrapped in its cuddle cloth and blanket, and placed it in his arms. "She'll be called 'Katie' after her grandmother Kathryn Killian. Both mother and daughter need watching through the rest of the night. I planned to stay up with them, but Kiri says you can tame this feisty little thing better than anyone, so I'll leave you to it, if you're willing. I'll snooze in the guestroom. Call me if you notice anything unusual." She disappeared as quickly as she had come.

Henry studied the baby's face, comparing it to the portrait staring at him. The eyes would remain a mystery for some time yet, but the remaining features bespoke a miniature Michael. His finger brushed her pudgy cheek and her lips already learning to pout. He lifted the sleeping infant to MT's favorite place in the crook of his neck, but this contrary babe squiggled and squirmed her way across his chest to his other shoulder and exercised her grasping reflex to loop a tiny finger through a buttonhole and anchor herself for sublime slumber.

Reassured by a gentle sigh rather than a squawk from the tiny girl nestled against him, Henry spoke in soothing tones of all the wonders she would experience in the days and years ahead.

"Planning Katie's life for her, are you?" Kiri asked as she labored to walk to the sofa. Her gray, sunken eyes and drawn face startled Henry. "I'm forbidden from my tub or from doing anything motherly with my baby, other than feeding her, for the next eight hours. Maeve neglected to mention sleeping in the same room with her, so I'm going to snooze here until Katie is hungry… if I'm not interrupting your intimate conversation." She smiled weakly at him as she lay on the sofa. "I thought I'd never get to lie on my back again without an elephant on my stomach. This is heaven," she said, drifting off to sleep.

Henry flushed slightly, embarrassed that Kiri overheard his private hopes for her child. He leaned back, put his feet up and waited in silence until she slept soundly before he resumed his monologue. He shifted his gaze from the baby who captured his love instantly to its mother who claimed his devotion bit by secret bit… and locked stares with Michael, sitting on the floor beside her.

At first Henry thought he saw double, but the two visages were markedly different—the one, confident and full of life and the other, pallid and somber. "This little wonder was hard… on both of us," Michael said, nodding toward the baby still latched onto Henry's buttonhole. "She is so precious, I couldn't bear to part with her. But when I witnessed Kiri's agony at the prospect of losing her, I had to let go. I won't put either of us through such pain again."

A gentle smile broke across the gloomy face. "Katie is a firecracker. She will give her mother fits. Even alienate her for a time. I wish I could tell Kiri that her little girl will grow one day into a lovely, compassionate woman… and she will tame her wild curl." He appealed to his friend. "Help Kiri practice patience with this little hothead."

"My pleasure," Henry said, unsure whether he spoke to himself or an apparition. He kissed the top of her fuzzy head. "My pleasure."

"I know what's in your heart, Henry. Don't let your past paralyze you. *Your* future can be as bright as the little one's you're holding. You have a right to happiness."

Guilt flushed Henry's face.

"I feel your longing, and I can tell you for certain that we are all connected… but it's up to you to discover your history and find your place in this family. I trusted you with my life. Now I entrust the lives of those I love most to you." The vision rose and approached the recliner. He tilted his head near the baby's. "Truly a treasure." He blew a gentle puff into the wee one's nose that caused her to twitch and open her pursed lips. Then the father blew a long soul-breath into his daughter. "Don't bother to look over your shoulder. I won't come again for a long time."

Henry wiped his eyes with a corner of the baby's blanket and when he let it drop, Michael was gone. He glanced over at Kiri to see if she sensed Michael's presence. Her fingers worried the edges of the old circular ornament he saw the last time Michael visited, and a black feather lay on her shoulder.

She stirred and stared blankly past him. "Katie will be baptized in six weeks, and *you* will be the godfather."

Henry did not report the unusual phenomenon to Maeve.

*   *   *

Spunky Aurora Kathryn entered into the family certifiably O'Connell as evidenced by her DNA profile. Grandfather Thomas proudly displayed the proof to his assembled children and announced that all talk of little Katie's parentage, legitimacy and rights to inheritance should cease immediately. End of discussion

"I still say she's Henry's," Anne complained. "Any lab assistant can make a mistake—twice."

When Kiri announced that Katie's baptism would take place in six weeks, outside in the courtyard at St. Mary's, and that Henry was godfather, Thomas objected vehemently.

"Henry? Has he been baptized in the Church?"

"That makes no difference to me or my daughter."

"He's not even family!"

"He's *my* family."

"The font outside? I've never heard of such a thing."

"The flowers are beautiful this time of year. Early rites took place outside church buildings, you might remember. If your God sanctioned His son's baptism in a river, Katie's will be fine in open air." She did not add that Henry seemed very uncomfortable with attending a ceremony inside a church, even for her daughter.

Following the ceremony, the proud grandparents strutted around the courtyard, each with a little one in hand. "This is our second grandchild, Paula. *Ours*. I know the fault in it, but when I look at Michael Thomas, I see the son we created together. And already I see in little Katie the embodiment of every other child we might have had."

"You foolish man," she smiled. "Don't ever confess that to anyone but me."

"Not a chance," he laughed, taking MT with him to mingle with the family.

Surprisingly, Meghan swooped in to scoop up her new niece and carried her around to show off to other guests. Paula politely attended to refreshments while engaging Bishop Byrne. Henry and the other guys kept to themselves. Young children scampered hither and thither, and the older texted and tweeted, oblivious of all the activity. Kiri sat by Brendan on a bench.

"You've been very kind to pay extra attention to MT these last few weeks."

"No problem. He's an easy kid to get along with."

"If you resent his place in the family, you hide it very well—not that I've ever approved of places within a family."

"No problem. I never wanted the job of looking after all of my cousins. Would you? If I can be honest, I don't think Uncle Michael would want his own son to be leader of everybody. He thought everyone in a family should get along with and help everyone else because each one had a special strength or talent to contribute. His gift was helping us learn that."

"How true."

"I get upset, though, when Grandfather rides me about teaching MT this or that—as if I'd not do it out of spite or something. Of course I'll do what's best for the family. Whenever he gets like that, I reach into my pocket and touch this…" He pulled out the knot made from his uncle's bootlace. "…and try to imagine what Uncle Michael would tell me to do. He'd probably remind me that Grandfather is getting older and is worried about keeping the family together after he's gone. So I try to be polite… and then do what my *uncle* would want." He smiled and nodded toward a mature man with unruly steel-gray hair trying to be a part of the group. "That's how I handle Phillip too."

"How are you adjusting to life with a new stepfather?"

"He's okay. Nice enough. He's old, though—maybe twelve or fifteen years older than Mother—in his mid-fifties. So he's not much of a do-fun-things-with guy. I use the same with him—rub my knot and try to do the right thing. I've pretty much stopped shrugging and rolling my eyes. That's helped."

Kiri laughed and gave the embarrassed young man a big hug. "You know you can take refuge at my place for a few days if you need to. We can always think of a good reason, like 'MT needs you.'"

He laughed back. "I already have. What do you think the dance party and camping with MT every few nights last summer were all about? I have to look out for myself, too. *I'm* family."

"That's exactly what your uncle would say."

They sat silently for a few minutes, soaking in a golden autumn day. *Michael is here with us,* Kiri thought, *sending September smiles to all of his family.*

Brendan rubbed the knotted lace uneasily. "Since I'm being honest with you today, I should warn you that MT will be two years old soon."

"I think I'll remember his birthday," Kiri chuckled.

"But will you remember that Grandfather believes young children should become active members of the church family at that age—the every Sunday program? Without Uncle Michael, Grandfather will assume the responsibility—or pass it to me when he can't—of taking MT every Sunday. You could, but I hardly ever see you there and besides, he thinks bringing the family is kind of a man thing."

Gold turned to gray and smiles frowned on Kiri's cheery afternoon. She knew Thomas would try to take her son away from her one day. She did not realize it would be so soon. Katie would be next. Then private school… university… the family business. Only two weeks left with her son and two years with her daughter. She wanted to run but did not know how to manage fleeing with two little children. *Michael! I can't bear to lose them so soon. I haven't had a chance to be a mother yet. Please help me!*

When she arrived home, she found a nettle on her pillow.

Kiri hosted an informal—and very joyous—reception at her home following the official one. Henry and the guys showed up. Devin brought his girl friend, and for the first time Doyle did too, prompting raised eyebrows and a few jeers meant to embarrass them both. Paddy popped his head in, and the cake ladies and other neighbors brought their good wishes to the new addition to the house on Quincy Street. Brendan was invited as long as he could produce a permission slip from his mother. He joined in the hearty toasts and cheers that he neglected to mention when he produced a paper for Meghan to sign. The star of the show was Henry, the only one who could quiet little Katie long enough for the others to admire her.

Gus turned her antics into a great story that had everyone laughing. "And mister control himself, Thomas, seemed almost relieved to hand the squawking wee one off to Henry for the rites and reddened mightily when she hushed immediately like a docile newborn… until the old man touched her again." Gus demonstrated by goading the baby into angry cries each time he jabbed her gently in the ribs. "Henry's got the magic touch with her, he has."

Guests out the door and feedings, baths and bedtime successfully accomplished, Kiri sat cross-legged on her bed, staring at the nettle. The bristly leaf puzzled her. Over the past four years without Michael, her heart interpreted every irregularity as a sign from him, but reason told her otherwise.

In a yard full of trees and birds, feathers blew everywhere. An old nest might be lodged in the eaves or the attic. She opened windows wide almost daily, so no magic brought an occasional feather to her. She placed the Celtic ornament in her bedside table and withdrew it at night sometimes to ponder its meaning, so she could have left it out to catch on her clothing and turn up in another part of the house. Her purpose for needing Michael's portrait during Katie's birth was to shift her focus from forcing to relaxation.

No logic explained the sudden appearance of the nettle on her pillow, however. None grew in her neighborhood, and she found the leaf immediately on her return, before any guests arrived bearing plant matter on their shoes. If she could determine its significance—why this, why now—her heart would win this round.

Like working out a puzzle, Kiri examined each piece for its placement. A nettle has more negative connotation than positive, so it was not a symbol of celebration. What negative thoughts crossed her mind on this joyous day? Thomas! Thomas usurping her children's upbringing! Now, find the connection between Thomas and the nettle. Thomas… nettles… Glendalough! Michael forced his desired life lesson when he tricked Thomas with a nettle in the game of St. Kevin and the blackbird.

That must be the clue. Change the rules of the game on Thomas. Outwit him. Pre-empt him. Force him to concede 90% to gain 10%. Certain of the nettle's message, Kiri headed for a long, hot soak in her tub to hatch a plan before Katie awoke for a feeding. *If you are behind this Michael, next time could you please be more obvious. I'm not as good at puzzles as I used to be.*

Sis: Mom shared phonecam photos of Katie's big day. Beautiful! Henry made a handsome change from the grumpy O'Connells. Tell Katie and MT to prepare to welcome a Koyle cousin into the family next summer. TA DA! Kurt

After Katie's christening, Kiri resumed a regular work program. She retained Maeve's sister on a permanent, part-time basis at the aquacenter where Paula continued yoga sessions twice weekly. She dedicated Tuesdays after bedtime to reconciling the business accounts of her neighborhood enterprises... and Charles. Henry was back on schedule for tea every Monday at four, and Thomas... Thomas fumed at the restrictions Kiri placed on his visits with her son.

"Kirin still will not allow me to take Michael Thomas beyond the top of the road on my own. I know she has spies who will call her if I do. Why doesn't she trust me with my own grandson, Paula?" Thomas grumbled his protests as he tried to secure his seatbelt around his expanding midsection. "Our boy is almost two. A father... a grandfather has responsibilities to a boy at that age. As tight as she's holding onto him, Kirin may not even let us take him to feed the ducks on his birthday!"

Paula burst into tears as he backed out the drive. "I'm sorry, love. Didn't mean to shout," he said. "I'm sure we'll come to some agreement for that happy day." He patted her knee as he turned the corner, but she continued to dab at her eyes. "What did I say that set you off?"

"It wasn't anything you said. It was something I saw today... at yoga."

"What could you possibly see at yoga that disturbed you so?"

"An elephant."

He gaped at her. "An elephant?"

She nodded and wiped her nose. "When the sky darkened, the instructor turned on the lights and we saw our reflections in the windows. An elephant stared back at me."

Thomas pulled over to the side of the road and stopped the car.

"I was so shocked that instead of 'being in the moment,' I really examined myself during our *sun salutations*. When I raised my arms, saggy flesh hung down, and folds of wrinkled skin covered my hands and forearms. We moved to *plank*, the folds shifted in the opposite direction and my thighs and chest sagged too. In *downward dog*, my eyes locked on my knees and I didn't recognize them. My skin is suddenly two sizes too big for me. It's like I turned seventy-one and got an elephant's hide for my birthday." Embarrassed, she turned her face away from him. "I'm disgusting."

He coaxed it back with his fingers under her chin and did not see wrinkles in her eyes—only hurt. "Get out of the car." At her surprise, he repeated his command. "Get out of the car and stand on the walk."

She opened her door and stood there, expecting to be discarded along the side of the road like an old rag.

Thomas climbed out and joined her. He opened his arms wide and pulled her to him. "I want to press all your saggy, wrinkly bits into mine this very minute. When I look at you, Paula, I see only the beautiful, twenty-three-year-old woman who sang folk songs to me on the beach so many summers ago. She was toned and bronzed from the Spanish sun, and white stripes crisscrossed her back and feet where her swimsuit and sandals had been—an bedazzling zebra of a woman."

Surprised passers-by gawked at the couple locked in ardent embrace and totally unmindful that even mature public displays of affection were frowned upon. "The next time you go to yoga…" She shook her head. He nodded and forced her attention. "When you go to yoga, you will wear tighter tops and shorter shorts and celebrate every square inch of this marvelous, complicated organ that covers and protects the beautiful you inside. Then you'll come home to this wrinkly seventy-three-year-old man and convince him that he is as desirable and young at heart as you."

When they returned to the car, they found a text from Kiri. *Please come to tea at four on Friday.*

At precisely four, Thomas and Paula knocked on Kiri's door, unaware of the power struggle in play that afternoon. She greeted them dressed professionally in skirt, blouse and sweater and with her shoulder-length hair waved across her forehead and tucked smartly behind her ears. Her eyes demonstrated clear intent as she directed her mother upstairs to watch the children while she and Thomas discussed a few matters. When he started to seat himself in the master's chair in the living room as usual, she redirected him to the nook in her octagonal kitchen—a place with no head of the table, a place from which she drew strength.

"I invited you here today to ask your advice—and possibly a favor. Since Katie's christening, I've been struck with how quickly children grow and change. You know that from the five you've raised and from watching your grandchildren. Michael would be so proud of our two. I understand precisely what he intended for their upbringing and plan to follow his course as closely as possible. There is one aspect, however, I do not feel prepared to oversee, and that is where you come in."

Thomas' mouth firmed at three and nine followed by a "hmm."

"We developed a time line." She enumerated her objectives as if they were bullets on a power point, leaving no time for questions or comments as she moved swiftly from one to the next. "So there is no question that *I* will make *all* the decisions regarding our children's social upbringing and formal schooling with Michael's wishes in mind, but I am stymied when it comes to their religious instruction. We thought to begin when they reached three or four, but I think you'll agree that Michael Thomas is advanced for his age. He has a vocabulary beyond two. He can remain quiet and attentive for long periods of time and absorbs elements of his environment quickly. Would it be out of place for him to begin around two or two and a half?"

Thomas nodded. "Of course. Two would be perfect." His eyes smiled even though he tried not to.

"You know how I hate to be separated from him for more than an hour or so at a time, but with a new baby, I won't be able to sit still for even that long. I want for my son to have the full experience now so he will be prepared to make his *own* choices in the future, but I cannot do that for him. I hate to ask this favor of you… and please tell me if it would be an imposition… but would you be willing to oversee Michael Thomas' religious instruction?"

She paused just long enough to notice him brush a wisp of his white hair from his ruddy forehead and the tautness of his jaw and neck muscles relax. "Of course, I expect you to discuss this with Mom. I don't want either of you to be inconvenienced on your Sunday mornings. A two-year-old couldn't handle much more than that without a nap, so I trust he would return home by one."

Thomas raised his fist to his mouth to clear his throat in an effort to avoid seeming too anxious. "I think I can speak for your mother. We accept this responsibility gladly."

"Thank you. Michael would be pleased that his own father guided this *one* important aspect of his son's training." She let those words sink in. "My little boy will be two on Tuesday. Do you think he'd like to visit the ducks again? Maybe have a little picnic as well?"

Thomas' eyes twinkled now, and his face broke out in a broad smile. Confrontation over a simple outing was averted. "Your mother and I would love to entertain Michael Thomas for the afternoon. Give you and little Katie a chance to rest."

"Good. It's settled. Tuesday after an early nap and Sunday mornings beginning the following weekend." Kiri imagined the nettle twirling between her fingers to taunt the aging patriarch until he dropped his nest. Game over. "I truly appreciate your help. Care for some tea?"

Thomas backed out Kiri's drive after an abrupt cup of tea. "You're rather quiet," Paula said. "Do you feel ill?"

"I feel like a wrinkled old bull elephant that was nudged to the edge of the herd by a powerful matriarch guarding her young."

Kirin Aurora O'Connell spent MT's first Sunday morning away from home sitting under the evergreen tree, also named Aurora by her husband. She held their namesake as closely as the squirrelly baby would allow. "Let's make these mornings special—just the two of us, for the next two years. Maybe I can bargain for three, since you're such a squirmy little girl. Then your grandfather will claim your Sunday mornings too. In the meantime we'll find joy sharing these hours together." She gazed upward toward the branches and noticed a one-inch needled sprig sprouting from a second old scar… with a black feather clinging to it.

CHAPTER 7

Black feathers fluttered through Kiri's life from time to time, but as a harried single mother of two little children with a business to run and neighborhood enterprises to oversee, she was too distracted to pay them much mind.   She tossed each one into Michael's nightstand to contemplate… later. She could barely keep up with the journal she started to chart her children's growth and other important changes in her family's life.

Days, weeks, months and years passed by her like fence posts as she commenced a long journey afoot. She began by walking and marked each one. Life pushed her to jog, and she noticed every fourth or ninth. Forced to sprint, she noted beginnings and endings. For the long-haul marathon, her surroundings blurred and she only focused when she stopped at a relief aid station for nourishment or water. During those hectic times, she set aside each anniversary day to share with Michael.   Some years she catalogued, at a minimum, births, marriages, deaths and other major events.

The constants in her life were her children and the men who shaped and guided them. She marked time from her marriage to Michael, the man who passed his genetic material and personality quirks to both of them. In his absence, her son Michael Thomas belonged to and emulated his grandfather Thomas in many ways, while little Katie was every ounce Henry's. She imprinted on him from her first night of life cradled in his arms, clinging to his buttonhole.

Fifth Anniversary Year: Birth: Michael Thomas
Seventh Anniversary Year: Birth: Aurora Kathryn
I commissioned two miniature harps intricately carved from green Connemara marble. They stand next to Michael's on the shelf running along a bedroom wall, in line with the others from Thomas' family—one for each of his children. I scooted the remaining four together to close the gap created when Anne took hers without asking. My eye can't tell that one is missing, but inside I know that we cannot erase the hostility between us.

The two children were compatible and complementary in many ways, but in others they were polar opposites. At the same ages MT cooed; Katie squawked. MT relaxed and lingered at his feedings. Katie attacked her mother voraciously, then pushed away when done as if saying, "All through! What's next?"   Whether at the end of a nap or a night, Kiri found her little boy almost as she had left him. Katie fought sleep, and her mother never could anticipate which corner of the crib or position she would choose. When MT wanted an object out of reach, he pointed. Katie squirmed inside whatever contraption she was strapped into until she could grasp with her toes and pass it to her hands. MT crawled, then walked. Katie made better time by scooting rather than crawling and bypassed a walk for a run. When they were sick, all bets were off.

Eighth Anniversary Year: Birth: Kendra May, daughter of my brother Kurt and Tanya Koyle

Birth: Kiera Pauline, daughter of Meghan and 2nd husband Phillip. They call her Polly.

Marriage: Devin. His wedding present—my communications job.

Death: Maureen, neighbor Paddy's wife. She made our beautiful wildflower quilts.

Other: Quincy Clinic established. It provides house calls. Maeve had a sister, and her sister had friends. No fun for me to drive into the city with two screaming kids, and an impossibility for our aging neighbors.

Thankfully, the aquacenter is doing well enough to keep our heads above water. Ha Ha. I am determined to support my family with my work and use Michael's trust fund to support his vision of community.

* * *

By the time he was four, Michael Thomas was tall for his age and tried to match his grandfather's shortening stride when they walked. He observed and contemplated how interactive parts behaved. He thought before acting. Two-year-old Katie inherited her father's bulky frame and explosion of ginger curls. She liked to see 'what would happen if' and wore burnt fingers and scabby knees as badges of her catlike curiosity. She had no patience for thinking. Learn by doing—action—was her modus operandi, especially where electronic gadgets were concerned.

If the house suddenly fell quiet, her brother knew she had found his "pad's" hiding place. Then the hunt was on for both of them. She became very adept at tapping, sliding and swiping, and her giggles at the results usually gave her away. Kiri did not approve of electronic devices for young children, but Thomas provided one for his grandson designed with apps for religious teaching. Katie liked the colors and cartoon figures. Her mother worried about what she would get her hands on next.

Michael continued to be the moral compass in all their lives—everpresent to watch over them and guide them from his place on the wall. Around the house it was as if "Daddy" just stepped out for a few minutes and would be home soon. Kiri frequently cautioned her children with, "Would Daddy approve?" Katie did not pay much attention, but MT thought a lot about his father's function in the family.

Their mother took little time for herself. Between chasing after children and tending to her many responsibilities, she was too exhausted to think about personal pleasures other than a long soak in her tub and an early to bed. Maybe a few pages in a book, if she could stay awake that long. This night was different, however. She was going out—prearranged, reservations, no children allowed—to a posh but cozy place up the coast near Malahide. For the first time since she returned to Ireland, she worried about what to wear. For family affairs, she did not care how she looked. For business, she always donned some variation of "the outfit." But for their first nonessential, nonemergency evening alone together, she wanted to look perfect for Henry.

After an early, early supper for the kiddies to allow Kiri time to glam up her forty-year-old body, mother and children sat beneath the evergreen tree. Katie busied herself by picking blades of grass and throwing them into the breeze only to have them shoot back at her. MT sat cross-legged with his elbows on his knees and his chin in his hands, in serious contemplation. "Is it really true that I'm part you and part Daddy?" Kiri nodded. "Then which part is which?" he asked.

She touched her little boy here and there to demonstrate. "Every part of you is both of us. Every piece of your skin, every hair on your head, every snip of your fingernail, every beat of your heart is a part of me and a part of Daddy so well mixed together that you can't tell which is which."

MT tilted his head and crinkled his nose, confused, so Kiri tried to explain. "It's like mixing paint. When you mix yellow and blue together, what happens?

"I make green."

"Can you ever separate the paint again into yellow and blue?"

He shook his head.

"So, you've made a brand new color of paint."

He nodded enthusiastically.

"When yellow and blue make a baby, they combine so well with each other that they become this brand new person—you—and they will never be separate parts again."

MT plunked his chin in his hands to mull over that idea. Then he asked, "Mommy, which one are you? The blue or the yellow?"

"What do you think?"

After another thoughtful moment, he replied. "I think you're the blue because you love water so much." He reflected a moment more. "Daddy's yellow like the sun. The sun is always around, but you can't touch it... just like Daddy. You love to sit in the sun and feel warm like Daddy made you feel when he was here to give you big hugs."

Surprised by his cogent reply, she nodded wistfully.

"So, you're the blue and Daddy's the yellow...." A light bulb turned on in his head. "...and I'm the green!" He looked down at his sister blissfully tossing handfuls of grass into the breeze. "Is Katie parts of you and Daddy mixed together too?"

"Of course."

"Well, if you mixed you and Daddy together both times you made a green baby why aren't Katie and I alike? After all, we aren't the same."

He put his hands over his mouth and giggled with embarrassment. "I have dark brown hair and hers is red!"

"True. But every time you mix two things together, you create something a little bit different."

MT crinkled his brow and looked confused. "I don't get it."

His mother glanced at her watch to gauge time because she did not want to bypass this teachable moment. "Let's go inside, and I'll show you. I think we can be quick." She picked up her little girl, and the three returned to the house. She seated the children in the nook, disappeared into the mudroom and reappeared with paper plates, a paintbrush and two tubes of acrylic paint. Katie's big eyes communicated immediate interest.

Kiri added a glass of water and paper towels to the table and squeezed out a daub of blue and a daub of yellow onto one of the plates. Then she handed MT a brush and a clean plate and stuffed her hands into her pockets, resisting the impulse to help him. "Now, take a little bit of blue on your brush and smear it on this plate. Then wash and dry the brush."

He followed her directions carefully.

"Now, take a little bit of yellow and mix it with the blue." MT did as he was told. "What do you have?"

He looked quite pleased with himself. "Green. Like the bushes... and a Christmas tree."

"Good. Clean the brush and do the same thing again—a little blue, rinse your brush, a little yellow and mix... right next to your first sample. What do you have now?"

Katie watched her brother intently while he followed directions again and turned his face to her, beaming. "Green! Like green beans."

His mother asked, "Is it the same green as the first?"

He shook his head. "Not quite."

"So, it's different even though you used the same parts." MT nodded his head. "Just like you and Katie are different."

"Yes. Does that mean if you and Daddy made more babies, they would be different too?"

"Why don't you try it?"

MT cleaned his brush and started to choose yellow first. He stopped and gave his mother a "does it matter" look. She smiled and shook her head, so he proceeded very seriously, taking a daub of yellow and mixing blue into it. He turned up his nose and pinched an eye shut when he produced a bright chartreuse. "Whoa! That's disgusting!"

"Is it still green?"

"Yes... but it's icky... like when Katie gets sick. I don't think I'd like a brother or sister who looked like that! You better not have any more babies!" He tossed his brush onto his plate and jumped down from the bench seat to run for the bathroom sink. Kiri sat in his place and burst into laughter.

So did Henry. He arrived and let himself in somewhere between Christmas trees and green beans and watched unnoticed from a corner of the dining room. With every phrase of her embarrassed explanation once she spotted him, he laughed harder, until his normally serious eyes jitterbugged in their sockets.

"What's so funny about a simple science experiment with a surprise ending?"

"The surprise ending," Henry replied, nodding past her shoulder.

Kiri turned to look behind her, and green paint splattered her in the face. Katie wielded the brush like a conductor's baton, redecorating the nook with each beat. Her delight at sudden colorful transformations extended to her fingernails, nose, and two front teeth and to blue, yellow and green streaks in her mother's hair.

"Aurora Kathryn O'Connell!" Kiri shrieked at the little girl as she wrested the offending tool from her, receiving a green stripe down her face in the process. "What have you done!"

"Make evewyting pwetty," Katie beamed proudly.

Henry doubled up at the happy accident facing him. "I expected to walk in on some drama, but not a farce. You 'painted ladies' go clean yourselves up. I'll push back our reservation by a half-hour. Or should I make that twenty-four?" he laughed as they disappeared up the stairs.

Kiri was furious. She barely had time to scrub one grubby body, let alone two. Any pretence at glamour now would be obvious—no curls in a slight change of hairdo or glittery nails. She would have to make do.

MT followed his mother to witness what happened to naughty children—for future reference. Left alone, Henry planted himself in a chair to chuckle over the amusing scene that provided comic relief to his nervous anticipation of the evening ahead. In the ten years he had known Kiri, and the hundreds of hours in one another's company, the two had never been alone to develop the familiarity of a couple without a backdrop of intense action, tragedy or necessity of the moment.

Tonight was a big step for him and he planned carefully for it. He timed the drive for music and conversation. He checked the menu for a variety of her favorites. He reserved a snug table next to a window overlooking the water, out of the way of serving traffic—and most importantly, within a few steps of the dance floor. He confirmed that the combo scheduled for the evening included numbers in its repertoire suitable for guests of his age, just shy of fifty.

He reviewed his options—gentle guiding touches as he led her to the car and the exclusive club, holding her hand across the table, pushing a lock of her hair behind her ear after a sip of wine, taking some fresh air in the gardens, and dancing—close, of course. The parting was the problem. Adults their age probably did not linger in a car anymore. Sitting in her living room with Michael on guard from the wall was a mood-breaker. The deck in back at the edge of her garden offered a likely possibility. He could turn on music inside, and the fragrance of flowers enhanced by dew descending on them would enrich the atmosphere. The late evening's chill would force them together for warmth.

He walked to the door to peer out. Only two deck chairs—not ideal, but they would have to do until he could come up with an alternative. He turned back for a sofa throw to place by the door and stopped himself. *For God's sake, Henry! You are not planning a mission. Tonight is supposed to be a pleasant, private—bordering on intimate—evening with a lovely woman. Kiri... and bitter memory... will dictate the tempo of your dance.*

Beads of perspiration broke out on his forehead at the realization that any stimulus of sight, sound or touch could cause the intrusion of horrid memory. He splashed cold water from the kitchen sink onto his face when he heard the front bell sound—the sitter, one of the cake ladies.

"The neighborhood has near gone to its grave waitin' for this night." She smiled kindly. "You two deserve time alone together. Enjoy yourselves."

Henry flushed at the implication, then caught sight of Kiri descending the stairs. She appeared fresh and natural, her hair shining in waves around her broadly smiling face. She wore a celadon one-piece that flattered her figure and opened to a slight flare at its hem. A long, multicolored chiffon scarf looped loosely around her neck, and tiny spots of bright color adorned her ears. A single bracelet decorated her wrist—no watch to indicate that marking time this night was important.

Kiri made the first move. She stood close enough to place her hands on his lapels and meet his gaze. "Not too casual, I hope. I thought this would camouflage any spots of paint I missed."

Henry laughed and took the wrap she offered him. He placed the sensuously soft cashmere sweater around her shoulders and squeezed them gently. He leaned toward her right ear to whisper "stunningly beautiful"... when his phone sounded.

He tried to ignore the persistent call, but it did not stop. He lowered his eyes and reached into his pocket. "I... I should take this."

She could not avoid overhearing the curt but serious call. Trouble at work. Doyle, Frank, and Gus were at different points along a border waiting to extract half a dozen informants. The network contracted a surveillance drone to track them—a trial run for possible purchase. Devin, in communication central, lost all contact with the men and the drone. Not a blip. Not a crackle. Not a flash of light. He had no idea where the problem was, but needed Henry in the event it involved a foreign government or destruction of the drone. Henry looked at her with apology written all over his face.

"Go. I'm one of the few people in this world who understands when duty calls."

He fingered the waves in her hair. "I rather looked forward to removing green flecks from your beautiful brown curls this evening."

"I'll save some for next time," she smiled.

An affectionate parting seemed out of place with no prelude, so he tilted her face upward, kissed her on the forehead, and let himself out. Two missions gone awry.

*   *   *

Kiri hosted her annual pre-Christmas party for the guys. Their ranks expanded by three women—Devin's wife, Doyle's girl, and now Gus's special someone. "Soon to be my missus," he said proudly, giving her a squeeze. Black-haired, ruddy-complexioned and wholesome-looking like Gus, she flushed a deep rose immediately. Glasses clinked with hearty good wishes and congratulations.

"Michael has changed since we were last here," Frank said, nodding to the portrait above the fireplace. His crossed arms held a babe in the crook of each elbow, bundled in brightly colored wildflower quilts.

"Our colors change with our seasons." Kiri smiled at Henry, the first time she had seen him since their aborted date. "This must be my summer."

He smiled back, remembering the painting of his hand that invited her to find color in her life again.

Her eyes fell to the three small stockings hanging from the mantle. They should have been flat empty for the next few days, but hers was plump. She eyed it, and the five men surrounding her, with suspicion and removed an unmarked digital music pod. "Who did this?" The men all claimed innocence.

Before she could grill them, Katie snatched it from her fingers and ran up the stairs. She flattened herself against step eight and squeezed through the railing until she dangled from her hips. Henry reached out to catch her, but she was wedged in so tight she did not fall. She attached the pod to the correct port beneath her and shouted, "Play audio!" A jaunty tune popularized in the Sixties by the Irish Rovers, "The Unicorn Song," blared out. Katie was mesmerized by thoughts of alligators, camels and elephants. When the song was over, she squeezed back onto the step and ran to her mother. She pulled on her skirt and asked, "What's a unicorn?"

Everyone laughed at the little tyke. "A mythical animal with a horn on its head right here." She put her fist to Katie's forehead. "My name, Kirin, means unicorn just like your name, Aurora, is a fairy princess."

Katie gave her mother that "too much information" look, grabbed her brother's pad and shouted into it, "What is a unicorn?" When a picture popped up, she said, "Oh," dropped the pad and ran upstairs. The group was still laughing, especially Henry, when she returned dressed in her net tutu skirt and ballet slippers with a toilet paper roll clipped to the curls on the top of her head. She shouted, "Play audio," again and twirled through all the rooms on the main floor.

The guys traded secretive glances. Michael's little girl inherited her father's impulsive action gene—mighty useful in their line of work if they could nurture it.

Kiri lowered the volume and turned to Gus. "Are you really ready for this?" she asked as Katie whirled by again.

"Aye! And ten more just like her. I can't wait." His affectionate squeeze of his girl prompted another flush. "So I might as well tell you now. I'll be leaving the team... and the network... before we say our 'I do's.' My girl's father has an apple orchard near Armagh and wants to retire. Her brother will take over, of course, but they need another pair of strong arms to get the hard work done, so I'll be brewing gold-medal craft cider come next fall."

The jaunty tune and its twirling unicorn went unnoticed by the stunned group. Since the team's inception fifteen or more years earlier, no one had defected. Gus sensed that his friends felt betrayed. "I love every one of you. You're like brothers... and sister... to me. And I love my job. But I love family more." He stole a glance at Michael's portrait. "With all due respect to the choices *you've* made, *I* will not subject the love of my life and our children to the hell Kiri has been through. They are going to know where their husband and father lays his head every night and wake up to his stubbly face every morning."

Very clever, Kiri thought. Gus remained loyal to the team. He did not reveal the details of his job to his intended, nor would he... ever. She watched the look on Henry's face turn from surprise to realization to yearning as the little unicorn skipped by. She forced a smile and gave her burly rescuer a mighty hug. "I say we have another round and wish this couple a long and happy life together... and as many whirling dervishes as their house can hold!"

"Hear! Hear!" they shouted.

Kiri served up more spirits and food, put her children to bed, waved her friends goodbye and grabbed Henry's hand before he could slip out the door. "Dance with me? One 'White Christmas?' I've got to get that crazy Rover's tune out of my head or I won't be able to sleep."

He nodded reluctantly and stood stiffly while she cued up the selection. She knew he was unnerved by Gus's announcement and his heart was not in two-stepping around her living room. *How many more months will this take*, she asked herself as she tried to rest her head against his chest. With the last phrase, he gave her a gentle hug and left without another word.

She retrieved the music pod from the stairs and replaced it in her stocking. She wondered if Thomas had meant it for Katie as a backdoor introduction to Bible stories and had dropped it into the wrong one. A mischievous gleam in Michael's eye gazed down at her, and she realized the silly tune was no mistake. It was a message... or a warning... that sudden change—like a flood—was in her future and that her 'stand by to support' strengths would be needed. "Thanks a lot, but a letter would have caused less ruckus. I'm not much for surprises. I'd really rather have a decent hug for Christmas."

Ninth Anniversary Year: Birth: Kody Dean, son of my brother Kurt and Tanya Koyle

Marriage: Gus

Graduation: Meghan's son Brendan and Anne's daughter Grace

Other: Quincy Clinic expanded to include an emergency section in its all-night pharmacy. Products available: nappies, wipes, formula, bottled water, juices, healthy snacks and, of course, ice cream. That delectable treat became a necessity after my moppet's curious fingers accessed our communication system's "phone on" command one midnight. She pleaded for "Henwy to bwing ice cweam and wead a stowy." He spoils her by granting her every wish.

The grocer added a section of medal-winning ciders and specialty apples next to the gourmet cheeses and breads. He can barely keep it stocked.

Henry moved in across the road and two doors down. I admired the charming, old home and wanted to buy it for a counseling center when it came on the market. But before I could put financing together, it sold. The new owner remodeled it into bachelor apartments with a Georgian feel, and Henry snapped up the first unit. On a tip, Brendan applied for the maintenance position and got the attic studio as payment. Seems like the "family" is taking over the neighborhood.

CHAPTER 8

Kiri hustled down the road toward her home and her date with Henry. Her appointment with the hairdresser ran longer than intended. She could not remember the last time she had been to one—in her early twenties, probably—but this visit had an ulterior motive. She wanted to snoop.

The neighbor ladies—one of whom was minding her children for the afternoon and evening—let it be known that they appreciated the convenience of a stylist's shop so near, but that it might close soon. Business problems. Kiri decided that the best way to find out what was on the stylist's mind was to sit in her chair. And what better day than this when she wanted to look especially nice for another attempt at an evening out with Henry.

She tossed her curls from side to side in a girlish way as she looked forward to a long soak in her tub and doing her nails this time. The sight of two forms huddled on her stoop halted her in mid-stride. She recognized the tall one—Paddy from across the road. The petite one, shivering in a ragged woolen cloak, was a mystery. Flashes of a Dickens novel came to mind as she drew close enough to note the wispy hair and eyes half the size of her face.

Kiri sat down beside the frightened, wan figure and held her hand. "Who is this?" she asked her old friend sitting on the other side and holding her other hand.

"According to the papers what was pinned to her," he read, "this here is 'Kathryn Elizabeth Killian, born March 10, 2006. No good no more. Take to Thomas O'Connell, Dublin.' It's signed by a Malachy Killian." He handed Kiri the note. "What father would do such a thing? She's barely fourteen years old!"

Kiri sighed, stuffed the note in her bag and gently rubbed the scrawny child's back. "How did she get here?"

"According to the cab driver who got it from the bus driver when her father put her on, he gave over an envelope with enough money for the ride and a cab to deliver her to 'Mr. Thomas in the big house.' When they got there, no one was home."

"Right. He and Mom are visiting the islands off the west coast."

"So, talking to a neighbor, he was directed to Tommy's house. The lady there said they didn't know any Malachy Killian and she already had a house full of kids so take her to your place. You would know what to do. I caught the cabby just as he was going to leave her alone on your stoop, or we wouldn't know that much. So... what will you do?"

Kiri looked at the little waif and shook her head. "I have no idea."

"I think some hot tea and maybe some soup would be a good start. There's only half an apple and a crust of bread left in this linen bag hanging 'round her neck, poor child."

That phrase, the one Thomas used to brand Kiri, hardened her resolve. "I have no idea, but I will think of a way to keep her safe and bring a smile to her face. Thank you again, Paddy. You're a good friend."

"My pleasure... anytime. I get mighty lonely in my old house. It seems to grow larger... or me, smaller... everyday." He tipped his cap, straightened the binoculars hanging from his neck, and carried his stooped body back across the road.

Kiri led the child to the kitchen nook and washed her hands and face before putting food in front of her—a small glass of milk, a cup of tea, a small bowl of beefy soup and bread. The girl stared at her as if awaiting permission, so Kiri set a similar place for herself and began to eat. The surprise guest drank the liquids but watched Kiri take spoonfuls of soup. Is it possible in this day and age, Kiri asked herself, that some people do not use utensils? She put down her spoon and drank from her bowl; the young girl attacked hers hungrily. Both sopped up every last bite with bits of bread. Kiri dished out a second helping for the child and called Henry.

"Problem?"

"More of a mystery. I need to hire your team to trace a person of interest."

"Do you have a name?"

"And a body claiming to be a Killian... a relative of Michael's, presumably. I'd like to make sure this is not a mistake... or worse, a hoax, blackmail or a remnant from Michael's errant youth. The child obviously needs help."

"Killian is a fairly common name in some parts."

"Yes, but I have her birth date and her purported father's name for a start. I'll send it."

"Wouldn't a DNA test be faster?"

Kiri sighed. "Of course. I'll call Maeve, but if you guys can find a relative—common or not, and pray it's not Michael—I'll try to contact a family member. May I request a team meeting here in about an hour and a half? I'll need help with legal issues regarding her father and social services available."

"We'll be there. And later?"

"If you guys are as good as you claim, we'll have this tied up with a bow before sunset."

By the time the team arrived, Kiri had the young girl bathed and shampooed, sacrificing her own curls and luster to the steam. The child did not speak, even when questioned. Maeve took a DNA sample and had it delivered to the lab while she checked the girl over in the guestroom.

Devin held folded papers in his hand. "Before I give you the information you want, we want something from you." Frank and Doyle nodded. Kiri rolled her eyes. "We want you to join our selection committee." Her eyes popped open.

"As you know, we are now two men down, and we must find replacements—at least one—for Michael and Gus. Who better than you to help? Your counseling background makes you a good judge of character. You know the demands of the job. You have a knack for finding flaws, and you are objective when analyzing the big picture. In other words, you can spot right off who will fit in with this crazy bunch."

Kiri threw up her hands and shook her head. "I'm so busy now. I can't tell you...."

Frank took over. "But you'll have to give the applicants water survival training in any case. Why not combine that with interviews and at least rank candidates for us? Besides, you did give up communications three years ago."

"Of course, if you're not interested in what we found out...." Doyle raised his thick eyebrows to taunt her.

"Oh, all right." Kiri gave in. "But not tomorrow!" She grabbed the papers.

Devin summarized. "Michael Killian O'Connell and Kathryn Elizabeth Killian are not father/daughter. They descend from the same man, Fergus Killian, about six generations back, so yes, she is a *cousin* to Michael on his mother's side. Fergus was a farmer in the north during the time of the potato famine. He had five sons and three daughters. We only followed the two lines in question, but there is enough information here to trace the others if and when you want to. The bigger question is, is the person who showed up today the same as the person on paper? Only DNA will reveal if blood and paper trail match."

"What can you tell us about this mysterious person?" Henry asked.

Kiri shrugged and handed him the curt note of introduction. The blood drained from his face when he read it. "Not much," she said. "She doesn't talk."

"Oh yes, she does!" Maeve bustled in, all business, leaving the girl in the guestroom. "She doesn't speak English like you dolts who forgot everything you learned in school the minute you received your Leaving Certificate. She uses the old tongue—Irish Gaelic."

"And you understood her, I suppose," Doyle challenged.

"Of course. We have to learn Irish language to be licensed. You never know who will call in the middle of the night. She doesn't answer to her name because she doesn't know it. She's always been called 'Bitsy' because she was such a little bit of a thing when she was born. Still is, but she'll fatten up with a decent diet. Her mother died shortly after, so her sister hauled her around until she could walk. Since then she was left to follow along. She's led a very sheltered existence on a sheep farm."

Maeve shook her head at the girl's misfortune. "She has no life experience. She's never been to school, so she has no concept of reading or numbers. She knows nothing of cars or buses or cities with lots of people. She never took a bath in anything larger than a washtub, and not with hot running water." She shook her finger at Kiri. "And that hairdryer near scared the girl out of her skin!"

Kiri started to apologize when the doorbell rang. A courier handed in an envelope. Maeve grabbed it first and fished in her pocket for copies of other reports she brought along. She studied them all carefully, then handed them to Kiri and made the announcement. "Michael and Bitsy have the same percentage of like markers, indicating they are the same generation from a common ancestor. MT and Katie have the same markers as both in a lesser percentage, as would be expected, so proof positive, Michael has himself a cousin!"

"When do we get to meet this intriguing creature?" Doyle asked.

"I'll bring her in," Maeve said. "But remember, she is a five-year-old in an adolescent body. Mind your gawks and comments." She scurried away to return moments later leading Bitsy—dwarfed in one of Kiri's nightgowns—by the hand.

Stunned, the men couldn't have issued a word if they tried, but gawk they did. The girl, barely as tall as Maeve's generous bosom, displayed skin like cream, eyes a vibrant robin's egg blue, long fine blond hair... and an acute case of pregnancy.

The kindly midwife introduced her to each man in turn, and to a one, they found the presence of mind to shake her hand and say something in their limited Gaelic. Bitsy did not smile but dropped her eyelids bashfully. Maeve told her to wish everyone a good night before she went to bed. The scraggy girl did so in her native tongue, then followed the woman out.

"You didn't tell us she was expecting!" Doyle exclaimed in a shouted whisper.

"I didn't think it important," Kiri said. "Bitsy's ancestry was our primary concern. Her physical condition was irrelevant."

"Not important!" Frank was in her face. "In the case of an unwed, teenage expectant mother, Health and Social Services will consider her condition *very* relevant. If no one in her family steps up to act as guardian, she'll be taken away to a home for unwed mothers. At birth, the baby will be adopted out and the mother set to working for her keep until she can be placed. Scandals a few years ago uncovered mistreatment in these places. You can't allow family to be given up for adoption!"

"What am I supposed to do? I'm not family."

"If she is kin to your children, then you *are* family. You hold the proof in your hands."

Kiri turned to Henry for help. "I'm a single mother myself with two small children—one of which is as out of control as three. I can't add a five-year-old mother and her baby into the mix. I'm so busy at the aquacenter that I have to hire more help. I have a zillion projects in the fire and can barely keep up with their accounting. You just asked me to add another for you. What am I supposed to do?"

Henry glanced at Michael's portrait and then back at Kiri. "Do what we all have dedicated our lives to. Try to make a bad situation better."

Kiri understood instantly that she was beaten. No matter how she felt about Bitsy personally, or how the girl might complicate her life, she was warned more than a year earlier that dramatic change, like a flood, was in her future, and she was compelled to support the best of the bad options available. At the least, she owed the girl a measure of Celtic hospitality.

"You win. I won't call Social Services. I'll be responsible temporarily, until we can sort out the legal issues. I still want your help. I'm not convinced that Bitsy landed in the right place. Why would this man, Malachy, send his daughter to Thomas? Why not to the family of one of Thomas' wife Kathryn's brothers—another Killian?"

No one suggested an answer, so she pressed ahead. "Michael had lots of Killian cousins from his mother's family. I think we should track them down to see if they are in a better position than I to care for Bitsy— someone closer to her home and rural way of life. I'll canvass Tommy and the stepsisters." She turned away when her lips started to tremble.

Surprisingly, it was Henry who pulled her into a hug and patted her head. "Go ahead and cry, little girl. You're entitled... but not for more than a minute. We have a mission to plan. Who knows, this might be a blessing in disguise." He nodded to the others. "Don't you have work to do?" They left without a goodbye.

"I'm sorry, Henry. My problems are petty compared to Bitsy's, but I really feel I'm in a good place. Colors look bright. Then, with one little setback, I'm an emotional and physical mess... again."

Maeve returned. "I think Bitsy's gone to sleep, so I'll be off. I'll check in tomorrow to see how you are getting on. I wouldn't let her out for a few days. She's like a little puppy that needs time to adjust to a new home. The city might be too much for her just yet. Sure, waking up to your two young ones staring at her in the morning will give her a fright!"

"Good idea. How much time do we have... to resolve the problem?" Henry asked.

"Six to eight weeks, I'd say. Hard to tell with her being so small. She might deliver early. Get the doctor or his nurse over to make some tests. Be sure we know what's coming. And she could do with a trim to smarten her up a bit, help her feel better about herself."

"Did her father...."

"Not that she says. Some village boy came along and talked her into doing something she didn't understand. I'm not sure she's made the connection even yet. She's probably never seen a human baby in her life. Now, sheep she knows about." Maeve smiled. "She's a sweet one, she is. You'll all get along just fine." She hurried out before they could think of a reason to keep her longer.

Kiri slumped onto the sofa with a sigh, and looked up at Henry, disappointment clouding her eyes. "I don't see how I can go out tonight. I can't leave Bitsy here alone."

He sat beside her and took her hand. "Of course you can't, and I'm one of the few people in the world who understands when duty calls."

"But I want to go out. I *really* want to go out… with you… tonight."

He tucked a limp curl behind her ear. "Me too." Momentarily emboldened by her weakness, his sedate manner turned playful. "Let's go out… now!" Kiri stared at him as if he were nuts. "I'll call First Chapter and order up an authentic Irish dinner for two, complete with wine and dessert, to be delivered by taxi. We'll go out… out on your deck! And after a lovely meal, I'll take great pleasure in checking for flecks of green in your hair."

*   *   *

Nice. No fancy adjectives needed. Their evening together was relaxed… comfortable and… nice, Henry thought as he walked the short distance to his apartment. Although doomed by the events of the day, the evening ended pleasurably. If Kiri had not called off the "date," he would have. The minute he saw the note introducing Bitsy, his stomach churned. "No good no more." He was that innocent child, spoiled through no fault of his own more than forty years ago, and the memory nauseated him. The pressure of trying to romance a woman he cared for turned him inside out until he was certain his nerves were exposed for everyone to see. When Kiri said "I can't," he relaxed and an idea flashed through his mind. Together they enjoyed a close, comfortable and congenial evening with no talk of work or children or the new challenge in her life. *Nice.*

At the bewitching hour of ten, they walked hand in hand two doors up to the neighbor's to collect her sleeping children. Each carried one, tucked them into bed, and peeked in on Bitsy, like loving parents. Then, very naturally, they shared a good night kiss. No surprise. Mutually desired. Mutually enjoyed. *Nice.*

The pleasure of his evening with her lingered, even as the image of Bitsy wormed its way into his thoughts. Only he could empathize with her desperate situation—how confused and abandoned she must feel. He had a mother for an advocate who loved him and spent many years trying to make his bad situation better. Bitsy had no one. Henry was uniquely qualified to understand and help her, but how? Any attempt of a single, mature man to befriend her would be suspect.

Kiri always referred to him as "Uncle Henry" in front of her children, so he and they would consider him family. Maybe it was time to assert his position as a nominal member of this family. Spend more time with them. He showed up for emergencies, special occasions and visited every Monday afternoon for tea when his schedule permitted but always at Kiri's home. They—the whole group, however many that encompassed—needed time together in a neutral setting, free from preconceived notions and behaviors. Thomas monopolized Sundays, so Henry would commandeer Saturdays. When in town, he would take Kiri, her children, and Bitsy "out" and use those opportunities to guide the unfortunate girl toward a transition to normalcy... someday. First he must convince Kiri to keep her.

Henry sighed and slipped into bed. His initial adult experience with total commitment beyond the job was MT, an intuitive, analytical little boy under the firm thumb of his grandfather. Katie wrapped her finger around his heart the first night of her life, and now he could not imagine a day without her skipping through it. Bitsy was his chance for redemption. And Kiri... Kiri was his dream... just out of reach. With his hectic schedule and the new and constant demands on hers, options for going out alone together dwindled quickly. Encouraged by their first step toward simple intimacy tonight, he vowed to take advantage of many late evenings... after children were in bed... to go "out" on the deck... alone together. *Nice.*

Nice, Kiri thought as she eased into bed. From girlish anticipation to surprise to frustration and disappointment to pure pleasure, the twists and turns in her day left her exhausted. After Henry's perfect departure, she peeked in to assure the little birdies were safe in her nest—all three, soon to be four, of them. To entice her tingly feeling to linger, she turned on music in her bedroom—Irish harp music—and replayed the events of the late evening. A comfortable cuddle while sitting on the deck sharing a blanket against the night's chill left her feeling very satisfied. To be held close in happiness rather than heartache was so... *nice.*

* * *

Kiri awoke with her brain squeaking into operation. She gazed at the skylight and made a mental list. Phone the doctor to request a house call for special circumstances. Phone the hairdresser to request a mercy mission here at the house. Phone Maeve to borrow hand-me-down clothing for a girl with expanding waistline. Call Tommy's daughter Caitlín to see if she will come after work with the cake ladies to make a trip to the grocer for her aunt. Find a substitute to take her patients at the pool. Immediate needs—health, food, clothing—done.

She sighed deeply with the realization that if Bitsy should not go beyond the yard for a week or so, Kiri should not either. The girl could not be left in the care of a stranger without a means of communication. She sighed again. Survival skills. Time for another long-range plan, just when she thought those days were over.

Week One: Communication. Teach Bitsy enough English for everyday and how/where to call in an emergency. Acquire a simple cell phone. Teach her to fend for herself in the water—a must for survival near a pool. The exercise will be good for her too.

Week Two: Walk up the road in stages. Introduce her to one or two neighbors a day. They will watch out for her—especially Paddy. By the end of the week, take her to a shop at the top of the road. Then add one per day.

Week Three: Childbirth education and childcare. Check the Internet for appropriate videos. Better idea—check with Maeve. She must know a new mother nearby who will allow her newborn to be observed.

Week Four: Family? Paula and Thomas first? Spare Bitsy the drama? Revisit.

Kiri yawned and stretched. A smile skittered across her face. Oh! Most important of all—call Henry! Thank him for the unexpectedly wonderful evening. Satisfied that she accounted for major necessities, she swung her legs over the edge of the bed... and nearly stepped on Bitsy, fast asleep on the floor wrapped in her cloak with a black feather caught in its hood.

CHAPTER 9

Kiri did not factor in her own children's reactions to the new houseguest. They ambled into the kitchen sleepy-eyed, climbed into the nook for breakfast and discovered a stranger sitting there. Kiri introduced her as "Bitsy, your distant cousin, who will stay with us for a while."

"Oh," they both said and drank their juice. "Does that mean she lives far away?" MT asked. "Like a long distance?"

"You could say that. She comes from the West."

"She doesn't say much," Katie said.

"She speaks a different language. We'll all have to help her learn English."

Before Kiri could finish, ideas for teaching English spilled forth from her children. MT was into nouns—naming objects throughout the house. Katie was all verbs—demonstrating every action possible. Bitsy was confused at being bombarded from both sides, so Kiri set ground rules— ten minutes each, in turn, and ten minutes for the young girl to sit alone with a snack and "digest" her learning.

By midafternoon and after breaks for the doctor, the hairdresser's daughter and Maeve with a bag of clothing, she called a halt to the vocabulary game and sent each to his own room for a rest, hoping they would fall asleep. She heard strange mutterings coming from MT's and could not believe it was her son who broke the rules. "What is going on in there? Are you and Bitsy talking?"

"No. Just me. I'm practicing her language. Every word she learns in English, she teaches me in her own tongue. That way, if she forgets I can help her remember. Mom, does her language have a name?"

"Irish Gaelic. Now, rest." Kiri closed his door and walked over to the pool to thank Maeve's sister's friend for substituting the rest of the week. She returned to jot down a list of items for Caitlín and found MT standing at the deck door with his electronic tablet in his hands. "I'm surprised at you. No play during rest time."

"I'm not playing. I'm investigating. I need a new app."

Kiri clapped her hands to her forehead. "Michael Thomas O'Connell! No apps! Your pad is a tool, not a toy. Now, back upstairs, and put that thing away."

Her son did not budge. "But this one *is* a tool. For helping Bitsy. It goes from English to Irish and back with pictures, letters, and sounds. Watch." He said the word "chair," and the screen showed one with a word printed to either side—English to the right and Irish to the left. He tapped the English word and the spoken word sounded. He tapped the other and a funny sound came out. "That is Bitsy's language. I learned 'chair' this morning. I don't know how many words it has but probably lots."

"How did you find this?"

"I asked my pad to 'find Irish Gaelic apps.' I tried a few, but this one made sense to me. Bitsy could learn to teach herself when we aren't around."

"You clever little boy." She tousled MT's hair. "I think you are absolutely right. I'll arrange it. Now, go rest!"

"Don't call me 'little!' Grandfather says I'm big enough to start school. When I get there, *I* will speak two ways and everybody else only one." He smiled proudly and scampered up the stairs.

Kiri made out her grocery list and brought some business accounts up to date. She was about to stretch out to rest when a sheepish little form appeared at her side holding scissors in one hand and a hank of curly red hair in the other. "Aurora Kathryn O'Connell! What have you done!"

"I wanted to have straight, pretty hair like Bitsy after the lady came and fixed it. Besides, I don't like this curl. It's always flopping in my eyes!"

Kiri smoothed Katie's hair back and found a bare spot where her favorite curl—Michael's curl—used to be. She took the scissors away and gave her daughter a big hug. "Your curls are special 'copper penny' curls, and not many girls have ones as pretty as yours. They tell everyone you have a fierce, powerful spirit. Next time, ask me first, and when you're Bitsy's age the lady will come and fix your hair too. Okay?"

" 'Kay." She handed her mother her hair and shook her finger. "But don't call me Aurora Kathryn anymore! I don't want to be a fairy princess or a tree. I want to be Katie Maureen Elizabeth Kelly Orla Bridget Taylor Sara Keeley Michelle Robin Henry Callaghan O'Connell!" She skipped away. "And maybe Helen too!"

At the end of too long a day with decidedly too many words, Kiri turned on the harp music and fell into bed exhausted, unsure of who learned the most.

*   *   *

Kiri awoke to find Bitsy lying on the floor next to her bed again. She tried to ask her why, but the young girl made no response. Perhaps she does not know the words for feelings in any language, Kiri thought, because she never had an opportunity to express them. She patted her on the head and tried to tell her that today she would learn how to swim.

Bitsy, who barely felt comfortable in a full-sized bathtub, balked at entering Kiri's pool. The two sat on the edge of the kids' corner with only their feet in the water while MT and Katie splashed about. Katie was all arms and legs trying to demonstrate the few strokes she knew. MT took the direct approach, attempting to explain each one and illustrate each step separately. When they tired of encouraging Bitsy to join them, they swam off to play.

Kiri finally coaxed her reluctant pupil to stand in the water and then eased her back into a float. When her baby bump rose above water line, no one pointed or made a rude comment, a compliment to the aquacenter's staff and clientele. Kiri prided herself in surrounding her environs with the best and knew Bitsy would be watched over by many pairs of accepting eyes.

After three short sessions that day, interspersed with breaks for a meal, snacks, and more language lessons, Bitsy floated with confidence in shallow water and with a modified back stroke, tried to keep up with MT while Katie splashed along beside. By the end of the week Kiri was satisfied that she could return to a shortened work schedule in the pool and her three young charges would survive.

She put everyone down for a mandatory rest period and intended to sneak one for herself when Henry called.

"How are they all getting on?"

"Pretty well. My two are trying to teach Bitsy English, but it is slow going. She can swim well enough to handle herself in my pool, and according to the doctor, her health is good. So, we're making progress. Bitsy seems comfortable enough with us, so I don't think she'll run away. I find her sleeping on the floor next to my bed every morning, so I now wake her and lead her upstairs when I'm ready to turn in and put her in bed with me. She likes that, but I wish she would smile... even once."

"She will. Give her time." He paused. "Work is slow enough around here that I can take the whole day off tomorrow, Saturday. I thought we could go out."

"Oh, Henry. I would love to but I can't leave."

"I don't expect you to. I meant *we*... all of us. Let's take a picnic and go for a short drive to a quiet place I know. We shouldn't be bothered by anyone, if you're worried about Bitsy and crowds."

"You are a savior! We... all of us... are delighted to accept your invitation."

Henry drove along a coastal road to what he called a "safe place." South of Kilcoole, he turned toward the sea and a picture postcard day opened up before the little band of relief-seekers. An old fishing pier jutted far beyond the shore inviting them to plop stones into the water or skip stones across it. Those seeking repose could lie on their bellies and count schools of baby fish swimming between the piles in the shallow water or lie on their backs and count seagulls flying overhead. A small, sandy beach tempted tiny fingers and toes to dig for crabby critters or to disappear with each miniature wave carrying sand to cover them. A knoll covered with marram grass beckoned to anyone hungry for a picnic or longing for a snooze. And for Kiri, brilliant colors splashed across the canvas of the scene.

Near afternoon's end, when Katie and MT fought drooping eyelids as they lay on the blanket and stared at clouds, Henry jostled Kiri's shoulder. "Bitsy and I are going for a walk. We won't be long." He took the young girl by the hand and they strolled to the end of the pier to sit for a private chat. Kiri noticed similarities in their builds—slender, same proportions of leg to trunk, like tilts to the shoulders and when they faced one another, the contour of their noses. By the time the odd couple returned, Kiri had surrendered to her own eyelids.

"Wake up, sleepyhead," Henry joked as he pretended to yank the blanket from beneath her, much to the delight of her two children. "Time to go."

She rubbed her eyes. "I have the strangest feeling I've been here before."

"You have... and MT too, although he didn't know it."

* * *

Kiri was not ready to introduce Bitsy to the family yet. She scheduled that for week three or four at the earliest. When Thomas arrived to collect his two grandchildren for their Sunday morning together at church, she tucked the young girl away in the mudroom to fold her own laundry. She hustled her two out the door and closed it firmly behind them with a sigh of relief. Then she remembered, her children would talk... a lot! No telling what tales they might tell of their mysterious guest. She needed a plan for Thomas' return.

She revisited her intention for a quiet morning. Bitsy needed more one-on-one practice in the pool to perfect her strokes. The other children's absence made this time opportune. Kiri would have only one body to watch. She also wanted to test the girl's skills in a kitchen. Surely she had prepared food for herself and maybe others during her growing up years, but she needed to experience modern appliances. The two of them would prepare lunch together—a light casserole, simple salad and fruit. Kiri decided the plan would work with a slight adjustment—move the usual bath after swimming to a bath before lunch.

Thomas returned Katie and MT at the stroke of one. He invited himself in. The two children ran for their rooms to change out of their nice clothes, leaving the adults face-to-face. "I understand you have a guest."

"Yes."

"MT says he is teaching her English while she teaches him Irish Gaelic."

"That's true."

"I'm surprised at how much he has learned. His vocabulary is very limited, but his accent is quite good—from the West, sounds like."

"And Katie?"

He chuckled. "Paula had her hands full trying to keep her from standing on the pew to lead the choir. May I meet your guest?"

"Sorry. Not today. She's in the tub." On cue, the stove timer sounded. "Time for lunch to come out. Thanks for taking the kids. Give Mom a hug for me." She motioned toward the door.

Thomas started to say something more, but Kiri's phone rang. She picked it up from the hall console table and waved goodbye with a smile, closing the door behind him. She leaned against it, relieved. Calling herself from her business phone in her pocket, and not pressing "send" until she wanted to end their conversation, worked perfectly.

* * *

Introducing Bitsy to the neighbors did not take as long as Kiri anticipated. Paddy spread word of the young girl and her situation up and down the road, so she was warmly welcomed. Some even spoke to her in the few phrases of the old tongue they remembered. Bitsy remained shy but not uncomfortable in their presence. Kiri knew they would watch out for her and point her home if she got lost, but a smart jacket and shoes might be necessary for the time being.

Those meetings went so well that Kiri advanced the schedule for visiting the shops. The grocer greeted the party of four and invited them to roam his aisles leisurely. She took note of which items Bitsy recognized and which seemed new to her so she could adjust their meals accordingly. MT was right at her elbow to name the various foods for her while Katie skipped about touching this and that. Each child selected one treat. Bitsy chose a cup of berries.

Next stop was the teashop. The ladies there doted on the O'Connell kids and accepted the new addition with delight. Each child selected one treat. Bitsy chose a square of chocolate. They passed the stylist's and waved to the woman who did Bitsy's hair. They were about to backtrack toward home when Kiri caught sight of a new shop and decided to investigate.

An old-fashioned bell above the door jingled as the four entered. A kindly man with frizzy gray hair and wire-rimmed glasses welcomed them with a twinkly eye and a smile. He opened his arms wide to present his range of wares—furniture and curios, many of them antiques. Kiri shuddered at the thought of Katie twirling her way around the shop and touching everything, so she held her daughter by the wrist while MT and Bitsy wandered off.

She chatted with the owner and learned that he specialized in estate sales. "The older folk have fine things that their children don't appreciate, so I buy them and sell to the younger generation as curiosities or starter sets for first homes. I just opened here a few weeks ago."

"Do you take any items on consignment? Heaven knows I have an attic full of pieces that would fit right in."

He raised a curious eyebrow, so Kiri explained that he would not pay her for an item but take a percentage of its price *after* the sale. "You invest your time instead of your money. I have several older neighbors who would be interested too."

They were at the point of exchanging names and numbers when a music selection caught her ear—Irish harp—a simple rendition, but touching. "I love that recording. I've never heard it before. Do you sell traditional music too?"

"That's not a recording, Ma'am. That's your girl over there." He nodded toward the window where Bitsy sat on a stool with a harp barely two feet tall perched between her knees and pressed against her protuberant tummy. She plucked gently at its strings. MT, cross-legged at her feet, was mesmerized by the sound. Even Katie stopped her jabbering.

"Bitsy! No!" Kiri shouted and hurried across the shop.

The owner stopped her. "No harm done. She plays well. How long has she studied?"

"Never, to my knowledge," Kiri said as she reached the girl and kneeled beside her. "How did you learn to play so beautifully?"

Bitsy looked at her with eyes sparkling an intense blue, skin as soft and white as a dove's belly, and a smile so broad it reached clear around her head to meet itself on the other side. In a voice as clear as crystal, English words spilled from her. "It just come to me like... like a fairy whispering in m' ear."

Stunned by the beautiful music filling the shop and the unexpected phrase of explanation, Kiri remained a statue poised over the young musician until time called them home. Bitsy refused to leave. She clutched the small stringed instrument to her chest and shook her head, tears squeezing through her eyelids—the first real emotion she expressed in almost two weeks.

"They say the ancient harpists were born with music in their souls—music that could lull men to sleep, bring them great joy and move them to weep. That gift can't be taught or bought." The shop owner smiled. "Looks like you've been blessed with one."

When she caught her breath, Kiri paid the man handsomely for the antique in less than pristine condition and hurried her family out the door. Bitsy led, clutching her instrument firmly and having no difficulty winding through the crowds of a late afternoon. She found her way without a second look and turned down Quincy Street, leaving the others to double-time after her to keep up. She went straight to her room and began to play again. The harp showed up to dinner, watched over bath time, and snuggled under the covers held tightly in its new owner's arms.

Kiri shook her head in disbelief as she made her way to the living room and a conversation with Michael. She scowled at him. From her spot on the sofa, she stared into his portrait eyes pondering how to begin a serious conversation with a person who was not there. She often aimed an off-hand remark his way when she was frustrated or delighted by the children's behavior. She engaged in one-sided conversations with him on his birthday and their anniversary, carving out as much time as possible underneath their evergreen tree to bring him up to date on the family. She wanted to believe he watched their every move, but in case he blinked, and as much to remind herself of the incidental as well as the memorable, she carried on a lengthy monologue that confused her children when they toddled out to beg a bite of fairy cake. She still repeated her vows and burned a pledge to him every anniversary, but they were less sentimental than early on and more statements of survival. *I'm trying. I'm hanging on. Even my best fails me sometimes.*

This day's incident at the second-hand shop, however, called for a real conversation, a two-way, with questions and answers. Bitsy's innocent and clearly spoken phrase, *like a fairy whispering in my ear*, could only have come from Michael speaking through her. Numerous others—family and friends—spoke of sudden thoughts *popping into their heads like a...* but could never finish the statement. Bitsy was the first—an emissary—but her message was a heavenly garble.

"Don't you think you've gone a bit overboard here to convince me to send Michael Thomas to a *gaelscoil*? You know I want to wait another year or home school until Katie is ready too. Suddenly this waif of a girl shows up on the doorstep speaking only Irish and now revealing an innate ability for the Celtic harp. MT is enchanted with her and is teaching himself Irish faster than his tongue will move. I have no choice but to send him to an Irish language school where English will become his second language... so you win this round.

"I really try to abide by your wishes for watching over the nieces and nephews, even when inconvenienced. I think I've got love, safety and a measure of joy covered, so I don't understand where Bitsy fits in. Taking on the obligation of an uneducated teen mother and her baby is quite a price to pay for a fairy's whisper that tells me to send our boy to *gaelscoil*, so what am I missing? I admit, there is something special about this girl, but I'm not getting the connection.

"I want answers! Why did you send Bitsy to Thomas—as I believe you did—when you knew he wouldn't be home? Why did she end up with me? Why is she really here? I want answers, and I intend to sit here and stare at you until I get them. Do something! Wink. Illuminate a candle. Touch my shoulder. Send a fairy's whisper to *my* ear."

Kiri sat and stared... and sat... and stared. Nothing changed. After interminable minutes she sensed a hovering behind her and shuddered. A gentle touch on her shoulder tingled to her toes. *Michael?* She reached for his hand—just one more touch to last a lifetime—and met Bitsy's delicate fingers tapping her. "Music for sleep," the girl whispered in her ear. "Music for sleep."

Bitsy took her new aunt's hand and tugged to pull her up. With the other, she carried the harp. She led Kiri upstairs to the octagonal bedroom and said again, "Music for sleep," pointing to the nightstand.

It wasn't my company Bitsy sought in the night. It was the music... the harp music I played. The music stirred something inside her. Kiri disconnected her player and followed Bitsy back downstairs to set it up in the guestroom. As soon as ancient strains filled the room, Bitsy crawled into her bed with her new harp and fell asleep.

As Kiri passed Michael's portrait on her way upstairs again, she nodded. "Message received. Don't question the blessings I've been given. Be grateful for them."

Immediately upon waking, Kiri phoned Henry. "Call off the investigation of Killian cousins. I'll gladly act as Bitsy's guardian if we can sort out the legal issues."

"This news is a surprise."

"Long story. I'll tell you next time you come."

"About Saturday..."

"Sorry. We can't tomorrow. Mom is hosting one of her grandchildren activities for ten and under with Meggie and Breeda helping. My kids are committed for the afternoon."

"I was about to say, since my Saturday is impossible this week, why don't I take you all out for ice cream this evening? You can tell your long tale then."

"Great! We have a surprise for you."

Henry arrived shortly after supper. The minute she heard his car in the drive and recognized his step on the walk, Bitsy ran out to meet him. She took his hand and pulled him into the guestroom without allowing him a hello to anyone else. She sat on the edge of her bed, uncovered the harp, placed it in front of her belly and began to play. When she finished a simple but merry piece, she smiled broadly at him and said, "Music for joy!"

CHAPTER 10

A frazzled Kiri cursed herself when she pulled up to Thomas' house and regarded the sulky child in the seat behind her. Katie developed pouting into an art form, and Bitsy picked it up fast. The young girl was patient when dragged along to deliver MT and Katie to Thomas' house earlier. After a series of errands at the shops, a mandatory rest and almost no time on her harp before being hustled into the car again, she displayed her displeasure well.

Kiri needed her to be the sweet, ethereal creature they came to love over the last two weeks, for this afternoon she would meet family—a giant leap to week four. Paula's rule—come in to get your kids and confirm they are just as you left them. Kiri forgot that she could not leave Bitsy in the car alone when she picked up her children, so she cursed herself... again... and trembled at the thought of running into her stepsisters.

Katie was the first to notice when the two entered quietly. She leapt around the living room announcing, "Bitsy's here! Bitsy's here!" MT took the girl by the hand to introduce her to the other cousins. Meggie stepped in to help, being the oldest there and nearest in age to the young teen. When she finished her round, Katie came to a halt beside her mother who was just within earshot of the stepsibs.

"So this is the rumored 'guest' at Kiri's house."

"Looks like there will be more than one soon."

"I'd be embarrassed to let her out in public."

"Kiri *would* adopt any knocked up orphan who came along just to humiliate the rest of us," Anne sneered.

Katie turned her boxy frame toward her rude aunt and planted her feet in a wide stance. She crossed her chunky arms on her chest and jutted a determined chin out and up, her fiery curls quivering. "Bitsy's not 'dopted. She's family just like you and me. So be nice!"

The high-pitched command caught Thomas' attention. The sight of the small, strong-willed figure standing up to an elder recalled his son Michael at the same age, and he suddenly realized how little attention he paid to Katie's personality quirks in favor of Michael Thomas. That little boy tugged at his hand to present Bitsy.

Initially repulsed by her condition, Thomas recovered to quiz the girl in Irish. The more he spoke, the more comfortable she became in sharing the few details of her background. When she mentioned playing the harp, punctuated with a luminous smile, he was astonished. How could this simple child grasp the significance of the instrument?

Kiri ordered her children to the door. "Sorry, Mom. Talk to you later. I can't stay where my family is insulted." She directed a glare toward the stepsisters.

Before she could escape with her brood, Meggie came forward. "I'd like to be Bitsy's friend, if you'll let me. I know what it feels like to be left out."

Kiri gave her niece a hug. "That's very sweet of you. Perhaps next week. She'll learn about childbirth and childcare then and may need a friend."

Meggie smiled and squeezed Bitsy's hand. "I'm very good with babies!"

*   *   *

"Don't look back, Paula, but I think we're being followed." Thomas spoke softly as they strolled, arm-in-arm, along the diagonal of the Green.

"Your imagination is playing tricks. No one is behind us. No footsteps."

He sneaked a peek low to the right. "He's still there. I see his shadow."

Paula took a bold stance, turned and laughed. "That's you, Thomas O'Connell!" She rotated him slightly in the late afternoon sun. "Wave your hand." The shadow waved. "See?"

"Can't be," Thomas flustered. "This one walks with his chin three steps ahead of the rest of him and wears a backpack in front."

"As do you, silly man. Follow my finger's path on the shade." She traced from his forehead, down his nose to his chin, inward to his chest and outward along the curve of his stomach. He shook his head. Paula nodded hers. "Yes, that is you. You lean forward when you walk as if you want to hit the pavement nose first, and that pack you carry holds second helpings of potatoes and the snacks you sneak when I'm not looking."

He shook his head again. "I used to stand erect, chest out." He inhaled deeply, puffed it out and slapped it.

"You used to be twenty-five years old." She took his arm again. "And I could barely keep up with you. Lately, you've begun to lag."

"I don't see the point in hurrying." He walked more and more slowly to irritate her. Then he sped up to a near jog. "Unless I'm anxious to arrive." And stopped suddenly when he grew winded.

"What are you so anxious about today?" she asked when she caught up to him.

"Talking to the new girl, Bitsy. A week and two Sundays have passed, and Kirin won't let me in her house. If I do get a foot in, she says Bitsy is 'unavailable at present.' I don't understand. Does she think I'm going to devour the girl or send her away to a home for unwed mothers?"

"No," Paula laughed. "She's being protective. She doesn't want Bitsy to become an object of family gossip." When Thomas started to protest, she arched an eyebrow.

"Hmm. Tomorrow will be different. Tomorrow we'll do our gardening in the morning when we're not expected," he said with a twinkle and jogged a few more steps toward home.

*   *   *

Thomas peeked over the fence before opening the gate to Kiri's back garden. He spotted her in the pool next door with a patient and her two children paddling nearby. Bitsy leaned back in a lounge chair beneath the evergreen tree with her harp propped between her knees and against her tummy and right shoulder. She tossed her hair, still damp from a swim lesson, and placed her open hands against either side of the strings, thrumming her fingers lightly against them. He smiled when she bent her ear near to investigate the sound.

He put his finger to his lips to quiet Paula who carried garden tools toward the gate. "Shh. Let's watch for a minute. Lovely, isn't she?"

Paula nodded. "Very. But she won't be friendly if she catches you spying on her. Be the kindly, gentle man I know, and you won't scare her away." She opened the gate quietly and smiled at Bitsy as she hauled the tools to the garden. "Don't mind me. I have a little work to do over there." She pointed to the far side, knowing the girl could not understand but might judge her tone as friendly.

Thomas approached Bitsy slowly and spoke only in Gaelic. He greeted her and reintroduced himself. She nodded. He asked if he could pull up a chair and listen while she played. She nodded again and began to pluck the strings. When she stopped, he asked if her tune had a name. She shook her head. He wanted to know if anyone else in her family played... if she brought the harp from her home in the West... where she got this one... if she had heard harp music before she found this one in the shop... and how she knew what to play.

"A feeling inside me tells m' fingers what to do," she answered shyly in Irish.

He examined the instrument as closely as he could without getting too near and showed her how to use her fingernails on the brass strings to produce a bell-like sound, almost like a harpsichord. He watched her discover she could play faster using them. Then he leaned back in his chair, interlaced his fingers across his belly and told her about the harp.

"Many years ago, long before you took your first breath, the harpist was a very important person... one born with the gift to make music without written notes. When a bard told a story or a poem, the harpist played music to go with it. Do you know what a story is?" She shook her head. "Then, let me tell you one, and when you have a feeling that goes with the words I say, play a little bit." She nodded. "Do you know 'rabbit?'" She giggled when he tried to demonstrate. "Do you know 'bird?'" She nodded with a smile. "Do you know 'ocean?'" She said Henry took her there. "Do you know 'island?'" She shook her head, so he decided to place his story about puffins and rabbits on the ground next to the ocean.

Paula watched and listened from across the yard but did not understand a word of their conversation. She gleaned the gist of the story from Thomas' parodies of action and emotion and their musical accompaniments ranging from happiness to sadness, fear to fatigue to pain, and from a sunny day to pouring rain to a terrible storm. She was in stitches when they finally arrived at a joyful finale.

He wiped his glistening forehead with his handkerchief. "Very well done! You told the story beautifully with your music. We'll tell another… after your baby comes."

Bitsy giggled again and touched her belly. "I'm the ewe and this is my lamb."

Oh dear, Thomas thought. What this child could do with a range of experience to draw on. He rose, took a euro coin from his pocket and showed her the symbol on the front. "Keep this to remind you how special your harp is when you're not allowed to carry the instrument with you." He patted her on the head. "You play what you want now. I'll listen from over there." He pointed to the patio sofa on the deck. "*Go mbeannaí Dia duit.* May God bless you."

Her eyes turned a melancholy shade of blue. "He won't. I'm no good no more," she said in a tiny Irish voice.

Thomas gulped to choke back a cry. He tilted her chin upward and kissed her forehead. "Of course He will. He chose *you* to be our heavenly messenger with the harp."

Paula joined him on the deck when Bitsy resumed playing—a gentle melody with a touch of yearning in it. Within moments, tears were streaming down Thomas' face. She had no idea what brought on such emotion, but she held his hand tightly and left him to it.

Music that can make men weep, Kiri thought as she witnessed the scene from the pool side of the fence.

*   *   *

Kiri knew the day would arrive but dreaded the conversation. Paula insisted they stay for lunch, and she would prepare it. With the three young ones fed and bedded down for a rest, Kiri saw no way to avoid another of Thomas' inquisitions. Paula warned him to tread carefully or her daughter was likely to clam up. After all, they did break in uninvited with an obvious purpose in mind, so Kiri had every right to ask them to leave.

"Bitsy tells me you found her harp at a shop nearby." Kiri nodded. "Judging by the woods used for the neck and soundbox, and the craftsmanship, I'd say the instrument is similar to a Brian Boru but only about two hundred years old. I counted twenty-two strings, which gives her three octaves to work with. At a little over two feet tall and being so light at less than ten pounds, it is perfect to carry along as a folk instrument to accompany singing and storytelling. Not many of these small harps are still around. The nicks in the pedestal and forepillar, and its lack of much carving and decorative details, saved it from being snapped up by a collector. You have a very fine instrument on your hands."

"Thank you."

"Bitsy also tells me she grew up on a farm in the West, and her father sent her here to the city. How did you find her?"

"She was delivered to my doorstep like a package dropped in the post. She was addressed to you, but you weren't home."

Thomas seemed baffled, so she reluctantly showed him the note attached to the girl's cape. He examined it carefully and clapped his hand over his mouth to stop a profanity. The words "no good no more" stung him, causing him to well up inside rather than out. He took a deep breath and recovered enough to say, with tears in his eyes, "She's a *Killian*."

Kiri nodded. "Proof positive."

"And *you* took her in."

"Michael would have done the same."

"My dear, dear Kirin. You have no idea what this means. Is there anything I can do to help you... to help her... *anything*?" He could barely get the words out.

Kiri thought for a moment, considering her two options. She did not want one more reason for Thomas to wedge his way into her life and weighed that against the emotional scene she witnessed earlier. She studied her mother's deep green eyes to discern her preference for another phantom Killian, or a present one, in her life.

"If it isn't too much trouble, will you take Bitsy along with my two children on Sunday mornings? She won't understand a word yet, of course, and the crowd may make her nervous... but I think the music will fill her heart with great joy."

CHAPTER 11

"Has the baby come yet!" Meggie shouted as she ran through Kiri's front door after school.

"Not yet, love," Maeve said as she bustled from kitchen to the stairs. "It may be awhile, so you are a welcome sight. The two young ones are a bit underfoot and ready for a swim at the center."

"I'll say a quick hello to Bitsy and then take them away... far away," the perky thirteen-year-old said as she followed Maeve to the floor above. She spent a few minutes with the expectant mother and then confided in the midwife. "Bitsy seems worried and uncomfortable. Is she in pain?"

"Nothing she can't handle. I'm afraid I'm the one who's brought the jitters on with all my talk of birthing being just like on the farm with the sheep and the lambs. We spent several days with a newborn learning to diaper, bathe, swaddle, clothe, and comfort him. She observed the baby nursing, but she can't get it into her head that she's got a two-legged creature inside of her instead of a four-legged one. Poor thing has worked herself into a fright."

"There must be something we can do."

"We haven't found the magic secret so far."

"Has the baby come yet?" Katie squealed on her return from the pool.

Kiri stopped her at the top of the stairs. "Not yet. Bitsy's trying to rest, so we all need to be quiet. Here are your clothes." She handed a bundle to each child. "Bathe and change downstairs while Meggie fixes your supper. Depending on how Bitsy feels, you may get to say good night. Now, scoot."

"Has the baby... uh... come yet," Thomas asked over the phone.

"No. Not yet."

"Trouble? I hope you have a medic unit standing by."

"Bitsy is fine. Just nervous, but nothing Maeve and I can't handle."

"Should your mother and I come? Maybe we can help with your young ones."

"No, Thomas. Meggie is sitting with them. We'll call you when there is news—if it's not too late."

"Call anytime... anytime. We'll come right over to welcome the new little one."

"You know Bitsy needs her space or she'll get flustered. She'll need to rest. We'll let you know at the first convenient moment."

He paused. "Remind her of the coin. It might help her nerves."

"What coin?"

"Just do as I ask!" he shouted, then paused. "I'm sorry. Please remind her of the coin. Thank you."

"Has the baby come yet?"

"Aurora Kathryn O'Connell! What are you doing down there?" Kiri was startled by the sight of her moppet scooching along the floor on her belly toward her mother's bed.

Meggie's head poked through the doorway, followed by MT's. "I'm sorry, Aunt Kiri. I was reading them a story in the living room when Katie disappeared and sneaked up the service stairs. I'm very good with babies, but Katie isn't a baby anymore."

"No problem. They can say their good nights now. We'll move Bitsy to the tub soon."

Bitsy's moaning and whimpers upset the little girl. "Mommy, she's making funny noises. Is something wrong with her?"

"She's frightened and tired. She'll feel better soon. Now, to bed."

"Wake us up when the baby comes? Promise?"

"I promise. Now, go!"

MT piped up. "I know why Bitsy's upset. She needs..."

"I think Maeve and I know what she needs. Off with you, or you won't wake up when I call."

"Has the baby come yet?"

"Michael Thomas O'Connell! What are you doing out of bed?"

"I know what Bitsy needs. I can understand what she says. She needs her music."

"I don't have time right now to give you a science lesson on what will happen to a harp exposed to steam for a long time. Go to bed and let us do our jobs."

MT did not budge one inch. He stood up tall and tightened his jaw. "Mother! Listen to my grownup voice! Bitsy needs her music... and I have it on my tablet. I made videos when she practiced. If you play these for her, I know she'll feel better." He forced the electronic gadget into his mother's hand. "Good night!"

"Has the baby come yet?" Gus's hearty voice bellowed into his sister's ear.

"Just. A little girl, and I mean little like her mom. But all systems function, so she'll be just fine."

"And Bitsy?"

"We found the magic secret. Once we got her music going, she calmed right down and relaxed. Next you know, we had a baby in our hands."

"Nice going, Sis. I'll spread the word. Give Kiri a hug. Oh, and we'll expect a proof of life in the morning."

"Has the baby come yet?"

"Henry! What are you doing up at this hour?"

"I just got home and noticed your house lit up like a Christmas tree. Well?"

"A little girl, almost as mellow as MT. We're about to take Bitsy down now to get the two of them settled in her room."

"How will you manage that?"

"Very carefully, but with the two of us, we'll make it work."

"Hang on for a minute. I'll carry her for you."

"How long is a minute?"

"Long enough for you to slide down the banister and open the front door." The bell rang and there he stood, all smiles.

With Bitsy back in her own bed, her harp propped against the wall on one side, her daughter on the other and the euro coin back underneath her pillow where Kiri found it, the new mother was ready to receive her first guests. "Shouldn't we ask her if she feels up to seeing your children tonight?" Henry suggested. At Kiri's nod, he asked Bitsy if she wanted to invite MT and Katie to meet her baby. She smiled shyly and said "yes."

"Would you grab Katie and hold her tight? I'm afraid she'll be so excited that she'll make a running jump for the bed, scare Bitsy, and bounce the baby onto the floor."

Henry chuckled and followed Kiri to the little girl's bedroom. Her delighted squeal sounded clear down the stairs. MT came quietly, holding Meggie's hand.

Katie pressed her little fists to her mouth so she would not wake the new baby, but her bright bug eyes showed her amazement. MT sucked his lips in so he would not make a sound. Meggie, her wavy, strawberry blond hair flouncing around her face, looked on in awe. "This is way better than seeing a new baby in a hospital! May I touch her?"

After Maeve's translation, Bitsy nodded. Meggie stroked the tiny cheek and fuzzy head with her little finger. "She is so precious. You must be very proud." Bitsy smiled.

Katie wiggled in Henry's arms and whispered in his ear, "Me too." He bent to hold her just close enough to touch. "She's soft, but she doesn't talk."

"Babies can't talk until somebody teaches them." MT rolled his eyes and moved in for his turn. "We can all help with that job."

"Can I hold her?" Katie asked.

Kiri shook her head. "Maybe tomorrow. A baby needs to get used to its mother first, but if you promise not to move, you may stand quietly at the edge of the bed." Henry eased her down but kept his hand twisted into the back of her nighty just in case she tried to hop up.

"What's her name?" Katie asked. They all looked from one to another and shrugged. Katie demonstrated by patting her hand on her chest. "Katie." She pointed. "Bitsy." And pointed again, waiting for the new mother to fill in the blank.

"Baby," Bitsy said in English with a smile.

Katie let out a deep breath and tried again. "Katie… Meggie… MT… Henry… Bitsy… and…."

"Baby!"

Maeve tried to explain in Irish that a name was what you called someone. Katie tried again. "Katie… Meggie… Henry and…"

"Lamb!" Bitsy shouted proudly.

Maeve dropped her head to her hands and shook it. "Mercy. What have I done?"

Katie giggled. "You can't name a baby after an animal."

"But you can name a sister after a tree," MT taunted.

"I'm not a tree anymore!" Katie shot back. "I'm Katie Maureen Elizabeth Kelly Orla Bridget Taylor Sara Keeley Michelle Robin Henry Callaghan O'Connell… but I will share one of those with the baby." They all tried not to laugh. "She can't have Henry, but she can have Bridget or Sara."

"I like Sara," MT said. "It's easy to spell for when Bitsy learns her letters and how to write."

"I like Sara, too," Meggie agreed. "Sara is a pretty name for a pretty girl. Besides, the kids at school will tease her if she is called Lamb."

Katie nodded and tried again. "Katie… Bitsy… Sara!"

Bitsy shook her head. "Lamb!"

Kiri agreed that Lamb would be an outrageous choice, but she did not want to override the new mother's first major decision. "I think we all need to go to bed and let Bitsy decide in the morning after her mind is refreshed."

"No, Mommy," Katie whined. "The baby has to have a name now so we can add her to our prayers."

A calm, serious voice of reason added his opinion to the melee. Henry spoke a sentence at a time—first in English, then a repeat in Irish. "I think Bitsy should use both names. 'Sara' is very pretty, for a pretty little girl. It means princess. 'Lamb' is special to Bitsy because it reminds her of where she grew up. A lamb is an innocent, gentle animal. A very old story…"

Bitsy's eyes lit up when Henry mentioned "story."

"A very old story tells of a powerful Irish king called Brian Boru who was greatly loved by his people. They liked to sing and dance and listen to the music of harps when they honored him with stories of his greatness. Many years later, a fine lady—we'll call her a princess—found a very beautiful harp and wanted to buy it. 'Nay,' said its maker. 'I fashioned this special—one of a kind. I call it the Brian Boru in memory of our ancient king.' She begged him until he agreed to sell it for twenty lambs and twenty ewes, on one condition. She must play beautiful music telling the story of old Ireland for her children every night in memory of the great king."

All the children were fascinated, so Henry continued. "Many people today have two given names like Brian Boru, and I think Sara Lamb would be a very nice name for this baby. She could use Sara most of the time, but when she grows up to be pretty as a princess and meets a handsome young man, he will ask her for her name. She'll say, 'Sara Lamb,' and he'll ask, 'Why Lamb?' 'My mother named me Lamb to remind me to be gentle with all the people I love,' she'll say. When she goes out in the world and has a job, she will call herself Sara Lamb Killian, a very distinctive, professional name, and people will think she is a kind-hearted and important person. I vote for Sara Lamb Killian."

Nods all around expressed agreement, but none were more emphatic than Bitsy's. She picked up the small pink bundle and cradled it in her arms. "Sara Lamb," she whispered softly to her sleeping baby. "Sara Lamb," she smiled at everyone with great joy in her eyes.

"Very clever, Mr. Callaghan," Kiri said, moving to his side.

"A practical solution," he replied. "The world at large will assume that Lamb is a family name—like Kirin Koyle O'Connell—and not think it strange at all."

"What gave you that bright idea?"

"I don't know. It just popped into my head." Henry felt Kiri shudder as if she had seen a ghost. "I think everyone should know where he came from and how he got his name. Bitsy will embellish the story as she tells it over and over. Someday maybe her father sending her away won't be the defining moment in her life, and Sara will grow up knowing only gentleness and love."

"You are very good with children."

"I'm learning, but right now I wish they'd go to bed. I can't hold onto Katie much longer."

Kiri started to hustle her children out. Bitsy protested when Maeve tried to put Sara in her own little cradle. "Maybe I should sit the night with her so she can keep the baby longer. Take Sara away when Bitsy falls asleep."

"I'll do it!" Meggie volunteered. "I can lie in a sleeping bag by the bed. Oh, please let me stay the night, Aunt Kiri. Please."

Kiri watched Meggie nearly burst with excitement. "You know the rules. Your parents…"

The teen ran from the room and down the stairs, returning with her backpack. She handed Kiri a note. "I asked Mother for permission… just in case. Please can I stay?"

Kiri smiled. "Help me get my two to bed. Then Maeve will show you what to do."

"Yes!" she almost shouted, then turned to reassure Bitsy. "I'm very good with babies."

The house on Quincy Street finally succumbed to dark and quiet with the exception of a lone candle burning on the deck table and Henry rustling in the kitchen. He assembled a platter of sliced bread, meats and cheeses, finger veggies and fruit. His search for a celebratory libation took him to the pantry where he found an open bottle of ale and wondered if Maeve nipped a little on the side. When he sniffed, it was odorless, so he thought it had gone stale and was about to pour it down the sink.

"No!" Kiri cried as she entered. "I need to save that!"

Puzzled, Henry set the bottle on the counter. "Whatever it was, it's gone to water now. I was looking for something that befits the celebration of a new life in our midst."

"How about this?" She selected a white wine. "I might even splurge and have three fingers. The other is special... for a new baby's first wash." She recapped the bottle and hurriedly put it back in the pantry. "You're a handy guy to have around. Not only are you the master of calm when it comes to children, you throw together a pretty fine spread. Thank you. I'm starving."

Once seated on the deck sofa, Henry poured. "A toast. What shall it be?"

"To Bitsy and Sara, of course. May they both find gentleness, love and music in their lives."

They raised their glasses. "To Bitsy and Sara." Henry smiled and took her hand. "Nothing is so exhilarating as witnessing a new life come into being—a clean canvass on which anything is possible. Innocence. The essence of purity. Sara has the possibility to experience a childhood Bitsy never had, thanks to you."

Kiri shook her head.

Henry cocked an eye at her. "Oh, yes. Less than two months ago, we sat in this same spot. You felt put upon by a poor girl needing help and complained about having no time in your life for her. Somehow, you survived and she flourished. Tonight she is blossoming with a baby in her arms, and you are positively glowing as if you brought that infant into this world all by yourself."

She flushed. "You're a little giddy too."

He laughed. "Only a little? I can't tell you how much an evening like this one means to a fifty-year-old single man who never expected to be welcomed within ten feet of a ten-year-old, let alone a newborn. And to hold your two within minutes of their births was... indescribable. I now consider myself a first night specialist."

After snacks and more wine to steady his nerves, Henry took Kiri's glass and set it aside with his. He curled an arm around her to edge her nearer. He stared deeply into her blue eyes, daring his demons to show themselves. "This one is for inviting me to enjoy MT's first night." He kissed her with measured emotion and opened his eyes. No demons. His other arm found its way around her back. "This one is for Katie's." He allowed his desire to rise and kissed her with undiscovered zeal. Still no demons. Heartened by her reaction, he pressed his body into hers and whispered, "This one is for…"

"Aunt Kiri, I don't mean to interrupt, but…" A very embarrassed Meggie stood in the doorway. "…Bitsy fell asleep after feeding Sara, so I changed the baby and put her in the cradle. But they are both so quiet I'm afraid I'll fall asleep too. I'm already starting to nod off."

Henry pulled away immediately. Kiri's hopes deflated with a sigh. She turned toward the anxious teen. "I'm sure you'll awaken if you need to, but maybe it is time for a catnap. Henry and I would love to hold the baby while you do. I'll wake you when I bring her back. How does that sound?"

Meggie nodded and left for Bitsy's room.

"Hold your thought." Kiri put her hand on Henry's shoulder and squeezed it. "I'll be right back with another first night job for a specialist."

When she returned, bundle of baby in hand, she found him in the living room settled in the recliner but still disappointed by the interruption. "Maybe this will help," she said, placing Sara in his arms.

He cradled the baby gently and bent his head close to inhale the sweetness of a newborn. He raised Sara to his shoulders, trying her on each. This baby seemed to favor his left one like MT. He leaned back to savor the feeling while he and Kiri chatted softly about all the wonders they would introduce into her life, punctuated with smiles and endearing glances.

"Ooh!" She stretched. "I'm yawny too. Do you think you can mind this little girl all by yourself while I splash some cold water and freshen up?" At Henry's smile, she rose to kiss Sara on her tiny head and bussed his cheek as well. "Back in a few," she said with a twinkle.

Henry eased the baby into his lap and opened her blanket to expose her dimpled knees slightly drawn up, her legs crossed at the ankles and her wee pink toes curled under. Her hands were tucked under her chin beneath a heart-shaped mouth, and her eyelashes fluttered with each shallow breath. When a tear worked its way to the corner of his eye, he bundled her again and rested her on his shoulder. He closed his eyes just for a second.

When he opened them, a familiar figure stood only feet away—wide stance, arms crossed over the chest like an obstinate Katie. "Welcome to the fold," Michael said. "That's quite a little bundle you have there. She'll grow to be clever enough to take care of her mother, so you won't have to watch over her for long. You did a nice job with her story."

The apparition made no move to advance toward the child this time. "You're a loyal trooper, Henry, but I would expect nothing less from you.

Family shows up in times of need, and *we are all family*, you know," he said with a wink and disappeared.

Henry broke out in a cold sweat and shook himself awake. The two previous times he conjured Michael's form, Kiri was asleep on the sofa nearby while he held the babies—logical for his mind to play tricks. But this night, Kiri was upstairs and her children were asleep in their own beds. He could not imagine what brought the vision to mind. What was the connection this time?

Kiri reappeared, all smiles and emanating freshness. "If I can tear this little one from you, I'll put her to bed and save my turn for tomorrow... so we can continue our... conversation."

Still disoriented from his encounter with a vision, Henry hugged little Sara and handed her over. Kiri carried her away, tucked her in, and jiggled Meggie awake. When she returned to the living room, all that remained was the stub of a candle, and the house on Quincy Street surrendered to the dark.

*   *   *

Kathryn Elizabeth Killian and Sara Lamb Killian were baptized together on a sunny day in the courtyard of St. Mary's. While Paula concealed her from view, Kiri added a sprinkle of spirit water to the font. Thomas, declared honorary godfather because of his insistence, stood proudly with his hands on Bitsy's shoulders, and Henry, named godfather to both, held Sara. All the cousins attended the simple ceremony. Their parents did not.

Tenth Anniversary Year: Birth: Sara Lamb, daughter of Bitsy; a girl to Gus, the first of many, I assume.

Graduation: Meghan's son Connor and Anne's son Ronan.

Other: Bitsy (Kathryn Elizabeth Killian), cousin to Michael, came to live with us. Guardianship in process.

Convinced Paddy to convert to community living. He now shares his house with a couple of friends who contribute to expenses. He and his housemates take turns patrolling the neighborhood, to keep it safe for the children, he says.

Established neighborhood delivery service for food and health products. Maeve had a sister who had a son.

Sponsored Quincy Cuts and Curls for men and women. First and third Thursdays are half price for seniors. House calls on second and fourth Thursdays. Services much in demand, and business now shows a profit.

Partner in Grandmother's Attic—Antiques and gently-loved second-hand furnishings. Accepts items on consignment.

CHAPTER 12

The battle was on for Bitsy and her baby. Thomas, whose expertise was Celtic and religious heritage, demanded more time with them. Henry, whose interests lay in historic and cultural heritage, requested more time with them. Bitsy, bereft of positive adult male role models in her early life, was overwhelmed by their attentions. When the stress of being tugged by both men affected her appetite, Kiri put her foot down.

Thomas was allotted Sundays out of the house and Wednesday evenings at Quincy Street. Henry was granted Saturdays out of the house and one other weekday evening at Quincy Street due to his unpredictable work schedule. Kiri reserved Monday afternoon tea with Henry for herself. Any outing that did not include MT and Katie required permission. Take it or leave it. Thomas grumbled, but took the deal. Henry accepted gratefully. Bitsy ate heartily again.

She thrived on routine. Learning to speak and understand English took priority in mornings, followed by swimming for exercise. Afternoons were devoted to manipulating a tablet computer, rest, and playing the harp. Childcare and child development were interspersed throughout. When school began in the fall, tablet exercises with MT took place for thirty minutes after his return. Katie and Meghan's daughter Polly, best buddies and pre-schoolmates, claimed the next half-hour for creative play and baby games which Bitsy had never experienced.

Two years later, Bitsy helped out at the pool. Maeve's sister said that the sixteen-year-old mother had quite a talent for soothing the disabled children who came for water therapy. "She hums to them and they calm right down and don't fight the water." Her English improved, but reading and writing were a slow go and math was a no go. Kiri decided that her young ward needed to learn a marketable skill and arranged for her to help the cake ladies two days a week. In the process she learned measures, times and temperatures and how to follow a recipe—practical applications that made sense to her.

Katie and Polly turned their creative play toward entertaining Sara. MT made it his mission to assure that she was not disadvantaged by limited facility with English. He taught her sounds and words, and soon had her babbling in sentences. Thomas bragged about his intelligent and sensitive grandson. Henry delighted in sitting on the floor to join in games. Kiri and Paula chuckled at them both.

By the time Sara was four, she spoke with the vocabulary and understanding of a six-year-old and began to read. Her mother tried to teach her to finger the harp, but her daughter did not have the touch. The little girl created amusing puppet shows for entertainment on special occasions. Thomas marveled at her active imagination. Henry was frequently cajoled into playing an impromptu part in her productions.

*   *   *

Bitsy's eighteenth birthday celebration was eagerly anticipated by all in the neighborhood. They watched her transformation over four years from abandoned waif to self-assured young adult woman. Still slight and delicate with tranquil blue eyes so deep they held the joys and sorrows of a people and wispy blond hair that floated on the gentlest breeze like dandelion puffs, she developed a vigorousness adequate to spirit herself, her daughter and her harp with confidence throughout the homes and shops within her comfort range.

Paddy and his cohorts followed behind to assure she did not lose her way or come to harm. The shopkeepers knew she would arrive with a list and the authorization to charge to Mrs. O'Connell's account. Taking advantage of the naïve young mother never occurred to them, for losing Kiri's good will was not worth the few pennies they might gain. The cake ladies and their friends engaged her in conversation to share helpful bits of the old ways as she passed by. "When she plays for us after a long, hard morning in our kitchens with the cleanup yet to do, all the aches and miseries of age vanish."

Kiri set the date to stage the event—late spring after Bitsy attained legal age and Sara turned four—to take advantage of warm weather and blossoming flowers in the garden. She whispered to Paddy that all were welcome to the outdoor buffet... but gifts were not. Anyone who felt uncomfortable coming empty-handed could bring a family favorite for the food table and a hug. Paddy and his housemates spread the word. "The party begins when the shops close. Bring only food if you want, and an instrument if you have one. We'll have a *craic* like this neighborhood hasn't seen in years. And Bitsy's baking the cake—all by herself she is, from start to finish!"

Kiri worried that the stress of such a huge project would undo Bitsy as she worked for three nights and a day on her cake, but the determined young mother refused all offers of help. "Stay away, please! I'm making a surprise. I can do it by myself. I know I can!"

The evening, pleasant weather and guests all arrived on cue. The table was laden with traditional favorites enough for a banquet. Cider flowed, gaiety abounded, and Bitsy paced, excited to unveil her cake. Henry and Brendan carried the three-tiered creation and set it in the center of the food table where it rose nearly to Bitsy's height—barely five feet on her tiptoes. The lower two tiers were frosted with an effusion of bright flowers. The top one was simple by contrast, iced in meadow green with no frills and with two hand-painted porcelain figurines placed in the center—a mother sheep and her lamb. Bitsy displayed that wrap-around smile of hers and exclaimed, "I did it myself! I knew I could!"

Her guests applauded with approval and burst into two choruses of "Happy Birthday," one for Bitsy and one for Sara. Then the feasting and merriment began. The young mother started the entertainment with a couple of traditional pieces. Fiddles and penny whistles joined in, and some added their voices. Thomas sang along from his seat under the evergreen tree, his feet tapping. "This is just like a *craic* from the far west. Oh, how the music takes me back!"

Kiri busied herself straightening the table when a black feather floated onto its corner. She started to whisk it away but pocketed it with a smile. Brendan approached and handed her a thick envelope. "There's one for you, one for Bitsy and one for Sara when you think they want or need the information. Everyone has a right to know where he came from." He kissed her on the cheek. "Thanks, Aunt Kiri. This research project earned me top marks in the class."

Henry overheard and beckoned her over. "New information?" When Kiri did not reply, he asked, "Is there any chance I can increase my visits?"

Thomas overheard and, not to be left out, joined them. "I was about to ask the same. We should decide soon on a school for Sara. Could I have another afternoon?"

"You'll have to ask Bitsy herself. Now that she is of legal age, she'll move into her own apartment in a couple of weeks and control her own schedule."

Two pairs of eyes exchanged disbelieving looks.

"The cake lady who stays with Bitsy while we're in Colorado approached me with a problem. Remodeling her second floor into an apartment and taking in a tenant seemed a logical solution; Bitsy and Sara, the perfect tenants. Win/win all around, wouldn't you say? Bitsy is fully capable now of living independently, and we're close by in a pinch."

Henry recovered first. "I'd like to help with expenses. Maybe pay Sara's pre-school fees."

"No, no!" Thomas interrupted. "*I* will take care of Sara's schooling." His face began to show its infuriated plum color.

"No, no, no!" shouted Bitsy, hurrying toward them. "I can do it myself. I have two jobs. *I* will pay for my daughter to go to school. That is *my* gift to Sara on her birthday." She turned and left them dumbfounded.

When the party ended—way beyond bedtime for young and old alike—Kiri sat with Henry on the patio sofa to recount the highlights of the celebration… and there were many. "Well done, Kiri," he said, pulling her closer and nuzzling her hair. "Very well done!"

"So many helped to make this day possible, but I can't stop wondering." She smiled and fingered the feather in her pocket. "What part in the puzzle does Bitsy play? What is the real purpose of her coming into our lives at this particular time? It isn't just so we can throw a party." She leaned into Henry and closed her eyes to count all those who contributed in some way and came to honor Bitsy—all the shopkeepers, all the neighbors, and Kiri's own family. All the cousins came, too. Their parents did not.

* * *

During their teen years, the nieces and nephews prodded their Aunt Kiri to keep them on track toward the safety, joy and love their uncle promised. She supported them at school programs and athletic contests and found them summer jobs at her pool, in the shops at the top of the road, and in her neighborhood. She required volunteer service to the kindly neighbors who tolerated their pool parties as well as Sweet Sixteens. Best of all, she treated them to spins around Michael's Raceleigh Track in his speedster.

The entire niece/nephew generation learned to swim well, including Sara, so that only left trips to see the buffalo for the harried aunt to chaperone. Since Bitsy and her daughter were unlikely to set foot on a plane anytime soon, Kiri broke the "eight years old and up" rule to invite the only one who had not been to Yellowstone with the Koyles. Even though Polly was only seven and Katie eight, the two were inseparable. Brother Kurt's daughter Kendra was the same age as Polly, so the trio of little girls in elbow-to-elbow proximity 24/7 promised either disaster or delight for the entire trip and thus ushered in the summer of " 'Kay."

MT, almost ten years old, was not thrilled about having to pal around with Kody who was not quite six, but he reasoned, "Grandfather taught me about 'familial responsibility.' If I am the oldest grandson in a group, then I must take care of the others. I guess I'll survive, but please can we not stay too long this time?"

Kurt outfitted the horde with sleeping bags and boots, packed all eight humans into a van and made the usual swing through the Park before returning for the Fourth to Paula's house on the hill where his family now lived. The three girls became a delightful disaster. Within minutes of meeting, they were best friends and could not be separated. They took on the mannerisms and behaviors of one another. If one wore a ponytail, the others did too. If another painted her fingernails purple, the others did too. If the third giggled, the others did too whether or not they understood why. When they sat quietly for five minutes and Kiri had a chance to compare them, she saw similarities between Katie and Kendra and between Katie and Polly, but Polly and Kendra really did not look alike until all three were together. Then they were triplets and were only distinguished by the colors of their hair.

The triplets begged to bed down in the library where they could sleep in a circle with their heads in the center "so everyone can hear and no one will feel left out."

They did everything in tandem: brush up first, then down; take a bite of meat first, then salad, then bread—all together; put on the left shoe first, then the right. If one said, "Let's wear blue tops tomorrow. 'Kay?" the others replied " 'Kay" and giggled. "Let's watch a video. 'Kay?" " 'Kay." "Let's go outside and run down the hill. 'Kay?" " 'Kay." Fireworks were a hoot. "Let's say 'Ooh' for the next one and then 'Ahh' after that. 'Kay?" " 'Kay."

MT rolled his eyes a lot, turned his cap backwards, and counted the days until he could find peace in his own home.

Weeping and wailing at the trip's end caught the parents by surprise. When the girls realized it was their last night together, they sat on the floor in a circle and gripped each other so tightly that they nearly drew blood. Their high, shrill voices vowed not to let go or fall asleep—ever! Kurt finally suggested Kendra return to Ireland with Kiri, and in a couple of weeks he would fly over to get her. "I'd like to visit with Mom. She said they won't be home this summer because Thomas was 'slowing down,' whatever that means."

Kiri was reluctant. "Won't the girls replay this same dramatic scene again when you come?"

"Nah. If they do, we'll throw them in your pool and hold them underwater until they get the message that they won't live to see each other ever again if they don't cooperate!"

Kiri ended up with a houseful again. Bitsy and Sara out. Polly and Kendra in. Katie insisted. "If I get to be with Kendra all the time and Polly has to stay at her house, it won't be fair!" Meghan was quick to agree; she and Phillip were happy for more alone time. Kiri set the girls up in the sitting room so they could do the "circle the sleeping bags" thing again and waited for their alliance to crack, but it did not.

City trips were not very successful. A triplet obstacle along footpaths with the girls dodging spot rains created a hazard for Dubliners who walked extremely fast to get where they were going, no matter the weather. Instead, several short trips to the zoo and parks replaced leisurely strolls in the city. After the first one, MT begged to be excused. "I would rather spend a quiet afternoon with Grandfather reciting the catechism in Latin than listen to those girls giggle for one more minute. And they're not even teenagers yet!"

Brendan came by one day after work to check on his half-sister Polly. Kendra fell in love! By the time he left with a wink and a smile, she had her whole life planned with him if he would only wait for her for a few years.

"Hold on," Katie said. "You might be related. If I'm related to Polly and Brendan, and you are related to me, then you might be related to Brendan and that would be illegal. 'Kay?"

"I don't care," Kendra said. "He's worth getting arrested!" The twenty-four-year-old did not oblige by inviting her on a first date.

Sensing Kiri's distress with only two hands and three girls to rein in, Henry rode to her rescue in a rented van. He drove the whole crew to his safe place where there was plenty for both boys and girls to do, Bitsy and

Sara included. The young mother, matured after just a few weeks on her own, was not impressed with the giggly gaggle of girls in the back seat. Sara was fascinated by them and tried to tag along. Henry spent more time with MT to give them both relief from the triplets.

While sitting on the sand letting gentle waves lap at their toes—right feet first, then left—Katie tried to unravel their complicated familial relationships for Kendra who wanted to know how Bitsy and Sara fit in. "They are my cousins because we are all Killians. Polly is a Killian too, so we are all Killian cousins, 'Kay?"

"I thought you were O'Connells."

"We are, but we're also Killians. Bitsy isn't an O'Connell, but she's still our cousin, just like you and I are both Koyles so we're cousins."

"How can you be three things?"

"It's complicated. But if you are my cousin and Bitsy is my cousin, you must be related."

"How about Uncle Henry? Is he a Killian too?"

"No. He's a Callaghan, which is *almost* Killian. One time I named myself Katie Henry Callaghan O'Connell, so we must be related, and if we are, you are too, so you can call him Uncle if you want. 'Kay?"

" 'Kay. He's very nice. And handsome for an old man. If I can't marry Brendan, can I marry Henry?"

"I don't think so. If you are related to me, and I'm related to him, then you and he must be related and that would be illegal. But you can still love him. 'Kay? Everybody loves Uncle Henry!"

Kiri burst out laughing, and Henry did too when he caught the end of the conversation.

Bad news. When Kurt arrived to take Kendra home, the girls met him with a declaration: the next summer, all three of them would stay together for one month in Colorado, one month in Ireland and one month at their own homes to get ready for school. Parents optional!

Fourteenth Anniversary Year: Birth: a second daughter to Gus; a son to Devin.

Marriage: Doyle

Graduation: Tommy's Caitlín and Fíonna, and Anne's Gemma

Other: Connor took over Brendan's attic studio and maintenance job in Henry's building. Frank leased an apartment there.

I was elected to the advisory board of Quincy Education Foundation, sponsors of a multidemoninational primary school, Quincy School, near our neighborhood.

I must remind myself not to wait so long between entries, but I've gone from a jog to an out-and-out run trying to keep up with these kids who grow so fast. Whew! The triumvirate shows no signs of dissolution. I'll write again soon, I promise. 'Kay? 'Kay!

CHAPTER 13

"At last! I finally got my house back," Kiri mumbled. "And not a minute too soon, for Henry and I are going 'out,' and if all goes well, we may come back and go 'in.'" She shot a sly, sexy smile at her image in the rear view and reminded herself to keep her eyes on the road or she would go up a tree.

After surviving the summer with giddy girls and frustrated boys, all children were now in school. Sara was a junior infant and Katie in third class at Quincy School. MT attended fifth class at a *gaelscoil* not too far from the girls. The three would meet up after classes to walk to Bitsy's apartment until Kiri sent for them. They all wore GPS trackers, but Paddy followed behind them daily just to make sure "they get where they're meant to go."

This evening the landlady volunteered to take care of all three for the late afternoon and evening, giving Kiri time to pamper herself a little before going "out." She arranged to pick up her two later… or later still… or very late depending on how the evening unfolded. She smiled again at the prospects and turned to the young woman riding next to her.

Bitsy worked four days a week during school hours—two at the aquacenter and two for the cake ladies who made use of her recently discovered decorating talents as their once-steady hands failed them. The fifth weekday she spent at leisure in the morning and with Kiri in the afternoon at a session with an orchestral harpist.

"Hardly anyone plays with nails on wire strings anymore, so I cannot help her with technique. She plays naturally from the heart, so learning music theory or to read music is no advantage to her. What I can do is show her how to retune her instrument. With twenty-two strings, she can play in only one key. If she can learn to retune, she'll have others she can use depending on the mood she wants to create."

Bitsy's harp was originally keyed to C. Since the beginning of school she had added F and G to her repertoire. Thomas added a case for her instrument, and Henry, GPS tracking for Bitsy, the case and the harp itself to relieve the worry that it might be lost.

By the way her passenger gripped the case between her knees, Kiri doubted that would ever happen. "How was your lesson today?"

"Very fine, thank you. My teacher says I can do the two new keys fast enough now without listening to a piano that I can learn a new one next week. I like the way she made each one a different color so I know where to start. Maybe MT can help me find out how to do this and I can learn one all by myself. I'll ask him tonight. That would make my teacher happy."

Kiri smiled when Bitsy used the term "my teacher," since she was obviously proud of going to school like the others. She was about to say that Bitsy's music made everyone happy when a call came in from Paula. She touched "accept" on her dash and her mother's distressed face showed on the screen. "Mom? Something wrong?"

"It's Thomas," she cried. "He's had a heart attack! We're at the hospital." Her hands and her voice shook so violently, she could not say more.

"I'm on my way. Sit down. Keep me on the line until I'm standing in front of you." A million thoughts ran through Kiri's mind as she tried to make sense of her mother's incoherent babbles. *The kids. Bitsy. Henry! The family. Paula!* No one is ever prepared for the worst, she knew, and the worst usually comes without warning. She screeched to a halt in the parking lot, transferred the call to her cell, and motioned to Bitsy to follow at a run.

For a few minutes of role reversal, Paula collapsed in sobs in her daughter's arms, and Kiri held and consoled her mother. "I can't lose him, Kiri. I can't! At our ages, we know the odds, but I'm not ready to accept that our life together will end today… in this way."

"It won't, Mom. Thomas is too stubborn to leave you without a fight. He's probably arguing with the doctors right now."

A faint smile crossed Paula's face, and then she erupted in tears again. "I'm sorry, Kiri. I'm so sorry."

"Sorry for what? You contacted the EMT's immediately. Thomas arrived here within minutes. What more could you have done?"

"No. About you. I'm sorry for the way I treated you… when Michael was killed. I did not understand how deeply you hurt. If you experienced a fraction of the pain I feel now, I don't know how you survived… and I'm sure you endured much more. I'm so sorry."

"This isn't about me, Mom. This is about you and Thomas. Right now, you need to sit here, calm yourself and send him positive vibes until we hear from the doctors. He will feel you praying for him."

Paula tried but was not very successful as she filled one tissue, then another and another while Kiri held her and tried to ascertain if she had notified anyone else in the family. Paula shook her head. Their priest? Another shake.

"Don't worry. I'll take care of it." Kiri prioritized—family first, then the priest. Tommy first, then the others in birth order. Did she really need to call each stepsibling since the word would spread like wildfire once she notified Tommy? Yes, she decided. As much as she hated to talk to them, that's what Thomas would do—make personal contact. A group text would not count. Otherwise they would find fault with her mother.

"Tommy? Kiri here. I'm calling on behalf of Paula. Your father suffered a heart attack just a while ago and is in the hospital. No word—good or bad—yet, but we should hear from the doctor any minute. I'll call again as soon as we have an update." "Anne? Kiri here."

She ticked them off her list. Next items: Call the priest—a new one since Bishop Byrne passed away a couple of years ago. Call Brendan. As leader of the grandchildren—at least until MT turned twenty-one—he should be notified personally. Calm her mother enough to face the onslaught of the stepchildren with some strength and composure so Anne did not try to take charge. Tea. Tea would help. There must be a teacart somewhere on the floor, but she did not dare leave her mother to look in case the doctor came with news. Paula could not be expected to recall details in her state.

She caught sight of Bitsy sitting nearby and looking very worried. Kiri had no choice but to press her into service. She dashed off a quick note with her name, location, cell number and order and gave it to Bitsy along with several euro. "We need your help. Down one of these halls you will find a teacart. Give this note to the lady and ask her to come as soon as she can. Call me if you need help getting back. Got it?"

Bitsy nodded. "I can do it. I know I can."

Kiri watched the diminutive figure toting a harp case disappear around a corner and hoped she would not get lost and confused. She turned her gaze back toward Paula and noticed a lanky figure dressed in navy scrubs and crocs approach from the opposite direction. After several minutes of discussing the particulars of Thomas' condition, the report boiled down to "Not mild, not critical, somewhere between moderate and severe. We'll know more in a couple of hours. Then, once he has stabilized, we'll let you visit for a few minutes."

Paula slumped back into her seat, relieved. Her sobs were infrequent now.

Kiri noted the doctor's name, thanked him, and asked if he would send Mr. O'Connell's nurse at her earliest convenience to discuss the family's visitation. She sat beside Paula and took her hands. "See? Positive vibes," she smiled. When she looked up, she spotted Bitsy down the hall carrying her case broadside like a tray with a cup of tea balanced on top. "That's quite a trick," she said, helping the young mother set her precarious load down on an end table. "I didn't expect you to carry this back yourself, but thank you."

"The lady said she will have to make more before she can come. I said Paula needed hers *now*, so I brought this. The rest will be here shortly." Bitsy seemed satisfied that she completed a very difficult task all by herself. Then she showed concern. "Many people in this building are suffering. Is Grandfather Thomas in pain too?"

"The doctor said he feels better but not good enough to see us just yet. The nurse will come with more news soon, but we may have a wait before we can visit him. The tea helps."

"Sara…"

Frazzled Kiri clapped her hands to her head. How could she forget the children? And Henry! Prioritize, Kiri, she told herself. Call each stepsib personally with the update. Then call the cake lady. Then Henry. She reached for her phone and began. As she spoke with each one in turn, she could detect Bitsy's mind churning deep behind her blue eyes. After alerting the children's kind sitter that they were delayed and why, she asked to have Sara given the phone and watched Bitsy's face light up as she chatted with her daughter. Before she called Henry, Thomas' nurse came.

Kiri tried to explain as diplomatically as she could that when visiting time arrived, it should proceed as she suggested: Mrs. O'Connell, the *present* wife, first; then the following in birth order—Tommy O'Connell, Anne Geary, Meghan Daly, Emily Flynn and Brendan Daly. One at a time for only a couple of minutes. No spouses. The priest, at Thomas' will. "Believe me," Kiri said, handing the woman the list of names. "The more firm you are, the easier this will be on everyone—especially Mr. O'Connell."

"Which one are you?"

"I'm not on the list. I'm Mrs. O'Connell's daughter, Kiri O'Connell." The nurse's eyes widened. "*The* Kiri O'Connell? Everyone says…"

Kiri hardened her stare. "I'll decide after Thomas has seen everyone else. Thank you for your cooperation."

"No problem. We're taking good care of him." She retraced her steps, and halfway down the hall checked her pager and began to run.

Kiri thought nothing of it and called Henry. "Henry? Kiri here."

"You aren't going to beg off on me are you?" he quipped.

"I'm sorry. I…" She started to tear up. "Thomas had a heart attack this afternoon. I'm at the hospital with Mom. She's in a state, so I don't dare leave her alone to face the sibs who should arrive any minute. I don't know how long we'll be here, so yes… I'm going to beg off. I'm sorry."

"Don't be. I'd give you a good scolding if you didn't stay. I can't leave for about another hour, but what can I do to help? The children?"

"At Bitsy's apartment. I'm not expected 'til late, so best to leave them there."

"Bitsy?"

"She's with me." Kiri looked around and did not see the girl or her harp case. "Or was. She must have gone to the ladies' or to get more tea. I'll call if she wants to go home. Thanks for offering."

"No problem. I'm free tonight." He heard her sigh. "Sorry. Nothing is humorous right now, is it? Have you called our friend the doctor? He might be able to sneak in and get more specific information for you."

"No. That hadn't occurred to me."

"I'll call him. Be on the lookout for a very suave scrubs-clad fellow."

"Thanks. Henry, I… I… I think I hear the sibs. Later." Kiri wiped her eyes, ran her fingers through her hair, straightened her outfit and returned to her mother.

Evening arrived before the doctor did. The two camps of O'Connells grouped on opposite sides of the corridor awaiting news. The circle of Thomas' children—temperate Tommy with wife Margaret, arrogant Anne and Charles, mellow Meghan and Phillip, and emotional Emily with Stephen—alternated between tears, wringing of hands, wiping of brows and glaring at *those Americans*. Paula's head rested on her daughter's shoulder while Kiri massaged her mother's hands. Brendan floated between. "Thanks for calling me. No one else thought to."

Only Kiri noticed the nurse approach and motion her around the corner. "Mr. O'Connell gave us a scare a couple of hours ago. His vitals went haywire for no reason we could determine. The doctors worked frantically until, all of a sudden, they stabilized. When everyone quieted, we heard the strangest sound... like bells or harpsichord music. Our patient became so calm that he looked like he could have walked off the street with only a splinter in his finger. When I opened the door and the sound flooded in, his entire body mellowed as if he were hovering in another world. Outside I found a girl sitting on the floor playing a small harp."

Kiri peeked around the corner and realized Bitsy had never returned and no one noticed. "That is my ward Bitsy. I have no idea how she found Thomas, but they share an intimate connection."

"Mr. O'Connell motioned her in and labored to speak. She leaned very close, and the two whispered back and forth in the old tongue. She pulled a chair up beside his bed and began to play again so beautifully. Tears came to his eyes, but a serene smile graced his face. Everyone in the room moved with ease, as if we were in slow motion. I've never seen anything like it before."

"Bitsy has a way of sensing stress in a person and a gift for relieving it. I'm sorry she interrupted," Kiri said nervously, hoping none of the others overheard.

"A gift is right! She played for about an hour. We monitored his heart all the while, and it pumped along with no irregularities, as if he hadn't had an attack at all. The doctors feel you should visit now, then they'll watch carefully to determine whether this is an anomaly or a trend before they say much more. Mr. O'Connell told the girl to wait quietly outside until the rest of the family leaves and then to come back in and play more before he falls asleep. Bless her heart, she sits across the hall with her harp back in its case and resting in her lap with her hands folded on top of it. She looks so... agitated. I thought you should know before I take the family to visit."

"Thank you. We'll let Thomas decide whether to mention her or not. Think you can keep this crowd under control?" Kiri winked and nodded toward the circle of O'Connells.

"Watch me."

When Henry arrived with their friend the doctor in tow, Brendan and Kiri stood outside Thomas' room listening to Bitsy's second concert of the evening. Paula sat in the room with them. The rest of the family had gone. Several hospital staff lingered in the hallway with tranquil smiles on their faces.

"I'm so glad you made it for some of Bitsy's debut performance. The nurse said that all patients within hearing range have experienced a drop in blood pressure. Even I feel a difference. I'm not as jittery as earlier. And look at Mom. Her worry lines faded. We knew Bitsy had a natural talent, but who could have predicted this?"

"The doctors are baffled as well," their friend said. "I've spoken to one and reviewed the tests. There is no logical explanation for Thomas' turnaround. They agree there is damage and treatment is necessary, but your girl bought them some time to reassess. If he remains placid throughout the night, they'll retest in the morning with an eye toward stent implants. Probably two placements, but now that they have time for reevaluation, they may decide on another one or two."

"Complicated or risky?" Kiri asked.

Their friend shook his head. "Not really. Pretty routine, but they'll want to keep him for several days. At eighty-one and with his family history of heart disease, they will be very cautious. He's off pain meds for the moment, but that may change."

Kiri grew pensive. *Family history. Would I be in my mother's place at Michael's bedside, had he lived? My son? Some stories of one's family are not gloried around the fire.* She shuddered when the music stopped. "Looks like Bitsy is ready for a taxi. Thanks, Henry." They exchanged hugs and waved goodbye to Brendan. "I'll be home as soon as I have Mom settled."

The nurse followed Bitsy out. "Mr. O'Connell wants to speak to you. Then you can take your mother home."

Kiri balked. "My mother will stay with Thomas tonight in his room."

"I'm sorry. That is not allowed on this floor." The nurse fidgeted with the pen in her pocket.

Kiri did not back down. "Then move Mr. O'Connell to a floor where it is."

"That would not be appropriate for his condition."

"Thomas will not sleep without my mother in the same room. *That* will not be appropriate for his condition. You find a cot for her, or I will bring a sleeping bag and camp out on the floor with her myself!"

The nurse scurried back into the room. Henry's friend the doctor followed. Within seconds, he returned. "Your mother's cot is on its way. Now, go in there and find out what other battles the old man wants you to fight for him today." He gave her a pat on the back. "It's nice to see that you haven't lost your spunk." He waved a goodbye, and Henry and Bitsy followed him down the hall.

Kiri entered Thomas' room, took his hand and spoke softly. "You gave us quite a scare today."

"Thank you... for Paula... for Bitsy."

"My pleasure. You deserve the best, and they are the best."

"I want to see... Michael."

Kiri shivered. *How can I remind a man near death that his son is dead? Must be the meds.* She shook her head. "Michael is away. He can't come now. Can I call someone else for you?"

Thomas swallowed hard and sadness crept into his eyes. "No... no. Bring Michael tomorrow... and Latin Bible. He reads to me."

Before leaving the hospital, Kiri searched out the nurse with whom she was so abrupt to apologize for her insolent behavior. "Now you may understand why the family and I have difficulty communicating. I'm too assertive for them."

The nurse smiled. "No offense taken. More patients should have strong advocates like you."

Kiri was relieved to find lights on in the living room—and only the living room—as she turned into her drive. Henry must have picked up the kids when he dropped Bitsy off and somehow managed to get them to bed, she thought. *Thank you, Henry. Maybe we still have time to carve out a deck date tonight.* She glanced at herself in the rear view and shook her head. Not even a sexy smile would help.

Henry greeted her with a gentle hug, a peck on the forehead and a bottle of his favorite stout. When she shook her head, he said, "Doctor's orders after any stay at a hospital. This brew is good for your health, you may remember. Come into the kitchen. I have a snack waiting." He caught her glance at the deck door. "Not tonight. You're too tired, and a chill is coming on."

Not until she finished eating—more than she intended—did Kiri notice that furniture was out of place. The recliner shifted to the opposite side of the room near the deck windows with its back to the fire and Michael's portrait and with its footrest extended. A couple of cozy throws hung over the armrests, and a bowl of candles burned outside on a table. "A compromise," Henry smiled as he turned out the lights.

He eased into the reclined chair, broad enough for two to snuggle comfortably, and invited Kiri to join him. One arm curled around her; the other pulled a throw up to her shoulders. "You can have this spot here," he said, patting the right side of his chest. "Katie's favorite place."

She inched her arm around his middle and nestled comfortably against him. When she felt his cheek against her forehead, she heaved a sigh, allowing him to carry the burden of all the day's tensions. "Thank you for being here. I'm desperate for a safe place. I feel so vulnerable... so terrified."

"Imagine how Thomas must feel with tubes and wires all over him and machines bleeping incessantly. For a man whose identity is synonymous with control, he must feel very threatened by having none. You did a good thing to insist that Paula be allowed to stay."

"Thomas will survive. It's Mom I'm worried about. I've never seen her so helpless. She was absolutely nonfunctional this afternoon. In my eyes she is a vibrant woman of forty, able to power over, under or through any obstacle with determination and emerge victorious. This afternoon, I looked into her eyes and saw a frightened woman of one hundred." She sniffed and rubbed her eye against Henry's shirt. "I don't want to lose her."

He remembered his mother that way too—a rock—always out front, clearing the way for him—fearless. Over time, her vigor also diminished, and he empathized with Kiri's fear of loss. After all, she barely survived a similar tragedy only twelve years earlier. He clutched her tightly. "Your mother needs as much time to recuperate as Thomas does, and you'll be there to help her regain her youthful spirit."

In an effort to soften the atmosphere, he kissed her gently and stroked her arm. "Bitsy played well tonight for the first time out of her comfort zone. Her maturity and self-assurance are really a... How do you Americans say it? '...a feather in your hat.'"

Kiri grinned. "Cap. A feather in my cap. Call me crazy, but I think Bitsy's arrival on my doorstep was no accident. Somehow she sensed Thomas' distress and was guided to his room to help him."

"You *are* crazy!" When she laughed, he turned her face toward his. "But craziness becomes you." He pulled her close, brushed her hair away, and planted a gentle kiss in a place he found becoming. He welcomed her response in kind but kept one eye open for the demons. He reached to coax her nearer and his eyes jerked open to see... Kiri next to him. His confidence renewed, he strengthened his move... and stopped. Once again a familiar song played in his mind asking if it would be a sin to stay. He could not toy with her affections and then walk out. Honor demanded a man commit... and at this moment he could not.

"I'm leaving for London in the morning. I'll be gone for a couple of months, maybe more." The disappointment in her eyes wrenched at his gut. "I'm sorry. I should have told you sooner. The network, and especially our department, are undergoing a technological restructure. Since we cannot cross a hostile border, we must develop a method of camouflage—an illusion—to protect our informants if they need to escape in a hurry." He readjusted the two of them into a comfy cuddle. "Wait for me? Save some craziness until I get back?" Her lips conveyed her answer, and then the two held each other tenderly and trusted sleep to quell their mutual yearning.

A bright ray of sunshine shot through the deck window and pierced Kiri's eyelids to shock her awake. She reached out for Henry, but her arms did not move. The throw was tucked tightly around her... and Henry was gone. He was right, of course. She would feel used had he flashed, dashed and disappeared for who knew how long. She comforted herself with the thought that a pleasant taste left one longing for more, and she hoped he felt the same.

She wriggled out of the cover and pushed the recliner back across the room, glancing at Michael's portrait as she went. Henry's rearrangement indicated his discomfort at expressing emotion beneath his friend's eyes. Even without Michael looking on, each time they attempted intimacy, some outside force conspired against them. She scowled at her husband's portrait again. "You're behind this, Michael. I know you are. Every time I work up the courage to add a new dimension to my life, I'm stymied by some call for help. Thanks a lot!"

She clomped up the stairs and into the shower, allowing the tepid water to wash her frustration away. She warmed with a replay of her short time spent with a gentle man. Henry's mention of a feather struck her as strange. When she found the last one at the party, she questioned Bitsy's purpose in their lives. At the hospital, the young woman revealed a clue.

She has a natural talent, but she also possesses a sixth sense for the inevitable, and her gift is to alleviate the anxiety of the inevitable for others. She has no ability to change the outcome, but her sudden appearance at an invalid's bedside is a premonition. Her purpose? She is an emissary for peaceful passing. "Good thing I didn't hit Henry with that one, or he would have called me more than crazy!"

She wrapped herself in a robe and sat at her dressing table. As she gazed at her image, a disturbing thought niggled at her—something she should remember. She picked up her hairbrush—the one made of beautifully grained wood from the revered hazel tree—the one her husband Michael gave her on the day they secretly wed. The memory flashed before her eyes. Today was their anniversary—their fifteenth anniversary—and the only one she thought about all night long was Henry.

* * *

"Where did that contraption come from?" Thomas demanded as Paula wheeled him to the foot of the stairs leading to the second floor... and their bedroom. "You won't find *me* strapped into that bloody thing!" He glared at the stairlift installed onto the staircase wall.

"Mind your language. There is a woman present," Paula responded. "Kiri arranged the lift for *me*. Whether you borrow it from time to time is your choice. She made me promise that every third trip up or down the stairs would be a ride. She doesn't want me ending up in the hospital from running up and down all day long. Thoughtful, isn't she?"

Thomas harrumphed and fiddled with his sweater.

"She also set up the den as a sleeping room for you, since you won't be climbing a full flight of stairs—and certainly not more than once a day—for a while yet. You can live upstairs all day or down, or alternate—your pleasure."

Thomas harrumphed and pulled at his eyebrows.

"This model is very fancy. It is voice-activated, has three speeds, a pause function, and this carrier attachment for... stuff. If you fix morning tea, you can send it up to me," Paula said with a smile and a twinkle. "What do you think?"

Thomas harrumphed and steepled his fingers under his chin. "Will you... stay with me at night?"

"Of course I will. You're my husband. But I don't want to be chained to one floor all day long any more than you do, and I can't run up and down the stairs all day for both of us. I must take care of myself too. Kiri insists."

Thomas glared at her. "You manipulative... conniving... devious... conspiring..."

"...woman who loves you very much and plans to for many more years, if you'll show sense enough to take advantage of the aids available so we can build your strength and get back to normal." She sat in the chair and its safety bar closed automatically. "Now, if you'll excuse me, I'll bring our travel kits to the bathroom down here for tonight. You make a list of the clothes you want." She said, "Fast," and zoomed to the top of the stairs, giggling all the way.

Without getting out, she zoomed back down. "I forgot to say goodbye." She rose from the chair, took his hand and kissed his disgruntled face. "I love you very much."

He tugged at the knees of his pants. "How will we wean me from this... apparatus?"

"Four steps up and down, three times a day without getting winded. Then eight steps. Then twelve, and so on, until you can walk up and down the stairs without huffing and puffing three times during a day for three days in a row."

Thomas gazed at Paula wistfully. "Can we..."

"When you are able to walk from here to the third floor playroom three times during a day without getting winded, I'll meet you there, and we'll... 'play.'"

He flushed when she arched her eyebrows. "Will this confounded machine carry both of us?"

"Get over there, and we'll see."

He walked the few steps to the chair and sat. She pulled out the side-seat. He wrapped an arm around her and shouted, "Fast!" They giggled all the way.

CHAPTER 14

Out of sorts, Kiri sat under the evergreen tree on a chilly November afternoon hoping to find some solace. Henry left over a month ago, and she rarely heard from him. He called the children regularly to check up on their progress in school and to apologize for missing another Saturday expedition, but small talk with her via video chat was not to his liking. Intimate conversation was better served face-to-face, and that would have to wait until his return. No date given. She began to think she misjudged the signals, and her children were more important to Henry than she was.

"Oh, good. You're out here," MT said on his return from Thomas' house. "I can always count on you being in a good mood when I find you under this tree." He sat on the ground cross-legged and hung his cap on his knee.

"What's on your mind?"

"Grandfather, of course. He's much better now. Hardly ever uses his walker or the stairlift except to ride doubles with Grandmother. They giggle a lot. It's embarrassing." He wiped his nose on his jacket sleeve. "Anyway, he thinks I should be confirmed—soon—so he can be my sponsor."

"Aren't you a little young for that?"

"I think he's anxious for me to be… you know, a full-fledged member of the faith… because of his scare… so he says maturity is more important than physical age, and that I am very mature. I know what it means to do the right thing, and I can read the Bible in English, Irish, and Latin. He says I have Grandmother's genes because I have a talent for learning languages and understanding meanings of words. Did you know she wrote books about that?" he asked with a look of mild amazement.

Kiri smiled. Their early years as mother and daughter never played much part in her dealings with her own children; her youthful experiences in Colorado, irrelevant to their lives in Ireland.

"He says I should learn lots of languages and choose a job that uses them to make a difference in our global economy. That's what my dad would want me to do."

"For once, I think your grandfather's advice is very sound."

MT ran the zipper on his jacket up and down nervously. "I don't want to talk about my job someday. I want to talk about my name now. I don't want to be called MT anymore. It's stupid. It doesn't tell who I am. The guys at school…."

"Tease you? Make fun of your name?"

He flashed a sly smile. "Not since I invited Uncle Gus to lunch one day. I want to be called Michael, just like my dad."

Kiri's eyebrows shot up. "What brought on this sudden desire for your given name?"

"A feeling inside me. Michael is my name. You named me Michael Thomas. I was baptized Michael Thomas and it's on all my records, so there must be a reason you named me that."

"What do you think the reason was?"

"I think you and Daddy chose my name a long time ago because Daddy wanted a son someday and wanted to name him Michael after himself. That's kind of how they do it in his family. And you loved him so much you said yes. You didn't count on his dying so that hearing his name would make you sad."

The words of her little boy who did not want to be little anymore tugged at her. "Why do you think I call you MT?"

He crossed his arms on his chest and thought for a minute. "Well, I think besides making you sad, you didn't want to call me Michael because you were afraid I would grow up thinking I had to be like my dad and never could be. I know I'm not like him. I'll never be a hero like they say he was, but I might do something else important to make a difference someday. I feel inside like I could."

"Have you thought for a long time about using your real name?"

"No. The idea just popped into my head when Grandfather talked about confirmation." He sighed. "Let me see if I can explain how I feel in a way that makes sense to you. You've always told me that I'm a part of Daddy and a part of you mixed into a unique human being. I think I'm old enough now to understand that and I don't have to be afraid of his shadow. I can be proud to wear the same name and be my own person at the same time." A mischievous grin played on his lips. "If there can be many shades of green, why not many shades of Michael?"

Kiri leaned down to tickle him. "You little imp! Is there anything else you want from me on my good mood day?"

"Well, there is one other thing." He looked into his mother's eyes to see if he dared. "I want you not to be sad when you *say* 'Michael.' Twelve years is long enough to be sad about Daddy. I think he would want you to feel happy when you said *our* name. And I think he would feel happy to know that you found enough room in your heart to love *both* your Michaels—differently."

Kiri wiped her nose and dabbed at her eyes. This would not be an easy transition for her. "Well then... *Michael*. Are you too grown up to give your mother a hug?"

He smiled and grabbed her, his arms now long enough to reach all the way around. "Never!"

She watched his lanky body—so much like her mother's and brother's—stride toward the house with his head held high. "Michael," she called after him. No response. "Michael!"

He swirled around and clapped his palm to his forehead. "Yeah, Mom."

"Just trying it out."

Not ten minutes later, Katie came running out, plunked her hands on the arms of her mother's chair and shoved her nutmeg curls into Kiri's face. "MT says I have to call him Michael now! Why?"

"Michael Thomas is his given name, and he has chosen to use it."

"Who gave it to him?"

"Your daddy did, just like he named you Aurora Kathryn."

"Well, I'm going to give my name back because I don't like it. I'm not a tree!" She stomped her foot, then crowded onto the edge of the chair. "Mom, why do I have a daddy when everybody else I know has a father?"

"Because you are part American."

"Which part?"

Kiri did not want to launch into another paint experiment, so she replied, "The Koyle from Colorado part. Do you think there is a difference between a daddy and a father?"

"A daddy is a person who never hugs you or kisses you or reads you stories or takes you places because you never see him because he is dead. A father is with you even when you are sick and snotty and brings you ice cream and he loves to do all those things with you and he tells you how much he loves you—like Uncle Henry."

Kiri's breath escaped her in a sudden poof like a soap bubble landing on a thorn. She had no idea Katie harbored such a strange misconception. "Why these questions about fathers?"

"I need one. For the father/daughter dance at school next month. All my friends have one." Her disappointment splotched onto her freckled cheeks.

Kiri trembled with anger at the Board of Quincy School for approving the dance. She voted against it arguing that not every female student, third class and above, had a living father. The Board was insensitive to make those girls feel different.

The chairman pasted on a patronizing smile and said, "This is not America, Mrs. O'Connell. In Ireland every little girl has a brother or cousin who will stand up with her."

"I'm sure your brother… or one of your cousins… will be happy to go with you. Who do you want to ask?"

"None of them! I want a father like everybody else! You don't understand anything, do you?' she screamed and ran to the house, tears streaming down her face.

Kiri barely stopped a flood of her own. Best to let Katie alone for a few minutes. They were both in such a state that they would not be much help to one another. Regain her own composure, then help her daughter reclaim hers. How different her two children were, she thought. Only minutes ago, Michael Thomas demonstrated maturity and understanding beyond his years, accepting the unusual situation in which he lived, while

Katie was detached from the realities surrounding her. She dropped her head into her hands and wept for her little girl in pain.

Katie rolled off her bed and wiped her face on the pillow. She washed up in the bathroom and brushed her unruly hair. She sneaked into her mother's room and put on a necklace, found some lipstick on the dressing table, and applied a beautiful smile to her chubby face. She tiptoed downstairs and stood in front of the communication system. "Call Henry," she commanded.

Henry's worried face appeared on the screen. "Hello, Katie. Is there a problem at home?"

"Will you be my father?"

Henry flustered a response. "Your mother might have something to say about that."

"No she won't. She doesn't care about me. I need a father for the dance at my school, so will you be my father?"

Henry tried not to laugh at the intense little girl. "You know I'm out of town working."

"Yes, and it's no fun around here without you."

"I'll check my calendar. When is this big dance?"

"The second Saturday in December. We're decorating and hiring music just like the big kids in Junior Cycle and it will be grand. All my friends will be there with their fathers. Will you come? Pleeease?"

How could he resist that painted smile? "I'll do my best to be there. I'll let you know for sure after I've talked with your mother and after I find out how long I have to work here. For the moment, I look forward to escorting you to the dance."

"I love you, Uncle Henry. You're the best!"

"I love you too, Katie. You're my special girl. Sleep tight."

Kiri walked in and witnessed the end of their conversation before Henry's face faded from the screen. "Aurora Kathryn O'Connell! What have you done? You know you're not allowed to contact Uncle Henry when he's at work."

"Don't call me that. You're not the boss of me! Uncle Henry is going to be my father and take me to the dance. He will be very handsome and I will wear a beautiful dress."

"This from my little girl who doesn't like dresses?"

"I'll like this one. Grandmother will make it for me. It will be purple, and I will be beautiful!" Katie ran up the stairs and slammed her door before her mother scolded her more for disobeying. She did not care. She had a father to take her to the dance… just like everyone else.

Kiri did not know what to make of her daughter's boldness or her defiance. Worst of all was the image of that tangle of copper curls clashing with a bright purple dress. She slumped onto the sofa to take stock. Her daughter's quarrelsome, uncooperative behavior over the last month was likely due to Henry's absence, she now realized. Plain and simple, Katie missed Henry and did not know how to express that feeling, so she lashed out at her mother.

She stared at Michael's portrait above the fireplace and wondered if she was wrong to use it—and him—as guidance for their children from the day they were born. Was she wrong to refer to Michael as if he were an active part of their lives and going to walk through the door any minute when, in truth, they would never know the man she fell in love with? Were her cautions—"What would your daddy say if...?"—helpful or harmful if they felt his eyes always followed them but his arms could never hug them? MT accepted his father's absence from his life. Katie never believed he was real.

"Attitude Adjustment Required. Is that the lesson I'm to learn from today's fiasco?" She challenged the man in the portrait to wink, blink, sneeze... anything, but he did not. "Okay. Time for a change," she sighed and removed the portrait from the wall. She carried it upstairs and hung it in her bedroom above the small fireplace, between the tall windows that Michael built for her to look out on their world.

"I should have done this long ago. You belong in our room where your spirit is strongest... where we can communicate." She dropped to the floor, leaned sobbing against the foot of their bed and invoked his lesson from St. Kevin when she cried out, "Oh, Michael! I can't bear to think how I've hurt Katie. I need help!"

*   *   *

The second Saturday in December finally arrived after heightened emotions, nervous anticipation, multiple fittings and tempestuous outbursts. Shortly after a mandatory light supper, Kiri opened the door to Paula who carried a garment bag upstairs to Katie's room with a "still a secret" look and Thomas who made his way to the living room sofa without a huff or a puff. He noticed the bare space above the fireplace now trimmed in holiday décor with three small stockings hanging from the mantle.

"Welcome," she greeted. "You look quite spry this evening." The last time she saw him, he was plugged in and lying in a hospital bed.

"Thank you. I am feeling good," he smiled. "Very good, thanks to your mother. She keeps me on a strict diet and exercise regimen. And you?"

"Busier than I care to admit. Always some crisis or other to tend to, and Katie's tantrums haven't helped. Her expectations for tonight are so high, I dread having to live with her if she is disappointed."

"She won't be. Believe it or not, my three girls went through periods of rebelliousness—not according to guidebook or schedule—and they came through all right. The other grandchildren, too. Katie will grow out of this stage in time." He stared at his daughter-in-law, no longer young in her mid-forties, but still lovely. "Speaking of grandchildren, all of them have been so attentive during my recovery. Not a day goes by without one of them showing up to visit, read to me, relieve Paula of a chore, run errands or drive us to church. We've even gone on a few rides into the countryside with one of them at the wheel."

"How thoughtful of them. They are a very nice bunch."

"I find it strange that every time I mention a desire, concern or need to Michael Thomas, one of the grandchildren shows up to take care of it. You wouldn't know anything about that, would you?" he asked with a glint in his eye.

"I'm sure they all love you very much and want to be of help. How about a cup of tea?" When he nodded, she left to fetch one.

After too much time in pointless conversation, the front bell sounded and Katie squealed from her room, "He's here!" When Kiri opened the door, a frisson of desire frisked through her at the sight of a very handsome Prince Charming. "You look most dapper, sir. Come in."

"Thanks to Paula. I sent her my measures and asked what would be appropriate for a dance at a primary school. She checked with other parents and reserved this getup for me."

"I could have…"

Henry shook his head. "Our outfits were to be a secret until the moment." He nodded past her toward the staircase. "And that moment has arrived."

Kiri turned to see his diminutive partner flounce down the stairs in a misty lilac dress accented with deep exotic purple bands extending from her shoulders in a V to the center of her waist, drawn together in a ribboned flower, then flowing outward in an inverted V to the hem. The back matched the front, a design that camouflaged Katie's boxy frame to give the illusion of an hourglass figure. A third flower made of lilac and deep purple ribbons fastened the severely slicked-back hair from the crown of her head. A mass of tightly wound red-gold curls bounced below, and her errant curl—her daddy's curl—was firmly clipped away from her forehead by a delicate baby orchid. The two posed for pictures, then waved an excited goodbye.

"Oh, Mom! You did a wonderful job. Katie looks beautiful!"

"My pleasure. Given time, these stiff fingers can still make it happen, although I doubted I would survive the last three days of practicing the hairdo."

"You shouldn't have indulged her. She's been a real pill lately."

"Much like her mother," Paula smiled.

"Mom! I was a good kid."

"Yes, you were… after you were a pain in the rear! Seriously, Kiri. You don't give Katie enough credit. She'll be a knockout one day." Thomas agreed with a nod, and the older couple left.

Kiri reviewed the photos when her eye caught sight of a rolled paper sticking out of her Christmas stocking. She removed it to read, *Your many kindnesses on behalf of a grumpy old man have not gone unnoticed. You will be greatly rewarded.*

She tried to keep from dozing while she awaited the return of the odd couple. When they walked through the door, Henry looked exhausted but Katie was a bundle of bubbles. "We had the grandest time! Uncle Henry was the best dancer of all and he let me dance on top of his *feet*! He was *very* popular and so handsome that all my friends wanted to dance with him so I got lots of dances with their fathers but they didn't let me dance on their feet. I have to go to bed now and dream of every minute again!"

The giddy young maiden started to run up the stairs, then turned and bounded from the fifth step straight into Henry's arms, nearly knocking him out the door. She clutched him tightly and gave him a big kiss. "I love you so much, Uncle Henry. You are the best father ever!"

He kissed her on the forehead. "I love you too, Katie. Anything for my special girl." He set her gently on the floor, and she scampered up the stairs with a haughty toss of her head toward her mother. At that moment, it became obvious to Kiri that she and her daughter were battling for Henry's attention and affection.

"Thank you for being Katie's Prince Charming tonight. She was thrilled."

"My pleasure. I'm embarrassed to admit that I did have a good time dancing with little girls."

"How about with their mothers? Do you have enough energy left to twirl this mother around the floor a time or two? I promise I won't step on your feet," she said demurely.

Henry smiled. "Of course… for you. But I can't stay long. I'm flying out to Geneva tomorrow morning." At Kiri's pout, he added, "I'll try to be home by Christmas."

"You set up the music. I'll check on Katie to make sure she's headed to bed and not still dancing." She climbed the stairs, peeked in on her daughter and returned with a chuckle. "You won't believe what she did. She crawled into bed with her dress still on and is fast asleep already."

Henry did not respond. Music played, but he was fast asleep in the recliner, his suit coat, lilac vest and shoes on the floor. As she covered him with a throw, she noticed how distinguished he looked with his coal black hair beginning to show gray at the temples. When she held his face in her hands and kissed him good night, he did not stir a muscle.

Kiri stretched out on the sofa nearby and pulled a cover over herself. She gazed on the kind and gentle man… the wonderful man… who devoted so much of his time to caring for her and her family. Who but he would fly home for one night to save her daughter from disappointment? Her thoughts wandered to her two beautiful children—one so bright and the other so spirited. She eased into sleep. *I have been greatly rewarded.*

CHAPTER 15

"I'll go with you, but I will not set one foot in the water!" Thomas protested.

Paula gathered their carryall bags and towels, delivered them to the car, and returned to gather him. "You'll do what the doctor orders."

"It's March. Too cold and drizzly. We'll catch pneumonia," he grumbled, refusing to put on his coat.

"You know the retractable cover is engaged this time of year, and both air and water are heated. No one has caught pneumonia at the aquacenter in the more than ten years it has been in operation. I doubt you'll be lucky number one. Now, into the car." He did not budge, so she removed a small notebook and pen from the hall console table, jotted a few words, and replaced them.

"What's that you're doing?"

"Listing all the times you do not follow doctor's orders. When you next go to see him and he asks if you've followed his directions and you smile and say, 'to the letter,' I'll pull out this notebook and show him when you put gravy on your potatoes at the restaurant, when you skipped resistance exercises, and when you refused aqua therapy."

He grumbled and put on his coat and hat. "Aqua therapy. Who ever heard of such a fool thing? I'm not a fish."

She helped him adjust the shoulders. " 'That fool thing' feeds your grandchildren and keeps a roof over their heads. Kiri's center is much in demand and one of the few certified for cardiac patients. She and her staff are highly qualified, and there is a waiting list for their services, so be thankful she agreed to squeeze you in."

Thomas harrumphed and walked to the passenger side of the car. Paula drove for them now. On the road, he did not engage in conversation, but the minute the car stopped at the center, he refused to get out. "I will not put on a suit and get into that pool."

"Then you can flip-flop your way up and down the edge as you follow me doing laps. That will be much more exhausting than exercising in the water." He did not budge. She looked him in the eyes. "What's really holding you back? You can't be afraid of the water... not a hearty sailor like you who nearly drowned me with his strength once."

His melancholy eyes revealed his embarrassment. "I'm not the man I was fifty-plus years ago."

She stroked him under the chin. "No one is." Then she flashed a sexy smile. "Some of us are better! I love you too much to lose you over some point of personal pride."

He patted her thigh affectionately. "Let's go see if that daughter of yours... ours... lives up to her reputation."

That daughter of theirs barely acknowledged their presence. Being forewarned, Maeve's sister glommed onto Thomas the minute he walked through the door. She was the only one on Kiri's staff hearty enough to out-bellow him, but she had a gentle way once it was clear that she was in charge. Paula swam laps in the lane reserved for caregivers who needed a relaxing break in their days.

Kiri attended to her own patients and kept her back to Thomas except for one instant when she caught a glimpse out of the corner of her eye. She noticed father and son were built the same—broad shoulders and chests, small waists, stocky thighs and calves tapering to thin ankles. Thomas lost muscle tone and carried his weight around his middle, but otherwise one would recognize Michael as his son. She wondered if her husband would have resembled his father in old age, then shook that unconstructive thought from her mind to file under 'one more thing I'll never know.'

"I have to admit, Paula, that workout was first-rate," Thomas said when the two met up on the patio after his session. "I might try that again sometime."

"That's good to hear because you have appointments scheduled three times a week for the next two months at least."

He would have protested, but his phone interrupted. By the expression on his face, he bore bad news. "That was Tommy. Margaret… another miscarriage." He could scarcely get those words out, so personal a pain did they recall for the two of them. "She's having trouble coming out of it. We need to go to the hospital immediately."

Within a half-hour of their hurried departure, Kiri received a call. Paula explained the particulars of her stepsister's condition and asked for advice. "Thomas thinks Bitsy would be a help… comfort and relax Margaret as her music did for him. What do you think? Would Bitsy be willing to play at the hospital again? For someone who has barely said one kind word to her in five years?"

"I don't know, Mom. All I can do is ask. I'll try to run her down and let you know. Has anyone contacted Brendan or her children?"

"Not to my knowledge. Tommy isn't much use. His father can't get one coherent sentence out of him."

"That sounds familiar. Never mind, then. A second call won't hurt. My next patient is here. As you saw, it's a madhouse today. Talk to you as soon as I can."

Kiri did better than talk. She arrived at the hospital with Bitsy and her harp. The young mother was reluctant to go until Kiri explained that Margaret, now in her early forties, lost a baby—her third in five years. When Bitsy thought of losing Sara, she agreed but was not sure what music to play for someone so sad.

After staring at Margaret's unresponsive body and taut, expressionless face, Bitsy sat in the hallway near her room and fingered a few chords with Thomas, Paula and Kiri gathered around her. She rose, stared into the room again, shook her head and sat to retune her instrument. After the second adjustment, Kiri asked what she was doing.

"Finding the music that works for her. Watch the muscles in her neck. See how tight they are? When I play this..." She plucked some strings. "...they don't change. I'm trying to find some that make her relax. When I do, then I will play."

Caitlín, Margaret's oldest, ran up the hall and invited herself into Kiri's arms. "Thank you so much for calling. My sister will be here soon. How is Mother?"

"We don't really know. Step into her room and ask your father. Bitsy will play for her soon. We hope that will help."

The young woman disappeared and Brendan arrived. "Thanks, Aunt Kiri. You'd think with instant communication today, we could do a better job of informing everyone. Fíonna is on her way. I'll pick up the others as soon as I get an okay. Bitsy's here?"

"Thomas thought she might help. We'll see soon."

Caitlín returned. "Father just shakes his head. The nurse says all of her vitals are normal. There's nothing they can do."

"She doesn't want to live," Bitsy said. They all stared at her, wide-eyed. "She's trying to decide if she should fight or not." Thomas clutched his chest and sat down with a heavy sigh, reminded of the choice his wife Kathryn made. Paula sat and held him tight. "Let me try this." Bitsy began to play.

Kiri watched through the window and gave Bitsy thumbs up when she noticed the muscles in Margaret's neck slacken. The young harpist played a few minutes more, then moved into music that was so sorrowful, Margaret and most of those present began to cry. Kiri motioned to Bitsy to stop, but she shook her head and kept playing.

"Her body and her heart need to weep to let go of her sadness. Then she will be open to healing." She continued while the family surrounded and held the grieving mother. After most of an hour, Bitsy moved into a soothing strain, the weeping abated, and Margaret's body relaxed. The harpist played another long session and then motioned Kiri over. "The power of touch will help her now... the massage you do for some of your patients... the one called Celtic circle."

Kiri drew in a shocked breath. "How do you know this when the doctors don't?"

"It comes to me like the music... like a fairy's whisper in m' ear."

Kiri shivered at those words but felt compelled to support Bitsy's assessment. She conferred with Thomas and Paula and then the girls. When they agreed her massage was worth a try, Kiri insisted she have permission. "Without Tommy's consent, I will not touch his wife."

Permission received, Kiri was about to begin when her phone sounded. "Henry!"

"I just got in. I have a couple of days. Are you free tonight?"

For the second time in as many minutes, Kiri could not believe her ears. Henry worked out of London for most of the two months since the holidays. They rarely found time together. Here was a chance, and once again she was embroiled in a family crisis. "Until a couple of hours ago I could have said yes, but at the moment I'm at the hospital with the family."

"Thomas?"

"No. Margaret. I'll explain later… if I can put you off for a couple of hours. Maybe a sit by the fire to catch up?"

She could sense his disappointment. "Right. Give me a call when you're ready to leave. The children?"

"Oh my gosh! I forgot the children! Bitsy is with me, so I'm sure they are with Sara at her apartment."

"I'll check. Come home to us soon."

"As soon as I can. Thanks, Henry. I'm sorry."

"No worries. Remember, I'm one of the few who understands when duty calls."

Kiri turned off her phone, summoned the two daughters and motioned for Brendan to pick up the other four. "Girls, I'm going to teach you an ancient massage technique. My patients like it. Maybe your mother will too. Bitsy and I cannot stay indefinitely, but if this method seems effective, you can take turns throughout the night until your mother finds her smile again."

Thomas and Paula looked on with interest as she explained the process. "The Celts revered the circle, you know. Your grandfather told me long ago that they believed the rhythms in nature and the divine followed circular patterns. Your mother's rhythms are confused and out of sync. We're going to massage her in a circle, with circles, to restore her natural circular rhythm. Bitsy's music will try to link your mother's soul with the divine."

She described briefly how she would begin on the left side of their mother's neck above the heart and with gentle clockwise motions move clockwise around her body from left shoulder to left arm to left leg and foot, then to the right foot and so on, up the right side of her body. They would then turn her over on her stomach, recommence on her back left side, and work counter-clockwise in both direction and motion, left around to right again. Then rest for about twenty minutes and repeat. "That motion directs her energy in a constant circle. Watch me first, and then follow me when we turn her on her tummy. Got it?"

At one year each side of twenty, and after working for their aunt at the pool, the two nieces knew how to follow directions. They nodded and entered the room. Bitsy played in circles too—a rondo so soothing that all spectators relaxed as well. By the time the rest of the family arrived, the atmosphere shifted from critical to manageable. Kiri and Bitsy left.

Thomas and Paula followed. Brendan took the two youngest home, and the two middle daughters spelled their older sisters once they were taught what to do. The hospital staff stood aside in awe.

Tommy sat in the corner watching his girls work on their mother, willing her to choose life. The harsh reprimand Kiri delivered to him privately before she left looped through his mind in a circle. "Do you love your wife? Why? When she comes back to us, send the children away. You climb up on that bed with her, hold her as tightly as you can and tell her all the reasons you love her and need her with you. Don't you dare say 'because of the children.' Margaret needs to know that *she* is important to *you* and *why*. She feels she is a failure because she has not given you a son. She's given you six beautiful daughters and lost three more. Is her life worth asking her to try again?"

Kiri found Henry in the recliner staring at the fire. She slid in beside him, and the two began the tender process of reacquaintance. Footsteps on the stairs brought them to a sudden halt. "Uncle Henry, I can't sleep," Katie said as she wriggled in between the two of them, forcing her mother out. *I was right*, Kiri thought. *In the battle for Henry's affections, my daughter and I are jousting 'round and 'round in a vicious circle.*

Fifteenth Anniversary Year: Birth: a son to Doyle; daughter #3 to Gus
    Death: one of Paddy's housemates
    Graduation: Emily's Meggie
    Jobs: Bitsy was offered a part-time position in critical care at the hospital. She refused. Thomas told her that her gift was to share, not to sell like a piece of chocolate. She volunteers one afternoon most weeks now that she no longer sees the harpist. The hospital provides transportation.
    Other: Quincy Clinic expanded again to include home health services providing temporary, part-time and full-time care, and supplies such as bath stools, grab bars, folding cane seats, walkers, wheelchairs, temporary ramps, etc., for rental or purchase. Free installation included. Electronic aids also available. The neighborhood has aged since we first moved in. Searching for a larger location.
    Quincy House Cleaners established—one-time, occasional, weekly or monthly, inside or out. See reference to aging population above.
    The cake ladies approached me with a problem: They are aging just like everyone else. Running back and forth between their four houses is taking its toll. They envy the house with Bitsy's apartment and wondered if they could do the same with their other three. I suggested they try community living like Paddy's group. Remodel one house into three apartments with common space. Another into a huge kitchen where all of them and any helpers could work together for savings on equipment, supplies, energy, and footsteps. Convert its extra space into a small

housekeeping apartment for someone to clean and watch over the place. Sell the third to finance the other two projects. Conversions underway.

Tommy and Margaret took their first holiday alone—away from the family—ever! They flew to the Cayman Islands in the Caribbean for a week in June. I wish someone would take me to a sunny island for a holiday.

Henry out of town lots. Mother and daughter continue jousting.

CHAPTER 16

Henry had a problem. Katie. The spirited whirligig he loved more than anyone in the world... except for her mother... did not know when to stop—at her bedroom door, at the top of the staircase or at the kitchen when she spotted them on the deck. Her interruptions were always ill-timed from his perspective; perfect, from hers. During excursions or evening visits she was delightful as always, eyes bright when she talked of her friends and of school, but as soon as her mother appeared on the scene, her eyes narrowed and she clung to him, monopolizing his attention, sometimes even telling her mother to "Go away!"

He wanted to wag a finger at her and tell her that such behavior did not become a sweet little girl, that she should cherish her mother's love, but he did not have that right. He was not related by blood or marriage. Kiri encouraged him to be firm with her daughter but when he tried, Katie turned all coy and giggly, much like the night of the father/daughter dance. That night when she introduced him to those unfamiliar, she called him her Uncle Henry *Killian*. Then she clapped her hands over her mouth, raised her eyebrows and said "Oops! Sometimes I get the names mixed up." That's when her obstinate behavior began—about the time of the dance— almost two years ago. That's when his regular times with her family were cut short by work. Perhaps that was the root of her problem—his frequent and lengthy absences, he realized. Perhaps Katie feared he would not return and did not know how to express feeling abandoned, and he knew the pain of that feeling well. She clung to him when he did come home because she was afraid of losing him again. The only solution for that was to be more present in her life... in all their lives... on a frequent, if not daily, basis.

That conclusion spawned a second problem. His job. Henry loved his job... or at least, his job as it used to be. With advances in technology, communications and surveillance, his time was spent setting up communication networks to eliminate groundwork and training IT guys in the systems that Devin, Frank and he set up. Doyle bailed shortly after he married; he did not like London. Henry contended that video chat interviews with prospective local reporters and sources in far away places compromised the integrity of objective journalism. A guy needed a face-to-face sit-down with an interviewee to stare into his eyes and soul and gauge body language to assure that he would not walk out the door and high five someone who paid him to support their political cause.

Extractions rarely occurred since network reporters seldom left the country these days. Surveillance drones permitted real time observance of events that could be reported from a comfy chair in London, while locals provided the in-depth. No need for interpreters or contacts. If a local employee requested to leave his country, he was responsible for making it to a friendly border where a Devin/Frank/Henry counterpart met him with documents and waved goodbye. No personal attention. No follow-up.

Training guys to utilize the communications and surveillance systems to the max was the worst. He no sooner hired and trained a techie, than the fellow was snapped up by another division or worse, by another company taking his knowledge of their systems and their secrets with him. While Devin substituted from Dublin, Henry started the hiring/training process all over again in London, thus requiring his long and frequent absences from Kiri and her family.

That had to stop. He needed a team of three or four to build and run the systems, vet and interview contacts on site or just outside their borders, and meet them if/when they decided to leave to glean as much helpful information as possible. The personal touch. He would never be cut loose; he knew too much. But the agency might shut down Dublin completely and transfer him to London permanently. Unacceptable. Time for an ultimatum—my way or no way, he decided.

He needed to talk to Kiri. Counseling others was her forte, never mind that she ran in circles with her own problems. He never discussed his personal issues with anyone, but she could suggest constructive alternatives. He had to take the chance that exposing his desire to grow closer to her family, and to spend *more* time with them, would not affect their relationship. Hearing "London! What a great opportunity. Go!" would be worse than the company demanding he make the move.

When Katie, Michael Thomas and Polly left for their month in Colorado, he asked Kiri to go on a short holiday to the Channel Islands off the coast of France—a short flight away. A few days alone in a neutral environment within the Commonwealth where he would not be surveilled would answer many questions for him… and them.

*   *   *

Kiri had a problem. Katie. Her delightful imp of a daughter, whose bouncing red curls and infectious giggle could turn frowns into smiles, perfected a glare especially for her mother. Her sparkle charmed an entire room and her flood of run-on sentences told a story in less than a minute, yet she had no time for her mother. She inherited her dad's bear hug and had plenty to go around, except for her mother. She never embarrassed Kiri in public because she knew word would get back to her grandfather, but she was brutal in private—enough to cause her mother to cry late at night when she thought no one could hear.

The mischievous preteen sat sullen through meals, then ran to her room and slammed the door, avoiding her mother as much as possible… until she heard Henry come in. Katie's built-in radar tracked him as soon as she heard his voice. She ran to him, monopolized his attention, and even after being sent to bed, she sneaked back to intrude on his private time with her mother. When he tried to scold, she tilted her head, crinkled her nose and twisted her finger into his buttonhole. She knew that aggravated her mother because she heard her tormented pleas in the night.

Kiri spent hours analyzing her daughter's behavior. "I'm a trained counselor, for heaven's sake, and I can't devise an effective strategy to deal with my own daughter. Why should my clients trust me?" She called out to her husband's portrait for help. "I don't understand Katie. I don't know how to help her. She rejects my love and I don't know why. Please help me, Michael. Michael!"

She and Henry were running out of options. Katie interrupted deck dates and recliner dates just long enough to spoil the mood. That might be the trick. If Henry were the lightening rod for her daughter's outlandish behavior, then he needed to spend *less* time with her and the family. The two of them should take their alone time away from the house and the neighborhood... maybe to a safe place. Kiri resolved to broach the sensitive subject during their long weekend in the Channel Islands—a perfect place to be alone... a perfect time to set a new course... for the two of them.

Henry announced his arrival from the bottom of the stairs. When Kiri observed the distress on his face, she realized immediately that she would have no need of her passport.

"I'm sorry. I must beg off. I received a call. My mother. She's had a stroke."

Kiri gasped and clutched his hand. "You must go! Immediately. What can I do to help? Do you want company?"

He shook his head, then grabbed her in an embrace worthy of a departing soldier and was gone. His revelation—that he had living family—stunned Kiri. He knew the most intimate details of her married and family life, saved her from self-destruction, experienced her transformational moments, lived her joys and sorrows as if they were his own... and she knew nothing of his. Henry had a mother... a family... a past... and never shared one detail with her. What did that say about his level of trust in her? About their relationship? About setting a course for their future?

* * *

"Kiri? Henry here. I'm calling from the airport. I just want to say... I'm sorry."

"No worries. I understand better than most when duty calls." She heard the suggestion of a chuckle. "How is your mother? Anything I can do while you're gone?"

"Thanks, but no. She's doing as well as can be expected." He cleared his throat nervously. "Besides the four days I've just used, I won't have another break for a couple of weeks. I'll go straight to the northwest to check on her and probably won't stop in Dublin. In fact, I may have to spend any free time I can wangle over the next couple of months to visit her. I'm sorry to put you off so long."

"Don't be. Your mother's recovery must take priority now. Why don't you move her down here? There's a wonderful rehabilitation center not too far away. I could watch over her while you're gone."

"Thanks, but no. She's best where she is... among familiar staff. I'll video chat with them... and her... every couple of days." He cleared his throat again. "Let me know when the children return. I'll text my apologies for not joining them on excursions while Kendra is visiting. I'll call again when I can."

Kiri was more disgruntled than disappointed. Henry refused her company and now, her help. She knew people—doctors, nurses, home health aides, friends and children to offer companionship to an ailing woman. She spent a fair portion of her workweek accommodating many neighbors with whom she had no connection, and she was very good at it. Why didn't Henry trust her enough to help?

"Kiri? Henry here."

"Henry! We haven't communicated in ages. How is your mother?"

"Doing as well as can be expected. That's what I'd like to talk about."

Finally. He's decided to accept one of my many suggestions of the last couple of months. "Can we expect to see her moved to Dublin soon?"

"No. Actually I... When do the children begin the fall session?"

"In a couple of weeks. Why?"

"If it's not too much to ask, I'd like to take them for an all-day next Saturday."

"They'll love that. We're all anxious to spend time with you again."

"I mean... just the children this time... unless you think it inappropriate. My mother wants to meet them." Silence. "Kiri?"

She was dumbfounded. The children? Didn't she count? She scolded herself. Henry wanted to fulfill his ailing mother's wish and was embarrassed to ask. "Of course. The kids will be delighted. They've never seen the northwest. When will you pick them up?"

"If I take the first flight out, I can be to your house by nine. The drive is a long one, there and back. I may not get them home until late, just in time for the last flight out."

"They'll be waiting. I'll pack snacks. Don't worry about time on this end. Relax and enjoy their company... if you can!"

Kiri did not inform the children of the excursion until a couple of days in advance in case Henry had to cancel. Katie would probably blame her mother if he did. When she announced the plan and its purpose, her daughter squealed with delight and ran up the stairs. "I'm going to wear my purple dress!"

The frustrated mother shouted after her that Henry's mother was very ill, and their visit was not a party. As the bedroom door slammed she added, "That dress won't fit. You've grown in the last two years." She sighed. Her daughter would discover that soon enough, and she prepared for the ensuing uproar.

The date and time arrived, as did Henry. Michael Thomas met him at the door, dressed in his school uniform as his grandfather suggested and with a basket of snacks enough for a growing twelve-year-old. Katie stood at the top of the stairs with her hair nicely brushed and held back from her face with a wide lilac ribbon. She posed in her purple dress under a white cardigan to camouflage the slit she made down the back—now held together with large safety pins—to add a couple of inches. The back bow was snipped away; the front one rode high to suggest an empire waist. She flashed a captivating smile and descended slowly for effect.

"I'm excited to meet your mother, Uncle Henry. She must be *very nice* to have such a wonderful son as you." She punctuated that last with a glare at her own mother, tossed her curls, and left with a swing of her hips.

Kiri fretted throughout the evening, awaiting her children's return. When she heard Henry's car in the drive, she opened the door to greet them. Michael Thomas was first in and headed straight for the kitchen. Katie followed, leading Henry by the hand. She grabbed him for a hug. "Thank you, Uncle Henry. I loved meeting your mother. Can we go again?"

"We'll see. Thank you for the ice cream. Now, off to bed." He mouthed a "thank you" to Kiri, followed by a "sorry, got to go," and left.

She turned to her daughter. "What was that about? Did you have a nice time?"

"A very nice time. Uncle Henry's mother was happy to see us—I could tell by her eyes—especially when I told her all about my dress and the father/daughter dance, but she cried a little when we left and that made him sad, so I held his hand and treated him to ice cream that I bought with my own pocket money just like he does for me when I feel sad." Pleased with herself, she dashed up the stairs before her mother could ask another intrusive question.

Kiri sought out her son for a more detailed report and found him in the nook building sandwiches. "Didn't you stop for supper?"

"Sure, but that was a couple of hours ago," he said, pouring two tall glasses of milk.

"Tell me about your day." She slid into the nook across from him.

He shrugged. "It was okay. Kind of interesting, actually. Katie gabbed most of the way, so I finally shoved an apple in her mouth to give Uncle Henry a chance."

She gazed on the son who inhaled food like his father. "Where did you go? Did he show you where he grew up?"

"Leitrim, not as far as the coast. No, he didn't mention where he lived. He mostly talked about the area and the Troubles in Northern Ireland. He really knows his history. He said Irish Catholics and Protestants fought each other there a long time ago when you and he were about my age. Can you believe that? He said he'd take me on holiday to the North someday when I'm older."

Kiri chuckled to think that her childhood was now considered ancient history. "What was his mother like?"

"Old. Pretty sick—worse than grandfather when he had his heart attack. Small like Bitsy. She can't move much, but she touched us with her right hand. We could tell she was happy to see us by looking in her eyes. Her speech was garbled and she used the old tongue, so Uncle Henry translated Katie's endless story about her dress and the dance. If I have to listen to that story one more time, I will p...."

She shoved a carrot at him. "Is the facility a nice one?"

He nodded. "Seems so. Clean. Quiet. The staff is nice. Funny thing, though. All the photos in her room were facedown on her bedside table like someone dusted and forgot to put them right again. She looked at me and Uncle Henry, then me again and made a little smile. She did the same with Katie and made a kind of question mark."

"What was her name?"

"He called her 'Mother,' and we forgot to ask. When it was time to leave, she had tears in her eyes. I took Katie into the corridor so Uncle Henry could have some private time with his mother. When he came out, he was pretty upset so Katie suggested we go for ice cream, and then we came home." He finished his milk, kissed her on the cheek and left with a "G'night, Mom. Love you."

Kiri treasured those precious words and wondered if she would ever hear them from her daughter again.

"Kiri? Henry here. I'm sorry I haven't had a chance to call since I borrowed your children two weeks ago."

"No apology necessary. They enjoyed their visit with your mother. How is she? Will we see you soon?"

"That's what I'd like to talk about. Does Thomas still have a hard lock on their Sundays?"

"Pretty much. He's too stubborn to give them up even though he has slowed down. Do you want to take them on a Sunday?"

"No. It's you I need and hoped Paula could keep them for the full day until evening." Pause. "My mother wants to meet you."

She calmed the surprise in her voice. "I'll arrange it. This Sunday? Same time, same place?"

"Actually... I need another favor. If you could meet me at the airport at eight, we could shorten the trip and get you home sooner."

"Consider it done. We'll take my car and save you time at the rental counter too."

"I'll text the details. Kiri, I... can't thank you enough."

"No thanks necessary. My pleasure to help *you* out for a change. See you Sunday."

Michael Thomas gave an accurate report. Upon entering the room, Kiri first noticed framed photos facedown on the table. Second was how frail Henry's mother appeared, and third was how her eyes told her story— a strong-willed woman seeking closure before she drew her last breath.

She struggled to make herself understood as her son spoke to her in Gaelic of his work, of Katie and Michael Thomas, and finally of Kiri who waited just outside the door grasping only a few words and proper names. She studied the invalid's eyes for meaning and watched them reflect lethargy and longing, then love, pride, delight and finally gratification when her son called Kiri in.

The mother reached out her delicate hand to the woman who held it gently while being examined by those eyes. Henry translated her garbles. "Mother thanks you for coming... She says you are very beautiful... She sees Michael Thomas in you and m... more so than Katie. The children were delightful... so well-mannered and loving... a credit to their parents." He appeared embarrassed and chose his words more carefully. "Mother wishes she had known them as babies... and hopes you will all come back soon so she can see..." He lowered his eyes. "...the whole family together."

"We would like that very much." Kiri smiled at the ailing woman, obviously exhausted by her efforts to speak. "We'll try... soon."

The mother sighed, relaxed into her pillow and let her eyes say "Thank you."

Kiri touched Henry's shoulder. "She needs to rest. Keep talking. I'll be right back." She found the nurse on duty and produced her credentials and a list. "I work with patients who have limited mobility and many are helped by these treatments. Is there something on this list appropriate for Mr. Callaghan's mother?"

The nurse smiled and tapped one. "This here. Patients love it, but we never have the time. The lady will be greatly appreciative. I would."

Kiri returned to the room and touched Henry's shoulder again. "Does your mother understand English?"

"She does, but the old tongue comes to her more easily now."

"Good." Kiri kept one hand on Henry and took his mother's hand with her other. She stared into her eyes. "I have a treat for you. I work with many people who find it difficult to move, and they often ask me for a foot rub. Would you like one?"

Reading the ailing woman's brightened eyes as a yes, Kiri stepped to the foot of the bed and used her magic fingers to massage the soles of her feet, hoping to touch her inner soul as well. Henry continued to speak in low tones and could sense his mother's tension subside. When Kiri finished, the sickly woman emitted a huge sigh of pleasure and blinked another thank you.

Kiri placed one arm around Henry's shoulders and the other on the side of his mother's face. She pulled him in close and leaned to whisper in the woman's ear. "You have a wonderful son... He is loved and admired by many... Thank you for sharing him with us." She kissed the woman on the cheek, tasting the salt of her tears, then turned to the son and whispered.

"I want to share a little piece of wisdom with you. If you have anything to say to your mother or ask her, do it now. From my experience, the unanswered and unspoken will haunt you for the rest of your life. No matter how painful, knowing prepares you to face your demons and conquer them."

Henry was startled by her remark. Did she suspect? How could she? He was so controlled.

Kiri took his strong hand and curled it around his mother's petite one. "Touch is important, especially now. I'm going to take a break while you share some private moments." She kissed Henry on the cheek, tasting the salt of *his* tears and said goodbye to his mother with her eyes.

*　　*　　*

Kiri double-checked her list. Casserole in the oven. Salad, bread and fruit ready. Wine—no, frothy dark ale—set out. Candle on the table. Lights low. Most important—children farmed out for the whole night! She really did not expect the evening to be a romantic one. Henry probably needed to unload, needed consolation and might want to stay the night on the sofa or in the recliner rather than spend it in his infrequently used apartment before he drove to see his mother the next day.

His call two days ago took her by surprise. They spoke not more than a dozen words on the return from visiting his mother three weeks earlier, and he called a couple of times to check in. Nothing to report, he said, other than they video chatted daily now. This time, he wanted to fly in early evening and stay the night in Dublin to depart for the west before dawn. "Are you free for a visit?"

"Of course," she replied. "Dinner will be waiting and the children won't." A visit? Why couldn't the man admit that he was desperate for a hug?

At the sound of a car in the drive, she lit the candle and turned on the fireplace. Since the motor was left running, she decided she was mistaken and started to blow out the candle when Henry burst in. His drawn, haggard face and hooded eyes foretold the evening. "Sorry. Got to go." His hands shook when she took hold of them.

"Your mother?"

"There was a message on my phone when we landed. 'Come quickly. She has... taken a turn.'" He could barely get the words out.

"Give me a minute and I'll come with."

"No. I can't ask... I'll be fine. I don't need any help."

"Then you're a first in the history of mankind. You shouldn't be alone at a time like this. I'm coming. I can spell you on the drive if nothing else."

"Please, no. I can't expose you... I can handle this. But before I go, I want to...." He grabbed her and held her so tightly that she gasped for breath. "I want to thank you for being so kind to my mother. Your tenderness gave her strength for a few more good days." He choked back his emotion and disappeared into the dark.

Kiri returned to her list. Turn off the oven. Put the rest of the food in the fridge. Shut off the fireplace. Blow out the candle. Douse the lights, and go to bed. She started her music, curled up with her pillow and stared at her husband Michael's portrait. *He* was the reason Henry would not admit his own need. He did not want to expose her to the grim reality of death again. *Well, I faced that demon and survived... only because Henry supported me almost daily for a year. He likely gave up time with his own family—the one I just recently discovered he had!*

She empathized with the desperation he must feel, anticipating the moment his life would change forever. No one should be alone at that moment. Henry needed someone... and she wanted to be that someone. That unflappable, self-controlled, selfless rock of a man needed a hand to hold and a shoulder to lean on whether he dared to admit it or not.

Kiri started a new list. Kids. She never thought she would feel lucky to have so many nieces and nephews. Meggie answered the call. Work. Thank goodness for Maeve's sister who could rearrange schedules in a flash. Clothes. Where did she put that blue-black dress Henry bought when...? One more thing. What was it... what was it? Bitsy! If her music created an atmosphere of calm that allowed a body to heal in its own way, failing that, surely her heavenly strains guided one through a peaceful passing.

The two departed at dawn.

* * *

Henry paced the room, then gathered his mother's personal belongings and placed them in a travel bag. He fingered through the photos with a weak smile and slid them into a side pocket. He checked the drawer in the table and registered surprise at the small, tin lock-box he found there with a label on the lid addressed to "My Son Henry." A key tied with a ragged purple ribbon hung from the handle. He started to unlock the box, glanced at the bed and changed his mind, placing it on top of the bag. He reclaimed his seat beside his mother and took up her withered hand.

Kiri watched through the doorway, fearing they were too late, but when he sat with his mother's hand in his, she followed his gaze to the minuscule rise and fall of the sunken chest. The ailing woman's change over the last three weeks was dramatic—from a frail woman with fight still in her eyes to a shrunken little doll with scarcely enough strength to hold them half-open. At that barest sign of life, Kiri signaled Bitsy to play her music.

Henry turned with a start, rage fighting with gratitude in his eyes. Kiri returned his stare with determination in hers. Bitsy continued to play, and within minutes the three of them witnessed the dying woman's state of being visibly alter. Her curled fingers and toes relaxed and spread, a spark charged her eyes and she whispered in halting English, "angels."

Her son bent over her, wishing her voice to sound again, for she had not spoken since he arrived. Her eyes darted around the room. "Angels?" she whispered. Henry motioned Kiri and Bitsy in, and his mother's focus came to rest on the young woman with long blond hair, rich blue eyes, and pale phosphorescent face who held a small harp in her hands.

"Mother, this is Bitsy," Henry said.

"Kathryn Elizabeth Killian, ma'am," the young woman corrected. "Here to play for you."

His mother gripped his hand with a strength he had not felt in many weeks. Her other sought Kiri's, as she struggled to pull herself up from her pillow. Her eyes stared into Bitsy. "Family," she whispered. "*Muintir.*" The aged orbs then searched the room frantically until they found the tin box. "Family," she whispered again. Her stare bore into her son as she repeated "*Muintir*… Family!" and fell back onto the pillow with a serene smile on her face.

Bitsy climbed onto the foot of the bed and resumed playing. Kiri sat on its blanket on one side of Henry's mother and held her hand. He, holding onto the other, sensed ease return to her body and calm envelop the room. Throughout several hours, the three bore witness to the strong-willed woman's journey from reaching closure with the trials of her earthly life to her dignified and peaceful passage into the next. Bitsy plucked a final, ethereal chord. "Your mother sends you her love."

CHAPTER 17

"I *hate* you! I hate *you*! *I hate you!*" Katie shouted at her mother, each repeat a decibel louder than the last. "Uncle Henry's mother was *my* friend... *my friend*... and I should have been there! Not you!" She turned her back on her mother, ran up the stairs and slammed her bedroom door.

"I'm sorry, Aunt Kiri. I shouldn't have told Katie why you were gone." Apology was written all over Meggie's face as she watched Kiri try to erase the humiliation from her own.

"No worries. Nothing I can't handle once I catch my breath." She handed her twenty-year-old niece an envelope. "Thank you for coming on short notice."

"Anytime, but you don't owe me." She attempted to return it.

Kiri insisted. "Do you not remember what I've tried to teach—fair compensation for a job well done? Take it and treat yourself." She waved goodbye and leaned against the door. *That embarrassing scene will rip through the family like a flash flood.* Deal with her daughter later. Now was the time for sitting under the tree to take stock. She fixed a cup of tea, grabbed a sweater and walked out to the chair permanently planted beneath the evergreen.

"Michael," she called, addressing her husband. "I've done it again... I can't seem to do anything right where your daughter is concerned. She thinks my purpose in life is to make hers miserable. How do I show Katie how much I love her when she won't come within two feet of me? How? I need your help... a sign. Help me. Please help me!"

A hand on her shoulder stopped her tirade. "Mom. What are you doing here?"

"Our granddaughter summoned us. She is packing a bag to run away from home... to our house. Thomas is upstairs with her now reminding her that O'Connells do not run from a fight. They stand their ground and find a way to resolve the conflict." She patted her daughter's knee. "So, how was your trip?"

"I'm glad Bitsy and I were there. I truly believe her music has fairy magic in it. Once Henry got over the shock of seeing us, he was grateful for our company. Watching a strong man let go of years of bottled-up emotion hurts. His mother's death did not affect him as much as her burial—a clergyman to say a few consoling words and the three of us. Neither he nor his mother wanted a full-fledged funeral. Our staying that extra couple of days gave him two pairs of shoulders to cry on."

"Did someone say 'funeral?'" Thomas asked as he ambled toward them with a smug look on his face. "That daughter of yours has the spirit of her father, for sure. I made it clear to her that she was not to disrespect anyone by the name of O'Connell again or she would have to answer to me. She's to find appropriate alternatives for expressing her displeasure." He smiled and patted her knee. "She's pretty upset about being excluded."

A vision of then twelve-year-old Brendan wanting so much to be a part of his uncle's rites flashed through Kiri's mind. Maybe she was wrong not to include her children. She reconsidered. No, Henry would have been mortified had they witnessed his lack of control... and his comfort took priority. Best to absorb her daughter's wrath.

"But I've planted a seed to help her deal constructively with her hurt."

"Thank you, Thomas."

"Reserve your thanks until we see what she concocts." He raised a crafty eyebrow.

"Maybe she *should* move in with you since you seem to know how to handle her."

He shook his head. "We love all our grandchildren dearly." And squeezed Paula's hand with a glint in his eye. "But at this time in our lives, we treasure our privacy too."

Kiri watched the aged couple depart without her daughter in tow, and resumed a mental conversation with the bits of her husband's spirit that resided in their tree. She appealed for strength and understanding... and an occasional hug from her little girl. Fortified with a couple of deep breaths and a vow for positive thought, she returned to the house and nearly collided with Katie in the kitchen.

Her daughter finished pouring a glass of juice and closed the fridge. "*I'm* in charge of the *Aft*funeral for Henry's mother—the part that comes at the rear end of the first one. Grandfather said so. It will be very nice and I will wear my purple dress and Uncle Henry and a few friends will come. *You* are *not* invited!" Katie stated with impudence, then froze with terror in her eyes as she imagined her grandfather's scolding countenance. She curtsied politely to her mother and went to her room... without slamming the door.

* * *

"Kiri...."

"Mom? I thought you were coming to the memorial today."

"I am. I'm sitting out front in the car while Thomas checks with Katie about sticking to 'the plan.' He insists she clear it with him or he will call the celebration off. He says she is so much like her father that she may have connived a way to blindside him."

"I hope not. I'm worried about Henry. We've hardly spoken in the last couple of weeks."

"Don't worry. Thomas cleared the event with him as well, and Henry set the date. Katie's tribute to his mother may even do him some good. She planned a short program, and I fixed her dress by making buttonholes down both sides of the slit and weaving a purple ribbon through them to hold the top together. What made her cut it up in the first place?"

"Some crazy idea about being beautiful for Henry's mother. I see them setting out chairs now. I hope she hasn't invited the whole neighborhood."

"She wanted to, but Thomas put the kibosh on that. He said she could have as many guests as her age. Since Katie was ten, she could invite ten people. That was the rule."

"Is there such a rule?"

"There is now! She tried to outsmart him by listing all the people who weren't really guests; they were family so they shouldn't count. The two of them finally compromised by overlooking anyone on the program but setting up only ten chairs for the rest. How she tried to manipulate him tickled Thomas. How are you doing?"

"For being banned from the main floor of my house and the garden, I'm doing fine. I plan to watch from my bedroom window."

"So I've heard. Do you want me to leave my phone on so you can listen?"

"Wouldn't that be cheating?"

"I won't tell anyone. Will you?"

Kiri listened to her mother exit the car and walk to the garden, her footsteps scuffing more slowly than usual.

When the principals took their places and all ten chairs were occupied, Katie opened with a short welcome. Bitsy played a loving, graceful—but not sad—piece on her harp. Katie presented remarks—in run-on fashion—concluding with the idea that since Henry's mother was loved and admired by him, then she should be loved and honored by all present because they all loved him and were part of his family… somehow.

Bitsy played another soothing—but not sad—piece. Michael Thomas read a prayer in Gaelic. Katie closed with an invitation to join in the planting of a memorial lilac bush. Henry would dig the hole but everyone could put a scoop of dirt on after. Michael Thomas led the assemblage in the Lord's Prayer. Fifteen minutes and done.

"Now, that's my kind of service," Kiri heard Thomas say. "Short and to the point. Let's go plant a bush, my dear."

Henry put his foot to the shovel. The bush was nestled in the ground. Katie pronounced it good and said, "We plant this lilac in memory of…" She looked at Henry. "What was your mother's name?"

He swallowed hard. "Kathryn. Her name was Kathryn."

"That's *my* name! I'm named after *your mother* too! I *knew* she was special to me."

Henry hurried to correct her, considering the Killian-O'Connells present. "You were named for your father's mother, Kathryn Killian.

Both mothers share the name Kathryn because they were both beautiful and beloved."

Katie accepted the explanation and continued. "We plant this lilac in memory of Henry's mother Kathryn who is related to us... somehow." She jumped up and down and clapped her hands. "Don't leave yet. We have ice cream!"

Kiri heard her mother speak to her husband. "Nicely done, Thomas. You taught your granddaughter well."

"All the credit goes to Katie. She said the ideas just 'popped into her head.'"

Thomas' last words rumbled around in Kiri's mind as she watched the reception wind down, guests pay their respects, shake hands and trade hugs, and the ice cream disappear. She wondered what flavor it was. Soon, only Henry remained, sitting near the lilac bush. She noticed him take his phone out... and hers sounded.

"Kiri? Henry here. I missed you this afternoon."

"I missed you too. I watched from the bedroom... where I am now."

He looked up, and she waved. He smiled and waved back. "Katie did a wonderful job. I was hesitant about her staging such an event, but I came away with a very nice feeling... a happy memory. You should be proud of her."

"I am, and someday she will believe me when I tell her. Would you like to stay for supper? Or go out?"

"Truthfully? I'd rather sit here alone and savor the memory for a while longer, then return to my apartment where some personal business awaits. I'll welcome an invitation when it's off my mind. Maybe tomorrow before I go back to London?"

"Of course. I'll wait for your call... and I won't spy any longer."

"Kiri? Katie is too young to appreciate how much her remarks and this plant mean to me, so I want you to know."

"Our pleasure. Enjoy the garden. We love you very much and hope you'll visit anytime you want to relive a happy memory." She shut off her phone and noticed a black feather float past her window, past Henry's shoulder and burrow into the lilac bush.

Much later, after Henry departed and the children buried themselves in their rooms with their electronic tablets, she strolled into the garden, fished the feather out of the fragrant shrub, and dropped it into her pocket. The plant, forced to bloom in autumn, reminded her that it was autumn— specifically October—more specifically mid-October, the most melancholic time of year for her... and now for Henry too.

* * *

Henry circled his dining table for the third or fourth time. He lost count. The tin lock-box sat at its center, awaiting his inspection. He reached for it and rotated it ninety degrees as if its direction would alter his fate for good or ill. He removed his tie and unbuttoned his collar. He circled the table again, stared at the box and rolled up his shirtsleeves. He ran his fingers through his hair and clasped them behind his head, tilting it upward to search the ceiling for a hint of the box's contents. Finding only a spider web clinging from a beam, he pulled out a chair, sat and drew the tin container forward. His hands shook as he turned the key in its lock.

A thin parchment paper lay on top of bundled documents. Henry opened it and read, *A child is entitled to his history,* and recalled his mother's departing words when she returned to her home village, "The rest I'll keep secret 'til the day I die." He clenched the fragile note in his hands and squeezed it against his eyes. *I've longed for this moment since my first memory of our flight in the night. Mother kept her promise. Finally I will learn my true story.*

The first packet contained photos in reverse chronological order: graduation from Trinity with his mother on his arm, holding his Leaving Certificate at the completion of senior cycle, the same for his Junior Certificate, and an assortment of primary school class pictures beginning about the age of eight. The last two were older and fading to sepia tones— one of his young mother and a man dated 1969, and the other of the same couple holding a baby dated 1970. *This man must be my father at their marriage and at my baptism. I got my height and widow's peak from him.*

He set those two aside and delved into the second bundle, copies of certificates from various levels of school from third class forward. The final document was an original of his birth certificate, a copy of which he used for entrance to schools and for proof of age on government and employment records. He smoothed it onto the table to examine for the thousandth time. Father: unknown. Mother: Kathryn Callaghan, DOB January 15, 1948, County Leitrim. Son: Henry Callaghan, DOB April 17, 1970, County Leitrim. Signed and Filed: Auxiliary Bishop Finbar Ryan, Dublin, September 2, 1978. Not a digit, period or comma had altered.

He set the document on top of the pictures of his parents and reached with trembling hands for the third, and final, packet wrapped in old newsprint. He unfolded it and read the headline: 11 August 1973. *Bomb Kills IRA Volunteer in County Donegal.* At first, he thought it just a scrap to protect the remaining items, but being a journalist, he read the article. *Authorities identified Dermot Henry Devane of County Leitrim as the IRA volunteer who died transporting a bomb in his car. The device exploded prematurely in Kilclean, County Donegal, killing the driver. His ultimate target is unknown. Family and associates of the bomber are being sought for questioning.*

Henry rubbed his chin, cracked his knuckles and opened the next paper—a second birth certificate. He skimmed it quickly. Father: Dermot Henry Devane... Mother: Kathryn... Son: Henry... Signed and Filed: Dr. Angus O'Gowan... He found his father's name! He reached for the next, a certificate of baptism, and the next, a marriage certificate for Dermot Henry Devane and Kathryn... His parents were married. He was legitimate! He laughed out loud at his good fortune. *Mystery solved. Thank you, Mother!*

He cleared a space on the table and arranged the items side-by-side: marriage certificate with picture on top, birth certificate from 1970 naming his father, certificate of baptism with picture on top, newspaper clipping. He paused at the twinge of regret he felt for not taking the time to mourn the father he found and lost in the space of five minutes. Later. He placed the final document on the table, the revised birth certificate from 1978, and wondered why he needed a second one and why his father's name was not recorded on it.

The revelation jolted him like the crack of a lion tamer's whip. He was eight in 1978, about the time his mother exacted a new life in Dublin and education for her son as payment for a priest's transgressions. Erasure of the boy's past was the Church's insurance policy against future exposure. With one stroke of a Bishop's pen, Henry became the bastard son of an unwed mother who endured that shame for the rest of her life in exchange for a future for her son.

His hands trembled as he worked his way down both pages. Father vs. unknown made sense now, but the mother listed beneath his father's name was Kathryn *Killian*... and their son's name was Henry *Killian* Devane! Impossible! He picked up the pictures again and examined them carefully. His mother's face was unmistakable. Why, then, and when did she change her name to Callaghan?

Dropping Devane might have been an act of desperation when the authorities searched for the IRA bomber's family. When Kathryn fled their home in the middle of the night, she carried only her son and her maiden name with her. The logical explanation for Callaghan years later was a sound-alike since at eight Henry would have memory of his true name. Little Katie said it herself, "Callaghan is almost Killian." Another parting gift from the Bishop made tracing the boy's birth records impossible.

His mother's last words when she heard Bitsy's name—"*muintir...* family"—was her final clue to his identity... his connection... his family. Henry reminded himself not to jump to conclusions. Surely, coincidence accounted for the same spelling, since the name itself was not uncommon in the west. But what if...? He allowed his mind to wander through the vast field of possibilities implied by blood relationship.

"Stop it!" he shouted aloud. "Supposition is not fact. I'm a truth-seeker. Concrete proof will tell the full story." He shuffled the litter of papers together to re-examine when the shock of their discovery waned. As he replaced them in the box, he noticed another piece of thin parchment stuck to its bottom. He peeled it away, taking care not to tear the ragged-edged missive—the type one might tuck into a family Bible for safekeeping.

He opened it gingerly to find a rough sketch of a family tree with his name in pencil at the bottom: Henry Killian Devane, called "Harry." He remembered now. He smiled at the memory of his mother's voice calling "Harry" to him when she came from working in the church kitchen. He traced the tree from his name through six generations to the time of the potato famine when Irish died in droves and their histories with them. Fergus Killian was his oldest known ancestor, and his oldest son Colm stayed on the family's ground in County Leitrim to eke out an existence that eventually gave Henry his.

Fergus. He recalled the name but not the context... until Bitsy's first night on Quincy Street flashed through his mind. She and Michael had a common ancestor named Fergus, and Devin uncovered enough information to track other lines from this man. "Only DNA will reveal if blood and paper trail match," he had said.

A sudden onslaught of sweating sickness caused streams of perspiration to flow from Henry's face and hands onto the bits and pieces of his identity. He rushed out into Dublin's cool night air and sat on his stoop. *I've searched my entire adult life for my story, and the one I've found is too implausible for belief.*

His gaze wandered across the road and two doors up where light spilled from the children's bedrooms and Kiri's silhouette roamed from room to room. All these years he lived not two minutes away from those who embraced him with love and called him family. Now, he wanted to shout, "I am!" For the second time in as many weeks, the unflappable, reserved, self-controlled man dropped his head to his chest and wept.

The goal for the day was to uncover proof positive, Henry decided when he dragged himself out of bed after a sleepless night. A million questions raced through his mind along the midline of a Möbius strip on both the upside and the downside of the never-ending track. He must find incontrovertible evidence of his relationship before he proclaimed it. To that end, he copied pertinent names and dates from the documents now in his possession and replaced the originals in the lock-box. A second thought led him to the side-pocket of the travel bag where he stored the photos from his mother's room. He placed those in the tin box as well, locked it and placed it on a shelf in his bedroom.

He first stopped at his friend the doctor's for a blood draw, then proceeded to his Dublin office in the network's basement. As the recently named secret chief of surveillance, data collection and analysis for the Middle East, Africa and Asia in the secret unit of a secret arm of a secret department of a very public broadcast company, he had access to personal information on almost anyone, anywhere. His intent to use that access for his own ends was, if not illegal, surely unethical, but he did not hesitate.

Henry hacked the medical records of Michael O'Connell and his two children for their DNA profiles and downloaded the files to his USB drive; Bitsy's as well. He accessed his mother's records and did the same with the profile he requested for her during her last illness. Once he had his own, there was a chance he could run it backwards to find his father's and use it to search data in the northwest.

He located the files Devin created to trace the two Killian lines back to Fergus, downloaded them, and used them to follow his mother's lineage to the same man. While awaiting his DNA results, he searched the vital statistics of County Leitrim, the least populous county on the island, for any records pertaining to a Dermot Henry Devane. He found nothing but the report of his death, not even where he was buried. The long fingers of the Church expunged his father's existence as well as his own.

No matter. Given more time he would search genealogical sites. Failing that, he would go old school from village to village asking questions. There were not that many villages or people in them to investigate. Surely someone must recall a Devane family. The idea excited him. Make Saturday excursions with Kiri and her family a treasure hunt for his; explore the beautiful lakes, mountains and rolling landscapes of his home county by back roads and the River Shannon by boat.

Henry rushed to print the downloads of pertinent records, place them in a folder and pocket his USB. Can't be too careful, he thought. He was always in and out of his office with papers and folders, so security cameras would reveal nothing unusual. He picked up his test results on the way home and laid them out on the table with Michael's, Bitsy's and the children's. No mistake. He was a full-fledged Killian, a cousin to them all.

He secured this vital proof in the tin box, grabbed some black brew from the fridge, and leaned back in his easy chair to consider the upside of his discovery. Legitimacy was paramount. For more than fifty years, he regarded himself as unequal to his peers and read in their eyes that they felt the same. Now he could take his place in executive board meetings with honor. He satisfied his longing for a family, and one in particular. No one could deny he had just reason to tend for Kiri and her family, for they were related to him *by blood.* The revelation would thrill Kiri and the children, especially Katie. He pictured her jumping into his arms, her curly copper tendrils of hair tickling his face as she hugged him tightly and announced, "I *knew* we were related... somehow!" They would spend more time together... days... evenings... every minute of Christmases and birthdays until he was so much a part of their lives that when he asked Kiri to join the Killian clan herself, she would not hesitate to say yes.

That thought brought him to the downside of revealing his lineage. Once exposed, the relationship would become common knowledge within the extended family. He would no longer be Uncle Henry, a nominal but revered elder, but Cousin Henry lumped together with all the others—including Michael's siblings—who made mandatory appearances at official family functions. He wanted to be loved... cherished... for *who* he was, not out of a sense of obligation because of specific markers in his blood.

Secondly, as Henry Callaghan he worked hard to build a reputation and was now admired and respected within his profession. As Henry Killian Devane he had no record of accomplishment. He could continue to use Callaghan professionally, but that would deny the very relationship he sought so desperately to claim. And claiming his name would unlock the secrets of his past, including the IRA connection, certain to raise the hackles of the British company for which he worked.

He feared telling his story to Kiri the most. Any future for the two of them must include full disclosure surrounding his name change. His sordid past would make no difference to her, he knew, but describing the events might cause the caterpillar eyebrows to come alive again, and shame with them. He doubted his courage to take that chance but had no choice.

"Kiri will understand. Kiri will understand," he repeated. "She said the unspoken will haunt me, but accepting the truth will help me conquer my demons." Truth struck him between the eyes like a maul. Facts, once revealed, cannot be recalled. Kiri would want to know the facts and how he learned them, and the fact was that he stole them... from her. He had the tools for prying at his disposal, and he used them. Without her knowledge or consent, he invaded her privacy to obtain personal information about Michael and their children. For her—and for their relationship—that act alone might be a deal breaker.

Henry tore at his hair with fisted fingers. Despite his efforts to be careful, he was not careful enough and let his heart get in the way of his head. He tried to examine his options but could not focus. If Kiri were his counselor, what would she advise him? She would say exactly what he told her: Following a trauma, one should not make a major decision for at least a year. Now, a year seemed an eternity to him. Within twenty-four hours he celebrated his mother's life with their family, found his father, discovered the connection that would change the rest of his life and caused that happiness to slip through his fingers.

Visions of tucking his family in at night... all of them... every night... evaporated, and tears filled their space. Once again the locked tin box guarded his fate. For the second time in as many days, Henry wept.

Seventeenth Anniversary Year: Birth: another daughter to Gus. He is halfway to a family with eight sisters! A daughter to Devin.
  Marriage: Not yet, but Brendan is getting close.
  Death: Henry's mother Kathryn; one of the cake ladies
  Graduation: Tommy's daughter Breeda and Anne's son Aidan

Other: Aidan took over the attic studio and maintenance job in Henry's building. He reports that Henry seldom requests help. Duh—he's never there!

Community living expands. Following the death of one in their group, the cake ladies found a friend nearby who wanted to rent her empty apartment and help with the baking. A waiting list attests to the high demand for Paddy's apartments as well. I've had several inquiries from friends and relatives of current tenants about converting other properties on the road. Quincy Street has earned quite a reputation for "aging in place." The whole group approached me about purchasing transportation and hiring a driver for trips to the park and errands and appointments outside the neighborhood. Ronan found us a great deal on a used electric minivan. He is finishing an apprenticeship with a family-owned garage four roads over. Fíona grabbed the driver's job. She loves to drive—the fastest around Michael's track yet, much to the chagrin of her male cousins.

Bitsy continues at the pool. I'm negotiating for her to take the written portion of her certifications orally since reading, writing and 'rithmatic are not her strong suits. She volunteers two afternoons a week and one evening at the hospital now that Sara is six. When Bitsy attends deaths, she always comes away with a sense of fulfillment. Sara spends those Wednesday evenings with us—Thomas' time with the kids, although he tires easily, so we go to him.

Established Quincy Hospice Center. Also, Caregiver Counseling Services. I'm very fortunate that Maeve has lots of sisters and they have lots of well-trained, caring children and friends.

The death of Henry's mother really hit him hard. Anytime I inquire about his being so glum, he doesn't want to talk about it. He did spend a lot of time with us during the holidays, and we went for a wonderful excursion to County Leitrim during a long weekend in late spring. He took off every so often while we explored a village for an ice cream shop. Then he caught up with us, and we'd go on down the road. I wish we could do that more often.

CHAPTER 18

Thomas did not bounce back quickly from his second heart attack. Paula stayed with him at the hospital, and Bitsy came every evening to lull him to sleep with her music, but the doctors kept him for weeks rather than days, and he spent a good six months of recovery at home. Kiri arranged for home health care, and all his grandchildren pitched in to help. His own children visited regularly.

With a full no-alarms year under his belt, Thomas felt ready to take on the world again—or at least Ireland. He spoke frequently and longingly to Michael Thomas about a place called Puffin Island, and his grandson passed that word on to his mother, although not so dramatically.

Kiri racked her brain for a means to grant his wish but determined the trip would be too hard on him at his age—eighty-five—and with limited mobility. His doctor, however, encouraged the journey provided she could procure proper care.

"Leave it to me," Henry said. "I know a guy."

On a sunny summer morning, Henry, Kiri and the kids piled Thomas and Paula into his car for a surprise drive in the countryside. It ended at a small heliport with a Gus-like guy and his wife—a medic and a nurse—waiting for the group. Flabbergasted, Thomas grew so excited that the medic—a broad and brawny man with legs like trees and hands that could hold the ailing man in their palms—set down the no-nonsense rules. "You keep yourself calm and under control or you go back home!" His wife attached sensors in several places on the elderly man and checked her tablet. She could monitor the function and movement of every part of his body, even down to his toenails! At her thumbs up, the rest of the entourage climbed into a small medevac, and away they flew.

Even with their eyes bulging out, the kids could not decide where to look first. Paula nervously held Thomas' hand. He tried to hold back his smile to keep the nurse's monitor from bleeping and flashing red when he realized the flight's direction. Henry and Kiri pressed together in the rear. The flight ended—after mere minutes, it seemed to the children—when the bird set down in a field of sheep. A van waited to transport the merry band to an old house on the northwest side of Valentia Island. When Kiri unloaded the hoverchair she purchased for Thomas following his recent attack, the medic called another "rules" meeting. He directed his remarks straight through Thomas' eyes and down his spine.

"One hour in the hoverchair each morning, one each afternoon, and one each evening. For every hour you spend floating six inches above the ground, you'll spend two back here at rest. You must be accompanied, and your partner must control the remote. If you go flying over the edge of the cliffs and on out to sea, I will not go after you. Got it? Wednesday we take a boat to this place you call Puffin Island. Nothing there but birds,

I hear, but we'll go anyway IF you've been good. Got it?" Thomas did not quarrel with the burly man in charge.

The house had bedrooms for everyone, even the medic and his wife. After the group settled in for rest and a light supper, and watched the sun disappear on its way to America, Henry and Kiri finally caught some private time in the lounger on the porch. "Is this crazy man your friend?"

"Not really. He came highly recommended, but he scares me to death!" he snickered, pulling her closer.

The couple watched the stars, listened to new sounds and enjoyed one another's company for the first time in months—maybe years—when Katie plopped down between them. "I can't sleep. The sky is scary dark and the ocean's too loud!"

Thomas spent his daily morning hour with his grandson investigating various parts of the island. On the last one he asked Henry to join him instead, puzzling everyone. Afternoon hourly sessions found Paula with control of the remote as the older couple rediscovered familiar sites, and they passed time in the evenings on a small stretch of beach where they sat in the sand and reminisced. The kids, Henry and Kiri followed along on the afternoon jaunts but walked to the village in the evenings. The younger set used their free time to explore, chat with friends on their tablets, and send pictures. The medic and his wife always followed Thomas at a discreet distance, her monitor unable to record the joy a man feels when his wish comes true.

A bright, fair-weather day arrived for the trip to Puffin Island. Thomas insisted on riding in the bow where he could feel sea spray on his face. The medic and captain wrapped him up in so much protective gear that he could barely see, let alone feel, spray or get an arm around his wife. Michael Thomas investigated every inch of the craft. In constant motion, Katie ran from stern to bow and back trying to find the best place for sea spray to sting her face too and tie knots in her hair. Henry and Kiri found seats along the side, safe from saltwater and kids. After circling the island once to pause at a barrier enclosing a calm lagoon, the captain dropped anchor for the older couple to stare at the huge hunk of rock and the sea birds that nested there until tides made lingering longer unsafe. The no-nonsense medic mandated an early to bed, followed by a day of rest for the elderly but grateful man.

Thomas lamented being too old to climb around like he used to. *"You might be old,"* Paula scolded, "but *I've* reached advanced maturity and am proud of it!" The happy clan returned from Puffin Island and the holiday pink-cheeked, invigorated and hopeful.

Kiri painted a picture for Thomas and Paula as a remembrance from their trip. She placed them on the crest of that rocky island, sitting on the grass together and looking out to sea with a few puffins nearby for good measure. A sick old man now, Thomas no longer tried to hide his emotions.

Nineteenth Anniversary Year: Birth: Son #2 to Doyle
    Marriage: Brendan
    Death: Paddy lost another housemate.
    Graduation: Anne's daughter Erin; Tommy's daughter Eileen
    Other: Grace has an engagement ring on her finger. Connor brought the same young lady to the last couple of family gatherings. Caitlín has that gleam in her eye.

Katie cleaned up a corner of our garden to dedicate to neighborhood friends who die. She invites a few from the road—not her age anymore, thank goodness—to plant a flower in remembrance. The neighbors seem to appreciate the gesture... and the ice cream! I'm never invited.

Henry continues to work from London a lot, but when he is in Dublin we see a lot of him. He hangs around almost morning to night. When he is gone, he continues regular video dates with the kids to help them with schoolwork and such. Sara too. I'm not in school anymore, so our chats are limited.

The trip to Puffin Island, and Thomas' reaction to it, caused me to reflect on my last days with Michael. If we knew our days together were numbered, would we have spent them differently? Would we have given up Saturday with the family on the excursion to Glendalough to stay in bed all day inviting our first child to take root? Would we have wasted time arguing about whether I should go on the mission? Would I have held him closer and not allowed him to leave me the night he...? Would we have found joy even in the rubble? Since the trip, I've asked Michael's portrait over and over again. He never answers. But I did find a black feather in my bag when we got home, so maybe he had his fingers in that jaunt too. I tossed it in his nightstand's drawer with the rest.

CHAPTER 19

Thomas called. Thomas never called. If he had business with his daughter/daughter-in-law, Paula contacted her and made arrangements for a meeting. When Kiri looked at her phone, she could not believe her eyes. Thomas called.

"Kirin? Thomas here. Would you be kind enough to come by the house at three? I have business to discuss with you."

"Of course. What's on your mind? Shall I bring anything?"

"Just yourself… and an open mind. See you at three."

Kiri entered the password on the keypad, and the door opened for her. She found Thomas in the living room sitting alone at one end of a sofa, his knees covered with a throw and his oxygen attached and running at his hip. He motioned her to take a seat beside him. She chose the opposite end of the sofa. "Where's Mom?"

"She's gone to your teashop for the fairy cake I love. She'll be back soon."

"I could have picked some up on my way and saved her the trip." Kiri swallowed her frustration. How could Thomas send her mother on a needless errand through heavy traffic at her age?

"It's you I want to talk to… while your mother's not here. Thank you for coming." When she raised an eyebrow, he plunged right in. "How many times have we sung 'Panis Angelicus' together over the last twenty years at the funeral of one of my friends?"

"I don't know. Five or six maybe."

"Eleven. You've joined me eleven times to help send a soul to its rest. Will you sing one more time for me?"

She regarded the frail man who barely had breath for a sentence and wondered how he would find strength to summon his renowned tenor voice. "Won't the effort be too much for you?"

"Not for me. I won't be singing. I'll be listening. You'll sing alone." He noted the confusion in her eyes. "Will you do this for me? Sing for me one last time? Promise?"

She considered. She never wanted to sing with Thomas… especially not for one of his cronies. She always felt that his friends judged her as the woman who married her stepbrother, the woman who had children without a father, the woman who separated herself from family and tradition and who owned her own business, for heaven's sake! But she always said yes because those charges no longer seemed important to him. *Yes, I can put on my blackbird dress, sit on the side aisle in uncomfortable company, stand in front of all those accusing eyes and sing.* She smiled. "Yes, Thomas. I promise. I will sing the 'Panis.' Who will I sing for this time?"

"For me. It's my soul you'll send to its rest."

Her smile dropped its lower half, color drained from her face, and her hands turned ice cold.

He wanted to reach out and pat her knee, but she was too far away. "Don't be so shocked. The good Lord has been tapping on my shoulder for several years now, and I've always managed to brush Him off. The doctor told me yesterday that won't work any longer. It's palliative care only for me from here on out. The next time I come down those stairs, I will be in a box."

Kiri gulped at his bluntness. "I'm sorry to learn your prognosis is... grim. Does Mom know?"

He nodded and a tear came to his eye. "We've discussed the possibilities over the last few weeks and have finally come to agreement. The other children will arrive for tea shortly, and we'll go public then, but I wanted to talk to you alone first... to warn you. I'll ask more than one favor of you today... many more."

Kiri drew her hands to her mouth and expelled a deep cleansing breath through her fingers. What more could this man possibly ask her to do?

He smiled weakly. "We've been at opposite ends of this sofa many times over the years, haven't we Kirin? You held your ground, got the best of me often, and on principle you were proved right. *I know* that if you make a promise, you will keep it. Your mother and I will ask you today to make and keep many for us."

Thomas paused to gauge Kiri's reaction. "I love your mother too much to put her through the firestorm that will accompany my death. We both hoped that our children would develop 'family' feeling, but after twenty years that has not come to pass as you well know. Luckily, animosity among our children—you and Kurt included—has not passed to the grandchildren, due in large part to your efforts. That is why we chose you to stand in her place—to protect your mother, her interests, and your children's, as well as all the grandchildren's interests. If anyone can prevent my four from devouring Paula when her defenses are down, that person is you."

He smiled weakly again and shifted his seating but not enough to reach the colored files on the coffee table in front of him. "Grab those folders, will you? And that pen. Open the red one first. This document contains what you in America call a Durable Power of Attorney for Health Care. I named you as my agent and include the directions for my final days."

Kiri's stomach lurched, but she tried to maintain focus. *This cannot be an easy conversation for the man.*

"Place your signature below mine on the last page, if you will. Mine has been witnessed, so the document is official. Adding your acceptance of the responsibility will put my mind at ease." He watched her hesitantly sign the paper. "I am confident you will read this carefully and be prepared to make the appropriate decisions when the time comes, no matter what pressures my children put on you. Remember, you are sparing your mother that pain."

When she tried to comment, he waved her off. "Set that aside for the moment and open the green folder. This document contains directions for disposition of my body, funeral, etc. I've stated and signed that you are in charge. Nothing for you to decide. Simply follow my directions. You'll notice your name beside the 'Panis.'" With a sly wink of his eye he said, "I knew you would say yes. I also want Bitsy to play her harp around you—intro, between verses, and at the end. Can you convince her to do that?"

Kiri nodded. "For you, I'm sure she'll play her best."

"Good. The blue folder contains my will. We'll go over that when the other children arrive." He took a slip of paper from his cardigan pocket. "Here are the codes to the suite and to my safe. Please make ten copies of the Power of Attorney and lock the original in the safe. Bring the copies down and place one in the back of each purple folder over on the desk. There is one for each child, including Kurt and one for your mother. They are labeled. You get the rainbow set since you are the workhorse. You'll need plenty of space for notes and the like."

Kiri rose to do his bidding. Making copies and organizing files she was good at. Orchestrating a dying man's final wishes she was not sure about.

He caught her hand and pulled her back down. "I'm not finished. Look me in the eyes. Promise me you will do all I ask to the best of your ability. *Promise!*"

His intensity frightened Kiri, but she nodded. "Yes, Thomas. I promise to do my best."

Visible relief showed in the relaxation of his face and hands. "Good. I know... Look into my eyes again... *I know* that you will keep any promise you make. Understand me when I say, *I know.*" He waited for the realization to take root. "*I know* you have kept every promise you made to my son—many against my objections. *I know* you are here in Ireland with us because of a promise made long ago. *I know* your children, my two beautiful grandchildren, are alive for the same reason."

Kiri could not believe what she was hearing. How could Thomas know? How could anyone? His eyes did not reveal how, but they did unveil the truth.

"I love all my children and grandchildren dearly, but there is something special about your two. If one could order up a boy with all the qualities he desired, Michael Thomas would be that perfect child. And Katie?" He chuckled. "Katie is a human magnet. She attracts and delights people wherever she goes just like her father. If hugs emitted a fragrance, her world would be bathed in it.

"You two have your problems, but they won't last forever. Michael went through that phase too. He was youngest and didn't understand when Emily got so much of their mother's attention. Emily, bless her heart, was not well as a child. She was an extreme child. Any cut, bump, fever, cough and childhood illness attacked her to the extreme. Her fevers spiked. A cut bled rivers. Her coughs rocked the whole house. There are no words to describe her bout with the chicken pox. Michael got lost in all the drama and acted out inappropriately until we hit on the reason. One day you will discover what nettle is pricking Katie's skin, and all will be well again."

He took Kiri's hand when she started to leave. "One thing more. Come to me and let me give you a loving hug—something we've not enjoyed for too many years." He pulled Kiri to him, held her as tightly as his waning strength allowed, and pressed her head into his chest. "My son loved you from the day you first stomped into this house, talked back to me, and slammed that bedroom door. He was right to fight for you, and he would be so proud of you and the children you've given us."

Kiri squeezed his hand and tucked those words of acceptance into a tiny corner of her heart to call on for courage in the days ahead.

Tears streamed down the ailing man's face. "Of all my children, you understand the true meaning of 'family.' From this moment forward, you will hold the delicate thread of my family in your hands."

Kiri's tears joined his as she struggled to speak. "Thank you, Thomas. Thank you for sharing Michael with me... for being such a wonderful grandfather to our children... and for making my mother's years with you her happiest. I'll do my best to take care of her for you."

Thomas fumbled with his sweater. "Why can't a man my age remember to put a handkerchief in his pocket?" he muttered, causing Kiri to snicker. That's how Paula found them when she walked in with the fairy cake—an emotive bundle of laughter and tears.

The children of Thomas Michael Eamon O'Connell sat on the sofas drawn up in a semicircle facing the family patriarch. They took their places in birth order with their spouses next to them. Paula, finally composed after a consoling sob with her daughter, sat next to Thomas, and Kiri took a chair to the side. Tanya and Kurt joined by videoconference. "Hi, all. What's up?"

"What are *they* doing here?" Anne asked with a sniff disregarded by the others.

"Almost twenty years ago," Thomas began, "Paula and I celebrated our wedding joining our two families. I threw a party before the vows to ensure that you all attended and paid attention. At that time I said, 'Nowhere is it written that family must love, like or even be friends with one another. You've proven me right!" He stared at each child severely.

" '*Dílseacht*—loyalty,' I said. 'Family is loyal. Family shows up and stands together in good times and in bad—not as tokens or spoilers, but as participants.' Today I'm calling on you to stand up loyally as participants and work together throughout the terrible time facing us."

"Divorce?" Anne whispered to Meghan.

"I wanted you together in this room at the same time to hear the same words so there will be no misunderstanding my intent. Today we'll share the reading of my will *before* the final 'amen' as I'm laid to rest."

Tommy and Anne stared at one another gapemouthed. The question mark on Meghan's face was directed at her father. Emily dropped her head in her hands and shook it back and forth. The spouses traded glances with one another not fully comprehending the implication. Kurt understood immediately when he saw his mother's eyes tear up and Kiri fidget with the pen in her hand.

At Thomas' nod, she handed out the purple folders and whispered to her brother as she passed by the screen, "Check your email for the electronic file. I'll send you the real deal tomorrow."

Thomas launched into his unpleasant task. "Paula, as my wife..."

"Father," Anne quickly interrupted. "We're well into the twenty-first century. Surely you are no longer compelled to follow every out-dated tradition. Tommy... any of us will..."

"I'm glad you agree with me, Anne." Thomas peered over the top of his reading glasses at his eldest daughter. "You'll be pleased to know that with this document I intend to follow your suggestion. Paula, as my wife, has declined to administer my will, so I have chosen the only one among you who has first-hand experience with the legal rigmarole that responsibility entails."

He peered again at the assembled children now on the edges of their seats, as he labored for a deep breath. "Open to part one, page one, please. Kirin Koyle O'Connell is named administrator of my estate. As such, I trust her to execute the provisions I have enumerated herein."

Audible gasps sucked the air from the room, none more so than Kiri's. Thomas failed to mention the additional duty that would triple the stepsibs' loathing for her.

"Moving on to part two. Paula has declined to accept any portion of my wealth. Her only concession is for a life interest in this house until her death, at which time it will revert to my estate."

Mutterings along the sofas indicated acceptance. The girls were certain Paula would allow them to take family keepsakes—even the valuable ones.

"Nothing. I repeat, *nothing*... not one end table... not one teacup... not one waste bin will be removed until that time."

Shoulders slumped.

"Part three. You O'Connell children received trust funds when you attained legal age. Paula insisted that *she* provide for her Koyle children.

Your generation... each of you has determined your own course. Therefore, I am placing my faith and my legacy in the hands of the next generation. The entirety of my estate has been put in trust for the grandchildren."

Eyeballs popped out everywhere.

"The only outright bequests—over Paula's objection that she be the provider—go to the two Koyle grandchildren, Kendra and Kody."

To a one, the stepsibs and their spouses turned and glowered at Tanya and Kurt.

"And Bitsy, Kathryn Elizabeth Killian, is to be considered a grandchild, equal in every respect and proportion to the remaining twenty."

"I can't believe this!" was passed in hissed whispers along the row like a game of gossip.

"Part four. The Grandchildren's Trust will be administered by Tommy..."

Sighs of relief.

"...and Kirin, the oldest and youngest of my children."

Gasps again.

"Tommy has keen awareness of changing trends in our community, country and world and of the advantages and limitations of our social order. Kirin has the business acumen to manage the day-to-day efficiently, profitably and justly. Together you two can assure the grandchildren's funds continue to grow, even in a difficult economic climate. Tommy, I trust you will work with Kirin to that end."

The sisters stared hard at their brother. This was the chance—an opening—for him to take a stand against their father's ridiculous charade. Tommy understood that intention, but when he looked at Kiri he saw the woman who saved his marriage and probably his wife's life. "I think... we'll make a very good team."

"You can't mean that!" Anne shouted at her brother.

"Good. My thought exactly. The family will be well served by you two—the bookends, first and last of your generation. Under the terms of the trust, any disbursal or transferal of funds must be for reasons outlined in this document and approved and signed by *both* of you. At Kirin's death, Michael Thomas will take her place. If Tommy should precede her in death, Kirin will become sole administrator of the trust and head of this family until she dies. Then Michael Thomas, my only *O'Connell* grandson, will become head of the family, sole administrator, and may disburse all funds or continue the trust as *he* chooses."

The girls' faces flushed in varying shades from Emily's pink to Meghan's deep rose to Anne's aubergine. Already her mind churned with schemes to invalidate her father's will or to eliminate Kiri and her son from the picture, including the use of sharp implements.

Kiri's mind roiled with anger as well as trepidation at the monumental responsibility Thomas thrust onto her shoulders. She shot the conniving man a "how could you" stare, and he returned one that said, "You promised." Short of wrapping herself around an oak tree, she saw no way out.

"Let's move to part five—my funeral. You all have a part, you'll notice, and I expect you to cooperate as you did for your brother. I've outlined a service similar to his. To spare Paula the task, Kirin will direct the arrangements."

Those were fighting words, and the daughters glared at their father for bypassing his immediate family in favor of an outsider to oversee one of the most important ceremonial transitions in a religious man's life. Anne opened her mouth to protest but was stopped mid-outburst.

"Until my last breath, *I* am the father in this house and head of this family! This is *my* will!" Beet-hued, Thomas stared his daughter down. "Part six! Directives for my end of life care. Once again, to spare Paula the pain, I've named Kirin as my agent. She possesses the objectivity to make hard decisions per my requests. I ask you to read this document carefully to understand what I intend and the decisions my agent is bound to carry out on my behalf."

Thomas' children were dumbstruck. Up to this point, they assumed the uncomfortable family meeting addressed a "general" when, not an "imminent" when. As they regarded their frail father, beads of perspiration sprouting on his nearly bald pate and his shaking hands unable to hold the papers in front of him, they realized his afternoon's performance was not a charade but a final bow.

Weeping was mild at first, then swelled to include even the spouses. Kiri consoled her mother and coaxed her away from Thomas so his children could crowd around their father with hugs and tears. Kurt and Tanya also seemed shaken by the scene and motioned Kiri over.

"This is too emotional for me. Thomas always treated me... and Mom... well. How will *you* ever survive?"

"Hope a fairy whispers in my ear. Wanna trade places?"

Kurt shook his head. "Take care of Mom... and yourself. Call if you need to unload. Love you, Sis. Stay strong."

Kiri disconnected the video feed and turned back to the group. The stepsibs began to whisper in twos and threes as they sipped tea to calm themselves. Paula served Thomas, but he shook his head, too exhausted to hold a cup. The overwhelmed agent studied the devoted couple and saw their eyes plead for this dreadful episode to end. She picked up her red folder—health directives—and noticed that Thomas added the date and time to her signature. Her duties commenced two hours earlier.

She inhaled deeply and stood tall, raising her voice above the whispers. "Your father... our father... Thomas is physically and emotionally drained from his presentation. His health is paramount now and supercedes our need to question and discuss with him. Let's all take a couple of days to review the documents he gave us and come together then to voice our concerns. Please express your love and good wishes, then allow him to rest for the remainder of the evening." The couple heaved a thank you sigh.

The stepsibs got the message. Kiri was in control... for now. They set their tea aside, picked up their documents and departed. No one touched the fairy cake.

*   *   *

Thomas called. Thomas never called. The last time Henry remembered communicating with the man by phone was during the preparation for his mother's aftfuneral. Their only other conversation that lasted more than a sentence or two was the morning the family departed from the island off the west coast, several months ago.

The man invited him on his morning hoverchair jaunt and did most of the talking. In a spirit of final confessions, he admitted opening the report of Michael's last mission but denied sharing it with anyone. "I've broken your confidence, I know, but as I face grave decisions about the future of my family, my transgressions don't seem as important as my connections to my children—living and dead. I hope you will forgive me."

Thomas interpreted Henry's nod as acceptance and expressed his thanks for being such a good friend to Kirin and her family. "They are lucky to have you in their lives—the more often the better, I say."

Henry remembered the man worry over how to dispose of all his son's files and how he wished his grandson could read them someday... when he was of legal age and old enough to appreciate the value of his father's life and work. The newsman told Thomas to contact him when the files were ready for pickup. Perhaps that was the reason for the man's call.

"Henry? Thomas here. I've a favor to ask of you."

"Certainly."

"All my children and their spouses will gather at the house later this afternoon. Our session is likely to be long and emotional. I've asked for Kirin's help, so she may be tied up here longer than she intended. I don't want her to worry about her children. She'll have enough to do with her mother... and me on her hands. Could you?"

"I'll see that they get home and fed, and I'll stay until she returns."

"You're a good man, Henry. I'm asking the Herculean of Kirin today. She'll need you... your shoulder. And I need you, too... to take care of her and my grandchildren. They need a righteous man like you to guide them." Thomas' choice of words smarted, but the man was clearly desperate.

"I'll do my best."

That call came midafternoon. Henry checked his watch again. It was now going on eight. He packed the car with water and blankets and had Cousin Eileen on tap to come mind the children as soon as he gave the signal. He watched his phone for the indicator that Kiri's car was on the move. When it flashed, he called Eileen, climbed the stairs for a final bedtime hug and reminded the children that he set their tablets to power off at nine. No whining. At thirteen and fifteen, they were beyond the age of whining but not beyond charming him out of an extra half-hour.

Kiri limped into the house looking as if she had been through an emotional wringer—the worst Henry had seen in years. She collapsed in his arms. "I'm so glad you're here," she sobbed.

"Not for long." He spun her around and marched her out to his car. They headed south from the city.

"Where are we going?"

"To a safe place I know." He smiled and watched her settle back into the seat, whimpering.

South of Kilcoole he turned toward the sea and off the road near the old pier. He grabbed a blanket to wrap around her. "Do you want me to swaddle you?"

She shook her head. "Just hold me, please. Hold me tight."

He opened all the windows to the salty tang of the night air, pressed her to him and tucked the blanket around them both. He felt her snuggle until her body melted into his. The setting was perfect, he thought. Just enough chill in the air for cuddling to seem natural. The sky was a brilliant backdrop for the fog bank waiting to pounce, and the lapping of gentle waves lulled even the seabirds to silence. He ran a hand over her shoulder and along her back noting how slim and fit she was for a woman past fifty. Must be all the swimming. His fingers crept up her scarred arm... and stopped.

Kiri is like a child tonight, frightened and vulnerable, seeking comfort and safety in my arms. How can I take advantage of the woman I love when she trusts me completely? Flashes of black robes and caterpillar eyebrows jabbed into Henry's eyeballs, and he drew back. *I'm no better than the man who used my trust to defile me. God, when will this end!* He smoothed Kiri's hair from her face and kissed her forehead. "Care to share what Thomas had on his mind today?"

"He's dying... and I'm supposed to help!" She described the family meeting, halting often to mop at her eyes with her sleeve. "When I put the signed directives in his safe, I noticed a large package with your name on it." She raised her moist eyes to fix on his. "What could that be?"

Secrets and lies. When will I be rid of them? "Old files of Michael's, I expect. You know he always gave Thomas backups in the days when he didn't trust the security of electronic files. No problem. No rush." He stroked her cheek.

She did not press the issue but continued with details of the other documents until she stopped abruptly and cried out, "I can't do this! I have a daughter who hates me, and I can't even keep my own laundry done. How can I take care of the whole family? Why *me*! Why did Thomas make me *promise*? This monumental responsibility is more than I can bear. I need help." She gave way to sobbing again.

Henry cradled her and tried to comfort her with a reassuring squeeze. "You're strong, Kiri. Thomas admires your determination and your passion for protecting your own family. You *can* do what he's asked. The grandchildren will help. I'll help. How long is your commission? Until the last grandchild reaches twenty-one? That's not even ten years."

"Forever!" she cried. "Thomas chained me to his wretched family until the day I die!"

CHAPTER 20

From day one after his pronouncements, Thomas' documents became Kiri's bible. She carried them with her all day, every day. Whenever she felt "the glare" from one of the stepsisters, she turned to the applicable page and paragraph to support her actions. Soon, they tired of glaring and she had the dratted docs memorized.

The morning after the conference, she contacted Quincy Hospice to arrange for twenty-four-hour care for Thomas at his home to begin the day after selected staff met with his doctors. She requested telehealthcare installation and bathroom modification. She also arranged for the neighborhood's car service to transport Paula to and from the aquacenter to swim laps once a day. She commissioned Ronan to disable voice commands for Thomas' cars. Even though vehicles hardly needed drivers any longer, a human could foul up the programming and end up in the harbor. Her mother was not in any shape to recall passwords and commands… and should not have to.

All household chores could have been hired out, but the grandchildren took it upon themselves to assist with the everyday. The younger generation took pride in even the simple acts that helped out during this heart-rending chapter in the family's life. Meggie moved into her Grandmother Kathryn's room at the end of the hall and spent nights there so Paula would not be alone with Thomas. A nurse was always in attendance, "but that's not the same as having family to hold your hand or call the relations," she said. "I'm very good with seniors." The others made their own chart for dividing up the chores—laundry, cleaning, grocery shopping, fixing meals and running errands. Their attitudes were not so much that they *had* to help, but making sure that they got an *equal chance* to help.

Katie, Polly and Michael Thomas rode a bus to the house after school to spend time with their grandfather. His eyes lit up as soon as he heard them come through the door. Katie climbed up on the bed right beside him, plastered him with hugs and kisses, stroked his hand and played with his fingers while she told him all about her day at school and the guys—plural—that she liked and was certain were "not related." The nurse was not happy about his granddaughter's liveliness, but Thomas always perked up when she came.

Polly giggled along, then told her own story while Katie did her daily chore—cleaning the grandparents' bathroom. Every so often she shook the toilet brush at her mother. "I hate this! Why can't we get a robot? Everyone has one."

"That's not true," Kiri reminded her. "We are part of everyone, and we don't have one."

"Why not?"

"Because there is value in hard labor. You should be able to take care of yourself if all the satellites explode and your electronics fail. Besides breathing, every human being needs to poop and pee every day, and a clean place to do that is important. If this chore is so distasteful to you, why did you volunteer for it?"

Katie marched off, brush in hand, shouting over her shoulder, "So none of my cousins would be stuck with the grubbiest job!"

Michael Thomas spent a couple of hours reading to his grandfather, talking with him, and helping him with his supper. Kiri worried about her son spending so much time with Thomas. He cut himself off from his friends and his beloved football. He explained to his mother that there were plenty of years left to kick a ball around with friends, but not enough time to toss memories around with his grandfather.

The neighborhood car delivered Bitsy every evening. Kiri or one of Tommy's girls gave Thomas a Celtic circular massage while Bitsy played and settled him for sleep. Other than an hour or so in the mornings and her hour of swimming in the afternoons, Paula was constantly at her husband's side. Kiri tried not to listen to their private conversations but noticed a recurring theme—a recounting of favorites.

A favorite day:

P: When you stopped to give me a lift in that sporty car of yours.

T: Our *first* time, in Rome. And when we met there again, the look in your eyes said that there would be many more.

A fond memory:

T: When *our* first grandchild was born.

P: The look on your face when you realized *our* second was a girl.

A favorite sanctuary:

T: Wherever we are together.

P: My house on the hill.

T: Come back to me, Paula. Promise to come back.

Thomas got along well with most of the staff Kiri provided. The one exception was his morning nurse. She stomped in early, opened curtains, scared Paula out of bed, and pushed, prodded, thumped and rolled her patient until his heart had no choice but to beat with vigor. Then she cleaned him, checked, tested, readjusted, monitored and gave him his orders for the day before she swatted him on the bottom of his feet, announcing "Guess we'll keep you around for another day!"

"Where did that crazy woman come from?" he asked. "She reminds me of that midwife of yours and her swimming sister."

"Another sister," Kiri replied.

"God save me... or take me... one or the other, for I cannot tolerate that woman one more day!" But it was clear from his eyes that he would smother her in a big bear hug if he could.

Kiri visited every morning while her mother bathed, dressed, had a leisurely breakfast and made lists for the day's shopping or errands. Thomas called that visit their "business meeting." Receiving a daily report helped him to feel he was still in control. He wanted an accounting to confirm that he was not receiving favors from her Quincy neighborhood businesses. She cut back her work schedule to near nothing. Thomas wanted to pay her a salary, but she refused. They compromised. He paid her substitute's salary—about half of what Kiri earned—and wanted receipts to prove she followed through. He did not lose his love for a good battle.

Thomas' clergyman visited every morning following the business meeting. His doctor communicated by live videoconference. Tommy stopped by every day after work. The sisters visited daily too—usually when Paula swam. The women passed one another civilly until they overhead Paula ask her daughter to help prepare Thomas' body for burial as she did for Michael. Protest was too mild a word for their attack. "Sacrilege! A disgrace!" they said. Kiri pulled out the directives and showed them where that order was buried in part six, paragraph seven, much to her surprise when she first discovered it.

The elder couple made it to their twentieth anniversary. The grandchildren threw them a low-key party while Connor, the storyteller of the family, told and retold the story of the unusual double wedding and the grandparents' escape in the blue sports car. Thomas could not take his eyes off the painting of the two of them on Puffin Island. Paula tried to hide her tears.

Thomas went downhill fast after that, like a ride on a toboggan. The morning nurse noticed the dramatic change first and did not smack his feet anymore. Paula stopped swimming. The grandchildren, even those with busy work schedules, spent less time tending to chores and more time visiting with their grandfather. Kurt and Tanya brought Kody and Kendra for the long President's Day weekend. Thomas' children came earlier and stayed later; their spouses were in and out as time allowed.

Kiri remained nearly around the clock, tending to Paula as much as to Thomas. Henry took off early from his job to pick up her kids, get them fed and to bed, then he settled down in the recliner until she returned... or did not. Bitsy played in spurts throughout the days and evenings.

The first time the evening nurse warned, "You might want to gather the family. Mr. O'Connell may not make it through the night," everyone came and waited, but by morning the dying man rallied. The second and third times, the same. The next time, with all the adults in the living room but Paula, Anne glared at her stepsister. "I don't know where you found these incompetent people. They obviously haven't a clue about judging a patient's condition. I say we spare ourselves the wait, get some sleep, and return first thing in the morning. Who's coming with me?" They all complied.

Kiri returned to Paula and Thomas. Bitsy played just outside his door, and her eyes were as worried as her fingers on the strings. The nurse watched the monitors nervously too. With Meggie in her room and the house now quiet, Paula climbed up on the bed beside her husband, cradled him and murmured lovingly to him. The last words Kiri heard him whisper were, "Come back to me, Paula. Please come back."

Anticipating her mother's heartbreak, Kiri sat with Bitsy for most of the night. When her beautiful music waned, then silenced, she looked into her aunt's weary eyes and said, "Grandfather Thomas doesn't need my music anymore." Kiri tiptoed into the room, threw a robe over her mother's shoulders and left the two of them together.

*   *   *

Kiri made the dreaded calls at the first trace of dawn. The family gathered shortly thereafter. Once the priest arrived, she and Paula stayed out of their way in the kitchen where her mother pretended to sip tea while Kiri prepared finger food for the others. The family reappeared a couple of hours later and helped themselves to nourishment. Kiri handed them copies of their funeral assignments as they left. Anne ignored her, but Meghan lingered after the others. "Thank you for taking care of Father," she said. "We don't know how to show you how grateful we are for your kindness."

Thomas' service proceeded without incident. Kiri's biggest worry was singing with Bitsy who refused to practice. "The music just comes to me. I don't know how to make it exactly the same twice." Their moving rendition of the "Panis" was so well received that Kiri was certain Thomas directed them from beyond. She marveled at her son's height when he stood with the other men in the family and the low, smoothness of his voice when he recited aloud. *When did that happen?*

At Thomas' gravesite, she handed Paula a small, Irish linen bag. "From your hillside of sons. I smuggled this soil back from Colorado last summer and added a handful of sand from Valentia Island for good measure." At the question in her mother's eyes, Kiri added, "Michael's story of St. Kevin. He said, ' 'Tis an Irish thing, to wish to be buried in sacred ground... a significant place in your life....' I thought these few pieces of earth might help put his body to rest since you two spent so much time gazing at the flowers and the sea... though I have no idea why."

She helped her mother's withered hands open the bag and sprinkle the sand, soil and small bulbs over his casket. Paula wept, burying her tears and their secrets with Thomas. When they arrived back at the house for the reception, she went straight to their suite. The grandchildren were puzzled by her absence. Their parents took no notice.

Twentieth Anniversary Year: Death: Thomas Michael Eamon O'Connell, age 86. If anything else happened this year, I can't remember. The whole family was consumed with Thomas' decline.

CHAPTER 21

If Thomas' life was orthodox, and his approach to death a paradox, then his afterlife was pandemonic, filled with wild animus and confusion. Kiri's first act as administrator of his estate was to reprogram the keycodes on the exterior doors of his house with new passwords... and not a minute too soon. The second she touched "apply," she heard frustrated voices at the door trying to open it with no success.

Anne bellowed, "Locked out of our own house! How dare she?"

Kiri opened the door quickly, and the stepsisters nearly fell in. "Good morning," she greeted. "How nice of you to come check on Mom so early. She's physically and emotionally exhausted—as we all are—so she doesn't feel up to visitors yet. *Call ahead* in a couple of days, and I'm sure she'll be happy for you to visit then. Thanks for coming."

The girls turned on their heels and drove off. If cars could still screech upon abrupt acceleration, Kiri felt certain the abrasive sound would wake the entire street. She made a call. "Devin? Kiri here. I need a security system for Thomas' house—one I can monitor from home... or from anywhere. Is there such an animal?"

"If not, we'll create one. I know a guy."

She thanked him and headed for the kitchen to make tea. Paula had not stirred from her room. *Keep Mom hydrated and let her sleep. She'll eat when she's hungry.* Kiri entered and delivered a hot pot. She lay beside her unresponsive mother and wrapped her arms around the diminished frame. "We all love you, Mom." She listened for the soft cries to pass into deep breathing before she left and made another call.

"Frank? Kiri here. I need a hacker. I need to get into Thomas' computer. I'm afraid to leave the house for fear I won't get back in again if he has the locks on a timed reset. My guess is, he has account numbers and passwords stored in the computer. I'm not sure what else I'll need before this crazy business is over. Do you know a guy?"

"I'm your guy. Be there this afternoon."

She thanked him and dropped her head into her hands. Thomas was very good about detailing what he expected her to do, but he did not detail the details. Implementation required a treasure hunt. Find his phone, she thought. Surely it was connected to the rest of his systems—a magic key. She searched his desk with no luck. He would put it in a safe place, she thought, but what was his safe place? She swiveled in his chair, and her eyes lit on his safe. Of course—if the code he gave her months ago still worked.

"Yes! I'm in!" she shouted. The vault was crammed with files, small accounting books and loose papers... and a phone. Kiri removed it and realized that an inventory of the safe's contents would take a full day. She propped the door open so it would not slam and lock accidentally before

Frank reset it, heaved a sigh and conjured a vision of her days ahead. Paula could not… and should not be moved from her house anytime soon. She could not be left alone. Kiri could not ask anyone else to stay with her; she wanted to be there for her mom. She had no way of securing the valuables—objects or documents—until new systems were in place. And she had not hugged her children—the child who welcomed it and the one who did not—in ages. She had spent more than twenty years wresting herself from Thomas' house, and now she was a prisoner in it!

Her first reaction was to cry until she remembered her mother's sorrow and chided herself for her selfishness. She made a call. "Henry? Kiri here. I need help."

"You're up early. How's your mother?"

"Not good. She needs time and mustn't be disturbed yet. The kids?"

"In school, unless they took a wrong turn."

"And you?"

"About to leave for my apartment to clean up for work. What do you need?"

"Another favor. You've been kind to take care of the kids for the last few days, but I think they should be here with me now. I'm captive in Thomas' house and can't leave—even for a jog—until Devin installs a new security system. Can you drop by my house after school, tell the kids to pack enough clothes for a week, and lock up the place for me? I'll arrange for a car about five."

"No need. I'll bring them. Anything for you?"

"A smile would be nice. I packed a bag the last time I was home, but it never occurred to me that I wouldn't be able to run back and forth and manage the kids as well as Mom. Thanks, Henry. You're too good to us, you know."

A playful smile appeared on her screen. "I know."

Kiri returned to Paula's room, lay beside her, and cradled her until her mother fell asleep again.

* * *

"Here? With you?" Katie pushed past her mother's outstretched arms, dropped her bag and scowled. "Uncle Henry said we would camp with Grandmother for a few days, but he didn't say *you* would be here!"

Henry entered behind Michael Thomas. "Sorry," he said sheepishly. "Seemed obvious to me."

"No problem." She turned to her children. "Your grandmother is very upset and needs for those who love her to be close by—but not too close. We need to be calm and quiet and let her sleep."

Katie harrumphed and slumped to a stairstep. "Where are we supposed to 'camp?' It's kind of creepy here without Grandpa."

"And lonely, too," her brother added.

"I know. That's why our keeping Grandma company is so important. You'll sleep on the third floor in your dad's old room where Kody sleeps, and Katie will take my old room across the hall where Kendra stays when she's not at our house."

"Where will you sleep?" he asked.

"On your grandmother's bedroom floor where I've been for the last few nights. I don't want her to wake up and be lonely or afraid."

"Where will Uncle Henry sleep?" Katie asked. "I won't stay up there without a man in the house."

"We'll be fine," Michael Thomas said. "I'm almost a man."

"You wish. Look in the mirror. You're only fifteen. I mean a *real* man... like Uncle Henry."

Kiri glanced at Henry's flushed face. "We'll discuss that later. Go upstairs and get settled. Start your schoolwork. I have a project for you after supper."

Katie's shriek from the top of the stairs was the only indication that they arrived at their assigned destinations. "I *hate* your room. It's *pink!*" A slam of her bedroom door followed. Their grandfather's absence impacted her children too.

"What is this project you have for us?" Michael Thomas asked, shoveling another bite of casserole into his mouth—his third helping.

"It better be fun," Katie said, choosing from the hodgepodge of leftovers from the reception.

"I don't know how much fun you'll have, but the job should be interesting. I'd like you to inventory the cupboards and closets on the third floor, then go to the fourth."

"There's a fourth floor here?" That realization sparked her son's interest. "What's up there?"

"I can't remember. I was only there once. Lots of old stuff. I want you to scope it out. Take pictures and make lists of what you find. Don't worry about blankets and towels, but look in boxes and label them as books, papers, treasure...."

Katie rolled her eyes. "That's ridiculous. Nobody buries treasure in a box anymore. But I'll do it if Uncle Henry promises to stay until we're finished. Who knows? There might be a monster guarding the treasure." She rolled her eyes again and grabbed her brother's shirtsleeve. "Let's get this over with."

"What possessed you with that bright idea to keep them busy?" Henry asked.

"I don't know. It just popped into my head like a...." Kiri gave him a sly wink. "But it buys you time to come up to the suite to collect your package." She recounted her frustrating day while they finished a pleasant meal alone.

Henry entered the suite with a "Wow! This room is spectacular!"

"The mountains? The mural on the wall is a photographic panorama taken from Mom's house. Thomas designed the place especially for her so she wouldn't feel homesick. He kept it locked when the family was here, even during his last illness. Michael and I were the only ones to see it. "Try the fireplace and make yourself comfortable. You're allowed to put your feet up here. I can tell by the worn places along the edges of the coffee table." They shared a snicker.

Henry turned on the fire, eased onto a couch and scanned the rest of the room. "I've never been in a home with so many books. Yours comes close, but this collection has some real oldies."

"A shared love of theirs. I have no idea what to do with them. Inventory first, I suppose and check online for value." Kiri clapped her hands to her cheeks. "I'm going to be here for months, aren't I?" She retrieved Henry's package from the safe. "Take this, please. One less item for me to inspect and inventory."

He accepted the sealed bundle and set it aside, grateful that he would be first to investigate its contents. "I'd be happy to help with the books. Some of the history looks intriguing—a love of mine."

The children burst in, interrupting Kiri's response. She put a finger to her lips to quiet their excitement. They hunkered on the floor in front of Henry and whispered their discovery. "This house has secret passages!" "We opened a door in the playroom." "We thought it was a closet, but it wasn't." "It was stairs leading up and down." "To the attic and to the pantry and even below the kitchen." "And there's a dark, narrow tunnel underground that leads toward the garage." "We got scared because we couldn't see in there." "So we ran back to the kitchen and up the front stairs to tell you."

Oh great! Just what I need. Who knows how many more breaches in the castle wall we'll find? One more thing to put on Devin's list.

Henry was more practical. "Were there lights on the stairs?" They nodded. "Did you turn them on?"

"Until we got to the bottom."

"Did you turn them off?"

The two young teens stared at each other, saucer-eyed.

Oh great! Just what I need. An electrical hazard and fire. Who do I call for that?

"Then you better go back and turn them all off," Henry said with authority.

Katie shook her head. Michael Thomas suggested he come with them "to make sure we don't miss one."

Henry smiled behind his fist and rose to follow them. "Where do we begin?"

Michael Thomas thought a minute. "At the bottom where it's already dark so there will always be light in front of us."

"Good idea. Let's go." Henry waved to Kiri as the trio tromped down the front stairs.

They returned shortly, huffing from the uphill climb. "We pushed a big shelf in front of the door in the playroom... just to be safe," Michael Thomas reported. Henry hid another smile.

"What do you think of your project now?" Kiri asked the children.

"I think we'll need more time... and headlamps... and someone to track us on our phones while we're investigating... and maybe some help." Her son glanced toward Henry.

"I think you need to shower," she said. "Get rid of those cobwebs you brought back with you."

Katie's eyes popped out again. "Cobwebs! Spiders! Ooh!" she shouted and ran out batting at her hair. Michael Thomas was right behind.

Henry brushed himself off and sank into the couch. "The children were right. There's quite a warren down there. No telling what we'll find. I'll pick them up after school tomorrow and bring some torches and headlamps, maybe a laser measure. Have them video our adventure."

Kiri sat down next to him. "You don't have to do all that. You have enough on your hands with work and running errands for me."

He looped an arm around her shoulder and kissed her forehead gently. "I'd like to. This old place holds secrets, I'm sure. We may find evidence that it was a hideaway during the Resistance or a cache for weapons. Who knows?" He slid her nearer and pecked lightly on her cheek. "Besides, now that we know the structure is more than it seems, it will have to be blueprinted and inspected before it can change hands."

Kiri's response was cut off when Katie ran in and plumped down next to Henry, her damp curls shedding droplets onto the two of them. "I just called Polly and told her that we're camping with Grandmother. She's never slept over in this house either. I told her that Grandfather's house is filled with secret passages and hiding places, and she wants to come and explore with us. I think she would be a big help. Can she come camp with us?" she asked him.

Henry gave her an "ask your mother nicely" look.

Her deep sigh filled the room. "Mom, can Polly please come and camp with us?"

"We'll see how Grandma feels in a couple of days. Maybe Polly can come for the weekend."

"That sounds like a good plan to me," Henry said. "Give us some time to clear out the cobwebs and old bones before you two get lost down there."

Katie shivered and hugged him tight. "Will you stay here tonight, Uncle Henry. Pleeease?" she begged. "I was kidding when I said there might be monsters here, but we could have stirred up rats or something when we stomped around." He did not seem convinced, so she tried a different appeal accompanied by doe-eyes. "When you tell us it's time for bed, you always say children need a good sleep so they'll be bright for school the next day. I won't sleep at all if we're alone in this scary house tonight."

Kiri shrugged. "It's fine with me. Heaven knows there are plenty of bedrooms on the third floor. I cleaned up Kurt's this afternoon after his visit for the funeral, and the two bathrooms are scoured and well stocked."

He squeezed both of his girls. "Are you scared of ghosts, too, Mrs. O'Connell?"

"Now that I know there are multiple unsecured entrances into this place, I will be uneasy until Devin has a security system operational. I've already foiled one family intrusion today. I'm too tired to guard against another. Pleeease?"

"I suppose a bed beats another night in the recliner," Henry replied with a grin.

"I agree," Michael Thomas said from the doorway. "The more men on hand tonight, the better."

After being escorted by the children to his new digs and shown the closet with nightclothes, robe and slippers awaiting Kurt's next visit, Henry shuffled them off to bed and returned to find Kiri dozing on the chaise. He kissed her gently. "Long day?"

She slit open an eye and smiled. "Sorry. I haven't had a good sleep in months."

"Dr. Henry prescribes bed rest for you too, whenever your mother is asleep."

"But there is so much work to do here."

"Yes, and it will get done in time, but that time doesn't have to be tomorrow or the next day. Your mother needs to grieve, and she must be your first priority. You cannot take care of her if you haven't enough energy to brush your hair or wash your face."

Kiri felt her head and clothes self-consciously. "I am a mess, aren't I?"

"In a word, yes. Let's get you to bed just like the kiddies. You haven't really been sleeping on the floor, have you?"

She nodded. "On yoga mats and folded blankets."

"That stops now! Help me move this lounge in. Is there room?"

She nodded again. The two hefted it up and along a short connecting hallway to a far corner of the dark room. They whispered an affectionate good night at the open doorway, and Henry climbed the stairs to the third floor to guard the castle from ghosts and ghouls.

No one noticed Anne parked in her car across the road. She wanted to try the door again in case the lock simply malfunctioned that morning. She came, hoping to find the house dark and Kiri's car gone—an indication that she took Paula to Quincy Street with her. Instead, Anne watched the lights go out on the second floor... then the third... with Kiri's car still in the drive... beside Henry's. "Slut!" she shouted and drove off.

A rustle and creak on the stairs brought Henry bolt upright. He prayed the noise would not wake the children and peered out his door to investigate. Katie's figure crept cautiously downward. Probably in search of a drink of juice or a snack, he thought.

When she failed to return within a few minutes, he went on a search to see what mischievous scheme the corkscrew-curled scamp was brewing. He noticed no lights on the main floor, so checked the suite and finally Paula's bedroom. He spied Katie snuggled under the covers with her grandmother, cuddling her, smoothing her hair from her tear-stained face, and whispering, "We love you, Grandma. Don't cry. We'll take care of you. We love you sooo much."

Near tears himself, he left quietly so he would not disturb the moving scene. That tempestuous box of a little girl had goodness and a heart big enough to encompass everyone, he thought. Everyone but her mother.

*   *   *

Kiri opened one eye and peered cautiously around her mother's bedroom. When she spotted two rumpled heads, one on each side of Paula's wavy, sugary-white one, she smiled, closed her eye and pretended sleep. She listened for Henry's heavy step on the landing to signal the girls to hustle back to their own room.

While waiting for his sound, she recalled the events of the last few days. The expedition below stairs was very successful, exciting even Henry with their finds. He showed up with requested headgear, the latest hand-held technology for exploring and measuring dark places and grubby clothing which, for him, was a button-down shirt with a frayed collar and slacks with a stain. "We found a veritable historical museum down there. Michael Thomas may cultivate a new hobby."

Kiri promised to listen to their stories attentively and to approve another trip down *if* the children promised, in turn, to spend the following afternoon and evening beginning their inventory. Michael Thomas nodded his acceptance of the terms.

Katie balked. "*If* Polly can come Friday after school and stay the weekend. I've told her everything, and she's anxious to help."

Her mother countered. "*If,* after an afternoon's tour below, you will both inventory Friday evening." Agreed.

Meghan seemed apologetic when she brought all three children from school. "Do you really want one more distraction when you have Paula to care for?"

Kiri assured her they would manage. "Henry is a great help."

Meghan raised an eyebrow and left. Maybe the story Anne told three mornings in a row was true, she decided.

The children kept their promise. They worked hard Friday night and finished cataloging the third floor. When they excused themselves for bed, Henry warned Kiri to be on the lookout for two young girls tiptoeing into Paula's room in the middle of the night. "Katie snuggled with her for the last three."

"I had no idea." Kiri was incredulous. "Why didn't I see her?"

"She scampered out before you woke up. I saw to that."

Kiri smiled. Amid all the sorrow surrounding Thomas' death, tiny rays of sunshine peeked through the curtains and caused two small forms to kiss their grandmother and scuttle from the room.

By midafternoon, the young teens were lost somewhere in the attic while Kiri and Henry tackled the books in the suite. He separated the keepers from the rest. Kiri cataloged the keepers first on Thomas' computer, successfully unlocked by Frank a day before. "Thomas used voice control throughout the interior of the house. I scrubbed his and replaced it with yours, so you can activate any device now... except your mother's computer. I'll fix that one when you say the word."

She said the word—"Keep Mom's; add mine."

"I stopped to check on your house and let Paddy know you may be away for a couple of weeks. He'll spread the word," Henry said from his place on a stepstool.

"Thanks. I forgot to let him know... and the aquacenter too."

"Did Michael Thomas tell you we found two tunnels to the outside— one to the garage and one toward the alleyway?" he asked.

"Uh huh."

"Devin says they probably date from the late 1700's. He'll extend the security system along the stone interior and block the exits with sheet metal until you decide what to do about them."

"Okay."

"He says that the house from the main floor up was likely built in the late 1800's. He'll show you how to shut off the old electrical circuits along the service stairs when you're finished working here in the house, in case the kids leave a light on."

"Good idea."

"He's upgrading your external system to activate by facial recognition. I told him to use yours and Paula's for now."

"Uh huh."

Henry doubted that Kiri listened to a word he said. He stepped toward her and bent to watch her face. "I'm feeling very comfortable here. I think I'll move in."

"Good idea." No change.

Now he was sure. He smiled slyly and tried again. "I've finally convinced the London office to give me the deal I want: three guys here in Dublin on eight-hour shifts, twenty-four hours a day, a fourth to cover days off and a fifth in the field on friendly borders. They'll rotate every two weeks. Survival training is required for everyone—myself included—in case an emergency calls more hands overseas. The execs got tired of my asking for leave to attend to "family matters," so they finally capitulated. Unless I have to fill in for someone, starting the beginning of the month I'll work in Dublin... regular hours... five days a week... indefinitely."

Kiri leaped from her chair and threw her arms around him. "That's wonderful! At last!"

The children discovered the two locked in affectionate embrace when they ran in carrying their own version of wonderful. "We found treasure!" Katie shouted.

Michael Thomas placed a ragged file box on the floor. The others crowded around as Katie blew dust from its lid and opened it with ceremonial flourish to reveal stacks of old photographs. "We found my dad!"

The teens reached eagerly for handfuls of photos and spread them out on the carpet. Katie found a black feather stuck to one, scrunched up her nose, picked it off with a finger and thumb, and tossed it aside. "The pictures are really old—taken with cameras that used film, like decades ago—but they are still pretty clear. We weren't sure what we found until Polly recognized her mother."

Michael Thomas broke in. "Then we looked for pictures with the whole O'Connell family and identified the aunts and uncle from the way they stood in a line. Grandfather was always first and the lady next to him must be our other grandmother—the Killian one." Henry's ears perked up. "Of the children, a boy stood next, then a girl, then Polly's mom, then another girl, and a little boy was always on the end. That has to be our dad."

"It was like a puzzle, trying to find all the pieces that looked like Mother," Polly chimed in.

"We looked for Daddy until we ran out of room and decided to come down here," Michael Thomas said. "We want to arrange the photos by age, if we can, so we can compare him to ourselves."

"I can pick him out easy now. He's the one with the bird's-nest hair and the scabby knees whose shirttail is always hanging out of his school uniform," Katie said, picking up another stack.

The children sorted and giggled at the childish antics of what became a very staid family. Kiri enjoyed watching over their shoulders to discover the young Michael for herself.

Henry was in a world all his own with two thoughts on his mind. He wanted to snatch a photo of Kathryn Killian O'Connell to compare with those of *his* mother at a similar age, and he was determined to find pictures of his father as a young boy. Surely there must be photos in a school or village library that he could search for images of a youthful Dermot Devane. The idea had not occurred to him until he saw Kiri's children pouring over the mound on the floor.

He had had some success in his quest to find other Devanes. A possible cousin had lived in Northern Ireland near Belfast and was a reputed IRA strongman and bombing organizer during the Troubles. He was killed a couple of years after Dermot's ill-fated ride. As Henry pieced a story together, his father might have been a courier for his cousin, transporting bombs and ammunition made or acquired in the west. Whether he was aware of his cargo or not, there was no way to tell. Maybe he thought he carried whiskey—a commodity as valuable as guns to many.

Henry's mind wandered to the similarity between his father's story and Michael's. Two young men, four decades apart who planned a future with families and children, became embroiled in a country's economic and religious internal conflict, their two untimely deaths the result of accidentally exploded bombs. Michael sacrificed his life for that of an innocent young boy playing with friends. Henry imagined his father reacting the same way by lurching to a sudden stop to spare a young boy chasing his football into the road. How strange the thread that connected his two kinsmen.

Michael Thomas' frustration jolted Henry from his reverie. "Mom, I don't look at all like my dad."

"You look more like Grandma and Uncle Kurt, that's true, with your long, lean body and prominent cheekbones. If you look at the youngest photo of your grandfather with Uncle Tommy as a baby, you'll find the hint of a cleft in your chin just like his. I don't know where you got your eyes. Your grandfather's were blue and Grandma's are green. Both your dad and I have shades of blue, but yours are blue-green like the sea—a genetic quirk, I guess. Very few people look exactly like one parent, you know."

"Maybe I should be collecting photos of Grandfather too. Do you have any of Grandma when she was young?"

"I'll try to find some for you."

Katie grabbed a picture in each hand and waved them in the air. "Daddy had a girl friend. Daddy had a girl friend," she singsonged. "She's very pretty… and blond."

Kiri gazed over her daughter's shoulder and noticed several pictures of the couple over a series of years, dressed for teenage dances. She motioned to Henry, and he nodded. They both recognized Michael's partner—a young Alice Richardson, Patrick Murphy's wife, the one Meghan once referred to as "expected to join the family." She was now exiled in the Falklands with her husband who betrayed Michael. The tiniest pang of envy struck Kiri as she realized that Alice might have enjoyed more years with Michael than she had.

Katie commanded everyone's attention again. She pointed excitedly at an array of photos of Michael on the first day of school, riding a bike, kicking a football, balancing on a stone fence, and throwing stones out to sea. "He was a kid, just like me!" she cried out. She clutched one in particular—a boy of about ten with wild ginger hair and a curl that flopped down over his right eye, bright blue eyes and a square face, freckles and a smirky grin, a boxy build and a wide stance, and arms crossed on his chest with an attitude that said "small but mighty"—a twin for the daughter holding his portrait. Tears filled her bright blue eyes, crowned on the right by a ginger curl flopping down. "My dad *was* real!"

Yes, he was real... a true treasure. Kiri rescued the black feather from the floor and pocketed it.

*   *   *

Kiri waved goodbye to a carload of kids bound for school on Monday morning with Henry at the wheel. Thomas O'Connell was buried one week earlier, and Paula had not left her bedroom since. Kiri entered the room quietly and bypassed her mother's morning massage to slip under the covers and press her body against Paula's frail back, cuddling her. She swept her mother's thinning hair from her face and whispered, "I'm here, Mom. You're not alone. I love you and want to help you if you'll let me." Hearing no response, as every morning for the past week, Kiri held her tightly and closed her own eyes.

Her mother's sudden arousal startled her. "We used to hold like this when you were little," Paula said weakly. "When you woke up frightened at night, you'd crawl into my bed trembling and I would surround you with my arms to protect you—to keep the scary things away. Now we've traded places."

"It's my turn. I want to be here for you"

"I should count my blessings, I know, but I can't find the strength yet. The girls helped." Paula rolled onto her back and gazed at the ceiling, a slight smile drifting across her lips. "They tried to come in quietly and not disturb me, but they argued over who got my front side and who got my back until I finally lay like this when I heard them coming so they could each have a side."

Kiri clasped Paula's hand between hers. "You should have shooed them away."

"Never. I couldn't refuse those loving grandchildren when all they wanted to do was comfort me, and they did help. The only feeling worse than emptiness inside is reaching out in the dark and finding no one there." She squeezed her daughter's hand. "But you know that."

Kiri remembered filling her bed with pillows so she would not feel alone.

"I can't imagine the strength it took for you to pull yourself back into this world after Michael's death... and to create such a remarkable and full life afterwards. I don't have that strength. Thomas was my soul mate, and I can't imagine another day without him. How did you survive without Michael?"

"Kind friends cared for me. And that's what I want to do for you... be your shoulder."

Paula turned her head to study her daughter, now a mature woman of more than fifty whose eyes revealed fortitude and wisdom she herself never possessed. "Forgive me, Kiri?"

"Whatever for?"

"As I look back over my few years with Thomas, I wouldn't have changed a thing except...." Her eyes filled with tears and her voice cracked. "I have one regret... that at the one time in your life when you both needed me most... I couldn't be there for both of you."

Kiri felt a welling up inside too. "You were. I knew you would come if I called. You're my mother."

"Forgive Thomas, if you can, for being so obstinate. He had no right to shoulder you with the burden of his family. He wanted to say more but was too emotional."

"Thomas needs no forgiveness. He was a good man, fully dedicated to his family. I'll manage... with your help."

"And forgive me for not sharing your burden. I need to go home."

"This *is* your home."

"No. This is the house I shared with Thomas. I once told you that who you are with is more important than where you are. With Thomas gone, my where is not here. I don't belong in Ireland anymore. Mountains on the walls are not enough. The Colorado landscape is in my blood. Please take me home."

CHAPTER 22

Kiri entered the upscale restaurant in Dublin's central business district for her first meeting with Tommy following his father's death a month previous. Neutral territory seemed wise for tackling the task at hand— inaugurating the administration of the O'Connell Grandchildren's Trust. She had no sooner opened her suitcase upon return from moving her mother to Colorado than her phone rang. Tommy proposed the get-together. She begged off for a couple of days—time to grind the details of the trust into her memory to prepare for their conference.

Paula transitioned to her home on the hill without fanfare. She packed a few clothes, books, some jewelry Thomas gave her and the painting of Puffin Island. "My other needs can't be met with things," she said. Her eyes scanned the suite for the last time, and then sought forgiveness from her daughter for burdening her with the rest, Kiri remembered as she noticed a man with Tommy's proud bearing rise to greet her.

"How is Paula?" he asked politely.

"As well as can be expected. Settled in with Kurt, at least."

Her stepbrother registered surprise. "She didn't return with you?"

Kiri shook her head. "She won't be back. Let's get started, shall we?"

Tommy sat. "I suppose we should begin with the house, if Paula intends to stay in Colorado."

Kiri did not blink. "According to Thomas' instructions, the house is not in play until my mother's death at which time it reverts to the Trust. Let's begin there."

The co-trustees examined the initial accounting, affixed their names to signature cards, discussed strategies and agreed to meet monthly to review. By the end of their session, Tommy's shoulders relaxed.

At their second such meeting, he approved reallocations Kiri suggested. She thanked him for the support.

At their third get-together, Kiri proposed that the grandchildren be included. "We're both in our fifties. This trust may not revert to them for two decades or more. If they have a hand in the management before they take control, they're likely to make more sound business decisions when the time comes."

"I thought your son would take over," Tommy said with a grump.

"He may become sole administrator in name, but I doubt he'll flaunt it. He'll ask for advice from his cousins. His grandfather expects that of him."

Tommy scrunched his eyebrows in thought. He did not want to be involved in any more meetings. "So long as it's more schooling than banking, I'll leave you to it."

Brendan, Grace, Caitlín and Meggie—the oldest grandchild from each family —were due within minutes. Kiri climbed the stairs to the sitting room to arrange seating for the group near her cluttered desk and ran smack into Katie dragging all the furniture back against the walls. "What do you think you're doing? You know I have a meeting here tonight with your cousins."

"Well, I need this room to practice for our play. Polly will be here any minute." Katie turned her back on her mother and continued.

"You'll have to move to your room. You can practice here tomorrow night."

"No! We need the communications' big screen so Kendra can watch us from Colorado and show us our mistakes. We have to be perfect *before* tomorrow. You move." She disappeared and returned with a handful of props.

"Katie, I'm using this room tonight. Maybe you and Polly can go to her house."

Her daughter turned on her and accompanied each shout with a stomp. "No. No. No!"

Exasperated, Kiri shouted back, using words she never expected to again. "Aurora Kathryn O'Connell! What would your grandfather say?"

Startled by the invocation of his frightful image, she clenched her fists and tightened her jaw. "He'd say to choose an appropriate alternative to express *your* displeasure." The two locked glares. "So if I can find an appropriate alternative for you, *maaay* I please use this room?"

Kiri backed down. "Five minutes, or you are out." She escaped to her room with her head in her hands. All the forces of Thomas' affairs tearing at her were nothing compared to the tug-of-war with her daughter. She raked through her hair with her hazel wood brush, splashed cold water on her face and returned to the sitting room to move her daughter out.

Katie was not there. She was not in her own room or her brother's. The laptop was missing from Kiri's desk. She followed the trail of scattered papers downstairs to the kitchen, collecting them as she went. She found the nook table folded out into its octagonal whole, never used that way by the three or four in their family. Dining chairs added enough seats for six. The laptop and remaining papers were neatly stacked in the center of the table, and Katie was at the counter hastily pulling out cups for the tea she brewed and setting out snacks.

"A little crowded, isn't it?" Kiri asked.

The young girl gave her shoulders a haughty shrug. "If, as you say, the cousins will work closely together for a long time, they might as well get used to being close now. Satisfied!" Katie hurried out and up the stairs to reclaim her stage before her mother could add a word.

Brendan was first to arrive, let himself in and find his way to the kitchen. "Brilliant! I didn't know you could open up the table like that. Just like old times at Grandfather's when we were kids," he said and slid right in. The three girls arrived shortly after. None of them understood why they were there. Their parents had not mentioned any Trust.

Kiri handed each one a binder outlining the fund, its terms and purpose. The young adults tried to hide their surprise at their grandfather's unusual arrangement. "Why?" Meggie asked. "Why would he choose us and not our parents?"

Unprepared for that question, Kiri brought the teapot and snacks to the table and fiddled in her pocket for an answer. "You have more years ahead of you to do good than we older folks do." She guided them through the documents and suggested they return with questions in three or four months. "Maybe we'll have time then to look at some of the accounts."

The grandchildren huddled. "We'd like to come back in a month, if that's all right with you," Caitlín said. "Maybe Paula will feel well enough to join us then."

"My mother did not return to Dublin. She plans to stay in Colorado."

The girls' eyes saddened. "But she can't," Grace said. "We can't lose her too. How can you stand not to have her close?"

Kiri smiled. "There's always Skype, and I plan to visit for a few days as often as I can." She resisted wiping her eye. "Thanks for taking time out of your busy lives to come this evening. Pick a date in a month and give me a call."

As the girls filed out, Brendan trailed behind. "I haven't been in the legal profession long, but I do know how to read a document. I find nothing in this one that refers to a Trust Committee formed from the eldest of each family. As I see it, you and Uncle Tommy are in control."

"I made an administrative decision that does not require a signature."

Brendan gave her a cunning look. "Gutsy move. Grandfather would approve." He patted her on the shoulder. "And Uncle Michael would be very proud of you."

When the Trust Committee returned in a month, they headed straight for the nook and settled in. "We've made an administrative decision," Grace declared. "If Paula won't come to us, we'll go to her. There are twelve of us out of school now. Fifteen, come summer. We've divided up the year so that one or two of us will visit her in Colorado each month for a long weekend."

"We investigated. Fast-Flights cut flight time in half and Speedy Security shortens that horrible wait time even more. A conveyor tube transports passengers and luggage together from curb to tarmac and uses 360° scanning sensors to safety inspect at the same time," Caitlín added. "But you probably know that."

"With the time zones, we'll arrive there before we leave here!" Meggie giggled. "I'm going over in three weeks. I haven't been to Paula's house since forever."

"Now that's settled, we have a few questions for you," Brendan said and started down his list.

Kiri did her best to answer them. She showed them the accounts, explained how she managed them and on what basis she made decisions. When their eyeballs dizzied in their sockets, she suggested the group run a trial. Each of them, Kiri included, would control an equal amount of money, hypothetically, to manage for a period of time—two to four months—and return to compare results.

"Caitlín tells me you're building an apartment for Paula above her garage. An octagonal one," Tommy said at their next meeting. "That seems a little strange."

"Four walls aren't enough for all the windows she needs to see her mountains, and she does need her own space."

He shook his head with a half-smile. "She's well and happy, then?"

"Seems so. She works in her vegetable garden and spends a lot of time sitting with her flowers."

He shook his head again. "How are *we* doing?"

Kiri showed him the accounts. "Up, except for this one. What do you think about moving half to this new one instead?"

Tommy pretended to look over the figures and seriously consider the suggestion. He finally nodded. "Agreed."

*　　*　　*

As soon as school was out for the summer, Kiri took the kids and Polly for an "apartment warming." The reunited triplets explored every nook and closet together. Katie went ballistic when she found Paula's personal robotic assistant. "Grandma gets a robot and we don't! That's not fair," she pouted.

"When you're her age, I'll buy you one too," Kiri replied.

Katie brightened with excitement, then did the math and rolled her eyes. "That'll never happen!" Once the novelty wore off and the young teens realized Paula preferred their hugs and kisses to the PRA, they decided she needed a dog for company and found a small, cuddly mutt at the shelter. Paula named it "Triplet" in their honor. Luckily, Kiri thought, the PRA was programmed to feed dogs as well as people. The addition of an exterior ramp also broadened its duties to carrying tools to and produce from her mother's garden.

Devin and Frank made a quick trip to Colorado during Kiri's stay to install a video communication/monitoring/security system in Paula's apartment. As far as the aged woman knew, a camera was only in the living room where she intended to chat long distance with her daughter, then flip the off-switch when they said goodbye. The guys set up hidden cameras throughout the rooms and a couple outside on the deck, unbeknownst to Kurt or his mother. These fed into Kiri's system in Dublin 24/7 so she could keep a constant eye on Paula anywhere on her premises without her knowledge.

"This surveillance system is probably illegal, surely unethical, and an absolute necessity as far as I'm concerned," Kiri said into Paula's screen through cyberspace to Henry who helped with camera positioning and connections from her Dublin house. "I'll probably go to prison for invasion of privacy."

"That will save you from your family responsibilities," Henry smiled back. "You might think about installing one in the aquacenter in case you do find yourself behind bars."

When Kiri returned home, she found such a system up and running.

*   *   *

Every dawn, Kiri thanked the good Lord for Henry and his new schedule. His emergencies and her monthly trips to Colorado alternated conveniently so her children could sleep in their own beds and maintain their routines without interruption. Henry often looked after Michael Thomas and a couple of his friends along with Katie, Polly and Sara Lamb for a weekend when Kiri visited her mother. He enjoyed the challenge and finally agreed to give up overnighting in the recliner in the living room to sleep in Bitsy's old room on the first floor as long as Kiri agreed to move the cradle out.

Katie excelled at gymnastics and drama—no surprise to anyone who knew her—and constantly required transportation to practices and lessons. Michael Thomas resumed football and took up choir. Between the two of them—Kiri and Henry—no child was left waiting on a doorstep or field or scanning a crowd for a familiar face on competition or performance days.

As promised for Michael Thomas' sixteenth birthday, Frank reassembled the old team—Henry, Doyle, Devin and Gus (no spouses, no kids)—to celebrate with a sixteen-layer plate-sized pancake and a pint of frothy stout in the center to hold the candle. The guys cheered what Michael Thomas vowed was his first taste of the brew, and he was proud that they treated him like a man... like his father... that day, sharing tales of their adventures as a team. The men masked their ulterior motive well—to assess his analytical skills and natural gifts for potential use in their line of work.

*   *   *

"My girls tell me they enjoy their trips to visit Paula," Tommy said when he and Kiri next met for their monthly review of accounts.

"She enjoys their company very much, too."

"Your mother is still well?"

The stepsisters are behind your constant interest in my mother's health. "Yes, very well," she said. "Thanks for inquiring."

"The accounts are still strong, I see. Just the one laggard. Any ideas?"

"I'll do some investigating and see what I can come up with."

"How are the grandchildren's trials going?"

"We've had three. The first was a disaster. The committee discovered that your Caitlín has a financial mind, Grace an objective one, Brendan a family first one, and Meggie a sympathetic one. They decided they might make better decisions working together and using everyone's strengths. The next round was more successful and last time they matched my gains. I told them that when they best me, they can move on to a new project. We'll see in a couple of days how they've done."

"Good. 'Til next month, then," Tommy said and left, happy that their meeting was a short one.

Meggie burst through the door first. "I know we beat you this time. I know it! You'll have to find something new for us to do so we can keep meeting."

The other three followed, opened out the table, and slid into their places in the nook. "You go first, Aunt Kiri," Grace said with a confident smile.

Kiri turned her laptop to display her accounting: a gain of 1.638% over the past two months, the best score of the trials. "Sorry, guys."

Brendan displayed the committee's result: a gain of 1.812%. "Sorry, Aunt Kiri," he said with a wink.

"I guess that does it. You've learned your lessons well. I will review your recommendations any time and see if I can convince Uncle Tommy to accept them. Little by little we'll give you an active part in management. Good job. Thanks for coming."

Meggie's eyes drooped. "Can't we at least have tea and snacks? And you said you'd give us a new project to work on."

"Ideas don't just pop into my head like that." Kiri snapped her fingers and realized that sometimes they did. "You should have a meaningful project, not just a pencil and paper exercise. I'll see what I can drum up before next time," she said and rose to gather refreshments. She bumped into Michael Thomas on his hourly trek to the refrigerator.

"Outta here, kid," Brendan joked, well aware that one day that kid would control the entire trust. "You're not twenty-one yet."

"Then you don't need to listen to my grand idea." All eyes turned on the teen. "Why don't you invest in yourselves?" Their eyes searched one another's, then focused on Michael Thomas again for an explanation. "Like you do, Mom, helping some of the cousins establish a business. If the Grandchildren's Trust will eventually support everyone, why not start now? Breeda asked you for a deal just last week." He grabbed a handful from the snack plate and left.

The four young adults had a vague idea that Aunt Kiri backed a couple of their cousins, but had no clue how that worked. Using Ronan as an example, she revealed her process. "With no middle man, he gets a loan for a fair interest rate. I make a small profit. He knows that if a payment is even a day late, he will have to renegotiate at a higher rate. And best of all, I know where the rascal lives, so he can't skip out on his obligations," she finished with a smug smile. Grace, Ronan's sister, snickered behind her napkin.

The committee asked more questions, especially about Breeda's "deal," and as their new project, decided to finance her catering business provided she make a formal presentation to include a sound business plan—and provided that Uncle Tommy agreed. They hugged their thanks to Kiri on the way out the door. She leaned against it with a sigh. With a simple question, Michael Thomas established his future role as the practical one in the group.

"I've come up with an idea for that laggard account of ours," Kiri told Tommy at their next meeting at the restaurant.

Brendan sat down next to the startled uncle. "We want to write a small business loan for a modest but guaranteed rate of return."

"To be paid off within eight years," Caitlín, Tommy's #1 daughter added as she sat down on his other side.

"We intend to use some of the money from that account that does nothing," Grace informed him as she joined the group.

"Even a modest return is better than *no* return from an investment," Meggie pointed out as she squeezed in between the previous two.

Tommy tried to maintain his composure, but when Breeda, daughter #3, walked up he lost it. "What are you doing here? What are all of you doing here? This is supposed to be a private meeting between your aunt and me. Can't we discuss your issue later?"

Kiri shook her head. "This *is* our issue today. The Grandchildren's Trust Committee has come up with an idea for our laggard account and wants to present it to you. Breeda is the spokesperson since she has applied for a loan from the Trust."

"Breeda," Tommy stammered. "What is this about?"

His daughter—fresh, bright-eyed and eager—smiled respectfully and handed him a folder. "Convincing you to believe in me, Father." She detailed the plan for her business, ending with "My mission is to provide traditional but healthful food not only for parties and special events, but also for the homebound in our community. My major obstacle is finding an acceptable substitute for that everpresent 'nob of butter.'"

At the end of her brief on-point presentation, her father vacillated. On the one hand, the idea was a good one—encourage the grandchildren to fund one another instead of draining their parents. Even if Breeda's business fell flat and the fund lost a little money, the committee would learn a valuable lesson. On the other hand, he had faith in his daughter. Kiri trained her well. She trained all the committee well. He just did not want to admit that his father Thomas was right. "Since this seems to be a committee proposal, I move that the first disbursal from the O'Connell Grandchildren's Trust be a loan to Breeda O'Connell to establish a catering business..." Ayes! interrupted him. "...with one stipulation." All eyes gaped at him. "That her loan include a release of liability clause... in case she poisons someone. Where do I sign?" he smiled.

Meggie urged her aunt to stay behind once the others finished their congratulations. "When did you last visit Paula?" she asked nervously.

"About three weeks ago. Why?"

"How did she seem to you?"

"Slowing down some, but that's to be expected. Why?"

"When will you see her again?"

"In about ten days. Why?"

Meggie was almost embarrassed to say. "Liam and Niall visited her last weekend, and they say she's... changed."

Concern clouded Kiri's face. "Did she slur her speech? Lose her balance? Forget who they were?"

"Not really. They said that Uncle Kurt was a lot of fun, as usual, but that Paula seemed detached, vacant... like she wasn't there. I hope this is nothing serious."

Kiri barely got a "thanks" out before she raced for home.

CHAPTER 23

Kiri burst through the door and ran upstairs calling her children's names to assure they were not home yet. They should still be at their after school activities, but with teenagers, one could not count on it. All clear. At late morning in Colorado, only Paula would be home; the rest of the family there, at work and school. She turned on her communication system and trembled as she did. *Admit it, Kiri. You are spying on your own mother!*

She activated all cameras and glanced quickly at the eight views displayed on her screen. Paula lay on her bed, eyes open and staring, with Triplet faithfully curled next to her while soft music played in the background. Kiri watched her mother breathe to confirm for herself that she did. Closer scrutiny revealed clutter everywhere in the apartment except the dining area and living room where she video-chatted with her daughter daily. Her PRA was absent. Outside, the garden screamed for attention. Paula's phone rang. She blinked her eyelids but did not answer.

"Mom, we're home!" Michael Thomas shouted from the front door. Kiri switched off her screen just as Katie whisked by and disappeared into her room. When her daughter's chatter indicated that Kiri's trickery was not discovered, she fixed and served her children dinner and hurried them out to the car for delivery to the evening's church activity. She could not return to her clandestine observation soon enough.

When she reactivated her system, she found Paula still in bed with the same music playing—no change until her alarm rang just before school was out, Colorado time. The aging woman roused herself, let her dog outside, fed him but ate nothing herself and scuffed back to her room pushing aside objects on the floor as she went.

That is so unlike Mom. She would never leave so much clutter about.

Paula dressed and tidied herself—sort of—and set a plate of packaged cookies on the dining table. She removed an apple from the fridge, looked it over and put it back as if it required too much effort to cut. Moments later, Kendra and Kody ran up the ramp calling, "Hi, Grandma! We're home." They sat for a few minutes to fill their grandmother in on their day, munch cookies, and run off to the main house.

Anxious to return to surveillance of her mother, Kiri played grumpy mom and hustled her kids off to bed as soon as Meghan brought them home. She found Paula exactly as she left her—sitting on the couch in the living room staring at the black screen on her wall. When it neared time for their evening mother/daughter video-chat—5 p.m. in Colorado/11 p.m. in Dublin—an alarm rang again. Paula straightened the room immediately in the camera's line of sight, sat again and waited. Kiri called, then watched her mother labor for a smile before she turned on her monitor.

176

"Hi, Mom! How are you feeling today?"

"I'm fine, dear. And you?"

"Busy, as usual. You seem a little tired. Did you exercise today?"

"I took Triplet out for a long walk this morning, and this afternoon we looked over the garden. A little early yet to plant but not to plan."

"Did you nap today?"

"No, no. No time for a nap. I made cookies to take over to Kurt's."

"Will you have dinner with the family?"

"Yes. I'll walk over as soon as we say goodbye."

"Are you keeping your PRA busy?"

"Yes. It keeps me tidied up."

"Liam and Niall visited last weekend, and I forgot to ask if you enjoyed seeing them. Did you have a nice time?"

"We did. They are such nice young men. Never would have guessed it when they were little tykes, always beating up on each other."

"What did you do?"

"We went for a nice hike along the creek, and they helped me turn some soil in the garden and clean up around the yard."

"Sounds like fun. Maybe I can help, too, the next time I come in a couple of weeks."

"Oh, you work hard enough as it is. You don't have to help here too."

"But I *want* to." She steadied her voice. "I love you, Mom."

"I love you too. Good night, dear." Paula switched off her monitor.

Kiri watched her mother make no move to go to Kurt's for dinner. She sat in front of the dark screen with Triplet on her lap until his squiggling caused her to let him out while she replenished his food and water. The two of them crawled back into bed by 7:30 to the strains of the same tune.

Kiri could not believe her eyes and ears. She and her mother traded deceptions, and there was no way to share that knowledge. She called her brother. "Kurt, we need to talk about Mom."

"Is there something wrong? I haven't seen her for a couple of days."

"Do you go to her house to check on her or does she come to you?"

"Lately, she comes to us, but I call her from work everyday. When she doesn't answer, I assume she's out walking or working. Why?"

"Did she join you for dinner?"

"Not tonight. The kids brought the message that she was tired and would fix some soup, then head for bed."

Well, she didn't! "How was your visit with Liam and Niall last weekend?"

"We guys had a good time. Kody enjoyed hiking with them to all his favorite places. We threw around a real football. That kind of stuff. The boys were a treat after all the girls who've been here."

"Did Mom hike with you or work in her garden?"

"Naw. She seemed tired, so she sat on her deck and watched when we were around. Why?"

"I thought she looked tired tonight too. Keep a close eye on her."

"Always, Sis."

Kiri determined to watch her mother during the entire night in case she awoke and exhibited other unusual behavior. By the time her kids greeted the day, their grandmother had not stirred. Once Kiri waved them out the door to school, she returned to minute-by-minute monitoring. No change throughout the remainder of her mother's night—not even in the music. The same song played over and over. Kiri vaguely recognized it from some school production and hummed along to pass the time. A mellow male voice implored Paula to remember the months of September and December and then, follow him. About 6 a.m., Paula made her way to the bathroom, let the dog out and in, and returned to bed. The same pattern ensued. The alarm rang just before the end of Colorado's school day and again before their video-chat. *What happens on weekends?*

Henry dropped by in the evening to look over the children's schoolwork. Even though they were both teens now, he could not shake the habit. After he hurried them to bed, he joined Kiri. "How is Paula today?"

"The same as last night. She just stares at the screen waiting for me to call. She hasn't eaten a thing as far as I can tell." She leaned against his shoulder with a deep sigh. "I don't know what to do. I can't let Mom know I'm spying on her—or Kurt. She'll never trust me again because I've not been honest with her, and Kurt will rip me apart."

Kiri's words cut deep into Henry as all his secrets and untruths circled in his mind. "Why don't you fly to Colorado and show up unannounced. Catch Paula and her apartment in their current state. Then you'll have good reason to confront Kurt with your concerns. Take the first flight out in the morning, and you'll be there before her afternoon alarm rings. She may not even hear you let yourself in." At the worry in Kiri's eyes, he added. "I'll handle things here. You can spy on me and the children from there if you want. I won't tell on you."

Kiri gazed at him with appreciation. "Thank you. I want to stay close to Mom and tell her every minute how much I love her... and my own daughter won't even give me the time of day."

*   *   *

"Mom needs special assistance, Kurt. I found her in bed in the middle of the afternoon. Her place is a mess, and the PRA is lodged way back in the cleaning closet. Fresh produce and wholesome foods are noticeably absent from the fridge, and empty boxes of snacks and cookies fill the trash. Mom would never live like this!"

"Are you accusing me of not taking care of her? I resent your showing up without a word and suggesting that I don't have a clue about my own mother."

"Not at all. I got worried after I talked to Mom last night—that niggly feeling that something wasn't right—so I came. I thought I texted you. Maybe in the rush I forgot to send."

Kurt shook his head. "I don't understand why I don't see the changes you do."

"Because she puts on a good show for you, but I know she is fading." Kiri did not share how she knew.

"She's not fading. She's old and slowing down. She has a different life now and new interests," he tried to argue.

"Her inactivity and untidiness are *not* new interests. They are symptoms. I want to arrange help for her. After all, that is one of my specialties—home care for those of advanced age. If you won't agree to that, at least let me take her to the doctor tomorrow. Maybe he'll prescribe something for her depression."

Kurt shook his head again. "She won't take any drugs. Neither would you," he shrugged.

"I'll pick up one of those gizmos that monitors when an elder opens the fridge or takes medication. Please?"

Kurt was in denial. He did not want to believe that his mother was less than the perfect mom he remembered. "Give it a couple more weeks."

Kiri yielded and spent the next couple of days cleaning Paula's apartment in between rousing her midmorning for a light breakfast, coaxing her to sip a few spoonfuls of soup at noon, and spending the warmest part of the day sitting with her among the flowers along the creek, the place Thomas called his hillside of sons.

"I see five healthy clumps now. One is for Michael, I assume."

"Tommy and Margaret lost three little girls, you remember."

"I do. I still ache for them. I can't imagine my two not in my life. And the last bunch?"

Tears came to Paula's eyes, so she changed the subject. "Soon Kathryn and I will be equal."

Kiri did not ask what that meant. She was too disturbed by the deep sorrow on her mother's face.

Paula's long term care remained unresolved when Kiri returned home. For the present, Kody and Kendra took their grandmother out for walks after school. Tanya offered to deliver healthful breakfasts and dinners each day and pick up Paula's dishes when she brought the next meal. She always found empty dishes rinsed and waiting on the counter when she came, and the clutter seemed controlled.

Kurt reported all was well, but Kiri had her suspicions. One night during their regular video visit, she proposed that she and her mother have dinner together. "I saved my chicken salad, so we can chat until Tanya brings your meal and then eat together. It will be fun!"

Paula's eyes darted around the room as if she were agitated, and then she nodded. "If you can wait that long. You must be starved by now."

Kiri snickered. "I confess. I've snacked all evening, but I've saved the best for last... with you."

Tanya arrived on schedule. Mother and daughter toasted with glasses of water. Throughout the meal, Paula took only a bite or two while Kiri wolfed down her salad. When they signed off—Paula thought—she scraped her food into the trash and rinsed her plate. Kiri smacked her hand over her mouth to keep from shouting, "Eat, Mom! Eat!" and risk waking her own children.

Midafternoon the next day, Kiri rushed home to watch her mother eat breakfast. Paula thanked Tanya kindly, but she did not even take one bite before she disposed of that meal as well. Kiri called Kurt and told him she was on her way.

Henry filled in for her at the Quincy house. He and Kiri communicated daily—late night in Colorado/early morning in Dublin—when everyone else was asleep. Three weeks later in early summer, he found her sobbing uncontrollably.

"I found Mom curled into a tight ball with her fuzzy little dog and crying with that infernal song playing. She refuses food and drink, and I can see in her eyes that she is willing herself to join Thomas."

"I'll bring the kids," he said.

Henry did better than that. He brought Bitsy and Sara too—their first plane ride. The three stayed in a small town nearby, and he delivered Bitsy during the day to play her harp while all the kids roamed the wildflower-covered hills.

Paula experienced periodic episodes of lucidity when her eyes grew clear and her voice, strong. She never discussed her intentions or her wishes. She only repeated phrases from the song that played incessantly in her mind, begging her to remember the significant months of her life. The words then faded into an echo of "follow" that never ended. During her last days she spoke vaguely of Thomas and his relationship to his grandson. She asked why Kiri did not question his favoritism for Michael Thomas.

"MT was his only son of a son," Kiri replied.

"Not *any* son," her mother said. "You returned *our* son to him."

"If he wanted a carbon copy of Michael, he should have favored Katie. Thomas told me often that she was so much like her dad in every way."

Paula shook her head and fumbled in a drawer. She retrieved an old, worn journal with 1968 embossed on the front and lots of papers stuck between pages. She clutched it to her chest, then handed it to her daughter. "Children have a right to their history…. When you're ready." Then she lapsed into her vague, distant state and did not return.

When Kiri called Kurt to the apartment, he was beside himself. "Do something!" he shouted at his sister.

"There is nothing we can do… except tell Mom how much we love her… and give her permission to go."

One night, not long after, Paula did… curled around Triplet with Kiri curled around her. Bitsy struck a final chord, and she was gone… to follow the man she loved and lost… and found to love again.

After a day of mourning when Kiri prepared her mother's body, she, Kurt and Tanya put their heads together to deal with the realities. Henry carted all the kids and Bitsy to see the buffalo because he had never been, he claimed. Paula left no last wishes. Kurt and Kiri agreed that she could return in a few weeks to help settle their mother's estate, but they could not agree on where to settle their mother.

"Since Mom did not give us any direction, she didn't have a preference for how or where she should be buried," Kiri said, "so it's up to us."

Kurt thought the obvious solution was Colorado, but Kiri held out for Dublin. "There is already a plot with her name on it, and the last words I heard Thomas utter were, 'Come back to me, Paula. Please come back.'"

"You're taking your duty to Thomas too far!" Kurt shouted, but he finally agreed when Kiri reminded him that Paula was obviously devoted to Thomas because she spent so much time either gazing at the hillside of flowers or at the painting of the island. *Where* settled.

In the midst of discussing the *how,* Henry returned with the kids. Michael Thomas overheard his mother and uncle agree on the lightest, smallest container possible to transport remains overseas. He protested. "You can't cremate Grandma just because it's easy. Grandfather wouldn't approve."

"What makes you think that?" Kiri asked.

"In his last days, Grandfather would look me in the eye and say, '*Our son* would never turn his mother to ash.' He repeated that sentence several different times. I think he meant you, Mom, but his words got mixed up toward the end." *How* settled.

The whole family agreed—Henry, Bitsy and Sara included—on a small memorial service on the flowering hillside the next afternoon. The kids planned it and the planting they would add, while Kurt and Kiri contacted a mortuary and started the red tape process. Henry, Bitsy and Sara left on the red-eye immediately after. The bereaved brother and sister contacted Groton's in Dublin to coordinate with the outfit in Colorado—only a graveside service one day after the family's return—whenever that would be.

Twenty-Second Anniversary Year: Death: Paula Koyle O'Connell, age 86. Mom lasted barely two years without Thomas. She lacked the strength of youth to carry her through her personal tragedy.

I'm writing this on our last trip to Ireland together—brother Kurt, my kids and I... and Mom. They are all asleep. I can't. The tempest that awaits my return will consume so much of my life that I'm afraid I'll forget our last two years together... and apart. I'm worried about the kids and how they'll deal with their second major loss in two years. There's bound to be a backlash. I'm having nightmares already about the days ahead. They'll have to squeeze in between the others I have regularly about the days and years behind. I no longer possess the strength of youth either, and I feel so lost knowing I'll never be able to call her again and say, "I love you, Mom."

CHAPTER 24

Henry unlocked the door to the aquacenter and climbed the stairs to check the monitoring system in the large, open area the nieces and nephews referred to as the party room. He assured the controls were in the off position and the screen black so the incoming group would not realize they were being watched. He questioned whether covert surveillance was necessary, but when Brendan said he wanted to use the room for a family meeting *before* Kiri returned from Colorado, he decided caution was warranted.

On the way out, he passed Brendan and Connor who came early to arrange seating for the more than twenty-five expected. Grace and Caitlín brewed tea in the kitchenette and set out cakes while Meggie searched for plates and cups. Sunday afternoon tea seemed an appropriate time for a family gathering, so Henry nodded his greetings and walked the few steps to Kiri's house. He let himself in and was about to activate her system and set it to record when he heard footsteps behind him.

"One thing before you go," Brendan said. "I need to pick up a box from Aunt Kiri's office." He returned barely a minute later carrying a recipe-style box crammed with wide strips of paper. "Thanks, Uncle Henry," he smiled. "We should be out within a couple of hours."

Henry smiled back and nodded. They still called him "uncle" even though they were adults now and rifts in the family fortress began to surface. He checked his watch. Kiri and family were due to touch down in four hours, so the group would be gone by the time she arrived home. Satisfied that the system was up and running and the recorder set, he changed the linens in the guest room/Bitsy's room/his occasional quarters to ready it for Kurt. He then watched out the window as the O'Connell family arrived, and he noticed Paddy across the road doing the same with his binoculars pressed against the window. Kiri could expect a full report.

He grabbed a pint of brew from the pantry and sat to witness the drama unfold next door. From the initial informal conversation, he gleaned that none of the parents had been inside the aquacenter before and that spouses and children of the younger generation were excluded. This was a core family meeting, and Brendan got right to the point.

"Please take your refreshments to your seats so we can get started." The thirty-one-year-old waited only a couple of minutes for the group to arrange themselves in birth order with Tommy, age fifty-nine, beginning the circle and Polly, age fourteen, closing it next to him. "We've asked you here because troubling trends are pointing this family in a direction we do not want it to go."

"Hear! Hear!" Anne shouted.

"Grace, Caitlín, Meggie and I, as the oldest in each family, met and agreed that it is time to address an issue we've watched fester for the last twenty years. We need to face you with a united front."

"It's about time," Stephen, Emily's oily voiced husband said.

"As you all know, Paula died a few days ago, signaling another change for all of us. Aunt Kiri is bringing her home to be buried tomorrow on Grandfather's left side. Grandmother Killian is on his right. That was his wish, not Paula's, and we hope you realize that for most of us, she was the only grandmother we ever knew."

"I say they all should have stayed in Colorado," Charles, Anne's blustery husband said, quite pleased with himself.

"We expressly planned this meeting to assure Aunt Kiri's absence. We did not want anything said here today to hurt or embarrass her or her children."

"If we're going to talk criticisms, I have a list," Phillip, Meghan's bespectacled husband said, trying to fit in. She smiled discretely, proud of her son for taking charge—the obvious leader of his generation.

"At the end, we'll present our proposal for a path forward. But first, we're going to break the ice with a game we're calling 'Who got permission, Who gave it and Why that was important.' Everyone will get a chance to select a slip from this box and pass it to the person named to explain. We'll begin with Uncle Tommy, senior among us."

Henry watched a scowling Tommy pull one out and read in a low even voice, "Grace" as if to say, "what's the point?"

"A good place to begin," Grace said, taking the slip from her uncle. "My mother Anne gave me permission to travel with Uncle Michael and Aunt Kiri to Colorado to camp in Yellowstone Park and visit the buffalo. That trip set two precedents. First, it was so successful that it became a tradition until all of us were treated to the same experience, even after Uncle Michael's death. Second, that girls were people too. Uncle Michael didn't want to take me because I was a girl and not expected to "rough it" without complaining, but Aunt Kiri supported me and thought I should make that choice, not he. I think I speak for most of us when I say that the experience added a new dimension to our lives."

The cousins exchanged nods and smiles.

"Aunt Anne, your turn."

She drew Liam's name. "My mother Emily signed this so I could take swimming lessons from Aunt Kiri. I can take care of myself in the water, know how to keep my friends safe and my own children," he grinned, "when I have them, and I've worked for two summers as a lifeguard near the boat rental at the lake."

"Aunt Meghan... Mother," Brendan continued.

She drew Breeda's. "My mother Margaret allowed me to hostess my sixteenth birthday dance right here in this room. Of course I had to share the night with Aidan, but we and our friends had a drug and alcohol free party and a really great time. That was a tradition too and showed us that booze doesn't make a great time. People do."

"Aunt Emily."

She drew Ronan's. "Aunt Emily, how could you? There must be a million permits in that box, and you had to choose the most embarrassing time of my life!" He took a deep breath. "My father Charles signed the judge's order that placed me in Aunt Kiri's custody rather than with a juvenile liaison officer when I was caught with my mate, an underage driver, drinking and with illegal drugs in the car. 'Ancillary guilt.' Everyone in the car got a penalty, and our penalties were the worst because we came from good families and should have known better. We all lost our learner's permits and were fined heavily. The driver drew a Detention Order for a year, another was sent to relatives in Cork for a year under a Care and Supervision Order, and I ended up with a GPS ankle monitor in Aunt Kiri's guestroom for six months. I think the juvie officer knew her."

The embarrassed twenty-nine-year-old rubbed his forehead. "Cakewalk, I thought, but no. I've never worked harder in my life. Up every morning early to clean the pool and the lavs in this building before breakfast, online school, lawn and garden in the afternoon, dishes after supper—no one did dishes by hand anymore but me—no electronic devices, and anytime I stepped outside her fences, alarms went off all over the place. After two weeks she allowed me an hour a day of Internet search on a topic of interest to me—no games or social media. I chose racecars.

"That led to a guy showing me all about Uncle Michael's custom sports car, then putting a boot on it so I could run it but not go anywhere, then being allowed to move it to the drive to wash and polish, then the promise of a ride if I made it to my seventeenth birthday with no more trouble, then a promise that I could drive it around the track at eighteen if I stayed out of trouble, then an apprenticeship with a garage up the road to learn more about maintenance and repair so I could keep old cars running, then a small shop of my own, and now a healthy business doing onsite emergency service for all the new hybrids and electric vehicles that don't have the bugs worked out yet."

He smiled at a sudden thought. "So I guess you could say, I owe everything I have today to that experience. Thank you, Father, for pawning me off on Aunt Kiri. Oh, and to all of you who got to drive that hot racer around the track when you turned eighteen or who called frantically in the morning because you forgot to plug in your vehicle or fill the auxiliary tank with petrol... you're welcome." He finished with a bow.

From his seat in Kiri's living room, Henry noticed Charles flush and focus on the rolling thumbs in his lap. The trusted family friend listened to the stories that followed. Many were of summer jobs provided for young teens with limited options to earn pocket money. Others involved volunteer experiences. Some included his name, and he remembered helping Kiri rescue stranded kids or place others with specialists in their chosen fields of study for their Transition Year before Senior Cycle. Some were particularly poignant.

"Gemma."

"My mother Anne signed this for my one-on-one day with Aunt Kiri," the reserved young woman began. "It's really hard to grow up as a middle child in a large family. When my aunt asked what I wanted to do for my special day, I said 'be alone.' She asked me what I liked to do, and I said 'draw with no one looking over my shoulder.' She took me to a small lake—I can't remember where—and rented a canoe. We paddled into a cove, had a picnic, and she brought out sketchpads and colored pencils for both of us. We waited quietly, and pretty soon the swans emerged from the reeds and grasses. Dozens, it seemed. They surrounded us, and we tossed feed to them.

"Aunt Kiri said that if I sat perfectly still with my hand on top of the water, they might come close enough to touch. Eventually they did, and I did... touch their white feathers and stare into their black eyes. Cygnets swam close by too, but I didn't try to touch them. We spent all afternoon saying nothing and sketching swans in their beautiful surroundings—the most perfect day of my young life."

"Is that why you bought the painting of the girl with the swans for your bedroom?" her sister Erin asked. "I love that painting. It looks just like you."

Gemma flushed and continued. "Yes and no. Aunt Kiri painted that portrait of me and gave it to me for my thirteenth birthday. I was afraid that hanging it up would cause a problem at home, so she signed it on the back and asked me how much change I had in my pocket. When I pulled out the coins, she took three cent pieces and said, 'Now you can say you bought it with your pocket money.' As you all know, today I teach art to primary students at Quincy School."

Connor removed a slip of paper towel. "Uncle Tommy, this one has Aunt Kiri's name on it with your signature, so why don't you tell us what you gave her permission to do."

With all eyes staring at him, Tommy had no choice but to respond. He thrust his chin out and spoke to the center of the floor. "When Margaret was so ill in the hospital the last time.... I permitted Kiri to administer a circular massage to her."

"You said the *girls* brought me around with massage," Margaret charged.

"They did... after Kiri performed the first one and taught them how. That and Bitsy's music led you back to us, and I'm thankful every day that they were there—no apologies."

Kean selected a slip. "Sis, this has your name on it."

"Please, please, please let it be the night Sara Lamb was born," Meggie, now twenty-five, pleaded. The disappointment on her face revealed that it was not. "My mother Emily asked Aunt Kiri to keep my brothers and me at her house on Quincy after Uncle Henry broke up a fight between my parents. We were there for two weeks while Mother stayed with Grandfather." She stared at her parents. "That was not the only time."

Everyone was embarrassed by the abuse no one dared acknowledge. "This game is over!" Stephen shouted. With his lips stretched tight and intimidating eyebrows aimed at his wife, he commanded, "Time to leave, Emily."

Brendan interceded. "Sit down! We said everyone would have a turn, and we've only a couple left. Nora."

"This one has Grandfather's name on it and is signed by a doctor, so I'll read it. 'Permission for Thomas O'Connell to travel to the west coast for a period of one week if accompanied by certified medical personnel. Have a grand time!' I guess if his doctor okayed the trip, no one can complain."

All the complainers were very quiet.

"Ríona."

"This one is for Uncle Michael and Aunt Kiri from Uncle Charles, so he should explain." The shy teenager handed her reluctant uncle the condemning slip of paper.

With no way out, he cleared his throat to speak. "About twenty years ago when our bank nearly failed, Michael rescued me and transferred all of our personal funds within minutes of the government's freezing them. My brothers, you'll recall, weren't so lucky and have struggled ever since. Michael and Kiri put me on a strict budget that allowed me to repay what I borrowed from Anne's trust account and continue a suitable life style."

"You borrowed from *my* trust fund without my knowledge?" she shouted at him.

His bristly mustache quivered. "That's a polite term for my action. But today, you are fully refunded and the trust has grown beyond my expectations. Kiri has seen to that."

Anne was livid. "How long did she have *her* hands in *our* pot?"

"She still does."

Anne's eyes bulged. "I suppose I pay her handsomely for her 'accounting services.'"

"Not one cent." Both grew sullen.

"Moving on," Brendan said. "Polly, you are last to pick."

The youngest child there selected, peeked, and slid the paper strip into her pocket. "You all know there are a million permits in that box with my name on them because Katie and I are BFF's and go everywhere together—including Colorado almost every summer—so drawing one with my mother's signature is no surprise. She takes care of Katie. Aunt Kiri watches over me. Brendan tends to Michael Thomas, and sometimes Uncle Henry takes us all on. That seems normal for a family, so I don't really get what the problem is between all of you and Aunt Kiri." She traced the family circle with a pointed index finger.

"Sometimes I feel like I have two different mothers—the one who shares transportation duties, greets our aunt in a polite way, and exchanges thanks... and the other mother who hasn't a nice thing to say about Aunt Kiri when she gossips with her sisters." Polly stared along the circle at her mother. "Maybe after I read this permit, you can explain that to me." She removed the paper from her pocket. "This is signed by both you and my father Phillip and is the reason I am here with all of you today. *I* will read it."

The two parents turned to each other, horror-struck.

"They gave Aunt Kiri permission to help them 'obtain medical advice and assistance for intervention in the natural process of conception, and in all prenatal directives for diet and exercise.' Judging by the date—not quite a year before my birthday—it worked!"

"Meghan! How could you?" Anne shouted to the sister next to her.

Sallow-faced Phillip flushed and had nothing to say. Meghan wrung her hands remembering her struggle between condemnation and new life. "Phillip and I desperately wanted a baby and, given our ages, weren't successful... so I went to Kiri for help."

Livid, Anne spat each word separately and distinctly. "Where... was... your... loyalty! You trusted Kiri more than us? I suppose you told Paula too."

Meghan lowered her eyes. "They both helped out when I had a couple of rough months."

"I see it now. You didn't volunteer for the church school's library project. You probably came here... to this very building... several times a week... for Kiri to work her 'magic' on you." At her sister's nod, she let loose with a salvo of charges. "You didn't tell *Father* the truth. You didn't tell your own *family*. The name... Kiera Pauline... I suppose you didn't choose it simply because you liked the sound. More likely, you wanted to honor your two secret collaborators!"

"Hey, I like my name!" Polly shouted.

Meghan stared apologetically at her two sons. "I'm sorry you found out this way."

Connor, now twenty-nine, replied with a shrug. "No sweat, Mother. We knew almost as soon as you did. Teenage boys have big ears."

Meghan turned toward her daughter.

"No problem, Mother. I kind of knew. Little sisters have ears, too, when big brothers try to keep secrets. But I don't see what the big deal is. I don't care how you guys *did it*... I'm just glad I'm here!"

Her seventeen cousins erupted in embarrassed laughter. Their parents did not. Henry spurted a mouthful of stout all over his pants and wondered how the young family man would regain control over a simple Sunday tea.

Brendan wiped his nose and eyes with a handkerchief and smiled. "I'm glad you're here, too, Polly. I'm glad you're all here. We've been silent and simmering too long. Ronan jumped the gun earlier when he thanked his father for signing a permission slip for Aunt Kiri to help his son."

He flung the remaining permits into the air to rain down on the astounded older adults. "This was our original intent today—to shower you with all your yeses so we could thank you for them. We decided to remind you how many times over the years you have condoned another family member acting in your stead—and we are richer for it. Every time you signed a permit, on some level you had to believe that the activity or event you allowed us to participate in was beneficial and well intended. You certainly would not have done so if you thought your own children would come to harm. You allowed—even *welcomed*—Aunt Kiri's influence on us, and we thank you for it. We think we turned out pretty great!"

Grace spoke next. "The difference between your generation and ours is that we know how to apply St. Kevin's lesson as Uncle Michael taught it—to holler for help if we've been dealt more than we can bear—and you are afraid or embarrassed to because that might show weakness or taint your reputation. Polly said it. Taking care of one another is normal for a family, so why should anyone be embarrassed to admit the need? Asking for help in difficult circumstances takes courage—as some of you know well. Answering the call takes courage, too. At his wedding dinner, Grandfather told us that members of a family don't have to love, like or even be friends with one another, but they do have to be loyal and show up when needed. We, your children, want to add 'show respect for one another' to his charge."

On the defensive now, Anne shot back, "That's a laugh. Kiri's own daughter shows disrespect for her."

"Perhaps she learned that from you, Mother," Grace said. "Katie looks to all her aunts and cousins to model proper behavior. If you bad-mouth Aunt Kiri in public, why shouldn't she?"

Caitlín, Tommy's eldest daughter, took up the sword. "Grandfather Thomas tried to *teach* us what it meant to be an O'Connell—to be family. You, our parents, *told* us not to disgrace the name O'Connell but to uphold the family honor. First Uncle Michael and then Aunt Kiri *showed* us how to be family—and name has nothing to do with it. There may be only one left to carry on the name, but we all carry the legacy. The kind of adults we've grown into speaks for us and does not require a label."

Meggie continued the agreed-upon message. "Aunt Meghan is not the only one who leads a double life. Aunt Kiri does too. She'd rather be left alone to live as she wants, take care of her kids, do her job and watch over her friends in their neighborhood, but her other life calls her to show up on our fun days, our angry days and on our desperate ones. To my knowledge she never said 'no' when we asked for her help, for which there is only one explanation—Uncle Michael guides her and gives her the fortitude to accept responsibilities she does not seek."

Brendan invoked his favorite uncle's spirit again. "On the night Uncle Michael was killed, he looked out from the television and asked, 'What do we want our children to learn from us?' As a boy, I wanted the men in my family to be proud of me. As a father now, I look over my shoulder and want my son to be proud of me. We need to look to the past *and* to the future at times like this and ask ourselves what we teach our children and grandchildren. I do not want mine to learn spite, contempt or disrespect from the family that is bound to cherish them."

He paused for dramatic effect. "I believe that Uncle Michael... and Grandfather... and Grandmother Killian... and now Paula... look down on us and ask over and over again what we want our children to learn. Whether they smile or scowl is up to us."

Connor, the storyteller of his generation, sat cross-legged on the floor amid the paper affirmations of family connection—the threads that held them together—and invited others to do the same. His cousins followed. Their parents looked on from their seats. "We began the afternoon with a game. In honor of Uncle Michael, we'll end with a retelling of his favorite story and a ritual."

Long ago, in Paula's ancestral land, there lived a people and a way of life on the point of extinction... Many tribes fought one another... Until you learn to keep peace among you... you will continue to suffer... Your good fortune depends on your good will... Pass the love of peace onto the next generation.

"Place your hands on the sides of your heads and curve them like the horns of the wooly buffalo." Connor directed them to snort, bleat and finally clap thunderously on their knees. When he shouted "Stampede!" the grownup children sprinted, with raucous laughter, for the last of the tea and cakes.

"Bravo!" Henry shouted from his place in Kiri's living room.

*   *   *

Paula's graveside service was proper and efficient. The priest recited the requisite prayers. Michael Thomas said a few words. The male cousins helped lower her casket into its final resting-place. Kiri and her two children emptied a small, Irish linen bag of beach sand, hillside soil and rich garden earth into the grave. The mourners departed solemnly, some placing flowers at the stones of Thomas, his first wife Kathryn, and Michael. All the cousins attended. Tommy and his wife Margaret, Meghan and Emily attended. Anne did not.

CHAPTER 25

Dinnertime together was sacrosanct—at least as much as it could be with two active teenagers and a working mother—so Michael Thomas and Katie were surprised to find their house locked when they returned from a free day with friends after their grandmother's funeral. Kiri wanted to reestablish a normal routine before the children started their summer jobs the following week, so she insisted their little family share at least one meal a day—kids choice—until that time. They chose dinner as usual. Neither one wanted to get up early enough for breakfast with Mom. Lunch was prime time with friends, so they agreed on the late meal of the day again as long as they would finish in time to go out after.

They retried the front door, but it did not budge. The facial recognition system installed after their grandfather's death had not malfunctioned before, but there were no guarantees with electronics. They tried the kitchen door with no success and finally the one to the mudroom. In each case they heard the locks disengage, but the doors would not give—as if they were barred. They sat on the deck to complain. Michael Thomas had a date with friends and did not want to be late. Katie scheduled a video-chat with Kendra in the privacy of her room to share the latest gossip from Dublin. After all, they had not seen each other for two days!

Katie glanced toward the aquacenter. "She can't be working. Everyone's gone."

Michael Thomas looked over his shoulder through the kitchen windows. "She's not fixing dinner. Let's check the garage. Maybe there was another family emergency." He shrugged when they discovered both cars in their places. "Let's call."

No answer, but their mother's distinctive ringtone sounded from poolside. They found her phone on top of an unused towel... but no mother. Time to call Uncle Henry.

He arrived in minutes since he was invited to family dinner too. Worry clouded his face until the teens described the doors as being barred. Then it changed to anxiety. Kiri was home, all right. She locked herself in. She had not used the old security system since Michael Thomas was born. Only desperation would drive her to throw the bolts again—bolts that would only release from inside the house. He turned to the boy and shouted, "Axe... garage! Go!" He ran to the deck below the bedroom window and called, "Kiri! I'm here to help. Kiri, answer me!" No response.

Axe in hand, Henry raced to the mudroom door where damage would be contained in a small space. The children followed, and he ordered them back to the deck. "Do not take one step inside until I call you." He hacked at the door, glass and splinters flying everywhere. When he heard a ping and the axe bounced back at him, he trimmed above and below the bar to create a space large enough to crawl through safely. He trod across the broken glass and skidded on a puddle of water, a sign that Kiri came from the swimming pool.

He flew up the stairs by threes to find her nearly immersed in ice cold running water in her tub. He pulled her limp, blue-lipped and –fingered form onto the floor, smacked her sharply on the back to restore normal breathing, and rubbed her roughly with towels to pink up her body.

"I tried to swim it off. Tell Michael… I'm sorry. Nest too heavy… too many children," Kiri mumbled and passed out.

Which Michael—the husband or the son? Henry swaddled her in a light summer quilt and carried her mummied body to the recliner in the sitting room. He turned on the fire and eased in beside her to hold her tightly. He heard a creak on the stairs and spotted four eyes peeking through the railing.

"Is Mom dead?" Katie's quavering voice asked.

Henry shook his head, remembering all Kiri's failed attempts after her husband's death. "She's physically and emotionally exhausted from the last few years. Caregivers need care too, you know."

"She looks like Grandma did before she died."

"Your mother is *not* going to die. She needs rest and loving care for a while." He stared at the two teens creeping closer. "I told you not to come inside until I called."

Her brother turned to go, but Katie stood her ground. "You didn't call soon enough."

Henry softened. "I didn't want you hurt by all the glass or to track it through the house. Please go down to the kitchen, clean your shoes and brew some tea. A hot cup for us all would hit the spot right now."

The children brought tea and sandwiches. "Mom said we had to spend dinner together," Michael Thomas explained. His mother was unresponsive.

They chatted quietly. "Won't we disturb Mom?" Katie asked.

"Hearing soft, familiar voices should soothe her," Henry replied.

Michael Thomas pulled out his phone and made a call. "Sorry, mate. I need to beg off tonight. Family issues. Maybe tomorrow. I know I've been gone forever, but family first in this house. Later."

Katie reluctantly pulled out her phone. "I guess I'm busy tonight, Kendra. I'll call tomorrow at 2/8." She looked at the other two. "We could sit on the floor next to the chair and play cards."

"Sounds good to me," Henry said. "Shuffle softly. And you have to let me win at least one hand."

A final tally showed Michael Thomas the winner, barely, over Katie with Henry lagging behind. He shifted Kiri's weight against him, pulled the quilt away from her face and felt her jaw—relaxed. "Your mother is resting now. She'll sleep like this 'til morning. Let's call it a night."

Michael Thomas rose and bent over his mother. "G'night, Mom." He kissed her on the cheek. "Love you." Shortly after he entered his bedroom, soft harp music wafted from it.

"Aren't you going to kiss your mother good night too?" Henry asked Katie who gazed intently at the blanketed bundle he held tightly against him.

She shook her ginger curls and walked away. "She's probably still mad at me for making a scene after Grandma's funeral yesterday when she wouldn't let me go home with Polly," she stated brusquely and slammed her bedroom door for good measure.

Henry hesitated to leave Kiri alone even for a minute, but when he awoke from a short doze he needed a break and wanted to inspect the damage to the mudroom door. He eased himself from her side and stole down the stairs. Not too bad, he decided on assessing the damage. He traced the line of the exposed bar, found the lever that released it, pulled and listened to the sounds of metal disengaging. Erector-set-simple, he smiled, but no one could have guessed. He swept all the fragments into a heap and bent to scoop them into the rubbish when a small blackbird swooped through the broken window, over his back and up the stairs without detection.

Satisfied that mild weather allowed repairs to wait until morning, Henry stretched his long limbs to prepare for the night ahead. Kiri had not lapsed into melancholy since her children were born. She was too busy. Her return now troubled him and begged for careful attention. He slipped back into the over-sized recliner and clasped her tightly again. A familiar creak broke the silence. Out of the corner of his eye, he caught sight of a nightgowned figure inching closer.

Escaping a sharp reprimand, Katie crept to the recliner, peered across Henry at her mother, and knelt next to the chair. "Why does Mom still look so sad?"

Henry patted the top of the girl's curly head. "She's grieving for all the lives lost, including her own. When your dad died, she watched her future die with him. When your grandmother died, so did her history… her past. She feels like no one knows her story anymore. All she has left is her present and it seems very empty to her. Our job is to fill her days with hope and love."

"I'm afraid she's willing herself to die like Grandma."

"Your mother would never do that. She loves you and your brother too much to leave you."

"My brother maybe… but not me." Her deeply sad eyes met his. "She doesn't love me."

A shocked eyebrow shot up. "Why would you say such a thing?"

"Because I hear her call my brother's name and talk to him at night. Sometimes she screams his name and begs him not to leave. You should know. Sometimes she talks to you, too."

Henry knew that was impossible and could not imagine Kiri favoring one child. "When did this begin?"

"When Michael Thomas got his name. He came into the house and told me Mom said I had to call him Michael from then on. And a few days later I heard them at night... in her room. And other nights too. She complained about me. 'Michael, help me. I don't know what to do about Katie.' 'Michael, our nest is too heavy.' 'Please help me, Michael.' 'Henry, I can't go on!' She never invites me to talk at night."

Poor little imp. Henry shook his head. She'd spent the last seven years living her mother's nightmares. Her confusion struck Henry and disturbed him. Michael the husband or Michael the son? There was no mistake this time. Katie must have heard her mother calling for her father, a clear signal to him that Michael was still very present in Kiri's life. But *he* was there too. Now to convince her doubting daughter.

"Did you ever peek in on them when they talked?"

She shook her head.

"Did you ever see me in your mother's room or look into your brother's room to see if it was empty when you heard voices? Did you ever ask either of them about their conversations?"

She shook her head again.

"Did you hear your brother's voice or mine... or only your mother?"

She lowered her eyes sheepishly. "Just Mom."

Henry did not want to say the words because he did not want to believe them—that Kiri kept Michael alive in her heart and mind by sharing her present life with him. But he now knew for certain that she depended on him, too. "Katie, your mother was talking to your *dad* Michael, not your brother."

The young girl's stubbornness reared up. "But he's dead! You can't talk to a dead person. I've tried. I talk to Grandpa sometimes, and he doesn't answer me. Neither does Grandma when I talk to her. So how can Mom talk to my dad?"

"One still maintains a relationship with a dead person after he is gone. She talks to your dad whenever she's worried or upset... or when she can't understand why you are so cold to her when she needs you now more than ever. She prays he'll answer... but he never does." Henry explained as gently as he could. "I'm sorry to say, Katie, you've been mistaken all this time. You've listened in on your mother's nightmares."

Tears streamed down her face onto his pant leg. "I didn't know parents had nightmares, too. I thought Mom didn't love me."

"Of course she does, more than anything in this world. She'd give her life for you and your brother." He took her elbow to edge her nearer. "Climb up here with us."

She sniffed and wiped her cheeks. "There's not room."

"That never stopped you before." He smiled and shifted his hips so she could squeeze next to him. "Now that you understand you were mistaken, what are you going to do about it?"

She stared into his kindly eyes. "Tell her I'm sorry?"

"Anything else?"

"Maybe give her a kiss."

"Anything else?"

She hesitated, then with a slight shake of her head said, "I can't tell her I love her. I couldn't stand it if I said 'I love you' and saw in her eyes that she didn't love me back."

Henry understood exactly what naïve Katie felt. Maybe Michael's ghost, as well as his own fear of the visions that might arise at the most intimate of moments, held him back from forging a closer relationship with Kiri—telling her how he felt and what he wanted for their lives. If he saw in her eyes that she did not feel the same, he would be devastated and could not continue their familiarity. Not only did he fear losing Kiri, he did not want to lose the family—the children—the life... the history they gave him.

He used the hand wrapped around Kiri to tilt Katie's chin upward. "Knowing that *you*—the light of her life—love her will help your mother heal faster than anything. Why don't you try?"

She pulled the quilt away with her fingers and smoothed her mother's limp hair away from her face. She cupped her hand to whisper in her mother's ear, "I'm sorry, Mom. I love you so much. Please get better. I love you." She brushed her lips across her mother's cheek and heard a whisper in her own ear.

"I love you, dearest Katie... more than you will ever know." Their gazes locked for an instant before Kiri succumbed to more disturbed sleep.

Katie's fingers searched for her mother's and clung to them. Her thumb found a home between Henry's buttonholes, and mother/daughter foreheads touched gently to rest on his chest.

Henry leaned back with a brooding sigh. He should be the happiest man alive spending the night with his arms around the two people he loved most in the world, but his inability to express his innermost longings nagged at him. Three heads together. Three points on a circle joining them. *Love spoken, love answered, love undeclared.* Until he summoned the courage of a fifteen-year-old girl, Henry's life would not advance along the circuit. He closed his eyes to join them in slumber, thankful for every moment they shared with him.

The blackbird perched on the corner of the mantle and watched over three wounded hearts trying to mend. At the first wink of dawn it disappeared to the lower floor and out the broken door, leaving only a black feather behind.

CHAPTER 26

The house on Quincy Street was abuzz on New Year's Eve, 2032/2033. Three giddy teenage girls giggled their way through primping for the gala evening in their honor—their sixteenth birthday social. Not all three were sixteen, but that did not stop the trio from finagling a joint celebration from Kiri.

"We want a party together. I'm already sixteen and shouldn't have to wait 'til spring. Polly and Kendra don't turn until next summer, but if we hold our party on New Year's Eve I'll be in my sixteenth birth year and once all the horns and whistles sound at midnight, they'll be in their sixteenth birth year too. You'll have only one party to sponsor instead of three. It's a win/win, Mom. Pleeease!"

Kiri gave up trying to poke holes in her daughter's convoluted logic many months ago. As long as Meghan and Kurt gave permission and the girls followed the established rules—chaperones, no drugs, alcohol or electronic devices, and permission slips for all guests—she had no basis for denying her daughter's plea. "You may find it hard to gather enough friends that night since it is a popular one for parties."

"No problem there, Mom. Everyone wants to come to ours, and with three of us celebrating we can invite three times as many friends!" Katie hugged her mother and ran up the stairs to deliver the good news to the other two triplets awaiting the word from cyberspace.

That was six weeks ago, and tonight was the night. Meghan and Phillip shared a drink with Henry while Kiri called Kurt and Tanya to join them by video. "You know we had to leave the ski slopes early to make this connection," her brother complained. "And a bowl game is due to start soon. Any way you can hurry the parade of party girls along?"

"Not a chance. Happy New Year to you, too."

"Oh yeah. Greetings everyone. Any snow in Dublin today?'

Kiri shook her head but was interrupted by Michael Thomas who returned from the party room in the aquacenter. "Sure is. Not outside, of course, but Devin and I have all kinds of winter going on inside." At his mother's raised eyebrows, he explained. "During my transition year internship with Devin, we explored augmented reality—creating holograms like the light sabers in that old movie about galaxies way out in space. He 'borrowed' some equipment from the network, and we set up filament screens outside the windows to reflect scenes you won't believe."

The self-assured young man paused to confirm that he had an audience. "When you look through the north windows, you see a quaint Irish village scene—falling snow piling up on thatch roofs, smoke curling from chimneys, horse-drawn carts clip-clopping by, all seemingly real as if you were watching the tele. The wall opposite refreshments is a giant fireplace that crackles and hisses. You can stick your hand in and not get burned because all the magic is projected onto a very fine screen there, too. If you look south toward the pool, it appears as a skating rink with a brightly lit Christmas tree at the far end and lots of skaters. The fireworks programmed for midnight are phenomenal and won't be seen or heard by the neighbors."

"You invited a bunch of robots to your sister's party?" Kurt asked.

"No way. My people are real people—at least they appear that way. No jerky movements from this guy. As soon as I graduate in the spring, I'll work full time perfecting my bodies for the net...." He caught a harsh warning stare from Henry. "I superimposed celebrities' faces on the skaters, so that will draw a laugh. I'm trying to create figures that are free of a screen... that could dance in the center of this room, for instance and fit in with everybody else... like Mom and Dad. If someone tried to cut in on them, like Uncle Henry, his hand would disappear into the image. I can age people too, like making Dad the same age as Mom is now. Next come voices. What do you think of that, Mom?"

Kiri did not know how to respond. She could not imagine an older Michael and did not know if she wanted to. She always pictured her husband as the robust young hunk she married. To be in his arms but not feel his touch or inhale his scent was unthinkable. The notion distracted her from the evening's excitement... but not for long.

Giggles at the top of the stairs heralded the parade of party girls. First came Polly, the youngest by a month, in Irish green appropriate for the season and with neckline and hem suitable for a fifteen-year-old. Kendra followed in medium blue, like the bright sky of a Colorado summer, and neckline and hem comparable to Polly's. Both sets of parents oohed and ahed at their comely young daughters.

As Katie began her descent, Michael Thomas placed his hands on his mother's shoulders and whispered. "Mom, she's beautiful!"

Kiri could not agree more. Michael's boxcar baby was a knockout. Her freckles faded, her ginger kinks calmed to golden waves and her curves found their proper places. Her light lilac, silk chiffon dress was more daring than the other two. The ruffled neck and hemline angled from left to right exposing a bare right shoulder and left knee like her father's dimpled one. The style accentuated her mature figure. Her hair was pulled severely from her face upward into a mass of curls covering the crown of her head and held by a circle of violet baby orchids with blue edges. Only her daddy's curl escaped onto her forehead. The rest of her tresses were left free to dance with her. The similarity to Kiri's stunning appearance the night of the Club Ball more than twenty years earlier was too striking to ignore.

Katie twirled in a pirouette in front of her mother. "How do I look? Please don't be angry. I only wanted to look pretty like you."

Kiri cupped her daughter's face in her hands. "You are lovely times ten. Where did you ever find the dress?"

"I sneaked yours from the back of your closet and took it to one of the ladies up the road to copy." Her lively eyes darted to the photo on the wall—the one of her mother and father dressed for the Ball. "You were so beautiful... and *sparkly*... that night. I wanted to be like you."

Flattered by her daughter's turnaround over the past year, Kiri took the bait. "Aurora Kathryn O'Connell, are you trying to con me out of my compass necklace?"

She batted her eyelashes coyly at her mother. "You have to admit, it would be the perfect accessory to highlight the gold in my hair and my bright blue eyes. Just this once, pleeease?"

Kiri fingered her rings and glanced again at the photo, then back at her daughter teetering between youth and maturity. "Just this once."

Katie hugged her mother—but not close enough to muss her hair. "I knew you'd say yes!" She stepped back with an ear-to-ear smile and opened her hand to reveal the antique gold ornament embedded with tiny diamonds and sapphires. She half-twirled dramatically for her mother to hang the cherished object around her neck, eliciting titters from the others.

Picture taking began in earnest with Michael Thomas doing the honors, first of the rainbow of party girls, then of Kendra with her proud parents via video, then Polly with hers appearing like grandparents. Phillip took over duties for Katie's family, first of the siblings—the tall, dark, handsome young man with solemn demeanor and mysterious blue-green eyes standing a head above his effervescent, petite sister. A shot of the spirited young miss and her nostalgic mother was followed by one of the three O'Connells. Katie insisted on one with Henry—a damsel and her faithful protector—and finally, one of her family—Katie, Michael Thomas, Kiri... and Henry.

"You girls better hurry on. I see vehicles turning down the road," Meghan said.

The three young maidens rushed to the door, smoothed their dresses, pinched their cheeks and shared a last giggle before exiting as young ladies. Katie squeezed Henry's hand and gave him a coquettish wink. "I'm counting on a dance with you, Prince Charming."

Kurt and Tanya signed off from Colorado. "Thanks, Sis, for helping our little girl make some more memories—your symbolic gesture for the year."

Meghan and Phillip followed with polite thanks, then took their leave. "Give us a ring when you want us to fetch Polly tomorrow."

"You two ought to pop in at the party later on. Take a look at my handiwork," Michael Thomas said. Kiri and Henry shared a secret glance. They did not have to go to the party to experience it. They planned on monitoring the affair through the surveillance system as soon as her son left for his own shindig. "May I take Dad's sports car tonight, pleeease?" he asked, mimicking his sister. His mother laughed and waved him away.

Kiri sank onto the sofa and motioned for Henry to sit beside her. "My children are grown and almost gone, Henry. When did that happen?"

He draped an arm around her shoulders and smiled. "When you blinked." They listened for the sound of the racer back out the drive and roar up the road—a sound rarely heard anymore. "What say we skip the bowl game and tune in to a holiday drama tonight?" he joked as he rose to gather up snacks and aged brew.

Michael Thomas sold himself short in describing the special effects he and Devin created. The venue's ambiance was truly one of a warm, old-fashioned Irish holiday. Gus provided a frothy spiced cider, and Frank was on hand to assure it was not spiked. The table was laden with meat pasties and other traditional eats. The teashop prepared sweets and its specialty holiday cakes. Brendan and Connor and their wives agreed to chaperone. Polly was their half-sister, after all, and their responsibility. Meggie and her husband volunteered. "I'm very good at consoling young girls whose favorite guys have wandering eyes," she explained. Other cousins minded the chaperones' small children. Every so often the music master took a break and turned on some fiddle music, inviting the young folk to try their feet at the old steps.

At one point, Frank came at a young man from behind and nearly crushed his wrist until he dropped the contents of his hand to the floor. "What's the big deal?" the lad shouted. "A guy needs a little nip to make a party special."

Katie was on him immediately. "*I* make this party special. No nips allowed here. Mom's rules."

"What is she? A dinosaur from the last century?" he asked, disgruntled.

"Don't you bad-mouth my mom. She's the best! If this party isn't 'nippy' enough for you, go find another one." Katie swirled away and onto the arm of another good-looking guy who did not need additives to enjoy her company.

"Confirmation," Henry said from his spot in the living room.

"Confirmation of what?" Kiri asked. "That I'm a dinosaur or back in my daughter's good graces?"

"A little of both," he laughed, squeezing her tighter.

The two agreed that the action onscreen was more exciting than any movie. Midway through the evening they overheard Katie explain that her Uncle Henry would arrive any minute to whirl her around the floor. "He's a very good dancer," she said.

"I thought parents were not allowed," her partner of the moment replied.

"Uncle Henry is way better than parents. He's my family!"

Kiri turned to Henry. "I think that's your cue, Prince Charming."

"Surely she wasn't serious. This is a party for teens. I'm over sixty. I'll be an embarrassment."

"Katie will be embarrassed if you don't show... and tremendously disappointed. You've been present for almost every major event in her life—including school plays and gymnastics competitions. Tonight is *the* most important in her eyes." She poked him in the ribs and teased, "I think this calls for donning your crown and your dancing shoes."

"But I'm not properly dressed."

"Take another look at that crowd. For the guys, casual is definitely in."

"Will you come with?"

Kiri shook her head vigorously. "Can you imagine Katie's reaction if I did? My place in her good graces would evaporate. I'll watch your missteps from here."

Henry chuckled and resigned himself to keeping time to the day's pop hits. He gave Kiri a peck on the cheek and left by the front door.

Kiri was so involved in eavesdropping on conversations that she did not realize how long it was before Henry appeared—a good half-hour—and a charming prince he was. Dressed in a dark gray suit and the lilac silk tie he wore to the father/daughter dance, he cut a refined and dignified figure, an image any young man there might covet. His salt-and-pepper hair added a measure of distinction and maturity to the handsome man. He must have gone home to change, she realized, instead of straight to the party. He never liked appearing in public in casual attire.

Katie squealed when she noticed him and ran—then slowed to a brisk walk—to take his arm and announce him. "*This* is my Uncle Henry. He came especially to dance with me." Henry flushed but played the well-mannered escort and led her to the floor. "I won't have to dance on your feet tonight," she smiled at the man who towered over her.

To his relief, the song had a gentle rhythm and words he could understand. Katie's face and eyes glowed with adoration for him, and he looked on her with loving devotion. The baby who clung to him the first night of her life now danced in his arms as a graceful young woman.

As Kiri watched Polly, then Kendra, claim their turns with him, her mind drifted to her first dances with Michael at Copley Castle their first New Year's Eve and with Henry two nights later at the Ball. He was the better dancer of the two, she remembered. They moved easily and naturally together. Then, as now, he displayed the grace and manner of a true gentleman but lacked the name and background to claim that title.

At the end of a second dance with Katie, Henry bowed and kissed her hand, saying "Sorry. I must rush. I have a pumpkin waiting." He shrugged apologetically toward a lineup of disappointed young ladies and departed.

"Isn't he the greatest!" By the time Katie finished her exclamation, he walked into the house through the kitchen door.

Kiri met him with a kiss. "Very well done!"

"I need a drink!" He pulled off his suit coat, removed his tie and unbuttoned his collar. After a long swig of his favorite stout he said, "I wasn't made for a group of teens."

"Oh, but you were. Every young guy there got a well-needed lesson in chivalry tonight." She wrapped her arms around his neck. "Are you made for a grateful mother?"

He wrapped his arms around her waist. "What does she have in mind?"

"A dance would be nice." She smiled and swayed with the music. "Or two or three. We haven't done this in years."

The couple made up for lost time by finding a rhythm meant for them in every number played. They moved in closer and closer to one another until not a fairy's breath could pass between them. "This is so much better than cuddling in the recliner," she said.

"We do fit well together, don't we?" he replied.

"We need to spend evenings like this more often."

"Now that the children are off on their own so frequently, perhaps we can… even go 'out' from time to time," he smiled.

She sang softly, inviting him to follow Presley's lead and take her hand, her life, as she could no longer resist falling in love.

A loud explosion jolted them apart. They turned toward the video screen to view the fireworks extravaganza and the excitement of the party guests, then to one another to share an ardent embrace and Happy New Year kiss. "Maybe this year will be ours for a change," Kiri said staring deeply into his mysterious gray eyes.

Henry reacted passionately, eager to prove her right. He welcomed Kiri's arms around his neck pulling him near again. She placed one hand on his cheek and with the back of the other, caressed his neck and jaw. A strange sensation sent a shiver down his spine—the touch of her rings… her wedding rings… pressing against his flesh.

Twenty-fourth Anniversary Year: Once again I'm on a plane bound for Ireland, this time after finalizing Mom's estate. And once again I cannot sleep so will play a little catch-up. I note that I have not recorded major events on the greater family front for the last 2 years. Yikes! Where does the time go?

Bitsy and I attended 9 weddings and almost as many births as christenings. Funny how I never seem to run out of spirit water. Thomas' grandchildren are sprouting kids everywhere. Following are Marriages (Births) in birth order: Brendan (3), Grace (3), Connor (2), Ronan (2), Caitlín (3), Gemma (2), Fiona (1), Meggie (1)—she's very good with her baby, Breeda (0). Gus—a son! and daughter #5, Doyle—a daughter, Devin—a son.

Graduation: Erin, Eileen, Nora, Niall, Liam, Kean and Michael Thomas (Yes!)

Death: Paddy, our faithful neighbor. He had to be near 100. His housemate found him passed away in his rocking chair facing the window with his binoculars around his neck—on duty 'til the end. We moved his housemate to another apartment further up the road and leveled the house in preparation for a parking lot. Business at the aquacenter is booming, so I need the parking to keep vehicles off the road. The house required too many updates to make it economically feasible to repair for new tenants or for sale. I will plant a hedge in front so the lot will not be unsightly.

Other: Michael Thomas went right to work on a project for Devin, so he did not make the trip to Colorado after graduation. He is enrolled in Trinity for the fall and told me what his major is. When my brain swirled with his "design your own program" description, he said, "That's okay, Mom. Don't bother yourself now. Someday you'll understand." He has a job waiting for him when he graduates from Trinity. He will move into the attic studio in Henry's building as soon as Niall moves out. He's really excited to be "on his own." I suggested we install a monitoring system in the studio, but Henry said NO!

Katie and Polly came with me as soon as school was out but stayed only a couple of weeks. Kendra returned with them so the three could work at the pool together to earn money for clothe$ for fall. Katie finished her transition year. Much to Meghan's dismay, Polly talked her into skipping a transition year so she and Katie can attend Senior Cycle together and graduate the same year. I don't know how long the triplets will last with two of them in the same class now and one far away and a year behind. We'll see.

With the children so busy, Henry turned his attentions to Sara Lamb. She is a computer inside a thirteen-year-old body, so he is working with her school counselor to develop a program that will challenge her. She is already taller than Bitsy and inherited her mother's sweet soul but not her talent for music. In fact, no one yet can match Bitsy's flair. She spends more and more time at the hospital and at nearby homes attending to hospice patients, but she still gives water therapy to disabled children. She mesmerizes them.

Henry and I share brief moments of affection as we pass on life's motorway going opposite directions. For the last few months he greets me differently. He takes my left hand and caresses it or kisses it, and then I get either a polite hug or a loving one depending on his mood. Wish I could figure out what causes the mood, but he never reveals much personal. I thought this year would finally be a good one for us.

CHAPTER 27

A barricade blocked the progress of a taxi as it turned down Quincy Street. Neighbors crowded the roadway to watch a covey of O'Connell cousins, spouses and friends maneuver wheelbarrows and crates through a maze of small earth-moving equipment. No one noticed the cause for the hubbub alight from the taxi and wheel her bag to the walk.

Kiri checked the calendar on her smartwatch, certain that she scheduled paving the parking lot for the middle of the month, not the beginning. Her agenda confirmed the appointment for two weeks hence, so she shouldered into the throng to discover the reason for the buzz of activity.

"So nice to see young folk workin' together on a project to improve the neighborhood."

" 'Tis a fine thing we're *all* doin.'"

" 'Twere our idea, remember, to make a garden there."

"Much better than the car park Mrs. O planned."

"I don't mind walkin' a few steps more if it means replacin' an eyesore with a spot o' beauty."

"Paddy turned in his grave when she tore his house down, for sure."

"Soon he'll be smilin' at us from his side o' the flowers."

The neighbor ladies shared an endearing chuckle while focusing their attention on the lively bustle across from Kiri's house. She gathered from their conversation that the parking lot was a no go and wondered who made the decision to replace it and with what. She did not have long to speculate, for she spotted Katie on a ladder in the middle of all the commotion pointing and waving her hands, shaking her head and directing traffic as if she were conducting an orchestra of cats.

Kiri snaked through the crowd of onlookers with her sunglasses on and her hat pulled down to escape detection. Her plan—to enter through the back and watch the project from the upper floor windows until she could corner the usurper of her authority—was stymied when her daughter caught sight of her and screeched.

"Maa...meee! This is a surprise! Hide your eyes!" Katie slid down the ladder and sprinted to push her mother through the door. "You're not supposed to be here yet! Uncle Henry is picking you up at the airport *tonight* and will bring you here for the grand opening."

"That explains why he didn't show up this morning and I had to take a taxi. Where is he?"

"He was here watching over us all day yesterday and said he had an appointment this morning in the west but would be back in time to meet you."

Kiri checked texts sent, and there it was. "Henry. Arriving 10 p.m." How could she make such a mistake? Mind and/or fingers losing touch, she guessed. She showed Katie the erroneous message. "Maybe *you* should let Uncle Henry know I've arrived." She watched her daughter's eyes roll. "But that doesn't explain the major project across the road that I do *not* remember approving."

"Hi, Mom." Michael Thomas greeted with a hug to placate his mother. "You're not supposed to be here, you know."

"Well, I am, and I'm mystified by who gave the authority to turn my parking lot into a garden party." She focused a severe stare on each child.

"You did.... No, we did and said you did," Katie tried to explain. "But we knew you would say yes when they asked, so we said it for you." She smiled brightly.

"Who asked what when?"

"The neighbors. A group of them came over late one afternoon to talk to you, but of course you weren't here, but they thought you were when they saw me, and Michael Thomas was home too, so we asked them what the problem was and they said they wanted to buy Paddy's lot from you and make a memory garden there because they'd rather look at flowers than cars. Since so many of their friends have passed, they feel like they are intruding when they come to visit our garden where they planted flowers in their honor. We knew you wouldn't say yes or no right away. You'd think about how to satisfy everybody."

"My turn." Michael Thomas waved a hand in his sister's face. "The problem was this: You needed parking space for your growing business. The neighbors didn't want to look at it and were willing to contribute to a solution instead of just complain behind your back. What they didn't understand was that you would never sell that piece of property even if they could meet your price."

Katie broke in. "Uncle Henry was very good about helping us. Over dinner, he came up with the 'find a different space' idea. We put our heads together, measured Paddy's lot for how many vehicles would fit there, and then it came to us."

Her brother took over. "If we broadened the alleyway at the back of each lot up and down the road, we could equal the space needed. We asked Brendan to investigate property owners and procedures for a land swap kind of deal—shortened lots for garden area. Turns out…"

Kiri dropped her head into her hands. What he was about to reveal was a secret she had kept for more than twenty years and was not ready to share with her children.

"…that besides your owning this house and the aquacenter, there are only two property owners along both sides of the road: the agent who owns Uncle Henry's building and the house on either side of it … and some organization called the Michael O'Connell Foundation! When were you planning on telling us about that, *Mrs. Michael O'Connell?*" He aimed a hard stare and set jaw in her direction.

Kiri was saved by Gemma who hurried in the kitchen door carrying a box filled with tools. "Excuse me. Just going upstairs to begin the tile work in the bedroom. Aunt Kiri! You're not supposed to be here!"

"Believe me, I want to be invisible." After Gemma disappeared, Kiri asked. "What tile work in the bedroom?'

"That comes later in the story," Katie said. "Once we figured out that you owned all their properties and could do anything you wanted no matter how the neighbors felt, we decided to float the land swap idea anyway to see what they said—three meters from the back of each lot in exchange for the inside perimeter of Paddy's fenced lot. We keep the middle for another house or for our family—our choice. No vegetables. Only flowers, and they take care of their own beds. Eighty per cent of the neighbors would be obliged to sign a Community Agreement—Brendan's idea to make the swap seem official."

"The neighbors agreed. We could have done it the easy way—said no, or just *given* them the perimeter ground, but they are all proud people and wanted some ownership of the project. That's the short version. What do you think?" Michael Thomas asked.

The only thing Kiri could think was that her husband would have done exactly that—found a way to accommodate the neighbors while maintaining their sense of worth. "I think…"

Ronan came in the back and called for Gemma. "We need you out here. We're ready to unload more paving stones and want to do it in the right place. Hi, Aunt Kiri. You're not supposed to be here yet."

"I'll hide out upstairs as soon as I understand what you are creating across the road."

"A labyrinth kind of footpath with reject pieces of Connemara marble to form the boundary between neighbors and family. Gemma has each piece labeled as to location. We're about halfway through. Then we'll border it with rolls of grass, so we should be done by the time you arrive tonight," he said with a wry grin.

"I better go help. I'm pretty good at aligning them. See you later, Mom." Michael Thomas followed the other two out.

"You'll love it when you see the finished product." Katie barely contained her excitement. "My brother and I chose memory garden instead of house. Buildings are too unemotional. Our park will be a beautiful extension of our home once Gemma sets the tiles for the house and connector."

"House and connector?"

"I'll explain later. I've got to go too. We're really busy. Don't come outside. You're not supposed to be here yet," she warned as she flew out the door after the others.

Kiri settled herself at her desk upstairs and peered out the window at the figure taking shape. Three octagons decreasing in size formed concentric circuits of polished green stones. A narrower path connected them, creating one winding walk to the center. That footway separated generous flowerbeds waiting for plantings to represent regeneration, rebirth and renewal, the spiritual essence of the geometric symbol itself. Worker bees cut away a strip of walkway and curbing on both sides of the road and roadbed in between, to lay with ancient green slabs. They tiled over her front stoop to the doorway thereby connecting the two lots.

Bright afternoon sunshine turned to dusky summer eve. Activity slowed, then halted, as the guys and gals cleaned up and brought chairs from the aquacenter. Breeda arrived with her catering van and food cart loaded with bangers and smoked fish, barn brack and soda bread, fresh fruits and veggies, and cheese and apple tarts. Drink, laughter and backslaps abounded. The fiddles came out. Bitsy added her harp to their music. Henry showed up to give praises and congratulations to the community effort. Michael Thomas and Katie exuded pride and gave thanks for the group's accomplishment. Kiri watched from her window.

She heard footsteps behind her and felt hands on her shoulders. "Why so misty-eyed?" Henry asked.

"I blinked again, and my little birds flew the nest. Michael Thomas and Katie are every inch their father's children, ready to carry on his work, and I am now a spectator to the lives they were meant to live." She swiveled her chair and watched carefully as he greeted her by taking her left hand and avoided her rings with a soft caress followed by a polite hug. "Something tells me you played a large part in today's production."

He sighed. "Not really. I planted the first seed—find a different space—and the children jumped on it. They became energized… inspired even… as they bounced ideas off one another. Then they stared at each other and with one voice shouted, 'a great idea just popped into my head!' I merely scowled when I thought they veered off-track a time or two. I didn't think you required a canopy or hover chair to cross the road just yet."

Kiri laughed at the thought and gazed through the window again as Henry drew up a chair beside her. "Off-site parking is quite practical for today's vehicles," he said. "Your clients can arrive at the center and program their cars to find spaces in the alleyway and return for them at a specific time.

"If you're worried about expense, the work in back will cost more than the garden. The children commandeered their cousins and cousins' contacts for materials, equipment and labor. The project grew into a family/community one with a couple of major issues decided by the group. Defining a boundary between neighbors and family was one."

"Who came up with a large octagon for a border?"

"Katie. Gemma proposed a circle with a triquetra in the center to give a Celtic feel, but a few days later Katie popped up with the design you now see. Bitsy suggested the green marble like the harps in the bedroom—whatever that means—and then the battle was on for whose planting would occupy the center. The family proposed Thomas, its head. The neighbors objected. Then everyone shouted together, 'Michael!' His vision transformed the tired, older neighborhood into a vibrant village. Problem solved.

"The latest conflict was over *what* to plant in the center to honor him. The neighbors suggested a fir tree like the one in your yard. Paddy loved to tell the tale of the day you two drove up with it poking up from the back of the sports car and of how you wrestled to get it in the ground. Katie objected. '*Our dad* would never want to stand taller than anyone else and have his shadow fall on them. *He* would consider everyone equal.' None of the family could remember what Michael's favorite flower might be—a traditional Irish one, for sure—until Meggie recounted her literal interpretation of 'not steppin' on any bloomin' shamrocks!' Everyone laughed and agreed that you will plant shamrocks in his memory tonight but that you can add something later if you want."

"I'll plant shamrocks tonight?"

Henry nodded. "Michael's is first in the center, then Paddy's arrangement outside the octagons where he sat in his rocking chair by his window as watchman and leader of the neighbors. His binoculars hang on the fence to mark the spot. Tomorrow a crew will transplant all the others from your back garden as determined by their friends."

"Your mother's lilac?"

"Katie settled that. 'Henry is family, so she goes with us. You don't get her!' No one dared question her decision."

Kiri chuckled at her daughter's undiplomatic response. "Have you chosen her spot?"

Now, Henry grew misty-eyed. "I'm thinking about it." He rose and took her right hand. "Are you ready?"

"For what?"

"It's time to drive you home from the airport. Be surprised, remember. I'm parked in the alleyway. How are you at climbing fences?"

*   *   *

Kiri gazed out her upper window at the near dark and near empty garden across the road. Following the two primary plantings and an ancient prayer of dedication—"May the fairies be kind and bless us now and then"—the neighborhood crowd disbursed quickly. She noticed the last to leave, Brendan, linger beside his favorite uncle's small patch of green and white. He removed a tiny item from his pocket, ran a thin bracket through it and pressed it into the earth beneath the bunch of shamrocks. He patted the ground lovingly and departed. *The memorials begin. Michael no longer belongs only to me.*

Katie bounced up the stairs and hugged her mother from behind. "The garden is more beautiful than I imagined! I can't wait to see how rain makes the green paving stones glisten and come alive. I hope you'll grow to love it and not be angry with us for too long."

"How could I be angry? You and your brother created a serene space for the neighborhood to enjoy, and I don't begrudge them the ground. But I am puzzled by your decision to proceed with a major project without my knowledge or consent." Her raised eyebrows made the point. "Such a large garden for us seems a bit frivolous."

"I figured that would be your reaction. That's why we didn't tell you. And frivolous is exactly the right word. I've never seen you let yourself go. You are so serious and practical that such a great idea would never occur to you—to create something purely for pleasure. You have one dress for weddings and christenings and one for funerals. You've only gone overboard with a feather collection hidden in a drawer. I bet you haven't changed your hairstyle in years or painted your toenails purple or danced barefoot in the rain in your blue ball gown.

"The last few years have been especially hard on you—and I haven't helped. You need a break from sad. You miss Grandma. I do too, every day. You can look out to her flowers from the deck in back, but you cannot distinguish *one* flower that represents her. When we plant one perfect columbine for her tomorrow, you'll feel what I mean. Grandfather used to tell us that we are all connected. You say the same, but you don't believe it. You need a physical symbol of that spiritual connection he talked about. That's why we joined the two lots—so you will feel the garden and its spirits are an extension of our home."

"Taking out roadway to make a point?"

"Think, Mom. Don't you know your Irish geology? Heat and pressure formed that green marble more than 700 million years ago. A little traffic won't hurt it. The roadway will break up long before it does. And it adds beauty. You'll see tomorrow when we transplant the rest of the memorials."

"How did you con your cousins into helping?"

"If you think about it—and I'm sure you haven't—my cousins are as much a part of this neighborhood as we are. All of them have spent more happy times together *here* than anywhere else—more than Grandfather's house, even. The neighbors encouraged them as they grew up, and as kids they helped the neighbors—just like family. I told the cousins about the garden and reminded them that they would attend more funerals than weddings in the coming years, and visiting a gorgeous garden was far more pleasant than tripping over old stones in an ancient graveyard. Spirits would much rather hang around a flower than a rock. The neighbor ladies believe in the old magic—that spirits reside in all things natural. They say the flowers whisper at night 'so don't be sharin' too many secrets with 'em!'

"After church tomorrow morning, a few cousins will help with the transplanting: Connor and his wife, Meggie and her husband, Michael

Thomas, me, Polly and Kendra, of course, and Kean. I think he's sweet on Kendra. He suggested you throw a pool party for all the helpers like you used to after summer cleanup. I think he wants to check out Kendra in a bathing suit!"

Mother and daughter shared a giggle as Katie paraded around the sitting room with a swimsuit model's strut. "So, what's the verdict, Mom? Thumbs up or thumbs down?"

"On Kendra in a bathing suit or your project?"

Katie propped her hands on her hips and rolled her eyes. "The garden, of course."

"You and your brother have done yourselves proud—well-planned, well-executed and supported by sound reasoning... with just enough frivolity... but I'm still curious about how you came up with the octagon."

"Gemma—our art teacher cousin—designed a triquetra in a circle but said it would be hard to replicate because angled slabs don't create smooth curves. She said a square would work better."

Katie paused and posed dramatically to reenact the bizarre scene. "On a drizzly day, I stood right where we are now and squinted my eyes to imagine what both might look like. The sun suddenly burst through and cast a shadow of the skylight in your bedroom onto the bare lot across the road—a perfect octagon, a compromise between a square and a circle, and the roof made a second shadow leading from the figure straight to our front door."

By all the laws of physics, light reflection and refraction, Kiri knew that such an image was impossible. Katie did not see a shadow. She perceived a mystical model of the stone foundation of Paula's house in Colorado.

"In an instant, the vision disappeared but an idea to recreate that design just popped into my head like... like..."

"Like a fairy whispering in your ear?"

"Exactly!"

With her exhausted teens in bed, Kiri prepared for the same. She was about to climb in when her eyes focused on tiles around the perimeter of the bedroom where molding used to be. She pulled on her robe and followed their trail along the walls and down the stairs to the front door. She hesitated. *I can't go out like this.* She crossed the threshold. *Of course I can. If the memory garden is an extension of my home, I can walk over there any way I want!*

She peered into the dark. Did she need a flashlight? No. Her bare feet would prevent her from straying. *But I do need a bottle of Michael's spirit water to christen the footpath.* She retrieved one from the pantry, turned up the collar of her robe and stepped from the house into the fog. She trod carefully, her toes gripping the glassy surface of stone slabs. She sprinkled water along the way watching the marble glisten, then disappear beneath soft wisps of fog. She followed the walkway as it folded back on itself through three circuits until it opened onto the center space.

Kiri knelt and listened for the whisper of spirits in the flowers. She felt the ground beneath the shamrock to discover what Brendan placed there and found a worn bootlace knotted around the bracket. A grown man now, he no longer needed a constant reminder. He knew he could visit this place again when he sought his uncle's counsel. She replaced the memento and began a chat within earshot of the blossoms.

"Michael, you trickster you. I was sure you inspired the creation of this memory garden until the design for a triquetra inscribed in a circle was rejected. Three points on a circle—like the Celtic ornament you left me representing mother, daughter and granddaughter—was a design with a flaw, wasn't it? No mother in the picture. Paula's spirit is not with us and until it is, the puzzle will not be complete.

"Katie misinterpreted your message. The garden is not a replica of *our* home but of my *mother's*. You designed our bedroom to pattern Paula's house—a fusion of O'Connell Celt and Koyle Coloradan, you said, a sanctuary for me on this side of the Atlantic. But Mom's sanctuary was never on this side of the ocean. Hers was always on the other, and until we create one here in her name, her conflicted spirit will not rest. The missing piece of the puzzle is the columbine I'll plant tomorrow so I can send her my love everyday on a whisper."

Kiri readjusted her footing and gave the earth around the shamrock another pat. "Please send me a sign that I understand your message... anything." Her resigned smile revealed that she did understand. There would be no message.

Henry, unable to sleep, walked up the road toward the new garden. He wanted a last look before planting time. He chose the farthest bed on the east side of the family section between Michael's and the small house next to his own apartment as the perfect spot for the lilac. His mother would like that. As he approached, he spied a figure clad in white—Kiri pulling a soft robe tight against the chill. He stepped into the shadows not chancing to frighten or disturb her and listened to a very private, one-sided conversation.

"We've done it, Michael—together. The economy of our corner of the city is sound. Your vision for modern village life spreads beyond our neighborhood. Your nieces and nephews, now scattered over the island, will return to this spot time and again with their offspring to remember the love and joy you wrapped around them. Our two beautiful children are grown and have learned your lessons well. Exactly like you, they will hold your extended family of devoted young people together as caring, compassionate citizens of the world. Your legacy will survive."

Kiri paused for a deep, longing sigh. "Michael, will you let me go now… please?" She sprinkled the rest of the spirit water on the shamrock, ran her fingers through the earth beneath it and turned up a black feather. She removed her wedding rings, kissed them, touched them to the white flowers… and slipped them into her pocket with the feather.

Henry stood at the corner of the garden and watched her move through the fog to her house. *Maybe this will be a good year for us after all.*

CHAPTER 28

Kiri padded to the north window of her sitting room in bathrobe and slippers and blew a kiss to the columbine in the memory garden. She finished with a whispered "I love you, Mom," as she had almost every morning for the last two and a half years. In that time, the neighbors' perimeter plantings increased to form a lovely border around the family area that had not lost any members since its christening. Only the columbine, shamrock, lilac and a lily for Thomas like the ones on Paula's hillside in Colorado spread to fill their plots luxuriantly. After a moment's meditation, she dashed into her busy day—two days, in fact, of family celebration centered around her son's twenty-first birthday.

She wrapped one of Paula's woolen shawls around her shoulders, grabbed a cup of hot tea, her journal and a pen and strode out to her chair beneath Aurora, the wounded evergreen tree. She set aside her twenty-sixth wedding anniversary specifically to catch up on her documentation of the years racing by. Tomorrow she and others would commemorate her son's entry into adulthood.

Twenty-Sixth Anniversary Year: Birth: Son #2 to Gus and 5 more christenings.

Marriage: Anne's Aidan and Erin, and Tommy's Eileen. Brendan is now a father to three and, at 35, a year older than his uncle at his death. Seven more nieces and nephews have been married longer than the three years Michael and I had together, making them the experts on achieving connubial bliss. I have no experience to help them through turbulent times, only a shoulder, an ear, a box of tissues and an open door.

Death: 4 more neighbors

Graduation: Riona, Katie, Polly and Kendra. Only Kody and Sara to go.

Divorce: Emily, from Stephen Flynn. The whole family breathed a sigh of relief.

Other: Katie and Polly finished their first year at Trinity without declaring a major. "How can you expect us to know what we want to do for the rest of our lives when we've only begun to live?" Point taken. She and Polly have an apartment three houses up the road beyond the aquacenter. They immediately replaced the fence with one six ft. high on my side to keep me from spying. When I asked if they obtained the owner's permission, Katie said, "What are you going to do, Mom? Take your daughter to court for improving your property?"

Kendra begged to attend university here in Dublin, but my brother Kurt put his foot down. "Two years in the American system first. Then we'll talk." Kody has no interest in the Irish option. He thinks we're all crazy for drinking warm beer—not that he knows the difference between warm and cold beer at his young age of 17!

Michael Thomas fast-tracked his studies and graduated from Trinity a year early this spring. He's been very hush-hush over the summer about his guaranteed job. We may hear an announcement tomorrow. More and more, as he grows in stature and ability, the cousins look to him as leader of their generation. Diplomatically he defers to Brendan, but they still seek his input for most major decisions, including the issue of Thomas' house—their first major undertaking.

Tommy insisted on being present for the committee's discussion about what to do with the property after Mom's death. None of his siblings really wanted the old house, he said. They just didn't want anyone else (meaning me or mine) to get it. The trust's pseudo administrators investigated costs of upgrading to sell vs. selling price in the current economy vs. keeping it in the family with minor upgrades.

Practical Michael Thomas strolled through and added an off-hand comment. "If you could think of a way to generate enough income from the house to pay for taxes and repairs, you would have another option. When Katie and Uncle Henry and I explored the place after Grandfather died, we found underground tunnels and all kinds of historical stuff. He said it was a great place for a museum. Something like that."

The Grandchildren's Trust finished refurbishing Thomas' house so it is now livable. Work is set to begin on the museum soon. The keys will pass from generation to generation tomorrow on my son's twenty-first. Despite their parents' objections, the grandchildren do not begrudge Michael Thomas his position as inevitable head of the family. They respect their grandfather's wishes.

The grandchildren asked for Uncle Henry's help since he was the eldest member of his generation, never mind the relationship they don't understand. As a historian he had many ideas for creating an interesting and interactive museum experience—a necessity in this day and age. Michael Thomas is contributing his holographic talents, which should pull in school groups and tourists. Entry will be from the alleyway (wonder where he got that idea?) with no direct access to the house proper. The museum will consist of three main sections housed in the two tunnels and the rooms below the main floor—Celtic age, Viking invasion to 20th century, and Irish Free State to the present with particular emphasis on the Troubles of the 1970's and 80's—considered ancient history to today's kids!

Henry is consumed by the project and spends most of his free time researching Thomas' vast library. When he can tear himself away, WE carve out time for the two of us—satisfactory for the present.

Since tomorrow is a day for passing on keys, I wonder if I should give Michael Thomas his dad's sports car.

Satisfied, she returned to the house to prepare her list and shop for supper. She, her children and Henry would spend the evening recounting the night of her son's birth complete with Katie's colorful renditions of all principal characters as passed on to her by Cousin Brendan—especially of Grandfather Thomas and Maeve the midwife.

*   *   *

"Imagine giving a mere boy an historic Dublin home—and a half-blood at that!" Anne complained to her sisters from her place on the stoop of Thomas' house. "I don't know why we must be here to witness such a travesty."

"Because we agreed," Meghan replied. "We all voted. Our children won. Tommy asked us to accept the decision graciously. Father would expect as much."

"In truth, none of us really wanted to take over this old place," Emily added. "We like our homes and we don't need the space because all of our children have moved on. Passing it to the next generation is fine by me. I just don't understand why we must make such an occasion of the transfer, birthday buffet and all."

"His mother's idea, no doubt, to rub it in our faces. Michael Thomas will probably turn it into a bachelor's playhouse," Anne snorted.

The subjects of their conversation arrived in separate cars—Kiri with Katie, Bitsy and Sara first, and Henry with Michael Thomas close behind. The men remained in Henry's vehicle for a few moments in serious discussion before they exchanged packages—one thin and one fat. The young man emerged wearing a conservative suit, pinstripe shirt and tie that blended with his blue-green eyes, dress shoes, slicked back hair and a broad smile. Henry followed, and as the two joined the multi-aged group in front of Thomas' house, Kiri realized that her son had grown taller than all other men in the family except Henry.

His cousins flocked around him with congratulatory hugs and handshakes for his initiation into the club of adults. As he regarded the crowd he realized he belonged to the sandwich generation between recent grandparents and their new grandchildren, and by a trick of fate he inherited the responsibility to keep that circle in tact. He smiled at his mother, now a great-aunt, squeezed close by Henry, now an esteemed great-uncle.

His Uncle Tommy beckoned him to the stoop for the ceremonial passing of the keys. He kept his remarks short and to the point. "Our father, grandfather and great-grandfather Thomas O'Connell charged us to remain loyal to our family. It was his wish that his legacy be passed to a strong, youthful generation. By joint agreement, we abide by his decision and, in a symbolic gesture, pass to Michael Thomas the keys to our dear patriarch's legacy—his home and his family."

Michael Thomas reddened with embarrassment but graciously accepted the jailer-sized, rusty iron ring bearing an assortment of skeleton keys. Face and voice recognition systems still operated the doors, so the keys were only tokens of his accession—Meggie's idea, no doubt. He cleared his throat nervously.

"Thank you, Uncle Tommy, and thank all of you for the confidence in me you've shown by your support. I trust that will continue with the decisions I make on behalf of the family." Nods affirmed acceptance.

"At the rate Uncle Tommy's daughters are marrying, I may soon be the only named O'Connell left…" Laughter interrupted his remarks.

"…and I will not live forever, so I thought it appropriate, as my first act, to remind every sojourner here of the spirit that will always reside in this house." He nodded to Henry who passed the thin package through the crowd. The young man removed the wrapping from a bronze plaque and held it up. "Therefore, I proclaim this O'Connell House, established 1885." Amid whoops and applause, he hung it from hooks near the door already secured for the purpose.

The family's prospective leader ran his fingers through his hair and stroked his chin with his fist, just like his grandfather. He glanced quickly at his mother before inhaling deeply and continuing. "It is said that effective leaders delegate responsibility. For my part, I will follow the footsteps of other O'Connells into the family profession—bringing truth to the eyes and ears of the public. Today I signed a contract with Dad's network."

During a pause for whistles and cheers, he sneaked another peek at his mother who controlled her facial reaction remarkably well but gripped Henry's hand for support.

"A home needs giggles in its cozy corners, bare feet along its hallways, smelly football socks and corned beef, and a warm hearth for wayfarers. I'm not there yet, so I delegate the O'Connell tradition of Celtic hospitality to the man who mentored me in the importance of family loyalty… Cousin Brendan… and pass the symbolic keys of the house to him so he can fulfill that responsibility."

Gasps, then squeals followed as the rest of the cousins realized that Brendan, their assumed leader for so many years, would live in the house filled with shared memories. Within minutes, Michael Thomas abided by their grandfather's wish that the oldest son of a son should head the family, then shared his birthright with his cousin—the mark of a perceptive leader. Meghan tried to hide her delight for her son, and her sisters nearly choked on their envy. Brendan, taken by surprise, grabbed his young cousin in a signature O'Connell bear hug as the others crowded around the two.

"Let's not go crazy here. I also delegate responsibility to Breeda to feed this crazy crowd. I'm ready to cut cake!" Michael Thomas shouted above the mob.

The youngest rushed the door with their parents not far behind. One lagged and took Brendan's hand. "Father, if you have the keys now, does that mean I'll get to sleep in this old house some night like you did when you were little?"

The ecstatic oldest cousin smiled at his son. "Some night... and every night for a long time. But we'll always leave a light on for *your* Uncle Michael." He flung his other arm around his cousin's shoulder. "You've made a young family very happy today."

"No problem. It's in my job description," Michael Thomas smiled as they entered their newly dedicated O'Connell House together.

Choruses sung, candles blown, and cake cut, the family filled their plates in the dining room few of them had seen in the nearly six years since Thomas' death. When they had had their fill, the little ones scampered to investigate while their parents tried to keep up and wipe frosting off the side tables and banister. The older generation gathered in the living room to admire some of the original family furnishings that were recalled into service after two decades in the attic.

Kiri finally caught up with the man of honor. "You are filled with surprises today."

"The job. I know, Mom. We'll talk later at home under the tree."

"You made your mother... and father... very proud today. Your exchange of symbolic gestures was inspired."

"Thank you. I was so nervous. You know that the cousins really wanted to keep this house—Brendan most of all—even though it was not a smart business decision. But I don't belong here. I belong in our neighborhood. I've been worried for days about how to reject the offer without seeming ungrateful. When I woke up this morning, the idea just popped into my head like... like..."

"Like a fairy whispering in your ear?" Kiri smiled.

"Exactly!"

The old team congregated in a corner of the room from which they had escorted Kiri in a protective wedge following her blow-up with Patrick Murphy after Michael's funeral. They exuded the pride that their fallen comrade must share at this moment. "We groomed that young man well, and he is no disappointment. When he signed on with us today, he handed us our hopes in an Irish pot o' gold. Our team's survival and funding are assured."

Henry excused himself and joined a conversation between Kiri and Meggie whose excitement bubbled over with possibilities. "We could have a holiday gathering here. We would all help. Decorate. Maybe have a Christmas cookie party for our own kids like we used to!"

"Brendan's wife might have something to say about that," he said.

"Oh!" Meggie's eyes bugged out. "I'll go ask her right now. I'm sure she'll say yes. I'm very good at persuasion."

Kiri and Henry chuckled as she rushed off like the little girl she used to be. "How is the proud mother holding up?" he asked.

She leaned into his chest and relaxed as he put his arms around her. "Exhausted. Emotionally exhausted, but very happy that Michael Thomas found a diplomatic way out of a very uncomfortable situation. He'll be happier near us." Her arms found their way around Henry's waist.

The stepsisters watched from across the room. "Would you look at that?" Anne snapped smartly. "The widow and her constant companion are parading their sordid relationship in public. Kiri is as disgusting as her mother."

"Oh, put a sock in it, Anne!" Meghan shot back. "You don't have to love or even like Kiri, but find the decency to appreciate what she has done for you and your family. Emily and I have."

"Never!"

*　　*　　*

Michael Thomas found his mother exactly as he expected—sitting under their evergreen tree with a hot cup of tea in her hand. He approached, kissed her on the cheek and pulled up a chair to face her knee-to-knee. "Sorry I'm so late. I left the noonday birthday bash early but got lost in some research back at the attic studio before I realized the time."

"No problem. I always have time for you, but why were you so specific about meeting me *here*?"

He flashed a cunning smile. "It's my birthday. If I trap you under this tree, you never deny me a wish on my birthday."

Her fingers played with the keys in her pocket. "What will I grant you today, my son of twenty-one?" she teased.

He stared seriously at her. "I want you to believe in me... to accept my decision to work in Dad's line of business. I joined the network to continue his cause. Someday you'll understand."

An ominous tingle crept upward from her fingertips. She shook her head. "No, Michael. No!"

He took her hands. "Mom, listen. You've always told me to follow my passion and to have the courage to right wrongs. This is how I want to do it... through a network team. I have the skills. I can make a difference. I believe I can change lives for the good—like you and Dad."

She ripped her hands from his grip. "No. No. No! I cannot bear the thought of losing both my Michaels. I absolutely forbid it!"

"Excuse me, Mother, but you cannot. I'm of age now and do not need your permission or approval. But I want to have it... to feel your support. Remember, you're the non-hysterical, reasonable one in the family. I would expect you to hear me out."

Her eyes narrowed and her lips tightened. "Where did you get this crazy idea? Did Henry put you up to it?"

"No. The idea came from Grandfather... and you... and the cousins who knew Dad. You all told me stories about him, and they always ended with a moral... morals that still hold true: follow your passion, have the courage to right wrongs and change lives for the good, be strong enough to save yourself, and know that love doesn't die with you. By my early teens I took them to heart and wanted to become that kind of man."

"You're not prepared. Why would the network hire you?"

"I have the skills that are in demand now. In university, I took every course with 'International' in the title, and I can converse in seven languages. I've been in physical training all summer. They waived water fitness and survival because... well, because you trained me long ago." He smiled with appreciation at his mother who sat as rigid as a boulder.

"On my own I upgraded and refined the old hologram technology to be interactive like I said. I can obscure natural features and replace them with an illusion that immerses people in a situation and causes them to change their actions. The British military wants to acquire my rights."

He paused before disclosing the next, fearing the discord it might create. "Uncle Henry agreed to put off retirement for a few years to be my mentor. Devin will help me, too, and Frank. By the time they all step down, I will have perfected a medium to take place of a screen and a means to deliver it anywhere in the world. Then I can take over the department to orchestrate ops from beginning to end and assure that what happened to you and Dad on your last mission will never happen again."

Kiri stiffened and nearly pulled off the arms of her chair with her tight grip. "How... do... you... know... what... happened?"

"From you and Dad actually, by way of Grandfather and then Uncle Henry. Before he died, Grandfather gave him a package of sealed files for me to open when I turned twenty-one if you had never spoken to me about your assignments with the network."

Kiri dropped her head into her hands and remembered. *No, Son. I gave those files to Henry. Why? Why? Why?*

"Apparently Dad gave Grandfather copies of all his reports for safekeeping. He was afraid both of you might be... compromised... one day, and he wanted to make sure the information would always be available. Uncle Henry must have given him the account of your last mission out of habit. That was the only one with a broken seal."

Thomas! Thomas opened that file! He did know everything. That explains our conversation on the day he saddled me with his family.

"Details of every mission Dad was on—and you too—are in these files. The good and the bad. That's where I've been all afternoon— reading them. I don't understand why you didn't expose that guy—Patrick Murphy—after Dad's death."

218

Kiri lifted her head from her hands and stared at her son without seeing him. "Your father was so passionate about his work, he would never tarnish the reputation of something he believed in so deeply."

Then she caught her son's eye. "It was a hard decision, but ultimately I determined that the mission was a success. All the people we were sent to rescue—plus more, and children—crossed the border safely and now live among us. The death of your father—an employee who knew the risks—was collateral damage and did not affect the successful outcome of the mission. That ass Patrick should have been shot, and I would have done it myself, but it would not bring back your father once he drew his last breath." She chuckled. "Patrick Murphy was exiled to the Falkland Islands for life—as far south on this globe as possible, within spitting distance of Antarctica. He'll never darken our doorway again."

She took a deep breath to relax now that her son knew the truth of his father's death. "Was anything else in those files?"

"USB drives with maps, names, audio and video."

Unsettled again, Kiri was afraid to ask. "Did you watch any of it?"

Her son closed his eyes and nodded.

"What did you think?"

Several moments passed before he looked at her. "I witnessed the most horrible… the most gut-wrenching… the most sublime scene ever. I understand you so much better now, and I understand why you kept Dad present in our lives all these years. I'm so, so grateful that *you chose* to give me life. Grandfather always told me you were the strongest of all the relatives. I am proud to be *your* son—not just Dad's. I know he would approve my decision, but now it is even more important that I have *your* approval. I want to finish the work that you and Dad started, and I want to make *you* proud of *me.*"

"I am so proud of you, Michael Thomas. Never more than on this day." She reached for the car keys in her pocket.

"There's one more thing." He hesitated. "I'm leaving in a couple of weeks for field training. I need to understand what our associates deal with day-to-day so I can duplicate their movements and environs with details that pass for reality. I'll be gone for six to nine months in the Middle East and Africa. I fly out October 19th."

October 19th! The day her husband died! Kiri flinched as terror twisted around her heart, and she dropped the keys back into her pocket. Before she could cry out at her son, a whisper of her mother's voice drifted from her columbine in the memory garden. *Every time you part from a child, it should be with an expression of love.* She stretched out her arms toward her son. "*Go gcoinni Dia i mbois a láimhe thú.* May God always hold you in the palm of His hand," she said and smothered him with a hug to last a lifetime.

* * *

Henry let himself into Kiri's house. He expected to find her in the kitchen setting a light supper on the table. She was not there. He called upstairs to her room in case she decided on a rest first. She did not answer. He glanced across the road at the garden. No Kiri paced the meditative path. He walked out onto the deck in back and saw no one—only two chairs face-to-face. He looked toward the pool presuming no activity because of the evening hour. A painful feeling of dread welled up inside him when sharp slaps on a fluid surface reached his ears. Kiri escaped to water... again.

He found her swimming laps ferociously, her fingers like claws raking through the water. Nowhere near exhaustion she flipped and returned, ignoring Henry as he stepped near the edge of the shallow end. Back and forth, faster and faster she swam in her race against despair.

He pulled up a deck chair to wait her out. Having dealt with her downward spirals before, he did not have to ask what triggered this one—her son's surprising news. He watched her surface dive headfirst in the deep end, becoming nervous when she did not reemerge until he remembered how long she could hold her breath. His vision obscured by descending darkness, he walked to her expected point of reemergence and peered into the water. She shot up into the air like a whale breaching, rolled, and crashed in front of him, spraying water from his head down.

He wiped his face against his sleeve. "I think you better get out."

"I think *you* better leave."

"I'm here to help you."

"You can't help me with my problems anymore, Henry. *You are* my problem. Go away!"

"Can't do that. Your health and safety are my job."

Kiri backstroked to the center of the pool, out of reach, to tread water. "Your *job*! It's always been about the job, hasn't it, Henry? Don't jeopardize the mission—the team—the department—the network." She searched his face for tremors of guilt. "Send a guy off on a risky assignment. That's the job. Send his wife too. That's the job. More accolades for the team. More funding for the team. More job security for the team. Hide the truth about the outcome. That's the *job*!"

"I know you're upset, but please get out of the pool so we can sort...."

Kiri flung more accusations at the man, batting the water as she did. "Follow the widow so she won't talk. Keep her alive. Keep her sane so there won't be any questions about the job—no links leading to the job. Go after her. Coax her back to the city where you can spy on her to protect the job. Keep her busy. Don't let her form relationships outside the team. She might talk about the *job*."

Tense and agitated now, Henry stuffed his trembling hands into his pockets.

A sinister smile crossed her lips. "Pregnant? Children? That wasn't in the plan, was it? You didn't consider *that* possibility. No matter. Expand the circle. Include the children. Make yourself indispensable in their lives. Groom them to work—for the team. Give them a job—a job that will chain them to the team. But don't get too close to Kiri." She cackled. "If the relationship goes bad, she might expose you out of spite—and imperil the *job*."

Henry's nervousness turned to anger and hurt. He tore off his suit coat and tie, ready to plunge in and drag Kiri back to her senses.

"Don't you dare come near me. I can stay under longer than you, and you know it," she mocked. "I'll bet you bugged my house and my cars. Can you prove that you did not have me surveilled? That a search of your phone and text messages would not disclose orders among the guys to watch me, guard me, keep me from harming myself?"

In defense, he countered. "Someone had to. You were determined to end your life, you might remember."

"That's a laugh," she spit out. "Protect me from myself? Who's going to protect me from *you*?"

"I'm not a threat."

"Not anymore. I'm as raw and battered as I've ever been. Nothing you do can hurt me more than you already have. For all I know, you had my children followed... their electronics bugged too."

"That's quite a list of condemnations. Will you let me defend myself?"

"Not yet. If you didn't intend to involve my son, why did you give him his father's files? Who gave you that right?"

"The package was addressed to me. I did not need permission. A child has a right to his history. For the record, I didn't expect Thomas to read them. He was honor-bound not to."

"Well, he did, and so did his grandson. Now you will never let Michael Thomas go, will you? You knew if he read the reports—and he would—that he would be bound to the network forever, just like me. How are you going to silence him if he decides to go his own way? Send him off on some ill-fated mission to come home in a body bag like his father? You carried Michael's casket, for heaven's sake! Are you anxious to carry his son's too?"

Fizzing with indignation, Henry clenched his jaw. "That's... not... fair!"

In the dimming light, with her wet hair plastered against her head, Kiri's skeletal form cried out, "Dying for no good reason isn't fair! Chaining my family to your team isn't fair! Creating a job for my son so you can control his future isn't fair!"

To calm her, he tried reason. "Your son was made for this job. I see his father's passion in his eyes. He is brilliant, Kiri, brilliant. Some tech wizard must be working through him because the program he designed is inspired—camouflage, pure and simple, taken to a highly sophisticated level. It will revolutionize how we do our work—eliminate the need for guys on the ground and protect our associates who are. Genius. No casualty, no loss."

She splashed that off. "Now that you have Michael Thomas in your clutches, what job do you have in store for Katie? For Sara Lamb? Keep them involved so their mom won't talk... won't give up the team... until no one listens to her demented babble any longer. Who's pulling our puppet strings? Michael? Thomas? You? Or are all three of you in cahoots somehow? It's time I put an end to it and took charge of my own life—all our lives—for a change."

Henry feared the day his secrets and lies would resurrect themselves. He could not face losing *his* family now that he and Kiri were so close. "You are. You've always maintained control. But I want to believe I've helped... I've supported you and your family. I love your children as if they were my own."

"A parent—a *good* parent—would not voluntarily send his son into harm's way. October 19th! How could you send him away on the day his father died? To the Middle East? To be target practice for some sniper?"

"Now that you're in charge, what do you plan to do as Michael Thomas' mother? Will you fall on your knees before him and beg him not to go?" he challenged.

"No, I won't expose your purpose. For the next couple of weeks, I will spend every moment I have with my son cherishing him, telling him how much I love him. Telling him what a joy he is to me and how brilliant he is and what a fine man he will be. I will not undermine his self-confidence and plant doubt in his mind. His loss will not be on *my* back. *You'll* own this one!"

Visibly sickened, the man's head and shoulders drooped.

"Tell me, Henry. Have you ever thought of me and my children as more than an assignment?"

He raised his eyes to lock her gaze. "You are my family. Not everyone can express feelings with words. Some must demonstrate them with actions... as *I* have for more than two decades."

Kiri dove beneath the surface again with a splash. A somber Henry turned and stormed away. A nettle floated on the water in the wake of their battle.

Twenty-Seventh Anniversary Year: I once said that the happiest days in my life were the days my son and daughter were born. Not anymore. The most glorious was the day Michael Thomas walked through the door after nine months abroad and shouted, "Hi, Mom! I'm home!"

No deaths to report this year.

CHAPTER 29

"Hi, Mom! I'm home!"

Katie's exuberant voice brought Kiri on a run. They flew into one another's arms for a heart-to-heart hug that did not erase the three months they were separated. Kiri pushed her daughter to arm's length to appraise her state of being following an internship with the United Nations. All fingers and all toes were still intact albeit gaily painted, she noted, and Katie's classic cola-bottle figure retained its curves. A few ginger curls escaped their tight knot of hair in back to frame the pretty face surrounding her eyes of bright blue that had not faded a smidgen in twenty-one years.

"Welcome, welcome, welcome!" Kiri said, squeezing her daughter again. "You look great! I didn't expect such a happy sight for another couple of days."

"Me either, but a seat opened up on a relief flight, and Uncle Henry met me at the airport, and here I am."

Henry picked her up. That's my job! Kiri hid her displeasure behind a faint smile as she helped Katie off with her backpack.

"You look great too, by the way, and the house and the memory garden. I can't believe how much I missed being here."

"Let's take some tea under my tree, and you can tell me all about your adventure." Mother and daughter fell into a familiar routine sidling past one another in the kitchen to prepare a tray with goodies and stories to go with them.

Once settled where a warm late-summer sun persuaded resinous scents to seep from the fir tree, Katie told her tales of work with a fact-finding mission to underdeveloped countries. The team focused on issues of sanitation, clean water, disease, immunization and inhumane cultural practices. Katie's task was to document their investigations with video and to provide written follow-up.

"You wouldn't believe what we saw, Mom. You'd think everyone would have food and clean water by almost the middle of the 21st century and that conditions would improve for children, but they don't. Some kids have never been to school. We saw boys working in mines or toting weapons bigger than they were and children crippled by diseases that should have been eradicated decades ago. Some will never feel grass between their toes because there is no grass and they don't have toes! Girls way younger than me have babies and do women's work. Don't even get me started on sexual slavery and mutilation. I'll have nightmares forever!"

She stole a glance at her mother when she recognized what she said. "Why can't people help each other more? Everyone deserves a little joy in life."

Realizing there was no logical explanation, Katie fell into deep thought while munching on a biscuit. She stopped and stared at her mother with a gleam in her eye. "I've decided what to do with my life. I know Dad would approve, and Uncle Henry will be pleased." She displayed a coy smile. "I want to join the family business!"

Kiri's mug thudded to the ground. "No!" She shook her head. "No! Absolutely not. I forbid it!"

"Mom? Why the violent reaction? All I want to do is make a difference—a small difference. I know I can't save every kid in the whole world, but I'd like to help the few I can."

Kiri tried to regain her composure, but her shaking voice betrayed her. "I'm sorry, Katie, but I cannot support your decision. I had no choice with Michael Thomas, but I will not allow another child to be sacrificed for some grand ideal. Your dad's loss is enough for this family."

"Sacrificed? What are you talking about? I want to help more people with the family business. *Your* business. The aquacenter. Hardly risky."

A short spurt of laughter broke the tension. "I'm sorry. I assumed you meant.... I didn't realize that the aquacenter was a family business."

"It is if you own it!" Katie knocked on her mother's head. "Hello. Gears rusty up there now that you're almost sixty?"

"I guess so," Kiri chuckled. "But I thought you couldn't wait to escape this little island."

"That's what I thought too, but I missed home—lots. I'll settle for hard work here and short escapes." She flashed her winning smile.

"Wonderful! And, welcome! Glad to have you. Do you plan on swimming all day and sending me out to the meadow like an old ewe?"

Katie shook her head, and a light bulb went on. "Bitsy! That's it! She came to us for a reason, and it wasn't just to play pretty music. Your business is more than the aquacenter. You empower people to take charge of their lives. You counsel and educate and rehabilitate misguided youth and supervise job training too. Think of all the cousins who got a start in our neighborhood."

At a cock of her mother's head, she continued. "Think of Bitsy! I saw lots of girls just like her—hundreds, maybe thousands—who were forced into early marriage—or worse—by their families, with no chance for school or a childhood. I bet there are plenty right here in Ireland... in Dublin even."

The size of her pupils doubled with her excitement. "Unwed mothers are still sent to homes with no chance to improve their situations. Children are children only once, you know. They deserve a fresh start in life too. They'll need trauma counseling, basic education and training... and personal health and physical fitness. The aquacenter already offers most of that. Bitsy found her confidence and independence in our pool; others will too. We'll expand to provide a whole menu of services for them... nutrition... child development... ooh, child care and maybe temporary housing and…." She halted abruptly. "We'll need more than one of me. Polly and Kendra will help. They'll need jobs soon too."

Kiri could not help smiling at her daughter's enthusiasm for the impossible. "Sounds like a very worthwhile project—a volunteer service project. Facilities we have, but how will you finance livelihoods for three very charming young women?"

Katie's wheels ground to a halt, then started turning again. "Don't worry, Mom. A plan will pop into my head… just like Bitsy did." She clapped her hands. "I can't wait! We'll need a new name for our partnership." She grabbed her mother by the shoulders as her eyes darted around their shared surroundings. "Aurora Aquatics!"

Kiri laughed at the thought. "You don't like your name."

"I do now! Aurora—the dawn." She twirled around and announced in dramatic fashion, "Welcome to Aurora Aquatics, pathway… no… *Waterway* to a New Beginning!"

*   *   *

A plan did pop into Katie's head, but she kept it a secret from everyone but her brother. "I'm no good at writing about the horrendous things I saw when everything I saw was so horrible. If Mom knew, she'd be sick."

Michael Thomas agreed, and helped his sister with structural advice and technical expertise. "Get rid of all the run-on sentences and leave the accompanying video to me."

After more than a year of hard work and frustration awaiting communication from her lead professor and her supervisor at the UN, she was ready to unveil the results. She chose to announce them at Sunday dinner at her mother's house—Uncle Henry included. She refused to be deterred by the fact that he rarely came to dinner anymore and then only when both she and her brother attended too. Tonight was her night to shine, and she wanted her favorite people there to share the glow with her.

Henry locked up after the last guest left the museum. Director of the network's international security division in name only until Michael Thomas took his place, he used his free hours to bring the Trust Committee's vision of an interactive historical museum to fruition. Open for just months, the attraction proved popular, especially the holographic invasion of Viking long ships sailing up the tunnels to establish Dublin City with leather-helmeted warriors wielding two-edged broad swords. Rave reviews ensured its ability to support O'Connell House.

He strolled the tunnels to confirm all artifacts were in place for Wednesday's visitors. His pride, the Troubles exhibit, was routinely his final stop. There he traced the involvement of two families—one from each side of the conflict—displayed opposite one another along a tunnel wall. He passed news clippings of government actions and republican bombings and paused before an unlabeled reproduction of a young couple holding a baby circa 1970. Beyond, he straightened a larger, empty frame awaiting the photo of living family members. *Someday I will reveal my link to this family and this house… when I can speak the truth to Kiri.*

On the drive to her home for Sunday dinner, Henry shuddered at the memory of their confrontation at the pool, but he had to admit that many of her accusations were spot on and still applied. From the moment Michael Thomas left for his field training, Henry had eyes and ears on him. He packed a duffel and moved into the situation room to monitor the young man around the clock. Unbeknownst to either mother or son, he arranged with his contacts for short video chats from airports only. Ditto for Katie during her overseas tour. He felt responsible.

Building trust with Kiri again was a tricky proposition when they rarely saw one another, but he did not give up trying. He continued to be a major force in her children's lives and in the lives of their cousins. They sought his advice and invited him to major family events and what Katie termed Sunday "family" dinners. He never showed up uninvited, with one exception. He appeared on Mondays at 4 p.m. for tea as usual just to keep the lines of communication open. Kiri always allowed him in, but their conversations were rarely interesting—more civil. The two never stretched a hand over the wall that divided them.

He tried every tactic he knew to entice Katie to reveal her "plan," but without success. His contacts in Geneva kept mum; Michael Thomas, likewise. Anxious to see the results of her work, he hoped the celebration of Katie's success would soften her mother as well.

An animated young lady met him at the door and could hardly contain herself throughout the meal. She did not divulge much except to say, "When I submitted my report of the internship to my professor, he suggested I go a step further and create a short documentary to accompany it from the three months of video I took. He thought the UN would be interested. Michael Thomas helped me, and the result is our after-dinner entertainment." She beamed from ear to ear. "So hurry up and eat!"

The assemblage carried their desserts into the living room for the presentation. "My brother told me to focus on a few major issues instead of trying to show everything. I chose food and water, disease, education and safety from a child's point of view. You know I took all the video, so don't be too surprised when you see me in front of the camera interacting with kids and talking to them. Michael Thomas worked his magic and put my image there." The young man took a bow.

Kiri jumped with surprise when her pixie-like daughter introduced herself onscreen as "Aurora." A whisper in her ear disclosed, "There's a reason. Wait 'til the end."

Henry and Kiri both applauded when the short, compelling film came to a close. "Well, did you see it?" Katie asked.

"That last scene was very stirring—all those children describing what frightens them. Masterful work," Henry said. "Masterful work."

"But what did you think of the very end? My plan for financial independence? My earmark?"

The older folks traded confused glances, so Michael Thomas backed up the video enough to catch the credits. They saw the two children's names roll by, a few acknowledgements and then an appeal: "If you were moved by any of the needs described in this film and wish to help a UN relief agency provide them, click the links below." Titles included: food and water, immunizations and health care, education, and Childhood for Children sponsored by Aurora Aquatics.

"When the UN agency saw the video, they wanted to use it as a funding appeal," Michael Thomas explained. "But Katie owned the rights because she paid her way on the internship, used her own equipment and received no compensation."

"When they asked me if they could buy it, I said 'No,' but that I would sign a license agreement for its use and take an earmark instead—my brother's idea. That means anyone who likes my project for rehabilitating disadvantaged kids can support it. They'll remember my name, Aurora, because I repeated it a lot and it's unique," she beamed. "This is my life's mission, Mom. I sense it. To build a strong family here—at home—and to provide others with the tools to do the same."

"Katie goes viral tomorrow morning," Michael Thomas added.

Kiri scanned her daughter's face. "What were you exposed to?"

Katie pressed her palms against her mother's cheeks in frustration. "Keep up with the times, Mom. My pretty little face will be all over the Internet tomorrow... all over the world!" She squeezed in beside her mother and launched into a personal appeal. "Our partnership should provide the facilities, and I hope donations will cover expenses and salaries. Ideally we should lease the house on the other side of the aquacenter from you. We triplets will remodel for our living quarters upstairs and for classrooms and counseling on the main floor. We'll automatically have easy access to the center. We'll have to provide transportation, too, until our program grows enough to require housing... like maybe that big, old house down at the bottom of the road... but that's a couple of years off. We can explore grants for part of the funding too. So, what do you think?"

"I think I am very proud and very blessed to have you as my daughter." Kiri wrapped her quickly maturing little girl in a tight mother-hug. "What can I do to help?" Henry nodded his desire to be part of the project too.

Katie looked at the two adults most dear to her, sitting across the room from one another. "For starters, you two can call a truce. I need help from both of you to turn this 'plan' into action."

Thirtieth Anniversary Year: Birth: Gus stopped short of eight with five daughters and two sons—a basketball team and doubles tennis, he jokes. Both Doyle and Devin have two sons and a daughter. I attended six more christenings for a total of 28 great-grandchildren for Thomas. None of them carry the name O'Connell.

Marriage: Tommy's Nora and Ríona, Anne's Niall, and Emily's Liam. Kean (26) is holding out for Kendra (22), but Kurt says she's too young to marry so he better "know how to hold 'em." My two—Katie and Michael Thomas—are the only named O'Connells left in their generation and likely to be for some time. Katie is admired by many but has time for few.

Death: Oh, dear. Bitsy had a busy three years, and the family flowerbeds in the memory garden show many colors. We lost three men: Meghan's second husband and Polly's father Phillip (76), Anne's husband Charles (69), and Tommy (65).

Meghan's sisters helped her through grieving times. The other two triplets helped Polly. Brendan and Connor were respectfully supportive for the older man who never was a father figure to them. Anne's sisters helped her. The cousins flocked around the six in that family who lost a father. Both families used Quincy Hospice Services and Bitsy, of course. The cousins remembered to thank us.

Tommy's death hit the family particularly hard because it was unexpected. He collapsed onto his desk at work. For the first time in more than a century, his network had no O'Connell in executive position— the demise of that family business, since both my Michaels opted for their competitor. I delved into family medical records (without authorization) and discovered that for the last five generations, O'Connell men have died by the age of 65 from heart problems, except Thomas. He experienced a mild attack two years before he reconnected with Mom. I say that her taking the butter out of the sauces and gravy off the table, plus large doses of exercise and love, bought him an extra two decades. I wonder still if Michael would have succumbed in similar fashion had he lived, and now I worry about my own son.

Chaos reigned for a couple of months while the stepsisters came to terms with the fact that the family no longer had a male as its head. I hid my tiara in the closet and kept a low profile. Brendan, Grace and Caitlín separately sought my counsel regarding estate settlements. They were perfectly capable of handling affairs for their widowed mothers but wanted an objective opinion, they said. Mostly they wanted my shoulder, ear and tissues, so I left my door open. A hot cup of tea and a walk through the memory garden brought calm faster than anything I said or did.

Seamróg (shamrock) House established: Within about three months, Katie's appeal generated enough to turn her plan into reality. After another year she announced adequate funding to acquire a very reasonable loan from the Trust Committee to purchase the house at the end of the road—one of the few I do not own. I told her that I tried repeatedly to buy it but the owner would not sell. The agent for the property assured me he would make contact if/when it came up for sale.

"When I talked to him as a representative of Aurora Aquatics, he must have confused my name with yours—the advantage of a partnership!" Katie giggled. I asked if Henry had anything to do with her arrangement. "I never talked to him about it, other than at dinner that first night. He'll be pleased, though, that I did it on my own."

I'm pleased, too, that Katie has done such a great job on her own... and close to home. I feel so blessed to have my daughter near and NOT in that other family business!

Michael Thomas pursues his indescribable passion. He works at the Dublin office with occasional trips to London and one or two into the field for "trials" as he calls them. He succeeded in finding his medium and delivery system. That required a tweak to projecting images. I try to listen patiently when he explains his program. Normally, he says, holographic images are projected horizontally, like from a wall. He had to develop a system that projected from a ceiling but then "bent" light waves to appear as if the image came from a wall to trick the brain into believing that what it saw was true. Looking down from a drone onto a road, you usually see tops of cars, but his tech allows you to view them naturally from the side at ground level. "Smoke and mirrors," he calls it. Smoke is only one medium he uses, and the mirrors are his secret.

The "diversionary" augmented reality in his holographic simulations is like "old-timey video games with pop-up obstacles where a viewer becomes part of the experience. But there is no need for electricity, wireless service, a screen, head-gear or goggles to view them, and they can be used anywhere in the world." I really cannot fathom virtual crowds of people and/or vehicles projected not onto a screen, but onto a supercharged atmosphere like mist provided by a high-altitude drone and then "bent" to create an image that surrounds and camouflages personnel traveling toward a friendly border or safe house. Chase vehicles or rebels find themselves speeding along roads that are not there or avoiding ancient stone walls and market places that spring up before their eyes. No humans needed other than the rescue subject=no risk to life or limb.

When I go cross-eyed trying to imagine what he describes, he says, "That's okay, Mom. Someday you'll understand the long-term ramifications." The British military still wants to buy his rights, but he resists. Now he's searching for something that technology can't create—a brawny, fearless, crackerjack "details" guy with his feet on the ground and a touch of the tender. More power to him!

CHAPTER 30

Clayton Daniel Moriarty, a tech-savvy stud with brawn to match his brain, drove up to Aurora Aquatics at precisely 2 p.m. as directed. A series of similar young men replaced Doyle and Gus over the years. After extensive exams and interviews for the few select positions with the network's extraction team, all were subjected to the psychological evaluation and water skills test of Kirin O'Connell. He dressed smartly for his interview with the woman rumored to have cut short the aspirations of many with one word to Henry Callaghan. Taken half-a-dozen at a time and after having passed initial interviews, background checks, and physical testing, young recruits were given to her to assess and rank. Inevitably five fell short and one survived to tell his tale of torture at her hand—stories never to be repeated thereafter to other than his new teammates.

The broad-shouldered young man, clearly uncomfortable in business dress, ran a finger inside his shirt collar, straightened his tie and rubbed each shoe on the back of its mate's pant leg to top off the shine. He readjusted his sportcoat fresh from the cleaners and stepped confidently through the door of the aquatics complex. Its emptiness did not surprise him on a Sunday afternoon when most folks enjoyed family time, but giggles and shrieks from the rear did. He followed the din outside to the pool and spotted half a dozen teenage girls in various stages of impending motherhood surrounding one young woman who definitely was not.

"May I help you?"

A lopsided smile beamed from his square face. "I hope not! I don't have the proper prerequisites. Mr. Callaghan from the network sent me."

Katie sized up the guy with short-cropped hair on fire and obtuse triangle eyebrows whose peaks followed the direction of his pupils and the cobalt blue rings that surrounded them. "You're dressed quite smartly. Did you not receive instructions for this interview?"

"I did, but I wanted to make a good impression. I'm determined to land this job."

"You'll make an impression, all right." She turned to the girls who ogled them both. "Time to get out and leave this nice man to his torture." She followed them and stood on her tiptoes to holler across the fence. "Your next victim is here!" Her comely frame dripped past him on its way to the dressing room. "Good luck!" she winked and disappeared through the sliding door.

Clay walked to the pool's edge and peered into its aquamarine water imagining a swim with a copper-haired mermaid. He heard steps approach from behind and turned to notice a slight woman who looked to be in her early sixties—hardly what he expected from her reputation as a harsh taskmaster.

"Mr. Moriarty," she greeted and stretched out her arm. "If you learn one lesson today, it will be to follow directions." She grabbed him by his tie and flung him into the pool like a piece of cardboard.

The overconfident young man nearly choked on his surprise and came up gasping.

"Not quite the greeting you expected? If you intend to be part of this team, you follow directions and come prepared."

"Yes, Ma'am!" He shot straight up out of the water, grabbed her arm and pulled her in with him.

They traded shocked stares. "That was a bold first move for a job interview," she sputtered, shaking wet curls from her face.

Clay's flush nearly matched his hair. "I'm so sorry, Ma'am. Instinct, I guess. The first lesson I learned in training—never allow your adversary the higher ground. I s'pose that finishes me." He started to heft his fully clad body out of the pool.

"Not so fast," she grinned. "If that's the way you want to play it, catch me if you can!" She was out of her wraparound skirt in a second and flung it over the fence. Then she disappeared beneath the surface of the water.

He struggled to follow but was held back by that impressive outfit. In an effort to shed his clothing quickly underwater, he first yanked off his tie and tossed it behind him. Within a millisecond, a foot planted itself in his back, his air passages seized up and his head jerked from a powerful tug on a familiar strip of silk cloth.

"Too slow, laddy. I just broke your neck. Your arms and legs are now useless, and you will drown. Lesson Number Two: expect the unexpected." Kiri released her grip on the man and gave him time to strip down to his swim trunks while she treaded water and outlined the purpose of her tests. "Always consider your adversary a killer and stronger than you, so you must use your wits and finesse. Your objective is to *capture* an adversary for interrogation. Use deadly force only if it's your life or his. And, don't try to strong-arm me in this pool. Let's start again. Catch me if you can." She surface dove into the water before the befuddled young stud could stutter, "Yes, Ma'am."

"Blessed Mother Mary!" Clay shouted as he rested his chin on the pool's edge. "That woman must take jet fuel with her breakfast!"

"Giving up already?" Katie asked the young recruit when she passed by his head with an armload of towels fresh from the laundry. "You've been at it for barely more than half an hour."

"Me quit? Never! I *want* this job. Give us a hint here. Does she have any pace besides turbo?"

"Sometimes endurance trumps speed," Katie said as she left with a hidden grin.

The next time Katie spotted him from inside the aquacenter, Clayton spurted up with a yowl and slapped the water causing an arc of spray to shower down on her mother.

"Problems, Mr. Moriarty?" Kiri asked, swimming toward him.

"No, Ma'am. I thought I had you this time, but obviously not. I have to say, you're one fine swimmer."

"That's my job," Kiri said as she rolled onto her back to float. "I like your technique. You stayed close enough to me to surge when I slowed down, but you didn't waste all your energy trying to win a race."

"Win? I barely caught your foot before you got away again."

Kiri laughed. "Close enough for this fish. Two hours at fast speed is about my limit. Most don't make it this long. They give up in frustration, or fatigue gets them. I need to float a bit before the next round."

"You mean there's more?"

"Oh, yes! Go up near the patio doors, grab a towel and a bottle of water. Take five. I'll give you a wave when I'm recovered enough for a game of 'Hide and Seek.'" She gave a three-fingered signal to Katie who stood just inside those doors with her six charges in a line beside her.

Clay took his time. He rolled onto his back for a couple of strokes, then floated his way to the shallow end. He pulled himself out of the water slowly, stepped onto the tiles... and yowled again. He danced nimbly across them, his drips sizzling behind him, and leapt onto a tippy side table to try to balance. He scanned the sky for the bright sun that heated the tiles to broiling but found only a coyote-gray overcast. He spied six noses pressed against the glass doors and seven young women laughing at him. The eldest flipped one switch off and another on. He turned back toward the pool and found Mrs. O laughing, too. *Expect the unexpected*, he remembered and gave her a polite salute.

Katie handed him a towel and drinking water while sizing up his broad-shouldered and deep-chested top half, tree-trunk legs and thin ankles. "You're very quick on your feet for such a muscular guy. Do you dance?"

"Only when I'm tricked into it!"

"It's safe to come down now. I turned off the heat. Those who make it this far usually fall through the lounger with blisters on their feet or leap back into the water. I've never seen table-hopping before."

"I've never had to use it before. My question is, why? What's the purpose of heating the patio up like a barbecue just to find out how a guy will react?"

"The special features of this aquacenter are not for you. Our clientele is health-compromised, remember, so we climate control all aspects of the environment, from water temperature to pool walls and railings, to tiles, to towels, walkers and the pool lift. Even air temperature is controlled. When there is a chill out—which is most of the time—we engage the retractable cover and create an ambient climate all around. Use of the tile heater for testing is an additional benefit."

Clay nodded his head. "Clever. I wonder what Mrs. O has cooked up—no pun intended—for the next round. There's no place to hide in a swimming pool."

"You'll see." Katie motioned toward the water. "One of my brother's mixed reality trials."

A monkey's shrill warning-call attracted Clay's focus to the pool where a mangrove swamp sprouted up before his eyes. Stiltlike roots plunged into the murky water, providing shelter for fish, crabs and softshell turtles. Bamboolike grasses wove through woody mazes to the surface. From the center of the scene, Kiri waved to beckon him in.

"She thought you looked like a swampy kind of guy. Good luck," Katie winked hiding another grin as she walked to the far end of the pool for the portable lifeguard chair. She wheeled it into place at midlength, stabilized it, and climbed the two circular tiers. A swivel chair set at 42" above the pool's deck allowed her a full 360° perspective, but she needed only half that to keep her eyes on the two swimmers.

Michael Thomas' visual illusions camouflaged his mother perfectly within clumps of marsh grass and roots. The recruit still stood on the edge of the pool scratching his head, confused by the simulation. The burly guy gave the appearance of a toddler at the shore for his first time, afraid of being sucked away when the surf retreated. He stepped one foot into the silt to test its depth and stability. The illusion parted, then filled in when he removed his toes. He cupped his palm and scooped sand into it to examine and taste. Clear water escaped between his fingers. He slipped his arm just beneath the surface and watched rooty images play on his skin. He concluded that anything his eyes saw was meant to be a distraction, and he was about to close them and dive in when a crocodile swam by and snapped at him. Those nimble feet of his carried him away from the edge in record time until he heard Katie's laughter.

"You better learn to distinguish a fake reptile from a live one, if you plan to survive in West Africa," she shouted from her perch above the pool.

He pumped the air with a fist, flashed her a smile and made a running dive into the swamp that was not there.

Kiri hunkered down in the center of the pool. Her swimsuit in mottled shades of greens and neutrals blended with the surroundings, and likenesses of jungle plant life covered her skin and shifted when she moved. She watched intently for the trainee's approach, rarely rising for a breath, and smiled when his brightly colored hair gave him away. It was no trick for her to circle to his rear whenever he swam within five yards of her. Only once did the two come up for air simultaneously and exchange a challenging glare. Kiri used this game not to hide, but to judge a prospect's use of senses other than sight when in unfamiliar territory.

Clay could never get close enough to make out his examiner's form before it disappeared. He glided slowly on top of the water through the least likely hiding places, then raced through root thickets in hopes of a lucky break. When he realized that his bristly pate was a warning signal no matter how he swam, he walked on his hands on the bottom of the pool to disguise it.

Katie was a pro at tracking her mother's measured movements despite the murky environs. Clayton was impossible to miss. His head looked like a fluorescent orange tennis ball bobbing on the water, conspicuously incongruous. Taken together, their paths traced bright paisley swirls through the mangrove maze... until the young man upended himself. Next Katie knew, he was leaning against the pool's wall just beneath her chair.

"That woman's game is more Blind Man's Bluff than Hide and Seek. I can't see a bloody thing out there! That last was wasted energy. Causes too much disturbance when I come up for air. Time for a change of tactic." He jerked down his swim trunks.

"What do you think you're doing?" Katie screeched.

"There's no hope for me if I can't camouflage this carrottop of mine. If you're not interested, don't look." He pulled the trunks over his head and face, leaving only his eyes and nose uncovered through a leg hole. When he swan off, he wore only a faint, full-body jungle tattoo that transfigured with each stroke.

Katie watched the rest of the show with renewed interest.

Clayton positioned himself vertically in the most densely designed portion of the illusion. He moved just enough to maintain stability. He kept his head face down in the water and turned it imperceptibly to one side or the other to take a breath and try to gain a sighting of his very clever opponent.

Kiri did not spot him immediately when she came up for air. When she did, she circled around him to see how he would react. He did not. She narrowed the distance between them with each circuit she swam. He made no move to chase her. She advanced slowly and steadily from the rear and assumed a similar vertical posture. Not one masculine muscle twitched.

The young hopeful maintained position... waiting. When he sensed the slightest motion in the water, noted a minute change in the orientation of an illusory vine, and the hairs on his neck and arms tingled, he realized she was within inches. In one lightening, mighty motion, he flung his legs back in a wide scissors kick and clamped them around the hips of his astonished quarry. Then he nearly drowned trying to get his trunks back on in a hurry.

Kiri shot up in shock. Katie clapped her hands. And Clay turned pomegranate red from head to toe, camouflaging that flaming hair. "So sorry, Ma'am. I hope I didn't grab you too tight. You never did say who was the hider and who, the seeker, so I took a chance that curiosity would lure you in."

"No worries," she said after regaining her composure. "Rarely does anyone get close, and I usually call time after about half an hour. Your catch was a first for me. Well done!" Kiri rolled to her back for another restful float. She delivered a hand signal to Katie who left her perch to turn off the reality illusion and dial up the next surprise. "You have good instincts. I like your style. How are you in open water?"

"Quite good, if I do say so," he responded, treading water near her. "I grew up in County Kerry where the family is in the hostelry business and spent as much time as possible with the fishing relatives out of Dingle. I've done my share of swimming in those waters." He cocked his head toward the west in fond remembrance.

"Large family or small?"

"My family is as old as this island, so I can't begin to count how many of us there are."

"Are you close?"

"As tight as a ball of tangled yarn."

"Will your family worry with you out of the country so often?"

"Have you ever known a mother not to worry the minute her child steps out the door?" He flashed his lopsided smile at the woman swimming beside him. "But a guy's gotta live his own life, now, doesn't he."

Kiri bobbed her head in agreement. "Well stated. Take a break and meet me up on deck at the deep end in five."

"There's more?"

"I've saved the best for last." She swam to the edge and climbed out while the mangrove swamp disappeared beneath her.

Clay headed for the patio, felt the tiles before he got out and grabbed a towel to wrap around his shoulders. Late afternoon brought a chill to the air and a shiver from his wet and exhausted body. When Katie appeared with another bottle of drinking water, he emitted a deep sigh. "How much longer does this torture, as you call it, go on? I'm near freezing standing here."

She tried to hide a smile. "Not long. I call an end after half an hour if you haven't before then."

"Can you tell me what we'll be doing?"

"Breathing... or not," she said with a coy wink.

"You're as wily as that woman down there staring as if my five minutes are up. How about another hint," he requested as he trotted toward the far end, still clutching the towel.

"Think outside the box," Katie shouted after him.

When he arrived front and center, his examiner asked, "Cold, Mr. Moriarty?"

Noting she stood without one, he dropped his towel. "No, Ma'am. Fired up and ready to go."

"Good," she smiled with a gleam in her eye. "We're going to see how long you can hold your breath underwater. We'll jump in together. If you come up before I do, you have the option of going again. If I break water first, you've proven yourself and we're done. Thirty minutes max. Rings are planted along the wall to hang onto if you feel the need. You may try to muscle me to the surface as long as you don't use brute force. Any questions?"

He studied the woman barely half his weight. "Only one. Have you ever been injured during this exercise?"

Kiri stared straight into his cobalt eyes. "Three broken fingers, two cracked collar bones, and six dislocated shoulders. Those will end your career with this network and probably any other. On three."

Their feet hit the water together. Clay touched bottom, then exploded up, out and onto the deck. "Jeez!" he shouted. "That water's freezing!"

"Not quite, by about eight degrees." She reached her hand toward him for help out. "You finished?"

He shook his head. "On three." This time he grabbed a ring to stop himself from scrambling out. Both swimmers leaned against the wall counting seconds and then minutes. When Clay started to turn purple, Kiri motioned to him to rise and get out. She followed a couple of seconds later and received another hand up. He shook his head, inhaled deeply, and they were in again on three.

When the first ice cold wave hit, Clay let go of his ring. The powerful swell swept him halfway along the pool's wall, but he grabbed another handhold before his head broke the surface and held on through two more surges. Rhythmic, turbulent undulations followed. He used what little breath he had left to plan a strategy for their next jump. He knew now he could not outlast her, so he would have to outsmart her. Turnaround time per jump—about three minutes. Number of jumps possible in half an hour—ten, if hypothermia did not get him first. Figure on eight, to be safe. Three used. Five more opportunities. Spend the next one observing Mrs. O's movements in relation to water conditions. Then decide how much strength he dared use below her chest to unhitch her from that wall.

Jump four. He noted that the muscles in her arms and neck tightened when she anticipated a wave to hit, and she used her feet against the wall to stabilize herself during turbulence so the force did not thrash her about.

Jump five. Clay waited until after the first wave to swim up between Kiri and the wall with his rear to her front. When wave two hit, he pushed back from the wall with all fours as hard as he dared to try to break her hold. She wrapped her legs around his waist in a tight squeeze, forcing his breath out like a deflating balloon. He cursed himself for giving her the advantage of the outside position.

Jump six. He claimed the outside, his arms under hers, his legs around her waist, but he had no wall to push against to help wrench her away. Her abs tightened, and she had more air left in her balloon when his ran out.

Jump seven. After the third wave when the water calmed to mild turbulence, he darted beneath her, pulled her feet from their place on the wall... and tickled them. She doubled up and let go to shove him away. With one mighty thrust, he launched her to the surface. Game over!

Clay gave Kiri a boost over the edge. She flattened her stomach against the deck. He shivered over her. "Sorry, Ma'am. I tried not to hurt you. Are you all right?"

She nodded between slow, deep breaths. "Lie down with me..."

His eyeballs jumped up to his peaked brows.

"...like this." He fell to his knees and stretched out on his stomach. This time the tiles were toasty—not sizzling, but baby blanket warm—just right. Tingles slowly danced through his frostbitten fingers and toes and into his arms and legs.

She smiled at him. "Unexpected. Smartly played and by the rules."

When she stirred, he hopped to his feet. "Can I give you a hand?"

Still a bit unsteady, she accepted gratefully. "Thank you. Mr. Callaghan will contact you soon." She patted his goosebumpy arm. "It's been a pleasure, Mr. Moriarty. May I shake your hand?"

He smiled and instinctively led with his right and knuckled against her extended left one.

She smiled. "You must learn to adapt quickly in foreign environments." She poised herself for the walk back to the patio where Katie waited with warm towels and a hot mug of tea.

"Well?"

"Later. I'm spent. Getting too old for this job. When the man's gone, you'll find me soaking in my tub."

Clay followed at a distance but received the same kind treatment from Katie—two hot towels and a steaming mug of tea. He mummied himself, collapsed on the lounge, and inhaled the fragrant brew. After a series of deep sighs, he downed it in one gulp.

She refilled his mug and sat in a deck chair beside him. "Well, how did it go?"

His long face told the story. "I wanted to be brilliant. Guess I'm not as flash as I think I am."

"It's hard to be flash when stripped down to your tattoos."

"I don't have any tat...." He flushed. "I probably lost the job on that move alone—baring my backside to her."

"I doubt it," Katie snickered. "She's pretty open minded."

"Fact is, I played an *eejit* from the beginning. I tried to impress with my smart dress rather than my ability. I flung her into the water. I almost swore when I couldn't catch her and made a fool of m'self dancing on the hot tiles. M' camouflage headgear was, shall we say, unorthodox. But the big goof was not expecting the unexpected like she warned me—the heat and cold, the mock marsh and those horrible waves—so m' reactions weren't as smart as they could have been."

She giggled at the amusing show she had witnessed.

"I tried not to use too much force on that last test, but...."

"She never runs out of breath, so how did you make her let go?"

Clay lowered his eyes, embarrassed. "I tickled her feet."

Katie burst into laughter. "What gave you that crazy idea?"

He shrugged. "Dunno. It just popped into m' head. But that childish trick probably sealed m' fate."

When her laughter subsided, he said. "Enough about my shortcomings. What's your job here?"

"My cousins and I provide services for disadvantaged young girls. Families still shun unmarried, pregnant daughters, even these days. Others have no family to support them for various reasons. We house, educate and counsel them, get their health back on track, and provide job training until they're out on their own with a support system in place. Our results have been very good. We use the pool in the evenings and on weekends... unless there's a bunch of you recruits to entertain us."

He laughed. "Where are the young men?"

"We don't know how to deal with guys."

"You don't deal with boys. You give 'em a hug and point 'em in a constructive direction."

"We don't have room for separate facilities."

Clay tugged on his right earlobe as if to unlock inspiration. "Build a bigger house."

She stared at him, and an idea began to perk behind her bright blue eyes.

"I better get going. I have to say, that woman has a body and nerves of steel. I heard she was a hard one to get past, but I never imagined how hard."

"Be careful what you say. *That woman* is my mother."

His plastic mug plummeted to the ground, dousing her toes. "Gobsmacked, for sure!" He regarded her carefully. "You don't take after her."

"My name's Katie. Katie O'Connell. They say I favor my dad," she said, wiping her piggies on the edge of his towel.

"You're *that* Katie? *That* little girl? The one fathered by a dead man?"

She bristled and rose for a hasty exit. "Does that make me *different*?"

Clayton grabbed her hand and gazed tenderly into her eyes. "Oh, yes. It means *you* are very special because your parents vowed to create you no matter what. That kind of devotion is... sacred. Something for a man to aspire to. I didn't mean to offend."

Katie relaxed and removed her hand from his. "No offense taken. I assume you spoke from exhaustion. Hot showers are inside and to the left. Clean sweats are in a cupboard near the door. They'll get you home. Give the sweats to my brother when you're done with them."

"And who might your brother be?" Clayton asked as he removed his towels and stepped toward the door.

"The team leader. Michael Thomas."

He spun around, his mouth agape. "You mean, *he's* an O'Connell too? And I've been calling him Mr. Thomas for the last month because his namebadge says 'Michael Thomas!'" He clapped his hands to his forehead. "Who'd believe that a woman as fine as m' mother gave birth to a man of such little brain as me!"

Katie laughed at the sing-song cadence of his speech, typical of the southwest. "I'll bag your impressive clothes and give you a chit for the dry cleaners at the top of the road."

"Thank you. That's kind. But I doubt I'll be using it. Not for these. They're goin' in the back of m' locker—if I'm lucky enough to get one someday—to remind m'self that no matter how great I think I am, there's always someone to show me that you may find perfection in a flower but not in a man."

Her dancing eyes sparkled at the sentiment that spilled out of the near perfect example of one standing in front of her. "A pleasure to meet you, Mister...."

"Moriarty. Clayton Daniel Moriarty. 'Tis indeed *my* pleasure to meet *you*, Katie O'Connell." When she patted his arm, he extended his left hand to meet hers—the first correct—and the best—move he had made that day.

*   *   *

Kiri took only a minute to shoot a text to Henry before she slipped into her tub for a hot soak. *Clayton Moriarty—#1. Hire him! Best I've seen. For the record, the other five are ranked below, but don't give them another thought. Expect you for dinner.* The soles of her feet still tingled as she slid beneath the surface—a sensation she had not enjoyed since Michael caught her off guard when they swam in the sea.

After cleaning up the pool area, Katie found her mother still nose high in bubbles. "You had a long, hard afternoon. You OK?"

"Once my teeth stopped chattering. Thanks for helping. What did you think of that one?"

"Hmm." Katie pretended to consider and chose her words carefully. "He was well-mannered and not too cocky. Determined, for sure, but he tried not to let his frustration strong-arm you. His handshake was firm with a touch of tenderness to it. Positive attitude. From what little I know, I think he would fit in well with the other guys you've chosen."

"My thoughts exactly," Kiri said. "He was the best specimen of a man I've seen since your dad."

Katie broke out in a huge smile. "Good, because Clay is the man I'm going to marry!" She bounced out before noting her mother's reaction.

Kiri gulped for breath and could not find her phone fast enough. *Mistake! Clayton NOT the one for the job. Hire #2!!!*

Henry arrived just before the dinner hour and found Kiri pounding the memory garden path like a steam engine. Around the octagonal circuit she huffed, ending at Michael's center. She paused only long enough to shout at him, then raced her way out and back again. *At least she's not swimming herself to death,* Henry thought. "What's the problem?"

"That depends on you. Did you give the young man the boot?"

"Sorry. I can't. I sent him a text as soon as I heard from you. He stopped by the office on his way home from the pool and signed a contract. That man has as much exuberance as he has muscle. Clay's on his way to Central Africa with Frank as we speak. We all thought the guy was perfect for the job, so what made you change your mind?"

"He's too much like Michael."

"We noticed that from the day he first walked in. He has the physical attributes for the job. His first language is Gaelic, so he and Michael Thomas converse easily. He's clever, quick thinking, amiable and adaptable. Born for this line of work."

"He is *not*! Have you looked at his file?"

"Of course."

"I mean, really looked at it? He was born on October 19th, 2012!"

Henry shrugged with a "so?" look in his eyes.

"The day Michael was killed! It's a sign. I know it. The man is doomed. And he'll take the rest of you with him. Even my son!"

He brushed her anxiety aside. "You're making no sense. The longer we live, every date has a memory attached to it. You can't reject a person because of the circumstances of his birth." He squelched the *like me* that fought to escape his lips. "Clayton is perfect for the job, and you recognized that too."

"But he's *not* perfect for Katie!"

Confusion played along the furrows in Henry's reddening forehead.

"They only spent a few minutes together this afternoon but as soon as Clay left, she announced she would *marry* him. She can't! You've got to send him away, back to Kerry to his fishing boat... or hotel... and pray she'll forget him."

Henry shook his head. "Katie's offhand remark is not a good reason to fire a perfectly qualified man. She changes her mind a dozen times in a day."

"I read her eyes. She will not change her mind this time. My daughter serves this community importantly without the veil of secrecy around her every move. How can you condemn her to a lifetime of never knowing where her husband is… or do you plan to suck her into your sticky spider web with the rest of us? I haven't the strength left to nurse this family through another tragedy."

Henry tried to calm Kiri by reaching for her hand, but she jerked it firmly away and yelled at him. "How could you do this? Throw a man in front of Katie just to insure her loyalty to your precious network!"

"How can you accuse me of toying with Katie's life? I love her as much as if she were my own daughter. I would never *throw* her at any man." Henry turned a shade of red that Kiri had never seen before and shouted in a tone she had never heard from him. "How am I supposed to know what kind of guy your daughter fancies when her mother cannot choose between a dead man and a live one!"

He stomped off straight through the flowers, not bothering to follow any path.

Thirty-First Anniversary Year: Henry and I are history!

CHAPTER 31

Henry and Kiri began dating—others—in earnest, not easy for adults in their sixties who had been out of circulation for decades. Henry had not formally dated since his thirties and Kiri, since her twenties. They hardly knew how to go about it, but as word of their unattached status exploded around the city, both were sought after.

Kiri's suitors included an associate of stepbrother Tommy's from the society division of that other network, a dentist, a professor from Trinity, a Danish businessman with interests in Ireland, a banker, and a trout farm owner. Most were retired with time on their hands. Kiri made time for them, but her interest never lasted longer than three dates. At the end of six months she could not remember which name went with which face and/or profession.

Katie accosted her mother preparing for yet another evening out. "The only good that's come from your gallivanting around the city in the company of men you don't give a hoot for is your sense of style. That and your wardrobe have improved, thank goodness. But I'd trade your smart new look any day to see you and Uncle Henry together again."

Henry escorted a newspaper columnist, a clothing shop owner, a solicitor, a doctor and a local TV personality. All were mature and available to take the arm of a handsome, mysterious older man. When time came for him to express some measure of affection—after about three dates—he did not call back.

Katie and Michael Thomas huddled. "What's the problem between Mom and Uncle Henry? They can't divorce. That would break up our family."
"Silly girl, they can't divorce because they were never married."
"Why not?"
Her brother had no good answer.

Devin and Frank, the last of the original team and about to retire themselves, met up at a pub—not Ryan's.
"Michael's kids are top-notch. No more worries on that score. Katie attacks problems at the root, and MT tackles solutions. That pretty little girl's guy is canny and clever—an added bonus."
"We never intentionally groomed them for our line of work. I saw our function as custodial, to help them realize their God-given potential. I never expected Henry and Kiri to be the problem."
"Should we be worried?"
"Not unless any relationship becomes exclusive."

"Should we keep watching?"

His cohort nodded. "You stay on Kiri. I'll keep an eye on the boss. We're too close to our pensions to let those two slip up."

Kiri stepped out with a gentleman who loved the theater, another who preferred opera, one who joined in sing-alongs at pubs, another who liked to amble the Green Roads, one who opted for luncheons and long walks because evenings were too late for him, and a seafaring type. She cut back on her schedule and planned for semi-retirement.

Henry squired a socialite whose obligations required a distinguished escort; a soft-spoken woman when she dared to utter a word; another who uttered too many; one who was too young for him but who expressed a definite interest; one who was attached to her electronic devices no matter what the dance band played; and another whose major interest was birding—definitely *not* history. Unofficially retired, he spent much of his time at the museum. Officially, he planned to announce his retirement when Michael Thomas gained promotion from team leader to head of the covert department responsible for international security—the one that supervised security advisors and provided oversight and training for their journalists abroad.

Michael Thomas cornered Henry in his office—the one he rarely used anymore. "What's up with you and Mom? Katie has you over regularly for Sunday dinner, and I run into you here at the office. But the only time we see you two in the same place at the same time is at family events, and you hardly speak."

"Your cousins are kind to include me."

"They invite you because they want you to share in their good times. You are family, but you don't act like it. My sister and I are unhappy because you and Mom are unhappy. You're both professionals. Talk to each other. Figure it out."

A photo in the society section of *The Times* told the story. Henry and Kiri were snapped at his retirement party with their partners staring adoringly at them... while they gazed longingly at each other.

Devin and Frank met up. "What do you think?"

"OK for now, but let's keep watch until they have sense enough to get back together."

Katie bumped into her mother at the aquacenter. "What's up with you and Uncle Henry? You've avoided each other for almost two years, but it's obvious you still care for each other. You're behaving like teenagers."

"Mind your own business."

"Teenagers! You two are adults. Figure this out. I want my family back together!"

One day, they were—by accident. Kiri and her man of the day entered a popular restaurant for luncheon, and she spied Anne across the room. Anne with Henry! Anne *flirting* with Henry! Suddenly weak in the knees and queasy, she urged her escort to choose a different venue. Enamored as he was with the attractive woman beside him, he complied without question.

The thought of Henry and Anne... together... drove Kiri to return to the eatery every few days—sometimes with a female friend and sometimes alone. Was their luncheon a one-time coincidence? A frequent occurrence? Something more? Those two were near the same age, after all, and single, but the image of Anne batting false eyelashes at *her* Henry sent Kiri reeling.

She spotted Anne a couple of weeks later lunching with Alice Richardson. Startled at first, she remembered that it was the end of June, Alice and Patrick Murphy's two-week escape from the Falklands. For the past few years she had not returned to Colorado for the Fourth of July and forgot that she might run into them... *him*... in Dublin. An icy snowball cannoned into the pit of her stomach at the realization that he might walk through the door at any moment, but she stayed and spied. The two women gossiped like schoolgirls until Alice used a napkin to dab at her eyes, and Anne patted her friend's arm. Kiri dawdled over a dessert she would not ordinarily order until the two women left... without Henry or Patrick in sight.

Not a week later, she was on the prowl again, and her prey sat across the room with Henry. Henry! Every item on the menu sickened Kiri. The waiter was so impatient with her indecision that he told her to give him a signal *if* she decided to order. She could not. All she could do was stare at the two. Alice entered and joined them. Polite discussion followed until Henry shook his head... firmly... several times. Anne donned her aubergine angry face. Alice burst into tears. Henry spotted Kiri across the room and departed in a hurry without lifting a napkin, fork or cup of tea.

Thirty-Third Anniversary Year: Births: Thomas can now boast 35 great grandchildren.

Marriages: Polly; Kendra and Kean (to each other, once Katie established to her own satisfaction that the two were NOT blood related!)

Death: Tanya, Kurt's wife. She met a tree on a ski slope that wouldn't move out of her way. Newlywed Kendra wanted Bitsy in attendance before Kurt took her mother off life support. "I know her heavenly sounds will carry Mom away peacefully." My brother complied, and despite medical evidence to the contrary, we all sensed Tanya's essence surround her lifeless form before Bitsy's final strains drifted out the window.

Sara graduated from Trinity early and turned her technological wizardry to electronic modifications for household devices to help her mother. As word spread, others in the neighborhood requested similar alterations in their older homes to gain a few more months or years of independence. She hopes to refine her programs and market them to older clientele. "Not every elder can afford to live in fancy new facilities." In the meantime, she keeps accounts for many of us and contributes to MT's projects when asked. She's met a guy. Jon is a techie too. He calls her his "little lamb." They make a cute couple.

Michael Thomas obtained a loan from the Trust Committee and moved into the little house between the memory garden and Henry's building. Clayton moved in with him. Katie expanded Seamróg House to accommodate more girls and added another across from it, Tuar Ceatha (Rainbow) House. She used her persuasive charms with me to turn the property next to mine on the east into housing for at risk teen boys, Lon Dubh (Blackbird) House. "The time has come for our partnership to launch a program for the other 50% of the population," she coaxed.

"As long as it's a 'smart' house," I said. "I want alarm bells to ring here before the Garda come knocking."

"Don't worry. Sara can 'smartify' anything. Michael Thomas and Clay agreed to keep a sharp eye on the young men across the road from them if you will agree to the conversion."

"Will we invest in robotic tech to keep the place tidy and stomachs full?"

"Nope. Boys need to learn to run a household just like girls. And no PRA can replace a human hug." Katie has a way of getting what she wants.

Home front—the shocker! When Polly announced her marriage plans, Kurt agreed to come for the wedding, barely a year after Tanya's death. The following morning I stopped by Meghan's to return a family punchbowl and platter she used for the reception in the aquacenter's party room. The atmosphere was terrific, thanks to Michael Thomas' magic, but that's not the shocker. Kurt answered the door in his skivvies and bathrobe!

I called him on it. I tiptoed around my house all morning so I would not disturb him in the guestroom. He wasn't disturbed at all. He slept in someone else's! His stepsister's! Not as a guest!!

We argued. "Just because I've lost my first love, doesn't mean I can't find pleasure with someone else. I'm not dead yet!" he shouted. "You ought to know. Henry has kept you company for many years."

Foist his wrong on me? I shouted back. "How dare you imply that our relationship is more than platonic!"

"How dare you pretend that it is only *platonic. Thirty years, Sis, is a long time to keep a guy strung along. He must get something out of it," he smirked and closed the door.*

By challenging their judgement, I've lost the last two important men in my life.

CHAPTER 32

Kiri had not sought refuge in the pool in years, not since her son's twenty-first birthday, but nervous anticipation drove her there. She swam lap after frantic lap to exhaust herself before Clayton arrived for his scheduled appointment. He called. Wanted to speak privately with her. Name the time, and he would be there. She knew the topic and worried herself into a nervous fit. *How do I say 'yes' when I don't mean it, or 'no' and break my daughter's heart?*

The young man sat patiently in a deck chair.

"I felt like a workout. Sorry to keep you waiting."

"No problem. I expected as much." He gave her a firm hand out and stepped away from the edge quickly.

When she spotted Katie peering at them from the window of the aquacenter's party room, Kiri wrapped a warm towel around her shoulders. "Give me a minute to change. Have a seat under the fir tree in my garden, and I'll bring some tea." Reluctantly she did as she said and returned within a few minutes to the young man who still waited patiently, dressed in T-shirt, swim trunks and deck shoes. "Well, Mr. Moriarty. What's on your mind?"

He inhaled deeply and tried to appear confident. "I've come to ask for your daughter's hand in marriage."

She was not surprised, but all she could manage to say beneath arched eyebrows was, "Really?"

"Yes, Ma'am. 'Tis no secret that I'm not on the top of your list as a prospect for Katie. I'm likely not on your list at all, but I want to assure you that I'm devoted to her and will do everything in m' power to be the husband she deserves."

"You dressed rather casually for such an important mission."

"Thought I might have to swim against you to win her. Didn't want to get caught off guard."

"Who would have won, do you think?"

" 'Twould be me, no doubt. Today I have passion on m' side."

"What about the demands of your job?"

"I love what I'm doing, but I understand your concern. You, better than anyone, know the hazards. But your Katie has an angel watching over her, for sure. No one she loves will be lost before his time. I'm lucky that ethereal wing is wide enough to cover m'self as well."

Kiri studied the swirl of leaves in her teacup. "I don't know anything about you."

"That's not quite true, Ma'am. You know I won the job fair and square. You know I adore your daughter. And you have access to any other fact about me at your fingertips. So, how about I tell you something that's not in m' file."

247

The muscular guy with cobalt eyes leaned forward, elbows on knees, hands clasped, and stared straight into her golden-hued blue ones. "My dear granny, rest her soul, was a fine woman with a streak of the ancient in her. She claimed she heard whispers and could foretell a thing before it happened. When I'd come home from school all banged up and bloody from tussling with m' mates or taking a header off m' bike, she'd pull hefty me onto her tiny lap and wipe away m' tears with the corner of her apron. 'Clayton,' she'd say. 'They tell me I'm touched, and maybe I am, but from your first breath I knew that you were born with the soul of a brave and tender man. The one will lead you to a fulfilling life and the other, to the love of a good wife... but you've got to live long enough to grow into that man. Mind the rules. Mind the red lights. And don't you ever go near the edge of the cliffs!'

"As I see it, I've been blessed with that life. I *will* take Katie as my wife. And her angel will prevent me from straying toward the edge of those cliffs." Clay wiped a tear from Kiri's cheek with the hem of his T-shirt.

She tried to recoup. "You are very kind, but too mild-mannered. I'll share some private realities about *our* family with you. My mother acted spontaneously without forethought at stressful times in her life. I'm sure my daughter shared my oddities with you, including marathon swim therapy. Katie is an unpredictable firecracker—liable to explode in any direction at any time at the slightest provocation. What if she has inherited all the family quirks?"

Clay tugged on his earlobe in search of a tactful reply. "Then, we'll have to build a bigger pool."

* * *

Not an hour later, Katie bounded through the door and into her mother's arms. "Oh, Mom! Isn't this grand? Clay proposed, and we're going to be married!"

Kiri steeled herself to appear to share her daughter's exuberance. She winked at the couple and smiled. "Frankly, I'm surprised you waited this long."

"Ah, that daughter of yours! She set her mind to waitin' 'til her two cousins tied the knot before she'd listen to me. And you know that when that mind's set, 'twould be like movin' a monolith to try to change it."

"I couldn't let either Kendra or Polly be last and worry that they'd never find that special someone. I knew I had mine." Katie grabbed her fella around the waist and snuggled against him. "But I'm awfully glad they're finally settled so we can make *our* plans."

"Any major decisions yet?" Kiri asked, as Michael Thomas walked in on the happy announcement.

The beaming bride-to-be nodded her ginger curls. "I want Uncle Henry to walk me down the aisle."

When her mother's jaw tightened and her eyes narrowed, Katie made her case. "Uncle Henry has been by my side almost every day of my life. I want him there on the most important one." She glowered at her mother. "Can *you* think of any good reason why not?"

Kiri could think of lots of reasons, but they were all hers, not Henry's. She stammered. "I… I have seen him enter a church only once… when we buried your father. He never attends weddings or christenings inside. He always greets us outside after. That's why you were baptized in the garden there. I doubt that an outside wedding would go over well with your prospective in-laws."

Clay's stricken face revealed his surprise at a fact his fiancée had not shared about her past. The Moriarty contingent expected a proper church wedding, for sure.

"Don't be disappointed if Henry says 'no.' Accept his decision gracefully."

"He will say 'yes' if *I* ask him."

"Don't beg. Be prepared for a 'no.' I'm sure your brother…."

"Don't count on me to do it," Michael Thomas chimed in. "I'm busy that day."

"You don't even know what the date is."

"True. But I'll be busy. I'm Best Man at a wedding."

*   *   *

Kiri found semi-retirement quite to her liking—two days of work per week, one day devoted to family/neighborhood/Michael's Foundation business, and four days to fret over her daughter's future and the sorrow and despair that were likely to color it. She gazed from the window of her counseling office in the aquacenter and marveled at how some plantings in the memory garden across the road always seemed to be in bloom—an ancient gift of the neighbors' green thumbs, no doubt.

With the last client of her morning out the door, she looked forward to a leisurely lunch before her water therapy patients arrived—mental exercise in the morning and physical in the afternoon. She stretched, gazed again, and glanced at her appointment calendar before leaving. She blinked at a new entry on the screen: 11:45. H.K.D. None of her current patients had those initials. Perhaps he/she was a referral whose records had not yet arrived and one of her employees booked the appointment. She set up a new file for this mysterious person and leaned back in her chair to wait the few minutes for the unknown's arrival.

At the exact moment, Henry walked through the door. When Kiri clapped her hands to her mouth to stop a shriek incited by sighting a ghost, he quickly explained. "I'm here on a strictly professional basis—client to counselor. Will you help me?"

She dropped her hands, took a couple of deep breaths and nodded toward a chair for him to sit.

"I apologize for the surprise... a secret identity I use occasionally. I didn't want you to reject me on the basis of our past difficulties. Only you can help me resolve my present dilemma." He tried a faint smile. She responded with another nod.

"My family is worried about me and advised me to seek help. I'm involved with a woman—two, in fact—and we've reached a point in our relationships where I feel I'm playing one against the other."

Kiri could not hide her bug-eyes.

"I am a man with a long history of denial who was successful in adapting until now. A situation has arisen which pits these women against one another. I can't please them both, and I don't want to disappoint either one. How do I choose?"

His quandary finally dawned on Kiri with a thud.

"In addition, I risk losing them both because I haven't told them the truth... the whole truth... about my past. My secrets separate all three of us—secrets that will affect my ability to please either one. I'm afraid that anything I reveal to support a choice I cannot make will turn their heads from me, and at this pinnacle time in all our lives... all may be lost."

Happiness is such an elusive condition she thought, regarding Henry's nervous thrumming on the arms of his chair while he awaited her response. *How can I help a man who, after seventy years, can solve any universal problem but his own?* She reached for a prescription pad—rarely used in the present day—and scratched out her recommendation for him. "Try this," she said, handing him the folded note.

His disappointment filtered through the gray tint of his eyes as he left without saying another word. He did not need a pill. He needed to talk to her, to hear her soft voice and regard her kindly concern... to feel her touch. Not until he reached his car did he open the prescription. *Take this woman (the older of the two) to a neutral place—a safe place—and share one small, inconsequential secret as a token of your promise that others will follow. Repeat as necessary... one secret at a time.*

*   *   *

Henry's car drove itself south along a coastal road, then turned toward the sea and stopped at the foot of a familiar, old fishing pier. Its passengers remained silent during the trip. When they stepped out of the car, the seaweed scent and rumbling surf rushed to clear the air.

"I'm sorry I hurt you," he offered.

"That sentiment goes both ways. I'm guilty too," she replied.

They walked the worn planks partway to the end and sat along the side with their feet dangling just above the water. "We all have secrets, Henry. Let's trade one today. The rest will come in time." She stared into the blue-green water and saw her son's eyes. "I'll begin. I lied to you once."

"No you didn't. You just skipped over the truth about the compass in your pocket."

She turned toward him with a tilt of her head. "You knew?"

He nodded, and the tiniest hint of a smile crept across his face. "You made some clever remark about a rodent. A dead giveaway. But we'll let your truth-telling count as a secret."

"Thanks. Yours?"

With so many to choose from, he took his time to decide what tidbit was substantive but safe. "I grew up on Quincy Street in the little house next to Paddy's, the one that borders your memory garden... where Michael Thomas now lives.

She tried to remove the stun from her voice. "With your mother?"

He nodded again and took his turn staring at patterns in the water. "For about ten years from the time I was eight. I planted her lilac as close to the house as I could. End of confession."

The counselor in her respected his need for silence. The screech of a gull soaring on an air current broke it.

"I came to you in the hope of reconciling after that last horrible afternoon. Or at least calling a truce until after Katie's wedding. I want more than anything to walk her down the aisle, but I won't if that offends you. Frankly, your saying 'no' would relieve me of making a choice. As much as I want to, I'm not sure I'm physically or emotionally able." Torment clouded his handsome features. "I can't tell you more without telling all, and I'm not ready to do that."

Kiri slid from the pier into calf-high water and raked through the sand surrounding her feet. She raised her arm in triumph and opened her palm to Henry. It contained a smooth flat stone about the size of a dime. "Think about this stone, Henry. Think about where it's been and where it's going. Once a mountain, then a boulder, a rock, a stone and now a pebble—all due to natural forces it could not deter. Someday it will be a simple grain of sand and then part of the sea. Look closely. This pebble appears regular, but it is not. Its smoothness is slightly pitted. We are like this pebble—imperfect and blemished—still in process because of circumstances we cannot change."

Gentle waves lapped at her knees as she continued. "Very little in this world is perfect, but many things give the appearance of being so. Take my Celtic circle, for instance. The one Michael gave me. Its very name implies perfection. But it is not. A true circle is a set of points on a two-dimensional plane that are equidistant from a center point. Our senses find circular patterns very pleasing, but on closer scrutiny they probably are not perfect. I thought my future was foretold in that ornament. But with all the jigs and jags my life took, I doubted. A son as my firstborn. My daughter's war with her mother. Thomas' lifetime sentence. Our falling out."

As each wave receded, it tickled her ankles with grains of sand in a hurry to reach the sea. "Now I'm certain my life *is* imbedded in that ancient, handmade ornament. When I run my finger along its edge, I find a dip here, a gouge there, a part of its curve slightly smashed in and the writing on it barely discernible. That circle is not perfection. It's reality. This pebble is the same, and it's a symbol of your life—the appearance of perfection on the outside with secret blemishes on the inside. You can't dwell on the parts that are not perfect. Celebrate those that are."

Kiri grabbed Henry's foot and slid the small stone into his shoe, fingering it past his arch. "Accept this pebble as your totem. Wear it in your shoe everyday. For a while it may feel uncomfortable, unnatural, and your toes will play with it. But in time you'll grow to accept its pressure on your foot as doing your part to help it achieve the perfection it seeks— that you seek. And after time, you'll only notice when it is *not* there."

She looked up at Henry, her rock for so many years, ready to crumble. "Wear this pebble on Katie's wedding day to walk her down the aisle. I guarantee you'll make that trip without incident. Not because you're afraid to stumble but because you'll be filled with such joy at escorting our precious girl to her new life that you won't even notice the threshold you've crossed or the altar you're approaching." She smiled and patted his hand, noting the tears that teetered on the rims of his eyes.

"Of course my answer is a 'yes.' Session ended. You're welcome."

*   *   *

Henry made it down the aisle with beautiful Katie on his arm. He did not stumble. He held his head proudly at the part he played in escorting her the full length of the journey—from day one of her life into the loving hand of Clayton Daniel Moriarty.

Thirty-Fourth Anniversary Year: Marriage: Aurora Kathryn O'Connell to Clayton Daniel Moriarty.

While Henry and I danced the parents' dance together, he proclaimed that day the happiest of his life and asked if we might work our way back. We'll see.

Is it normal for a mother to be a little envious of her daughter's happiness—or does that failing make me a horrible person?

CHAPTER 33

For the first time in years, Kiri could not board the plane fast enough. She still dreaded flying and still could not sleep when she did. But this time nothing could be worse than what she had just endured—two weeks of UN conferences in Geneva examining the plight of underserved populations in the world. The presentations were all the same; only the vegetation in the background changed. Crisis devolved into crisis around the globe, repeating centuries of history.

She took pride in the roles her two children played in stemming the tides of conflict and want—if not completely reversing them… yet. Michael Thomas' methods to stunt the escalation of military actions were coveted by many, but he retained control in a constant effort to perfect them. Katie's project model spread and was effective where it took root, but when the geopolitical situation changed, increased need followed. The doting mother kept herself out of the kids' businesses except to glow with them when they experienced a success.

The recent UN conference called for the participation of its funding beneficiaries, Aurora Aquatics being one. "It's about time you step up and promote the project that carries *our* name, Mom," Katie argued. "That's *part* of being *part* of a *part*nership. Besides, all you have to do is turn the presentation on, turn it off, answer a few questions and schmooze with anyone who stinks of money or authority. Your chic look will be an asset because most of those who do smell are of the same vintage." At her mother's continued reluctance, she tried, "Or would you rather that *I* attend the conference while *you* go on my honeymoon!"

Kiri snickered again at her daughter's prompt resolution of the issue and recalled her own honeymoons—both of them—sleeping on a floor under a tree. She dutifully packed her bags and took a quick lesson from her son on how to power on and off the up-to-the-minute projection system he sent with her. No hitches. She schmoozed. And survived. As the airport's passenger conveyor track whisked her through security and straight to the plane, she longed for the comfort of her usual seat—first class, first row, right window—and for the uninterrupted relaxation it promised.

She greeted the familiar cabin crew, eased into her seat, slid out of her shoes and was in the process of deciding whether to recline her seatback by 20°, 40°, or a near recumbent 75° when a commotion broke out in the seat next to her. A young woman struggled with an older, disabled one in a wheelchair while the attendants were unsure where to place their hands to help.

"We have a system. Really, we do," the young woman apologized. "It just doesn't seem to be working at the moment."

Clearly, Kiri thought as the woman's rear bent uncomfortably close to her nose.

A little more shifting, lodging and fastening finally secured a satisfactory result for the older woman with a placid smile across a face that lolled slightly to the right. "I'm so sorry," the young woman apologized again. "We've just seen a specialist here in Geneva. He changed my mother's medication, and she hasn't adjusted to it yet. But you know how it goes with older folks. They're anxious for their own homes and beds, so we booked the earliest flight."

Yes, I do know how it goes with older folks. If I could get her mother into a pool regularly, I could increase her muscle strength enough for the woman to help herself some and bypass the side effects of strong medication. "As we all are," she said.

"I'll just go see about my seat now. I always sit across the aisle from Mother so I can help her take liquids and use the ladies." She glanced at the couple seated there. "Must be some mistake." She smiled sweetly at them and left to conference with the chief steward.

He listened politely, examined her seat assignment, and shook his head. "I'm sorry. No mistake. Nothing can be done. You may take your assigned seat or we'll transfer you both to another flight," he said with a patronizing smile.

The young woman pressed her case, grew angry and impatient, and took the liberty of requesting the couple across the aisle to give up a seat to her. The gentleman refused. "My wife and I always travel side-by-side. In case... you know... we will not be separated."

Kiri grew indignant. Even the slightest measure of Celtic hospitality required accommodating a stranger, but this couple apparently had no ancient blood. She raised her voice. "I'll switch," she said, gathering her things. "I don't mind sitting a few seats back *this once*." She moved to the aisle and smiled at the steward most familiar with her habits.

The daughter quickly assumed the window seat. "Thank you. You're very kind."

"Part of my job description." Kiri looked around for the empty space.

"I apologize, Miss Kiri, for your inconvenience and thank you for volunteering your seat. This flight is fully booked today. Probably the reason their last minute purchase separated them. The young lady's seat is in economy. Near the rear. Middle seat. On the left."

If Kiri's jaw were not so firmly set, she would have demanded her seat back.

"I'll make room for your carryon and bring you all your favorite drinks and snacks. We owe you that much." He took her small bag and led the way into the cramped, noisy section.

Kiri rolled her eyes and followed. "I deserve a black feather for this, Michael," she said, working her way toward the rear.

"Pardon?"

She shook her head and looked for the seat with no head bobbing above it. There was only one… between a quite large man blissfully asleep with his head against the window and a not quite so large man who slept noisily with his mouth open. *Oh, great. Little space. No armrest. And headphones a definite must!* "Excuse me," she said, glancing at the black polished boots blocking her way. "I'm seated next to you."

No response.

The steward pulled on the man's short-sleeved, checkered shirt. "Sir. The lady wants to take her seat, please."

His head rolled to the other side and his deep breathing continued.

"Excuse me, Sir. May I *please* get past you to my seat!" Frustrated by his continued lack of response, she stomped on his boots and pushed her way in.

That brought the man upright and angry. "Rack off, mate! What kind of a puhsen tramps on another puhsen's feet!" He moved awkwardly into the aisle.

"What kind of man doesn't see fit to move them when a lady asks politely?" she responded and fell into her seat. As he regained his, she took stock of his jeans, rawhide belt holding in the beginning of a paunch, and the gray invading his sandy, tightly-crimped hair. The gold watch around his wrist seemed out of place.

Once in the air, he resumed his snooze. Kiri donned headphones in defense and reclined to relax as much as possible in the minimal space allotted in economy. She jerked when that chunk of gold plunked onto her thigh. She started to slap its accompanying hand away but noted that its owner was still comatose. She slid a magazine underneath it and rolled it back onto its owner's lap before her friendly steward appeared with refreshments—her favorite blend of tea in a mug and a plate of fruits, cheeses and wheat crackers.

She nearly swallowed her tongue when, midway through her snack, the expensively adorned hand was back and helped itself to a clump of grapes and three slices of cheese. "Nice nibbles on this loine. When do they bring the drinks?"

Kiri nodded up the aisle where the service cart made its way slowly in their direction, passing out beverages and peanuts along the way. "Yours is coming."

"You mean, this choice plate is not to share? How d' you rate?" He tried to replace the cheese.

His lingo caught her off guard. "I put in a special order. Keep those, with my compliments."

He ordered whiskey—a double—to go with.

Her steward reappeared to collect her rubbish. "I'll take your carryon with me too so you can deplane quickly. Again, thank you, Miss Kiri, for your cooperation today. I hope your flight wasn't too unpleasant." He glared at the ruddy-faced man seated on the aisle.

"I managed."

"Miss Kiwi? I thought I was the only Kiwi flying thousands of feet above ground and miles from anywhere."

"The name's **Kiri**. Lots of folks slur their r's these days." *You included*, she wanted to add. "You don't look like a bird."

"I'm a New Zealander."

"I'm not," she said and stuck her nose in a magazine. *Why didn't you stay there? The rough flight from London to Dublin will be a pleasure after this!*

Kiri texted Henry: *No delay. Arrival 3p.m. Thanks for the lift.* With the flurry over the wedding and her own quick departure for Geneva two days later, they had not had much chance to converse. He offered to deliver her to the airport and drive her home. She accepted. No big deal. That's where their relationship stood for the moment. She looked forward to a short flight, a quiet dinner at home alone, and the taste of a casual evening fog closing in around her. Not gonna happen, she realized the moment she recognized a familiar face in *her* seat—first class, first row, right window.

She approached the chief steward on this second leg, also familiar to her. "Congratulations on your promotion." He smiled proudly. "You know I book this London to Dublin flight several times a year, and I always reserve the same seat. Did someone change my reservation without informing me?"

"Oh, no, Miss Kiri. We wouldn't do that. Must be some mistake." He approached the young lady occupying Kiri's place and asked for her seat assignment.

Her flushed face and downcast eyes told the story. "I'm sorry. When I asked who had this seat... and you were so kind this morning... I just assumed...."

Kiri was about to lash out with the same "never assume" lecture she gave new employees when she realized that the young woman might be Katie shuffling her own disabled mother around the globe some day. "Never mind." She patted the mother on the shoulder. "You are blessed to have a strong advocate for a daughter," she said and resigned herself to pretzeling next to a stranger again. Saving grace—no one could be worse than the lout on the flight to London.

Not so. She immediately recognized his checkered shirt, then his hair. The florid face was the same with the addition of wire-rimmed reading glasses focused on *The Times* held upright by a hand encircled below with a gold watchband. She double-checked the seat assignment and muttered, "Two feathers for this, Michael. Two feathers!"

The man dropped his paper. "Come again?"

"I'm afraid that's my seat... again." She nodded toward the middle.

He turned a deep crimson, jumped to his feet and stepped to the left. "Be my geest. It's the least I can do by way of apology for this morning."

Kiri settled herself in the aisle seat and buckled in with a sigh. *Reprieve.*

"I do apologize. I leeft Queenstown very early this morning… or yesterday… or tomorrow. I don't even know what day or toime it is now and I'm buggered from flying for hours. Darned snarky to grumble at you and nick your nibbles. Truce?"

She flashed a friendly smile. "We'll see how this leg goes."

After takeoff the man asked, "Do you floi back here often?" You don't seem the toipe."

Kiri bristled. "What do you mean by that?"

"No offense. Just seems you know a lot of up-front staff, and you're classier than the reest of the mob."

"I fly frequently for work, and I like to be comfortable when I do. I ran into a snag today. And you? Why Dublin? You don't seem the type."

He snickered. "What gave me away?"

"Gold and rawhide aren't usually paired as accessories."

"My wife gave me this…" He tapped the watch. "…to look shahp for business and important occasions, but the beelt…" He unbuckled it and tugged it to remove and stretch out across her lap. "This beelt is who I am."

When the shock of a man disrobing next to her wore off, she examined the leather strip and fastener.

"I'm a sheep man," he continued and pointed as he explained. "This buckle shows a Merino here on the leeft and a Perendale on the roight. I raise both. In different areas, of course. Wouldn't want them crossbreeding. The Merinos give wool for our world-famous undies and the Perendales, the best lamb to grace your table. The Merinos buy the watches and the Perendales feed nations. I'm headed to the weest of Oireland looking for rams—some new blood. I rotate my rams every two years to keep the flock from inbreeding and to cull out the old ones. One ram can service 150 ewes, you know, but after about teen years he's done for. I have a lead on some foine Texels near the weest coast—to 'sweeten my meat,' as we say."

The man launched into a fascinating dissertation about all things sheep: mobs, breeding, pasturing, mustering, shearing, selling, trading, and most important—dogs. He exuded gut-deep passion with his brows, eyes, mouth and hands all coming into play. By the time he stopped for breath, Kiri felt able to distinguish the breeds even if they were all penned together. His Merinos with long, spiral horns close to their heads and triple or quadruple neck-folds of thick, dark wool would stand out from the larger meat animals. His spirited conversation was the most delightful in her many years of flying.

The chief steward interrupted them somewhere between teasers and terminal sires. "It's our pleasure to serve you as usual. Your standard?"

Kiri nodded. Two plates, please, if you have enough. And the gentleman will take your best—a double."

"Mug or glass, sir?" the steward asked with upraised eyebrows.

"What real man drinks good whuskey from a mug? He's gotta admoire the color sparkling through."

"Very fine, Miss Kiri. I'll return shortly."

The man twisted in his seat to reach for his wallet, but she stopped him. "My pleasure to repay kindness with kindness, and you seem the kind who appreciates the taste of the best. Besides, it comes with the price of my ticket."

He nodded his thanks and began to expound on the three types of dogs who work as a team when the afternoon snack and beverage appeared—meat pie, apple tart, raw veggies, fruit, cheese and an assortment of nuts and chocolate. "I brought an extra straw in case the gentleman has a change of mind."

Kiri smiled and shook her head. "Thank you, but I doubt he will." She unwrapped her straw and placed it in the half-mug of tea.

He gave the short serving of her beverage a crosswise glance, shook his head, and turned to his own tray. "Cracker, this! I'll try to keep my fingers off your plate," he said and dug in.

She finished most of her lunch, checked her watch and asked, "Are you sure you won't take a straw?"

He scoffed at her. "Who drinks whuskey or a cuppa through a straw?" He put his glass to his mouth, tipped his head back to drink… and tossed whiskey and ice cubes all over himself and the woman in the aisle seat beside him.

"Anyone who knows that the plane usually hits a rough patch this time of day." She, and those nearby, laughed heartily at the man with the face as red as the tomato on his plate trying to mop up himself and her before the plane hit another rough patch. He did not move fast enough.

Embarrassed by the two calamities, he apologized again. "I'm awfully sorry. Both of us going off smelling loike a pub."

"That will be the least of your worries if you don't get this back on." Kiri handed him the belt with the buckle proclaiming who he was. "Will you take my advice and hold on for a bumpy landing?"

"For sure!" He flushed again and tried to decide whether to dress himself first or grab the armrest.

"I'm sorry it was at your expense, but I have to say that this flight has been a delight. Thank you." She rose to deplane and handed him a business card. "If I can be of any help to you, let me know. Good luck on your journey. I hope you find the perfect specimen."

He watched her walk up the aisle while he gathered his belongings, belt included. "I just have."

Henry's heart quickened when he saw Kiri approach. At first he thought she had been in a pub brawl with her shoulder, chest and lap damp with stains. But her smile was relaxed and natural—more so than he had seen in months. She welcomed a breeze that blew her hair across her face.

She tried to keep her displeasure about Katie's choice of partner to herself. After all, what could she say after she and Michael defied family wishes to marry? But Henry could tell… could see in her eyes that she was disappointed… frightened. Until today. Today her eyes sparkled. Geneva must have been the tonic she needed.

She burst into the car, gave Henry's arm a welcome pat, and regaled him with her latest adventure. Even a quick stop at the grocers to pick up an order she emailed in did not slow her. By the time he turned down Quincy Street, he knew all things "sheep," and shortly after they turned into the drive, he discovered why. The man himself sat on the deck dozing. His car, drawing stares from the neighbors, was parked in front of the aquacenter.

The stranger came to when he heard voices and the kitchen door open. "Don't know how I beat you here, but glad to see a friendly face." Then he launched into his adventure with the rental vehicle that only responded to voice commands given in proper English and repeated the message "input address." Since he had not booked a hotel ahead, he did not have an address to input and the car would not move until he did. He finally used the one on the business card Kiri gave him and the car took off before he could shift, brake, turn or holler HELP! "Without any eeffert on my paht, it steered its way to Aurora Aquatics—veering to the leeft and then to the roight as it raced through traffic—and pahked in front of the building neext door. A lady came out and told me to wait on the deeck. What a relief to hear voices with human bodies attached!"

"Meet the perpetrator in my adventure, Henry. Mr…"

"Jack MacKenzie." He offered his broad, strong hand. "But don't worry. I'm not related to that legendary sheep stealer Jock." He glanced quickly at Kiri's bare ring finger. "And you would be this koind lady's…."

Both laughed nervously. Kiri did not know what to say. Who was Henry to her now? "Henry Callaghan is my oldest and dearest friend. You are in the home of the O'Connells and welcome to it."

The two men sat awkwardly facing one another. "Would you care for some tea?" Kiri asked.

Henry nodded. Jack shook his head. "Too early for a big meal, but a cuppa'd be choice."

She shrugged her shoulders in "whatever" fashion and left the men to become acquainted while she put on a kettle. She watched out the window at the pas de deux developing between them.

Guarded Henry leaned back with his arms across his chest; Jack eased into a broad-chested "what you see is what you get" demeanor. Reserved Henry listened attentively; animated Jack talked incessantly. The older man sized up the younger one—about Kiri's age. His own tall, distinctive bearing contrasted with the guest's stocky but fit rugged look. Henry wondered what secrets lurked in this stranger's past; Jack, confident at winning the opening round, returned Kiri's bright smile when she served him first.

During Irish tea Kiri and Henry realized they had not learned all things "sheep" and added culling, droving, mating, lambing, and crutching to their vocabularies—not all of those descriptions being appropriate accompaniments to a polite afternoon tea in any country.

Jack tilted his chair back and stretched near into the flowers, allowing that belt buckle of his to glint in the late afternoon sun. "Buggered again. I need to foind a good hotel before I fall flat. Would one of you koind folks program my rental to geet me to the nearest one?"

"My pleasure," said Henry, and he rose to walk to Jack's car.

"I have a better idea," said Kiri. "Why don't you stay with us for the night?" She caught a disapproving glance from Henry. "I mean, I'll check next door at Lon Dubh House. I'm sure they will arrange an extra bed. It's far easier to leave for the west from here than from in the city." She left before either man could protest.

Within minutes she returned with a clean-cut teen. "Sean will show you to your digs for the night. Take a couple of hours to rest and freshen up. Please join us for a light supper about seven. You *do* know what supper is," she joked.

"If it has anything to do with food, I'll be here," he smiled with a wink and followed the young man next door.

Kiri caught up to Henry at his car, "See you at seven?"

"As long as it includes a cuppa." Her laughter trailed after him.

Jack entered by the front door this time. "Noice group of young meen you have for neighbors."

"They are more than neighbors. They are one of my daughter's programs for underserved Irish youth." Kiri gestured toward the sofa while they awaited Henry's arrival. "She provides a safe space for them to recover and guidance to become independent. The girls live further down the road."

"Pahdon me, but I'm not bloind. Not all of those boys are Oirish."

"Katie also takes in referrals of young immigrants and refugees from countries in political crisis who need extensive counseling to fit in. During the years we've lived here, our neighborhood schools have grown from being multidenominational to multilingual and cultural as well."

"Whoever they are, they're moighty puhsonable and mannerly. The older couple living there didn't lift a hand. They leeft my welcome and arrangements to the boys—a fresh bed, toiletries and a wakeup call."

"The O'Malleys are live-in hosts who help the boys become self-sufficient and provide hugs and handkerchiefs when needed. My daughter's husband is their male role model. He uses a strong right hand and a tender left one to keep them in line."

At Henry's arrival, Kiri ushered their unexpected guest to the kitchen nook for beef stew and brown bread from the freezer and a fresh salad. Henry guided the conversation away from sheep and toward his favorite topic—history. "How long has your family lived in New Zealand."

"From the beginning—or at least since the mid-eighteen hundreds when immigration began in earnest. Early seettlements were planned and founded by English Anglicans as an outpost of Britain. Oxford intellectuals and the chuch decided to establish a Utopian society and reproduce their homeland in the South Pacific by importing plants and animals familiar to them. They handpicked their emigrants to fulfill predetermined roles in new communities. My several-greats-back grandfather drew a lot to seettle agricultural land and feed the new population. Still today, lands or properties are held in family trusts, and the family is expected to live there and keep the business going. The land doesn't belong to us. We belong to the land. Not my choice, but you have to do what you gotta do for family."

His nerve-racking day took its toll on the congenial guest. "Beest be on my way. I've got a long day tomorrow. Would someone care to program that four-wheeled monster to geet me out of this city?"

"My pleasure," said Henry. "In fact, I have an idea. I'll lend you my standard vehicle and drive the rental while you're gone."

"Sounds good, eh."

"I have a better idea," Kiri said. "You can take my standard. I'll drive you partway and grab the Express back."

Jack shook his head, but a smile peeked through his statement. "Cannot ask you to do that."

"Celtic hospitality demands that I guide you safely toward your next stop. Right, Henry?"

What could he say but yes? "Of course. Give me a call if you need a lift from the station. I'll move the rental into your drive and keep an eye on it. Safe travels."

"Don't worry. She will be. I'm not of 'convict blood,'" Jack said with another smile that prickled Henry's skin.

That call did not come by midafternoon the next day. Nor the next. Finally a text. *We're in Galway. Home by Wednesday for sure. Jack's plane leaves Thursday early. See you then.*

A second text followed a day later... from Frank. *Rec'd word from Doyle whose cousin contacted him after some guy from New Zealand stopped by his farm looking for Texel rams. Accompanied by a woman calling herself Kiri O'Connell. Cousin recognized the name and passed the word. Thought our Kiri was the only one.*

She is.

The cousin said that the man named a top price, marked a few hoggets and said he would return in a couple of months to see how they put on weight. The ones he liked, he'd pay for. Substandard, he'd pay half just for holding the animals for him. Should we check into this guy?

Don't bother. Nothing to it.

But when Henry received a text from Gus a couple of days later, he was not so sure. *Kiri stopped by the orchard today for fresh apples and some jugs of cider. Had a guy with her. Been to several farms throughout the west looking at sheep, he said. He seemed happy, and she wasn't shy. Do we need to check into this guy?*

Don't bother. Nothing to it.

The final text of the series came from Kiri... on Saturday... long after Jack and his car's departure.

Please come for tea on Monday as in days of old. Much to talk about.

How much of that talk, Henry wondered, would be about Jack MacKenzie?

*   *   *

Henry stepped to Kiri's door at exactly 4p.m. Retired and with the museum closed on Mondays, he could have come at any time—even for lunch—but he was determined to stick to her game plan. He would not mention her extended trip with the sheep man until she did.

The door opened before he could knock. "Henry," Kiri greeted and gave him a friendly hug. "Come in. It's been too long."

He nodded. "Exactly. A warm welcome is... always welcome."

She poured tea.

He sat, smiled and began a neutral conversation. "The children?"

Kiri returned a polite smile. No one had heard from the honeymooners. They made it known that they would be gone for a month and did not want anyone snooping after them! Henry visited Michael Thomas at the network anytime he wanted. So, she chose a topic equally as neutral—the wedding. They reminisced, chuckled and grew misty-eyed. She did not mention her trip with Jack MacKenzie or stopping by Gus's orchard.

He did not either. Henry did not want her to realize that he had his own sources of information about her movements in the west. At the end of an hour, he rose to leave.

"You'll come again next Monday?"

"Love to. See you then."

A week later, the pattern was much the same. Polite, friendly conversation. The newlyweds were still off the map. Henry updated her son's progress—successful intervention of a diversionary hologram to allow a couple of freelance journalists and a photographer to elude being captured by rebel forces in Central Africa. "They shouldn't have been there, of course, but there's always that hunger for 'The Story.'"

Kiri wove a couple of long-awaited impressions into her response. "Jack tells a good story. I know he seemed over the top the first day you met, but after a good 'Oirish brekkie and a cuppa,' he was very pleasant and companionable. Once I turned him onto our famous black brew, he held it well and bypassed the whiskey. Despite that first impression, he was every ounce a gentleman."

Another week later, they welcomed back the newlyweds. The couple spent their month in Paula's octagonal apartment above her garage in Colorado. "I wanted Clay to see the Koyle part of me before we got too far into this marriage thing," Katie explained. While most of their time was spent "...getting to know that part better," Clay blushed, they did hike, boat, swim in high lakes, visit Yellowstone and the buffalo, and taste big city life in Denver.

"We didn't tell anybody because *we* wanted to be the ones taking pictures!" Katie added.

Kiri and Henry shared a guilty glance. She did not disconnect the monitoring system in her mother's apartment in order to keep tabs on the triplets who used it as their hideout during their sojourns to the States. She and Henry could have watched a very interesting miniseries, had they known.

"Uncle Kurt kept our secret and spent the whole month away in a hiding place of his own. That was his symbolic gesture in honor of our marriage," Katie said as she and her new hubby left in a hurry for their home up the road. Kiri had a pretty good idea where that hiding place was.

"Jack took lots of pictures for his electronic files," she said, pouring another cup of tea for Henry. "He was very down to earth. Curious. Stopped often along the way to photograph the landscape and examine the terrain. He walked into fields, scooped up handfuls of soil and ground them into the palms of his hands to smell, then smeared them onto an app on his electronic pad for analysis. He always replaced what he dislodged—a true steward of the land."

Other weekly teas followed similarly with friendly conversation set off by a tidbit of information: "Jack really knows his stuff. He weighed and measured the animals that interested him. Examined their teeth, felt their musculature and took ultrasonic scans for back fat and muscle depth.

He recorded all that data in charts on his electronic pad. He's very knowledgeable about more than sheep, too. He told me about the climate from examining the environment, and he tasted the flocks' pasture grasses. His passion for his work shines through."

Passion. Katie, Michael Thomas, and now Clay showed passion for their work—in their eyes, their body language and their speech, Henry observed. Kiri had that glow once. He liked to think he did too—show passion for his work and for Kiri—but when he looked in the mirror, his zeal hid behind his stormy gray eyes. The museum kept him going. That and the hope that he and Kiri would find their way to one another again.

"Jack is very personable and got along well with the farmers. New acquaintances became instant friends. He claimed distant relations all along the way and invited half the island to visit him in New Zealand!"

Henry would not describe himself as personable. Personable on demand, maybe, but he had too many ghosts to let his guard down around people he did not know well or trust.

"I did more trekking during that week with Jack than I had in ages. I returned feeling so healthy and young again. He made me laugh."

Kiri exercised regularly with her work, but her remark hinted that there was a difference between being healthy and feeling youthful and vigorous. Henry could not remember the last time he and Kiri shared a good laugh. When the children were little, perhaps.

"Jack always has positive news when we skype. He invited me to go along on his return trip."

Skype! Henry did not realize they spoke regularly. He wanted to shout, "What the bloody h*** are you thinking, Kiri? Jack is a married man. He told you so himself. Where can he talk with his wife and family around? In the bloody sheep pasture?" But he did not express his displeasure. He took a deep breath and said a polite goodbye until next time.

At their next get-together, she dropped a bomb. "Sorry to beg off for tea next Monday. I'll be out of town for about a week."

Henry felt Kiri slipping away, and he did not know how to hold on.

CHAPTER 34

While Kiri was on the road, Henry received a flurry of texts meant for sharing among the old team members. The first came from Doyle. *My cousin says that the NZ sheep man returned as stated. Inspected, then culled about half of those he marked. Had a billfold filled with euros to settle on the ones he let go. Due to return in another couple of months. Cousin asked why he wouldn't take them now. He said he didn't want to introduce them in midwinter—opposite seasons! Kiri along for the ride.*

Henry: Suggest you reconsider looking into this guy. Frank
Don't bother. Nothing to it.

I disagree. Can't think of one logical reason to come to Ireland for sheep when NZ has more sheep than people as it is. And more than IRE or US. Must be another reason. Bears looking into. Devin
Don't bother. Nothing to it.

My cousin checked with other farmers he knew. Seems this NZ guy worked his way through many farms in the west and north and offered the same deal. If he takes even half of what he's marked, he'll need a whole plane to get them home. Is this guy legit? Doyle
Only one way to tell. Investigate. Frank
Don't bother. Nothing to it.

Kiri and the NZ guy stopped at the orchard again. Not as much to choose from since we're waiting for this year's crop to ripen, but they loaded up anyway. Said most were for the kids. Those kids aren't kids anymore, are they? Gus
No, they aren't. One of them is a crack investigator. Frank
Spy on his own mother? Devin

Henry shuddered at that last one. No way could they involve Michael Thomas in tracking his mother or obtaining information about her latest companion. No way! That young man had access to every bit of data the team acquired over the years; he just had not bothered to search through it yet. No way could they give him a reason to. And Kiri would cut them all off if she got wind that they were snooping in her business. He could not take that chance.

Do not! Repeat, DO NOT involve MT in any way! No reason to question the man's intentions, or Kiri's. If she has anything to share with her children, she will. Her private life is no longer our business. Henry.

Henry said it, but he did not believe it. Kiri and the children *were* his business, and he could not risk losing them over a chase in the dark.

The texts did not stop when Kiri disappeared every couple of months for a week at a time over the course of more than a year.

The unnamed duo showed up again at my cousin's. Took their measures and culled a few more. Said next time through in a couple of months he wanted to see carcasses and get a list of pubs and restaurants nearby that bought and served his meat. Called it his taste-testing tour. I can't imagine lamb twice a day for a week! Doyle

Cousin said after a full round of taste-tests, the duo swung back through and culled a few more. A couple of the farms north of his got left out altogether but were well compensated for their trouble. These critters must cost that guy a fortune. No idea there was so much money to be made in sheep. I'm in the wrong business! Doyle

Do I smell a lead? Frank

Don't bother. Nothing to it. Henry

Cousin reported that NZ made his final picks and ear-tagged them with his own electronic chips. Kiri helped. Next pass through, they'll load the beasts up and ship them. Doyle

Kiri and NZ showed up matted with mud to their knees all smiles, joking about our sodden country. Been tagging sheep. He was all excited about shipping the rams home. 'My girls will be so anxious to see new blood, they'll stand in line for their turn,' he said. Going by air. Says he flies his 'chilled' meat all over the globe, so he shouldn't have trouble with a few live ones. They'll fly Dublin to Abu Dhabi. Spend a few hours. Then on to NZ. Abu Dhabi? Gus

United Arab Emirates. Middle East. I don't like it! We've gotta check this guy out. Frank

No. Absolutely not! We cannot get involved. Henry

Sorry, Boss. We're all retired now. You're not our boss any longer. We don't need the agency. We can get a good start on the Internet. We'll let you know what we find out. Devin

Don't bother. I don't want to know. Henry

You don't have a choice. We'll keep it simple for now, but we're calling a meeting. Tuesday next. Ryan's. 3pm. You're going to tell us everything you do know about this guy, and we'll be the judges! Doyle. Frank. Devin. Gus.

* * *

The old team—the quick and on the sly guys—met as scheduled. Not so nimble but still cunning, the men all displayed signs of advancing age— gray in Doyle's beard, wan Frank with an inability to calm his shaking hands, Devin losing muscle tone from too much time behind a computer, and Gus half again the man he was despite physical labor in the orchard.

266

Only Henry maintained his trim, distinguished look. The men greeted with friendly hugs and back slaps. Doyle brought a round with the traditional empty glass for their missing comrade. Then they huddled far away from the few midafternoon customers.

"You first, Henry," Frank said. "Then we'll tell you what's rankling us."

Henry gave a detailed and objective description of Kiri's encounter with the man on the plane, of his first conversations with Jack the day they met, and of the few impressions of him that Kiri shared during tea. He knew nothing more. "Really not our business."

The other four huddled again, then pleaded their case to Henry. Devin began. "We'll admit, Jack MacKenzie is squeaky clean from what we've found so far, but all that money and the Middle East still give us a queasy feeling. Their meeting seems an innocent coincidence, but when you add your new pieces to ours, well, consider this."

"Why would a guy with a gold watch and wads of money in his billfold fly economy on such a long trip? Why would the only seat left for Kiri on the plane be right next to him?" Doyle asked.

"Why would exactly the same setup occur on the second leg? Why would he charm Kiri with his belt buckle and stories? And why did he really end up at Quincy Street?" Gus continued.

Frank took over. "MacKenzie is obviously more intelligent than he lets on. He's a man with smarts and enough technological savvy to compare his sheep's data electronically and to check world markets. He has vast experience with all kinds of electronic testing equipment and machinery typical to any farm operation in a developed country these days. He has plenty of money and connections all over the globe. So, why would that man not be able to program a modern car?"

All the color in Henry's faced drained and pooled in his belly. How could he miss the obvious?

"Has the man touched her yet?" Frank asked.

"What do you mean?"

"You know exactly what I mean."

Henry flushed. "How would I know, and what does that tell us? He's a man."

"Exactly," said Gus. "And there's not a man this side of Mars who could keep his hands off our little lady, given the chance. If you just mention his name and stare at her, her eyes will tell you. My sisters.... Women are like that. If yes, she'll look away but if no, he has an ulterior motive for gaining her confidence."

"And we need to figure out what that is," Devin said.

"But Kiri would never.... Jack is a married man. He told her himself."

Frank leaned in and arched his eyebrows toward the shaken man sitting opposite. "*Was* a married man. I don't know what story he told her, but the man is a widower. His wife died in an earthquake eight years ago—double the casualties of the 2011 one. Maybe the Jack MacKenzie Kiri's taken up with is not the same Jack MacKenzie, New Zealand sheep expert, of record."

"Identity theft? But why?"

Doyle shook his head. "Don't know. But time to go digging."

Henry stammered. "I... I can't be involved. I can't let Kiri find out that I..."

"You won't be," Devin said. "You have two... no, three simple jobs. Mention the name Jack MacKenzie, watch the eyes, and text us, yes or no. Take a look at the pictures of the real Jack we send and text us, yes or no. Give us advanced warning of his arrival to pick up the animals. Can you do that much?"

Henry dropped his forehead into his palms, tore at his scalp with his fingernails and finally... nodded. The quick and on the sly guys tipped their empty glasses upside down, brought them to the table with a bang and lumbered out the door. Once again, they had a mission.

* * *

During those same months of texts, Monday tea with Kiri was only interrupted by her occasional trips around the country with Jack. After meeting with the guys, Henry had only a few days before the next tea to consider his actions and what seemed like an eternity to worry over them. He continued his schedule at the museum, but every other waking moment—every moment—he paced, wrung his hands, pounded his fists against the furniture and swore at the nausea that consumed him. If he mentioned Jack's name and Kiri's beautiful blue eyes with the hazel flecks averted his stare, he would be crushed knowing in that instant that he had lost her. If her gaze remained strong, she was in danger and he had no way to alert her. In truth, he did not know which was the better outcome.

He appeared on her stoop precisely as expected after 144 hours of agony. Perspiration soaked his clothing and made his hands clammy. They barely hugged.

"Come in," she said with a smile, then noted his unusual appearance. "We can postpone until next week if you aren't feeling well."

"No. I'm fine. I just don't handle a workout as well as I used to."

"You should come for a swim in the evenings. That will get you back in shape in no time, and there's always room for you."

"Thanks. I appreciate the offer. For the moment, a good cup of tea will hit the spot."

She poured.

Before taking a sip, he summoned his courage and stared deeply into her eyes. "How's your friend Jack MacKenzie? Did he finally find the rams he was looking for?"

No hesitation. "He did. He should be back soon to ship them to his sheep station. The animals need some time to acclimate before tupping begins—the mating season."

A wave of relief washed over Henry, followed by a torrent of dread. "Will he have time to stop over for dinner maybe? I'd like another chance to talk with him. Get to know the man better."

"That might be fun. We could treat him to the best *beef* in the city." She smiled and changed the subject.

Henry did not pay attention to any of her patter. His mind was like a bowl of spaghetti with possibilities and fears all twisted. Try to twirl the strands together and they fell apart. Try to separate them into some logic, and they clung together. He stirred when he felt her pat his hand.

"Henry. You need rest."

He tried to smile. "Perhaps I do. Please let me know when Jack plans to return. I'll call in a reservation for the three of us. See you next week?"

"Always."

Henry stumbled to his apartment across the road and two doors down. He collapsed in his easy chair and prepared for his unpleasant task. He was in up to his elbows now and tried not to squirm in the quicksand sucking at him.

Pic-Y. Eyes-N. Asked Kiri to inform me when NZ returns. Hope you uncover factual info and have a plan. Henry

* * *

Two weeks passed with nothing untoward on the Kiri front until Henry's phone nearly vibrated off the dining table. Text, email and call arrived simultaneously. *Cousin reports NZ and K turned up without warning early this a.m. in truck. Paid cash, loaded up and headed for Shannon airport. Due to fly out soon. Do not. Repeat, DO NOT let K leave country with this man! Doyle*

Kiri had not said a word to him about Jack since he proposed dinner, but Henry remembered hearing her peel out in the early hours the previous morning. He thought she just went for a drive, but on second thought, her car did not return home. She must have gone to meet the man. How could he stop someone clear across the country from getting on a plane? Call the Garda? Claim national security? Fake a heart attack? Didn't matter. He rang her mobile. No answer, so he left a voice mail. "Urgent. Call me." He texted. *Urgent. Call me.* Maybe he was too late and she was already in the air. When his phone finally did ring, his hand could barely get it to his ear.

"Henry. One of the children?"

"No. They're fine. Where are you?"

"Near Shannon airport. Why?"

"Don't get on...."

"What? What's so urgent?"

"You. The children... I... we're all worried about you. You left without telling anyone when or where. You know how children are."

"Sounds like you're one of them." She laughed. "I'm fine. Jack called from London early yesterday. Said he found room on a commercial transport plane with climate control due to leave Shannon this morning. Would I drive with and keep him company."

"Don't get on...."

"Sounded like an adventure to me, so I picked him up at the airport. He booked a rental truck—also with climate control—from a place just outside the city. Funniest thing. It was a branch of Ronan's auto services. No one recognized me, though."

Henry was desperate. "Please, don't get on...."

"We left my car and drove the truck on a route in reverse order to end up near the airport. Loaded from four farms yesterday. Spent the night camping in a pasture. Loaded from the last two this morning. The plane just took off."

Henry's heart crashed into his stomach.

"I'm on my way back with the truck. I'm crossing the river now on E20. Don't get on what?"

Then jumped back into place and rapped with relief. "The M7. Traffic is a monster this time of day."

"No worries. Jack programmed the return for me. I should be home by late afternoon."

"I... the children... we'll all be happy to see you safe and sound after your adventure."

"Me too. How about we have dinner together and I'll fill in the blanks?"

"Sounds good. My treat. I know a choice place for beef." Her laughter filled his heart with joy but only long enough for him to compose a text to the guys. *Jack gone. Kiri driving truck back. We need to meet. Henry*

*   *   *

Henry was waiting when Ryan's Pub welcomed the quick and on the sly guys for another huddle. He greeted them with a stern look. "I take issue with your plan to have me throw my body in front of an airplane as it taxis down the runway. Come up with something better next time."

"Sorry, Boss," Doyle laughed as he sat and Gus passed around the drinks. "I was almost out the door myself with a handful of tiny GPS trackers Devin 'acquired' for me to inject beneath the neck skin of my cousin's rams. The plan was to track the beasts to their final destination, whether that be in the Irish Sea, the Middle East or paddocks in New

Zealand. The man showed up sooner than expected and without advance notice. Your sacrifice was second choice."

Laughter broke out around the table.

"Did you learn anything new from Kiri?" Frank asked.

Henry settled back, but not with ease. "Nothing much to arouse suspicion." He told of her early call, sudden drive to the airport, picking up a truck and driving the reverse of the usual route. "At farm #4, they stayed overnight in a pasture—Kiri in the cab and Jack on the ground beside the truck." He let that fact sink in before he continued. "Your cousin's was the last farm they hit."

Devin pulled out his smartphone to take notes.

"Jack did urge Kiri to make the rest of the trip with him, but when she learned they would change transports in Abu Dhabi, she balked. 'I will never set foot on Middle Eastern soil again!' she told him. Besides, she did not have her passport with her. He suggested she travel to his place for lambing season—their spring, our fall—and she agreed to consider the invitation. He flew away. She drove back. I have no idea if, how or how often they communicate. End of story."

The guys huddled to compare notes, and then they revealed their findings.

"The man is for real—well-liked, with a solid reputation in his community and profession. He doesn't flaunt his good fortune. His money comes from family land holdings north to south on South Island. They don't own one sheep station, but many," Doyle said.

Frank took it from there. "He's the brains of the bunch and handles all the business. He follows the markets and trades in sheep all the time. He maintains global connections in the commercial transport industry and transports worldwide, not only lamb, but beef and farm-raised venison."

"I didn't know you could raise deer on a farm," Gus interjected.

"If he's such a standup guy, why tell Kiri not to leave the country with him?" Henry asked.

"We decided that Jack may be an innocent player in this drama, but a player all the same." Devin presented an intriguing possibility. "Why did he come to Ireland for sheep? He has plenty and connections everywhere. Who turned him onto Ireland when he'd never bothered to come before?"

"Maybe one of his many connections has a bone to pick and planted the seed. Think of how many reporters and photographers we've snatched from the hands of hostage-takers and quasi governments. We did good work, but there are a lot of folks out there who hate us. What if some group is seeking revenge and, hearing the name O'Connell, has made Kiri their target?" Frank posited.

Henry shook his head. "Doesn't make sense. Who half a world away would know about Kiri? Or us?"

Doyle straightened in his seat, placed both forearms on the heavy oak table and leaned in. "After four decades in the extraction business, word gets out. They wouldn't try a thing on our home turf, but in a foreign country... far away... say New Zealand... she's a sitting duck."

Gus broke in. "That was our first theory. But when Devin got to talking about how he wished we had better tracking equipment, like some of the things MT was working on, it hit us. Kiri's not the target. Her son is. And maybe revenge isn't the objective, but technology is. Every group in this world who has an inkling about the systems he's developed wants a piece of his brain. He won't sell or give that away on any terms," he said with assurance as he folded his arms across his chest.

"Any terms but one. We were all taught not to give up information whether that meant torture or laying down our lives. No ransom for the quick and on the sly guys. Michael Thomas accepts that risk too. But what if it were his mother's life hanging in the balance? We think MT is the target, his mother is the pawn, and Jack is an unknowing accomplice." Frank punctuated their hypothesis with a fist to the table.

Henry leaned back in his chair with his hands folded behind his head. He looked each man... each friend... squarely in the eyes and sighed. "I think the four of you are bored with retirement and spend too much time watching the tele. The last time I read such a far-fetched tale was in a book. You know, those things with words printed on paper that we used to hold in our hands. You need something else to fix your attentions on, and there are still some unanswered questions."

"Like?" The rest of the men reached for their smartphones.

"I want to know more about the commercial air transport company Jack used. Most commercial flights head west out of Shannon. Does this particular one fly regularly, to the east and/or west, or was this a one-time 'coincidental' flight?"

"Mine," Devin called and typed onto his phone.

"Does this air company regularly connect in Abu Dhabi or was it a one-time occasion? If frequent, which lines does it connect with? Any we've had adverse relations with or owned by someone we've outmaneuvered?"

"I'll take that," said Frank

"Delve into the family connection more closely. One of the brothers, sisters or uncles may have a connection that compromises us."

"Got it," said Doyle. "And I'll keep closer tabs on my own cousin, too. See if he hears about a return trip."

"What do I get?" asked Gus.

"You get the family because they know you best. There are O'Connell cousins spread all over this island now. I hear that many of them stop by your place from time to time to load up on produce."

Gus grinned. "The best there is!"

"Quiz them about MT and Katie. And especially Kiri for any hint of travel plans."

The kind-hearted gorilla-man nodded.

Henry paused to consider his next request. "I curse myself for asking, but we should know how and how often Kiri and Jack communicate. We *don't* need to know what they say," he added with a stern glare.

"I'll take that one, too," Frank offered. "And you?"

"I'll take Kiri. Try to learn what she hears from Jack and if/when he'll visit again or if/when she plans a trip to his part of the world."

"Remember to discourage her from going," Devin said. "Any travel to Colorado or Europe's capitals is probably safe for her. But, if there is any substance to our assumptions... if anything sinister is likely to happen... an area in conflict or off the main drag—like a sheep pasture—is the likely place."

Henry nodded. "Anything else?"

Frank ran a finger around the rim of his glass. "I'm still bothered by the hidden tech savvy piece. Can't imagine why the man would profess ignorance, then use it openly and expect Kiri not to notice. Maybe you could ask her to...."

Henry's chair fell back with a thud when he stood up and shouted, scarlet-faced, at his friends. "I will *not* intrude on Kiri's life one more inch than I already have. I nearly lost her and the children... twice... overstepping where I had no right. I will *not* do that again!" He marched out of the pub, leaving his stunned comrades without a goodbye.

*   *   *

The next weeks and months proceeded in normal fashion. Henry went for tea each Monday afternoon. He and Kiri went out for dinner occasionally. Kiri served Sunday dinner for her children, Clay and Henry a time or two. The older couple drove to the coast to share some secrets and west to Country Leitrim, still a favorite haunt of his. They became amicably comfortable with one another again.

If visits became frequent, communications on the research front were not so.

One-time—yes and no. Usually fly DUB, but for regular customer and right price, will do as requested. Half-loaded in Dublin night before. Flew to Shannon at first light. Loaded and on to Abu Dhabi. Devin

Abu Dhabi's allure—low petrol prices and airport fees. Yes, connecting flights and sister airlines. Frank

Jack back for a quick pass to see how our new lambs compared to last year's to calculate estimated breeding value. Trip also to see a goat-sheep born in County Kildare to a ewe from a buck goat. Rare occurrence. Most die before birth. Huh? No word on the relatives. NZ family tree more prolific than Gus's. Doyle

O'Connell cousins friendly and frequent. Never noticed how often they stopped by, but no one knows of any travel plans. Gus

Other than the excitement over seeing a 'geep,' nothing more to report. Henry

Not so... until Kiri announced Jack's return to escort her to his place in New Zealand. "He has a slow week now before lambing begins in earnest, so he's coming over and we'll fly back together. He arrives tomorrow and will stay overnight at Lon Dubh House. We leave the next day."

Thunderstruck, Henry tried to remain calm. "How long will you be gone?"

"Two... three weeks. Maybe a month. It depends."

He fumbled for a way to stop her. "Do you think that's a good idea? What about your clients? Your patients?"

"Already taken care of. I'm thinking full retirement is in my immediate future."

Her eager anticipation signaled that she had something more on her mind than sightseeing. Time to eagle eye Jack again, Henry decided. "Why don't I take you two to dinner? That good beef we missed last time."

"That would be very nice. Thank you."

At dinner Kiri excused herself for a minute, and Henry jumped at the opportunity to quiz her friend. "What prompted you to come to Ireland in the first place? There must be plenty of good rams to choose from in New Zealand."

"A friend tuhned me on to the idea when I expressed an interest in Texel crossbreeds."

"I hear you're connecting in Abu Dhabi. Why Abu Dhabi?"

"After I retuhned from my fuhst trip last year so buggered, a friend suggested this route. I took my neext trips in stages and was not bothered by jeet lag at all. Just takes more toime."

"Do you know that Kiri doesn't like flying and never sleeps on a plane?"

Jack nodded. "That's why we're making the trip in stages. To Abu Dhabi tomorrow. I've booked two rooms for the overnoight. Then to Sydney. Again a sleep over. Then on home to Enzed. I like to arrive early in the day, which is hard to do if you're always flying east towahd the dahk. I do the same for my loivestock."

Henry shook his head. "She tries to steer clear of the Middle East."

"No problem. She told me she would neever seet foot on that soil again, so I told her I would carry her if I have to." He shrugged. "Won't be necessary. The airport has elevated trams and the hotel is connected. I don't mean to upseet such a lovely lady."

Henry pretended interest. "Where exactly is your operation located?"

Well aware of the cross-examination taking place, Jack swallowed a guffaw. "Over our remarkable mountains and near the middle of the mystical middle of our earth," he grinned. "We're surrounded by our flocks and huhds, superior grazing land, family and good friends. Not many others pass through our territory."

"Over what mountains?" Kiri asked on returning. Dinner and animated conversation continued with Jack telling most of the stories and Kiri smiling brightly.

At its end, Henry made an offer. "Let me drive you to the airport in the morning. Save you some time and a few steps."

Jack accepted. "That would be great. Ta!"

Henry tossed all night. Jack was good-natured in a nonspecific way, he decided, but he did mention unnamed friends three times. When he considered the glances the other two shared throughout the evening, he resigned himself to Kiri's growing affection for the man.

With passengers and bags at curbside, Henry made a final appeal. "I don't think you should go. The trip will be too hard on you. Unsafe to be so far away."

Determination fought with her excitement. "I did not make this decision lightly. I want to go. I must." Worry in his eyes veiled fear. "I'll be fine. I'll call when we get to New Zealand day after tomorrow. Remember that's twelve time zones and half the world away, so I'm not sure what day it will be." She gave him an affectionate hug and was gone.

Henry spent more sleepless nights until her call came. "We made it. Went straight to the hotel in Abu Dhabi and collapsed. Spent time in Sydney and took tea at the Queen Victoria, an evening harbor cruise, and dinner high above the world. Sydney is a great place! My feet are on the ground in New Zealand, so you can stop your worrying."

"Glad to hear it."

"Let the children know that...." The tone in her voice changed. "What are you doing? Stop! Jack! No. Don't...."

Henry heard sounds of a scuffle and then Jack's voice. "No worries, love. I have a little suhproise in store for you." Next came the sounds of her phone's thud to the ground and a second, husky voice speaking in a language Henry had never heard before. Then Jack's. "No, I'll carry her. You grab the phone and staht the buhd." Then the signal cut out.

Henry struggled against nauseating dread and paralysis to shoot a text to his comrades. *Kiri flew to NZ with Jack. Taken by force on landing. Don't know who, where or why.*

CHAPTER 35

Once in the air and on their way, Jack replaced Kiri's blindfold with headphones to protect against the ear-splitting whir of the helicopter's engine. A heavyset, broad-faced man of Polynesian descent turned his head of black, wavy hair from his place in the pilot's seat. Big, brown eyes and sparkling white teeth smiled and greeted her. "Kia ora, Miss Kiwi. Suhproised?"

Apprehension faded as otherworldly landscapes formed by ice and lava opened up beneath her. The helicopter dipped for closer looks at shining glaciers on jagged snow-dipped peaks of the Southern Alps, the South Island's majestic mountainous spine. Turquoise lakes nestled below them surrounded by lush, green forests called "bush." Stunning vistas followed the contours of the land through sheer canyons and along pebble-bottomed rivers rushing to their destinations—the only evidence of haste in sight. Foothills dotted with flocks and herds of livestock opened onto sheep country—a quilt of green meadows alive with tussocks of rich dark grass.

Kiri's eyes filled with tears. "This looks just like home!"

"You're crazy. This land doesn't look anything loike Oireland."

"No. My *own* home. Colorado." She wiped the tears from her eyes. "I didn't realize how much I miss my own country."

Jack inched an arm around her and spoke through his mic. "I'd love to visit your Colorado someday to compare spectacular landscapes. From what I have seen, Oireland is loike a lily pad placed geently on the ocean. But when the good Lord finished creating all the lands and the waters, He took the leeftover bits or rock, soil and seed, squeezed them together in his fists until they oozed between his knuckles and flung that mixed-up mass over His shoulders into the farthest reaches of the sea to become the North and South Island of my country. Then He spat out all the hues of His palette to color His creation—Godzone."

The proud sheep baron gave the signal for Nikau, his Māori right hand man and occasional pilot, to head for home, and the helicopter banked hard to the south.

Kiri barely took her eyes from the spectacle below but did scan the man sitting next to her, intent on his electronic tablet. "What are all those specks on your screen?"

"Drones that keep watch over my flocks at night. Daytime too. The operation is spread out with some animals—deer and cattle, as well as the sheep—in high, rugged country, so I can't geet around to monitor them all as I should. The bugs spot trouble almost before it happens and relay the alert—like a late spring snowstorm during lambing season. All my animals are tagged, so I can teell how many and which ones are down."

"What good does that do, with you miles away?"

"With the house and headquarters near the southern edge of the Canterbury Plain, we're just a short heli jump to anywhere. I can load up this buhd and drop in a couple of mates, food, water, medical supplies, big tent and enough fuel to keep it toasty for man and beast until the llamas can pack more in, depending on the need."

Kiri rolled her eyes. "Llamas? How do they get to a faraway place in time to do any good?"

"They floi in the back of our transport heli with the freesh supplies." He turned toward her. "Have you ever peet a llama?" She shook her head. "Then you have two marvelous treats ahead—baby lambs and llamas in one trip."

Kiri considered the multi-talented man. "You use more technology and modern equipment than most people I know. Why did you say you couldn't program a car?"

"Strewth? I wanted to see you again and in my semi-inebriated state, I couldn't think of a beetter idea," he explained with a grin. "God's truth."

She mulled over the implication of his statement until they descended into a valley etched into the earth by some ancient, industrious glacier that emptied into a pristine, glassy lake. An old stone structure stood within walking distance of its edge. The complex included multiple wooden sheds, groves of trees, well-worn paths to nearby paddocks and a handful of two-legged animals near the helipad awaiting their wandering employer. "The earliest seettlers nearly destroyed the native forests, so my ancestors used what stone they could foind to build this house and plant in the English style around it. I keep the old place running in honor of their dreams. At least the plumbing works."

He turned her face toward his. "Welcome to Godzone, Kiri," he said and planted a long-awaited first kiss on the lips trembling in anticipation of his touch.

* * *

I am a stranger in a strange land, Henry admitted when he snaked through the newsroom on his way to Michael Thomas' office on the floor below. Officially retired for nearly three years and checked out mentally for ten, the elder barely recognized the reporters on duty. He identified faces and names from evening newscasts, but he could not remember a conversation with any of them.

The present crew monitored screens displaying scenes from around the world. When an anomaly caught a reporter's attention, he instantly flew to the site on invisible wings and landed on a young woman's *hijab*, a militant's shoulder, or a brick plummeting to the ground during an earthquake. He became a firsthand witness to the sights and sounds of action and to speech immediately translated by computer, minimizing the need for local contacts. Journalists no longer signed on with "…coming to you from here in Baghdad;" rather, "…bringing you the news from

Baghdad," with their images superimposed in a tiny inset at the bottom right of the screen in an effort to focus on the story and not the one who told it. No need. Advanced technology replaced feet on the ground or social media as the authentic source for information—for this network, at least—and the new generation of newsmen accepted the assignment.

Henry suspected that Michael Thomas was behind the system that placed his network's eyes and ears at a scene faster than anyone else's could arrive there. Competition was rampant throughout the profession and many other news services longed to get their hands on this technology, but only a select few within his circle knew the developer's identity. To the rest, the bright, young executive was the person responsible for international security at his network. No one questioned how he achieved that. Henry determined to find out now and plead with Kiri's son to bend the rules in the interest of his mother's safety.

The confident younger man shook Henry's hand when he entered his old digs. "You could have walked next door from your apartment to talk to me, you know, instead of asking for an official appointment."

"Official business. I've come to ask you for a favor." His serious expression and unsteady gait exposed his nervousness. "I'm worried about your mother's relationship with Jack MacKenzie. I'm afraid she's in danger."

"How so?" Michael Thomas leaned back in his chair, placed his elbows on its arms and rested his chin on steepled fingers like his grandfather used to do. He did not blink, sigh, or allow any emotion to flutter across his face during Henry's calculated description of the case for intervention. When he finished, the current security chief shook his head. "Your scenario would make a great thriller but is far removed from reality. Haven't you heard from Mom since that aborted call?"

Henry shook his head. "Have you?"

"A couple of texts. She seems to be enjoying herself."

"Any person can use her phone to send a text. We *must* confirm where she is and what she's doing." Henry's demeanor begged for action.

Michael Thomas regarded the man who had been father and mentor to him for as long as he could remember, the man whose chair and position he now occupied. "I can assure you that Mom is not currently in danger from any foreign entity that seeks to threaten me. I can't tell you how I know, but I am certain and will not take any *additional* action to confirm her current welfare."

Henry's failure deflated him. After heated discussion with the old team about the best course to secure Kiri's safety, he finally agreed to risk his good standing with her son to make the appeal that Michael Thomas so abruptly dismissed.

"You taught me everything I know about this business, Uncle Henry. You and Dad set the rules, and I've not seen fit to change them. We share information with need-to-know employees only. To my knowledge, he never broke that trust with his family, my mother included, until you hired her to work for you. You are retired and no longer on the payroll. I can't change the rules now for your peace of mind. I wouldn't be worthy of sitting in your chair if I did."

Henry grabbed at an opening. "But your mother *is* an employee of the network. Surely she deserves your help just like any reporter."

"Sorry. A week too late. Mom resigned before she left. Clay will do water testing and Kendra, the counseling, for the time being."

"Kendra? But she...."

"No worries there. We won't send her anyone who might compromise our work." He regarded the man folding in on himself. "Walk with me?"

The two left the building and ambled through the Green across the road. "I can't tell you how I know, but I *assure* you that Mom is doing what she loves." He paused as if grasping at a thought before it flitted away. "Imagine Mom swimming in the chilling water of a milky blue, glacier-fed lake so large that even she cannot reach its far end before tiring. Imagine her floating under a bright, unpolluted sky and smiling at the spectacular mountains surrounding her. Imagine that when she does tire, she waves an arm and a boat skims the water to retrieve her and deliver her to shore."

They stopped, and Michael Thomas turned to his mentor to stare deeply into his troubled gray eyes. "Lovely picture, isn't it? Believe me, Mom is well and happy."

Henry got the message. Somehow—he would never know exactly how—Michael Thomas had eyes and ears on his mother. Kiri was safe. The rules by which her son lived, as did his father before him, were intact. Henry and Grandfather Thomas used that same word play when his son was captured in Yemen. Visible relief swept over the man.

"You held me the night I was born and know more about me than any other person in this world. But did you know that as early as I can remember, I had an innate sense of my life's mission and that I was not in control? Grandfather called it 'responsibility to family.' You would define it as enabling journalists and others to do good things for society without compromising their own safety—like Katie, for instance. I sense that I'm destined to gather both under the same umbrella and ultimately work myself out of a job following my father's path. I will protect my home, my family, my own wife and children when the time comes, our village and beyond as far as my intuitive abilities allow me to reach."

Michael Thomas could tell that Henry was not fully satisfied. "We can discuss my first project because you were instrumental in supporting my fanciful idea. Augmented reality is commonplace for us now. Others have tried to replicate my program but have not succeeded. The skies are filled with drones, but government regulations for flight paths, speed, height and load limits hamper gathering and transmitting information.

Currently my work takes a new direction—inward—toward a smaller and undetectable system that I am not at liberty to share with you. A different spin on the camouflage that's served us so well." He added with a cagey glint in his eyes, "Astonishing how far we've come. 3D printers mass produce small, intricate devices very economically today."

He guided them to a bench by a bush swarming with dragonflies. "When you gaze out your kitchen window, do you ever see these sophisticated flying creatures that most people disregard? Aerodynamically perfect, they can travel great distances at amazing speeds. Watch their two compound, bead-like eyes capture every detail of the environment. Notice their four opalescent, gauze-like wings that are nearly invisible when they fly but remain still and shimmer in the sunlight when they perch on a bush—or on your shoulder, maybe—to rest. See those dark spots no bigger than a pinpoint, one at the tip of each wing? They could be sensors of some sort and their long slender tails, like antennae. Together they probably gather and transmit information to help them survive... or guide them back to their 'mother ship,' so to speak." He smiled. "Amazing creatures, don't you agree?"

Michael Thomas held out a finger to invite one for closer inspection. "Is it possible that some of these insects may be more than they appear? Mother imagines that blackbirds watch over her. Maybe dragonflies do too."

There was the proof positive that Henry sought. Michael Thomas *was* the mastermind of the network's new technology. If Kiri were in danger, her son would be the first to know.

"The basics of my job—of our job—have not changed. Remember. We're the quick and on the sly guys. We don't kill; we outsmart. In today's world that means we use illusions as a tool. I cannot stop a bullet, but technology allows me to foil the human being who fires it. I cannot stop a bomb from exploding, but I can interfere with its delivery. I cannot change a militant group's plan of action, but I can lay down a different road for it to follow. And I cannot watch over every sheep in *my* flock when they are now spread all over the globe, but I can devise more eyes and ears to help me."

At Henry's knowing smile, Michael Thomas returned a kindly one. "I understand and appreciate your concern. If it were up to me, I would program you and Mom to find happiness together, but to date I've not developed a technology to influence emotion."

Henry's flush betrayed him. "But how... what sparked your ideas?"

"Let's just say... a fairy whispered in my ear."

*   *   *

Kiri prepared herself for entering Jack's world, including his home. She anticipated finding signs and photos of his family life with his first wife prominently displayed throughout. After all, the first eye-catcher from the doorway in her home was the merlot wall displaying the For Better, For Worse and Forever photos. Jack must have noticed those but did not comment. She resolved to respect the memories living in his home by focusing on the two of them and not their ghosts.

Three weeks in and hundreds of lambs later, that plan had worked well. Neither brought up the subject of previous spouses. In fact, they and several other hands were so hard at work with lambing that exhaustion at the end of each day overcame any desire for chatter or closeness. Jack was constantly at her side with his arm around her shoulder or holding her hand with a vise-like grip unless he was driving, piloting or working on one end of a lamb while she held the other. She warmed to the attention but was relieved he had not made other moves on her except a few pecks during the day and his version of a passionate good night.

Kiri found that tramping the paddocks and hills among the wooly animals large and small was exhilarating. Hearing the bleats of hungry newborns reminded her of Sara Lamb's birth and naming story and how precious Bitsy's limited life on a farm was to her. She took lots of photos to make a collage and felt the urge to paint a picture of the wonderful scenes she witnessed in this beautiful, unknown land. Bitsy wanted for no things. She had her music. But images that captured the idyllic surroundings of her early life would please her.

During their many days of driving or flying from flock to flock, Jack carved out enough time for a river-skimming jetboat ride on the Shotover and a tour of the sights in Queenstown, especially a shopping center bearing her married name. "Maybe you have rellies here you didn't know about," he joshed. She could not imagine encountering anyone she knew so far away from Dublin.

One evening, after another long day with the animals, a keyed-up Jack led Kiri to lakeside to enjoy the full moon's play on the water. They found a comfy spot of grass. He scooted her close, and she responded by lolling against his powerfully muscled arm. His dogs went for a swim, then showered the two when they shook before settling down by their master and his new friend.

"You are one hardy woman, Miss Kiri. Even my dogs have taken to you. A sheep man's dogs are his most valuable possession. They mold and shape a flock and keep it together. I wouldn't make a move without their approval," he said.

He nudged a dog's snout away to fidget with her fingers. "When we shared a cuppa at the Queen Victoria, you looked every inch the puhfect lady surrounded by crystal chandeliers, gold-fringed chairs, foine table linens and choina, and polished silver tea service. I thought to myself that you were born for such a regal setting. After the days we've worked together here I've seen a true spirit for the land, too—a powerful combination in one female... the koind I'd like to keep in my loife."

Kiri started at his words and tried to change the subject. "The pulse of Sydney is exhilarating. Its bustle of activity calms when a breeze sweeps in. The city blends old English charm with all the amenities of modern culture. But I love it *here*. This pastoral environment takes me decades back in time when life wasn't so hurried and crowded with meaningless tasks. Your landscape is rugged but neat and ordered as well. Lines of evergreen hedges act as shelter belts, and groves of trees define paddock lines and windbreaks. Rolled bales of feed dotting alfalfa fields remind me of my grandfather's farm in Colorado where life seemed so calm and laid-back."

He chuckled and inched behind her to knead her shoulders. "Hardly calm and laid-back this trip. To weigh, measure and tag so many squirmy critters in a day saps the energy of man and dog, but that data guides decisions that keep my business at the top of the pack. New Oirish blood will give me another edge too, I'm hoping. You were roit in there with the reest of us, lightening the load 'til the end of the day. I didn't invite you for a farmstay to pitch in. I expected you to roide along in the ute and leave the back-breaking work to me and my mates, but you have as much spunk as my dogs." He turned her to face him, ran his fingers through her hair and scratched affectionately behind her ear as he would one of his furry friends.

"I came back so sweaty and dirty that even my Merino grunds needed a wash. While I anxiously sculled a couple o' jars before a hearty meal, you skipped off toward this lake, shed your grotty duds as if they were sheared clean from you, and plunged into the icy water for longer than humanly possible. When I picked you up with the Fizz boat, you were all glowing and refreshed, ready to staht over again."

A second throaty chuckle masked his nervousness as his intense eyes fixed on hers. "Fuhst a lady, then a laborer, and now a water nymph too. Makes me wonder how many other layers there are to discover... and how many days... and noits that will take."

Discomfited by his implication, Kiri fumbled for words. "A love for water was always in my blood and swimming, an essential part of my daily routine. So it's no surprise that it became my chosen profession. I swim for exercise. I go to water in times of stress..." She succumbed to the wave of pleasure that swept over her. "... and in times of joy."

Encouraged by her response, Jack kissed her gently, then stole a look at his watch and jumped up, pulling Kiri with him. "Time to rattle the dags. Tomorrow's the big day. The rellies are coming and their ankle biters too. They all live close by and want to meet you. If neighbors or hands drop in with a plate, we'll welcome them too. We never know how many mouths will sit around the table when we have a pahty." He guided her along the path toward the house. "My guhls will pitch in to put a traditional Enzed feast on the table—roast lamb and all the trimmings. You're in the land where the Kiwi man cooks the meat and makes the pavlova. If I don't get that dessert in the oven soon, we won't have sweets until midnight tomorrow. This man can't wait that long!

He allowed her to help with the specialty dessert. She separated the eggs and broke a yolk. He laughed and asked if she was "away with the fairies." Noting her agitation at the idiom, he explained that "even one drop of yolk makes foam break down" and with a wink and a grin, told her to start over. He asked her to find the caster sugar, and she had no idea what he meant. He snickered, called her "thick," and gave her a peck on the forehead. After being shaped like a glistening white angel food cake, the meringue went into a slow oven to bake for an hour. "Do not open that oven door!" he said, placing a bright red linen napkin on its handle.

After cleanup, Jack took her by the hand and led her outside onto a path that meandered from shed to shed on the complex. He set his phone to alert him at exactly the right moment to turn off the oven and leave its door ajar until morning. His dogs trailed along behind in case their master gave a sudden command to perform an important task. Lower in the sky now, the full moon's light cast long shadows across the landscape enhancing the mood of the moment.

They strolled hand-in-hand. Footsteps crunching along the gravel path followed by light four-footed padding were the only interruptions to clicking songs of insects until Jack said, "We haven't spoken much about our pasts."

Kiri knew that conversation was inevitable, but she did not want to have it now. The atmosphere was too serene—the first unhurried moments they had shared in days—but he pressed on.

"I don't intend to go there except to say that the pain of losing your fuhst neever goes away. You think that there is no room in your broken heart for another love. But that's not true." He turned to gauge her reaction and then stared straight ahead into the moonglow. "Remember the birth of your fuhst choild? Didn't you wonder how you'd ever foind enough love to wrap around that little boy? Then, how your life could ever be better than it was with him in it? The neext one came along. Same fears. And your love grew to fold that one in too. You discovered that every choild is different and as precious as the last."

At Kiri's nod against his shoulder, he continued. "Love is loike that too. We grow and mature enough to make room for another, even though that newfound love will neever be the same as the fuhst. Not better or worse… just different. We can all use more love in our lives, more dear ones to hug and cuddle, more sorrows to comfort, more good times to share." He dropped her hand to wrap both arms around her.

Kiri trembled at the thought of where the conversation was headed. She did not know how deeply she felt about Jack. The sensations he evoked were new to her. She did not know what to say and did not want to spoil his declaration, so she said nothing.

"I neever dreamed I'd see the day I wanted to share my loife with another woman. But with twenty to thirty years still ahead of me, I don't want to spend them alone. I long to go to sleep with someone dear neext to me again, to hold her toit and keep her warm. I want to wake up with her broit eyes staring into moine, invoiting the two of us to cherish each new day we're given." His eyes begged for a reply.

"You paint a beautiful picture, Jack MacKenzie. A compelling one. No two loves are the same, but I too believe a second can be equally as treasured as the first. We experience different types of love at different times in our lives. Some are blessed to discover them all with their first partners. And others hope they will be lucky enough to find new friends to share new fondness."

He exhaled deeply and smiled. "Kiwi women have a saying. 'That man can put his slippers under my beed any day.' I hope to hear those words again... soon... from one very dear to me." He pulled her into a goodnight embrace more tender and passionate than usual. They whispered an affectionate "Po Marie." Then at the sound of "time's up" they sprinted their separate ways in anticipation of a rousing family reunion the following day.

*   *   *

Emergency. Discovered a link. We need to meet. Doyle

The men convened at Ryan's as usual and lowered themselves into chairs with less gusto than three decades earlier, achy knees and hips taking their toll. "Seems we've been barking up the wrong tree," Doyle said. "Family tree, that is. After finding no questionable connection along Jack's line, and after Henry assuring us that Kiri was not in any present danger, I went on another search. You'll never guess what I found."

"Illegitimate children?"

"Two wives? Not unheard of in the early days."

"A cannibal at the top of the tree?"

"Worse."

"What? Tell us."

"You won't believe me when I do. I found a connection between Patrick Murphy and Jack MacKenzie."

The men's eyes jumped out of their sockets.

"Seems Patrick's wife Alice Richardson is second cousin to Jack's first wife."

The men looked from one to another in disbelief. "Is that a problem?" Devin asked. "Surely no one there will link Murphy to O'Connell. Jack's wife must have dozens of cousins."

"Not a problem unless the wedding and funeral photos I found on the web are displayed on a wall, shelf or photo album in his house."

"Should we warn Kiri?" Frank asked. "Or Jack, for that matter?"

284

Henry burst in. "No! Any warning would alert Kiri that we've spied on her again." In truth he wanted to shout "Yes! And I'll fly over and snatch her away myself!" But he could not. If she returned home and seemed serious about the man, he might start a conversation that would expose the relationship, but for the moment the guys were stymied as was he. He had had his chances with Kiri and allowed them to slip away. But if he truly loved her, he would wish only happiness for her. If Kiri found new happiness with Jack, so be it. "No. There is a chance she will not see or hear anything to disturb her."

"If she does see the photos, what will she do?"

"Any image of Patrick will send her into a spin near the edge. With no one to help her, she'll have to find the strength to help herself," Henry replied.

"The family connection?"

"She'll take a running jump over that edge or swim the lake until exhaustion pulls her to the bottom of it. Or save herself," Henry said.

"Maybe we should tell MT about the connection."

"No. He'll want proof and that will expose us too. We cannot intervene. We must trust that the dragonflies will do that for us."

The guys looked at Henry as if he had lost his mind. They calmly discussed other options and found no good ones. "Ironic, isn't it," Devin said, "that Alice's cousins—first Blondie dragging Patrick into Michael's last mission, and now Jack's wife—form the beginning and end of Kiri's tragic story."

"Poor Kiri." Frank studied his hands and shook his head. "Could there be anything worse than seeing photos of Patrick Murphy in Jack's house or realizing that the two men are related?"

Gus gave his shoulder a nonchalant shrug. "Having Patrick show up for dinner?"

Kiri: Come home soon. We all love you and miss you. Henry

CHAPTER 36

Reunion day started early for Kiri when she heard Jack's footsteps in the hallway before dawn. She pulled on her robe and followed him to the kitchen. Noting his surprise at seeing her, she explained. "I want to see your Kiwi magic at work."

He agreed reluctantly and allowed her to watch and learn while he played chef. He chatted amiably—no pressure or reference to their conversations of the previous night. He trimmed the fat from two milk-finished legs of lamb and slathered them in olive oil. Then he rubbed the meat with garlic and handfuls of rosemary. She looked askance at two more garlic bulbs he plunked onto the cutting board. "Sliver these," he said with a grin. "You do know what 'sliver' means?"

She grabbed a small knife and went to work, happy to focus on thin slices instead of the early lambs she met on her arrival whose departure might well be on her dinner plate. She was allowed a second honor—to slide the slivers under the skin into the insertions Jack made with his knife.

After another sprinkling of rosemary and a few sniffs to confirm that the meat was well seasoned, he placed the large open roaster into a very hot oven. When the timer sounded a short time later, he turned the oven down to near off and placed the bright red napkin over its handle. "Do not open that oven door!" he said. "This Kiwi man's job is done!"

"You have the day off today," he informed her while they cleaned up. "I'll be back before my guhls show up to get the late meal on the table. You try to soak that garlic off your hands."

Kiri returned his harsh parental stare. She hustled to raise her fingers for inspection, but he was out the door and shouted over his shoulder as he left, "Reest and relax before the rellies arroive."

She could not. She rolled under her covers again to try to sleep, but the implications of their conversations rumbled around in her head. Kiri MacKenzie. Kiri MacKenzie. The name looped through her mind. She tried it out over and again like an infatuated teenage girl writing in the margins of her notebook. Kiri MacKenzie was a little sassy and had bounce to it. Kirin Aurora MacKenzie did not. The long "o" in her present name flowed nicely from Aurora to O'Connell. But if she changed her name—which she was not quite ready to think seriously about yet—she would have to drop the 'n' and deny her meaning and destiny as a unicorn and 'Aurora' for the dawn and harbinger of hope in each new day. She would have to give up that part of herself to fit in. Was a name change a betrayal to herself or to her children's history? A MacKenzie as head of the distinguished O'Connell family would set the stepsisters on their heels, for sure.

What else would I have to give up other than my name and address? The question niggled at her throughout the day. Dinner with the relatives. She would be on show. She steeled herself for the responsibility. She could not let Jack down. As much as she liked the man, he came with baggage as did she. Despite what he said the night before—everyone was different and special in his own way—comparisons were inevitable. She determined to harness her mounting nervous energy into constructive action.

After a light breakfast of tea and toast, she wandered in and around the old stone abode, examining its construction and the beauty of the entire complex. She was always busy with the stock or swimming while Jack waited patiently before a meal together in the kitchen, so she had not taken time to explore yet. Bright light streamed in the house's small windows and a large modern one facing the lake. Its dazzle played with mountain daisies and drooping clusters of lemony yellow flowers of the Kowhai trees outside—a perfect opportunity for photos.

Kiri labored to capture shadowed patterns in uneven stone surfaces, polished from years of wear. The light caught hints of blues, greens, purples and oranges that warmed and cozied the environment. Woolen area rugs broke up the harshness of flagstone floors, even in the kitchen. Woolen rugs were easily replaced, she deduced, while worn stone flooring told the story of generations of inhabitants. All walls of the original structure were built from local stone cleared and gathered from surrounding fields. The exteriors of additions to the house were also of local gray-brown stone in keeping with the old style, but interiors were more modern. Two stone walls and two normal ones enclosed her bedroom. A massive fireplace with the family name carved above the mantle formed the focal point of the living area.

She walked about the complex for a few final shots of dogs and men at work, hoping to sneak up on a colorful wood pigeon too. With the sun now high in the sky and taking shadows with it, Kiri decided she was satisfied with the array of images she captured and returned to the house in search of another constructive pastime. Even though she and Jack had not spent much time inside the old place, with guests coming she decided to tidy up a bit. Nikau's wife who came once a week to launder and cook for her favorite Pākehā was not due for another two days. She grabbed a cloth to chase away the dust and left the other hand free for plumping pillows and straightening magazines and curios—the family's Koru, a blue-green glass symbol of new beginnings and loving protection, and an Irish shamrock pressed in a transparent cube, among them. Last on her list was the entertainment center with all its cubbies holding family treasures.

She approached the task systematically—down the left side, across the bottom and up the right, saving all the framed photos for the end. She was on her hands and knees when she spotted a couple of dried leaves on the floor and whisked them toward the hallway for pickup later. One clung to her cloth—a nettle. She wondered. Where did that come from? In all their tramping, she had not seen any others. Surely the British did not import their favorite weeds as well as flowers. She picked it off to toss aside and noted it was fresh. Another mystery.

A shout interrupted her methodic path upward toward the photos. "Geet off that floor! No one who has lived in this house is bothered by a little dust." Jack grabbed her hand to help her up. "Come with me. I want you to see a stunner just outside." He led her to a bush on the sunny side of the house and pointed to a swarm of dragonflies with their tiny wings vibrating at hyperspeed until they perched, in unison, giving the illusion of a diaphanous golden veil. "Neever seen this many before, not at this toime of year. Aren't they a brilliant sight?"

"Must be climate change," Kiri said and ran for her camera.

The daughters arrived—both of them. Ella and Zoe were pleasant girls with a fresh, outdoorsy look. After a friendly "kia ora" and introductions, they headed for the kitchen with bags of fresh fruit and vegetables. Accustomed to the oddities of the small room, they soon had the counter space filled with appropriate cutlery and dishes in various stages of completion. They chattered in a language Kiri only half understood. She wandered in and offered to help. They placed her in front of the bowl of potatoes, kumara and pumpkin and told her to cut them up for roasting. She quartered them like she did at home until one of the girls stopped her.

"Those will neever cook through in the time Dad takes to bring the meat up to temp. They should be boite-size. Dad's roast is so teender that you'll only use a knife to smash peas on the back of your fork. I'll do it," and she proceeded to cut one-inch cubes.

Next Kiri tried peeling down the leeks—"too far." She tried preparing the peas and carrots—"too many carrots for the peas. Just a few for color." She felt like she had acted in this scene before, but the girls' attitudes were not acerbic like her stepsibs, just patronizing.

They asked her to layer the berry pâté and tomato slivers on crackers. She had no idea where or what berry pâté was, and her slivers were "too thick." She asked what they were used for. "Our favorite entrée." Kiri thought the roast lamb and veggies were the entrée, but no. "They're the mains." She tried one of the rejects and it was wonderful—a pleasing flavor combination. Exasperated, Zoe gave their guest very specific directions for slicing fresh strawberries to top off the pavlova while she whipped the cream.

Jack strode in to check on their progress.

"Rattle your dags, Dad. We're almost reedy to make the gravy. I brought mint sauce from home."

He placed his hands on Kiri's shoulders and gave her a peck on the cheek—in front of his daughters. She flushed. They flushed. "How's the newcomer doing?" he asked, gazing fondly at Kiri.

"Two sammies short of a picnic, but we'll shape her up soon enough." They all laughed. Kiri was not sure why.

"Who's bringing the hokey pokey and afghans?"

"Lucas. The boys will be here soon."

Kiri dared to ask, "Are dancing and napping traditional after dinner entertainment?"

The girls laughed again. Zoe shook her head. "Our favorite ice cream and chocolate biscuits in case we run out of pavlova. Dad's is the best and disappears as quick as a brushtail possum up a tree when his grandkids are around."

Ella reached for her phone to read a text. "Cuzzie Alice says they aren't coming after all." She looked up to explain. "They arrived in Christchurch a couple of days ago, phoned and asked if we could geet together. I invoited them to dinner tonoit." She glanced at the text again. "She says they programmed the reental vehicle straight to our door, but somewhere along the way it made a wrong turn and they didn't realize it until they were halfway up a mountain. They are toired and frustrated, so cancelled for tonoit and want to come day after tomorrow."

"Good," Jack said. "I don't care much for that oaf of a husband. Hate to have him spoil our pahty." He removed the roast pan, added veggies and spooned meat juices "over top." He sprinkled more rosemary on, popped all back in the oven, turned up the heat and left.

The meal was more raucous and with as many or more faces around the table than at Thomas' in the old days. The food was superb; the lamb, the most succulent ever. Between jargon and accents, Kiri had trouble keeping up with the conversation. She found that smiling, nodding and laughing worked well. When the pavlova plates were licked clean and the ice cream and cookies devoured, the group retreated to the living area. Kiri studied Jack's three boys—James, Samuel and Lucas. Built like their father—not triangular like O'Connells, but as solidly square and erect as support beams—they were good-looking men with friendly wives. She could not match the grandchildren to their parents or distinguish the neighbors from the rellies because, as Jack told her once, "In New Zealand, we're all the same."

Kiri plastered on her charming and delightful face and joined in lively chatter. After the first couple of exchanges that ended with baffled stares, she abbreviated her résumé to a simple, "I run a swimming pool."

"The sporty type, eh. You tried any of our extreme sports? Ever feelt a rush of fear loike bungee jumping off a bridge?"

Numerous harrowing experiences ran through her mind. She dodged a *jambiya* to the throat. Would that count? She shot a man, pulled Libyan refugees out of a rough Mediterranean Sea in the dark of night, escaped a car bomb, scrabbled through rubble for survivors with attack jets screaming overhead, and ferried her dead husband's body through militant checkpoints in Syria to reach a friendly border. "No," she said. "Can't *say* that I have."

After an accepted length of time, Kiri excused herself and headed for the kitchen to clean up. She waved Jack off when he tried to stop her. "My thanks to you for the last three weeks of your famous New Zealand hospitality. You need time to relax as a family. Take my word for it. I've been there before."

She surveyed the mess and quickly categorized what would fit in the dishwasher and what she would do by hand—wash, dry and stack for Jack to help her put away in the morning. She wanted to leave the kitchen spotless in case Cuzzie Alice showed up before Nikau's wife did. Alice. That name had not come up for years. Another rellie for her to pretend to enjoy. That's what Paula would do. Leave another woman's kitchen with no room for criticism and with a smile for the relatives anxious to voice it.

Elbow-deep in warm suds, Kiri stared out the window at meandering paths linking sheds and their wooly occupants—so different from the view of her own garden. Could she adapt as easily as the Irish rams had to their new environment? How did her mother do it? What called her mother to do it—leave her beautiful home and life in Colorado for the unknown?

Thoughts of the horrors she had survived wormed their way back into her mind. She wondered if that was why Paula turned her back on her life so quickly—a way to leave tragedy and heartache behind and start a brand new life? To grasp at new happiness in her final decades? Am I entitled to do the same, Kiri wondered. If she followed her mother's path, would that be a betrayal to her family?

With the mess washed, scoured, wiped and stacked, Kiri looked on her efforts and called them adequate. On her return to the gathering, she found the guests departed, grandchildren engrossed in their electronics, and Jack and his five children corralled near the fireplace. He had one booted foot on the hearth, one hand on the mantle, and the other bearing his gold watch, in his pocket

"So, what do you think of the new lady in my loife?" The boys nodded reluctant approval. The girls remained noncommittal. He flashed his sly grin. "I'm planning to ask Kiri back for the holidays. We moit have an announcement to hang on our tree."

She froze in her tracks.

His eyebrows beckoned her to join him. "I just told my kids that I'm inviting you and your kids to floi over for the holidays. Bet they've neever had Christmas in the summertoime. Lots to do if they like extreme sports. Snow skiing in the morning and water skiing in the afternoon, too. Should be fun. Yours will geet along great with my clan!"

Kiri balked. She had heard that declaration before—from Thomas—and wanted to stop Jack from making the same mistake. Not all families behaved as fathers wanted them to. Instead, she smiled and said, "Something to think about... but not right now. Meeting you all was so exciting that I am worn out. I'm sure we'll have many more opportunities to get to know one another, but tonight I'd love to turn in and give you more family time. Do you mind?" she asked Jack and gently patted his shoulder.

"Of course not." He pecked her on the cheek—his endearment of choice. She flushed. His children flushed. "I'll be along in a few... to make sure you're seettled... and to say a proper 'Po Marie.'"

Kiri held her breath until she reached her room and felt the safety of a heavy wooden door separating her from Jack's family. She knew he was inching toward a relationship, but she was not prepared to face the pinnacle moment so soon. Her nightgown did not fall easily over her trembling body, and she nearly tripped on the clothes she let slide to the floor. She pushed those aside and slumped onto the chair in front of the dressing table. She ran the hazel wood brush through her hair—Michael's fingers—and realized she had not thought of him once since she left Ireland.

She regarded her image in the mirror... and did not recognize it. After days of working with Jack outdoors, her sun-baked skin was the toasty color of her biking and swimming youth, but she had to press her fingers to her cheeks and pull back to tighten her skin enough to find her features. Her eyes puffed from dust, and streaks of gray tried to hide among her curls. Her neck was still taut and smooth, but her hands gave away her age.

I am becoming my mother! At that sudden realization, Kiri spoke to the actively aging woman looking back at her. "I'm behaving like a twenty-something, escaping the nest to fly on my own in a chase after dreams and intimacy. I'm too blind and so caught up in the moment—electric sensations and new experiences with an intriguing man—to realize that I'm breaking away from my family just like my mother did. Why, Mom? Why did you do it? What connection drove you to cut ties with everything you knew and loved to be with Thomas?"

Hearing no reply, she moved to the window that overlooked the lake—the lake that invited her to swim as far as her strength would carry her each and every day; the lake surrounded by protective mountains that separated her from the cares and sorrows of her past; the lake bordered by vast fields of rich grasses dancing in a breeze that whispered "You are safe here." Moonbeams glinting off its surface sparked a myriad of possibilities open to her in this mystical land.

Her gowned reflection in the window bobbed on the lake's never-ending waters and urged her to look beyond its allure to verbalize her hopes and her fears. "What do you love about Jack?"

Kiri was unsettled by the sound of her own voice. Ordinarily her thoughts played mutely in her mind. She approached cautiously to look herself in the eye and replied, "I like Jack. I really do. His ruggedly handsome look hasn't faded with age. We get along well. Work well alongside each other. We would find happiness and enjoy a life together. We'd build enough affection to get us through the tough times—to face what it means to get older when our bodies, minds and emotional needs are not the same as they were."

Her reflection countered, "Don't reply with what you like or expect will come to pass. What do you *love* about the man *now*?"

She had to think twice. She never looked back with Jack, only forward. "Now" was that elusive space in between. "I love his compassion for man and beast. His dedication to stewardship of the land. He celebrates life everyday. His fun-loving spirit turns work into play. Jack doesn't allow problems to become obstacles. He sees them as opportunities to discover a new path. He is very affectionate and not shy about displaying his feelings, even when others are around."

"But is that enough? What about sex?"

Kiri could not believe she would ask herself about such a sensitive subject. But she did need to face it… and before Jack came to say good night. She took another step forward—the better to see herself—and two quick steps back, startled by the clarity of her image. "Of course, I think about sex. What mature woman doesn't? In the years after my children were born, I ached for intimacy with a man. I hoped Henry and I might… but over the years as love changed, so did our relationship. We glazed over the romantic years of playful flirtation to the companionable maturity phase. Our last several years have been so conflicted—hurtful—that now we're too close to remain just friends and too far apart to be more."

"This conversation is not about Henry. It is about Jack. Where do you stand on having sex with Jack?"

Kiri folded her arms across her chest and gripped her shoulders. Her reflection followed suit. "Sex can be awkward no matter how old you are," Kiri admitted. "Especially the first time with any man. I hope Jack will be as understanding as he is compassionate." She paused to study herself. "If I'm honest, I have to ask myself if sex with any other man is a betrayal of my vows to Michael." She shivered. In all the years she longed for closeness with Henry, she never considered that question.

"Whoa! You're veering off-track! This conversation was to focus on the immediate proposal before you. Now you've complicated that discussion by bringing Henry and Michael into the mix."

"Who I am now is a result of the men who helped shape me. I can't consider a life with Jack without acknowledging their influence."

"So, compare and contrast. You're good at that."

She inhaled a deep cleansing breath and slowly expelled it while considering the men in her life. "Henry and I have history. Jack and I don't. My children and I provided Henry with a family he never expected to have, and he filled a hole in our lives too. Jack and I will never have a family together—the bond of blood—so our loyalties will always be divided no matter what we claim. I have firsthand experience on that battleground! Michael and I... had a very short history with a good share of battles. In truth, we never spent much time... alone... together."

Kiri had not really thought about how a future with Michael would have played out. She incorporated him into whatever she and the kids were involved with at the time and assumed he followed along. When she did ask for his advice, he never answered. What would decades together have brought them?

"Out loud, Kiri. Voice your thoughts."

"My life with Michael would have included children, for sure, but maybe more than I was willing to have and fewer than he desired—an ongoing conflict. Our times together would be passionate and intense but few and far between. He would never give up the adrenaline rush of his job, despite the deal he offered. I know that now after observing his teammates all these years. Another ongoing conflict." She sighed deeply. "I've idealized Michael for so long that I can't admit the truth—our reality might have been completely opposite of my illusion."

"Good. That's progress. Is that why you are not wearing your rings?"

"I don't wear them when I travel. Old habit."

"Anything else important that you don't do?"

Kiri thought for a minute. "I don't wear my compass necklace. No occasion to. It hangs on my bedroom wall to remind me..."

"Of what?"

"Of the fairy tale I imagined with Michael."

"What else hangs on your wall to remind you of the 'happily ever after' that never came to pass?"

"Photos, of course, and the portrait I painted with Michael holding our children."

"You can hide jewelry and photos in the bottom of a dresser drawer when you move in here, but where will you hang Michael's portrait? On the wall of another man's bedroom?"

Kiri snickered at that silly thought. "Of course not." Then she grew wistful. "I would have to leave Michael behind in Dublin. And who said anything about moving in here?"

"One issue at a time. If you are willing to forsake the most important symbol of Michael's memory, what else will you give up? Your family?"

"No!" Kiri shouted at herself. "I can't! Katie expects her first child in February, and from the look in Clay's eyes, it won't be the last one.

Michael Thomas talks about marriage all the time. He just hasn't done anything about it. Sara is grown now and starting a business. The nieces and nephews keep my schedule full with their major events. The neighborhood...."

"So, what do you plan to do about all those obligations? Grow wings?"

"Frequent flyer miles are in my future, aren't they? I wish Ireland wasn't so far away."

"Will Jack travel with you every time Clay gets a twinkle in his eye? Will he stay as long as you feel necessary—months, maybe—or will you alternate time periods and hope Clay conforms to your schedule?"

"Six weeks in one place and six in another didn't pan out for Mom and Thomas. He eventually pared that down to two short trips a year until he couldn't travel any longer."

"The other men in your life?"

"Michael tried to move from Ireland with me, but he wasn't happy until we returned. My brother Kurt confessed that when Meghan expressed an interest in him shortly after they met, he cut her off because he wanted to stay in Colorado and knew she wouldn't agree. Henry would never move. He threatened to quit his job when the network wanted to transfer him to London, and London is just next door. And Jack? Jack is tied to his land and will not flit around the globe according to my desires. His work comes first and always will. Retirement is not in his vocabulary."

"You, your mother, and who knows how many other women in your ancestry are Ruths—'whither thou goest' women—bound to honor their loyalties."

Kiri pressed her face against the glass and peered through her head to the lake and the shadows of mountains beyond. "I do love it here. Apart from my feelings for Jack, I am renewed, young again, energized and even enlightened by the environment." She placed a palm on the window and felt the warmth of hand upon hand as she spoke the truth to herself. "If I'm honest, I must admit that I can manage a long-distance relationship for a time, but eventually my visits will diminish... and I'll have to make peace with that."

"Settled. At some point in the near future you will button up your life in Dublin, move to the wilds of New Zealand... and not look back. That would be too painful."

"Pain I can endure, but wouldn't it be selfish of me to turn my back on my family and walk away like my mother did?"

Her image shook her head. "Paula wasn't sel*fish*. She was sel*fless*. She traded one set of obligations for another. You'll do the same. After slogging through decades of dragging the chain of family behind you, you are entitled to put yourself first for a short time until your new obligation to Jack kicks in. Your choice is not between selfish and selfless. Now is your time to choose between the life you want to live and with whom… and the life you're expected to live. The gift of yourself to others is a given."

"The 'I do' in a vow."

"Exactly!"

Kiri and her reflection remained silent for a time as she contemplated the realities of a life with Jack and weighed the pros and cons. Her reflection broke the hush first. "Objectivity isn't all that's needed here. What about emotion? You haven't expressed any emotion. Do you love Jack?"

"I already said what I loved about him. His compassion. His…."

"Those are attributes. You were once a partner in a conversation about love with Michael and Meghan. Do tenderness, kindness and respect seem simplistic now? What happened to shared feelings and compromise—the verbs? Do you appreciate little things you do for one another and express thanks for them? Do you adore one another? Do you give as much or more affection as you get? Do you tend to one another's needs—emotional as well as physical? Do you listen? Does he add a new dimension to your life and you, to his?"

Kiri had not thought about New Year's Eve at Copley Castle for years. How naïve she was then to think that love, marriage and family could be neatly pigeonholed.

"Do you love the man? Do you tingle at his touch? Does your stomach back-flip in his presence? Do you long for him when you are apart? Does your heart quicken when you hear his footsteps? You better know before he stands beside your bed tonight wanting to leave his slippers there. Do you *love* Jack?"

Kiri nodded.

"A nod is not a declaration of love. Do you love Jack?"

"Yes. Yes, I do."

"Do what?"

"Love Jack."

"Say it like you mean it."

Kiri's eyes darted around the room and her feet followed, trying to find a place to hide. No matter where she stood, she could not escape herself. "I love Jack. I *love* Jack." She burst into tears and watched them spill like a waterfall down her reflection in the window and plop at her feet to disappear in ripples across the waters. "*I do love Jack!*"

"Good for you. You've reached the 'emotion' stage. One more to go. Stripped of your past, do you see spending your future—the rest of your life—with Jack? All three important and significant men in your life have shown love for you… and you, them, each in a different way. Imagine yourself in an empty room—a room locked for an indeterminate time. Your eyes are closed. Someone enters—a man, but you don't know which one. Picture each one in turn. Are you anxious, or do you look forward with anticipation to an empty space and unlimited time to fill it with just the two of you?"

Her reflection prevented any response. "Do not open your eyes now. Keep them closed in that empty room until you are ready to accept— unconditionally—the man you see when you open them."

Physically and emotionally drained from her embattled confrontation with her psyche, Kiri turned her back on her reflection to allow it to sink into the lake of possibilities. She flopped into her bed with ideas still tumbling around in her head. "Mom, I need help," she whispered in an attempt to channel her mother's spirit. "We need to talk. Am I so hungry for love and sexual intimacy with a man that I'm willing to endure the pain of separation from my children and my family? I need to understand what force was so strong to tear you away from us. Send me a whisper. Tell me what to do."

In silence, Paula's words returned to her daughter with a vision of a canoe gliding across a similar high lake in Colorado. "Who you are with is more important than where you are."

The only sounds were those of footsteps approaching along the stone hallway and a knock on Kiri's door.

CHAPTER 37

Henry: Arrive DUB 2p.m. Monday. Desperately need a session with my personal therapist. Kiri

Whatever the reason, it couldn't be good, Henry thought as he pulled in at the airport. Just in case, he had a mug of tea and a blanket in back to swaddle Kiri if need be. He had not done that for years, but after Doyle's news, anything could have set her off. Her approach confirmed his fear. She wore her healthy tan beautifully, but it did not mask her drawn face and nervous demeanor. "Home?" he asked.

Kiri shook her head. "Take me to our safe place, please."

Henry headed south. "Problems?" he asked. "Anything unusual or unexpected happen?" At a second shake of her head, he breathed a sigh of relief. Patrick did not pay a surprise visit to Jack's. He did not probe any deeper.

"I have a secret to share," Kiri said. They seated themselves at the end of the pier. She clutched the blanket around her shoulders against autumn's chill. Her faint smile broke for her to say, "Jack asked me to marry him."

Henry fought against his shock and dashed hopes. He felt compelled to reveal Jack's connection to the man who thrust Kiri into the cavernous sorrow of her earlier years. Telling her the truth would expose a second one, that he and the guys spied on her again—perhaps the final blow to their relationship. "There's something you must know about the man... his family. He is...."

Kiri gave him a disapproving look. "This is *my* secret. Let me share it in my own way." She turned from him and stared out to sea. "I love Jack. We agree that love later in life is different from our first loves, that we can never duplicate the same feeling and will not attempt to. But there is a place for fondness and intimacy in our lives now—companionship— and we are fools not to grab that chance for a few years of happiness before we die."

"Kiri, please. As much as it hurts me to do so, I must tell you...."

"I told Jack that I cannot marry him because I'm not willing to give up my family, the life we've built here. Besides... I love someone else more."

Astounded, Henry could not believe what he was hearing. He had not a clue she was seeing someone else, but he did not know everyone she went out with while they were estranged. He shook his head. "Don't ask me to approve or give my blessing."

She ignored his plea. "The man I've come to love is kind, gentle and attentive. He anticipates my needs before I reveal them and gives up his immediate needs for mine. He listens to me, soothes my hurts and fears, and shares my tears and troubles as if they were his own. Physical intimacy escapes us, but he says more with one look than…."

"Stop! Please stop."

"Through him I've learned that sex and love are not synonymous. The intimacy and security of a deep friendship are priceless and must be in place first before love, and then a physical relationship, follow. True friends share history and experience. They respect and are honest with each other and accept that any truth withheld is for good reason. Jack and I are not best friends first. The man I've come to love and I are friends at our core."

Frank flashed through Henry's mind—the only single guy left from the team other than himself. Frank lived in the flat above Henry's. He shared training, missions, her kitchen and constantly checked up on Kiri from the time of her tragedy even until her recent trip. At Henry's request, he was on standby when the boss was out of town, and he was the one who fought most vehemently to investigate Jack. Had Henry been blind all these years not to see their relationship develop?

Kiri had practiced her entreaty over and over on the interminable flight back to Dublin. She was not about to be dissuaded now by Henry's silence. "Caring and commitment aren't about the person who excites you on Saturday nights. They are about who you want in your life on a terrible Tuesday or a dull Thursday… that person who supports you every day, who knows your story and shares your memories. A loving relationship is not about who you sleep next to at night. It's about who you sit next to every day."

Near tears, Henry could barely find words to speak. "Do I know the man? Have I met him?"

"You see him every morning… in the mirror. *You* are that man, Henry. You fill my empty space. You are the 'who' I want to be with. You are the person I long for in my every day."

Henry was the only one standing in his way now, and his feet were as riveted to the ground as the piles that held them above water. He turned his somber gray eyes, blurred by a mist of emotion, to face her. "I have a secret too. I've longed to hear those words for thirty years." He choked back the tears that refused to hold their place. "But I can't be the man you deserve. Part of me is dead."

Kiri reached for his hand. "Part of me is dead too, but the part that is alive wants to spend the next thirty years close to you. Your terms. No expectations."

*   *   *

Your terms. No expectations. The words rang in Kiri's ears as she roused in the middle of a restless sleep for the third night in a row with no word from Henry. Not a call. Not a text. Not a wave as he drove by on his way to and from the museum. Face it. She took a leap of faith and landed in a face-plant at the bottom of a canyon. She pulled the covers over her head in an effort to escape into black sleep again.

A hand on her forehead roused Kiri for a second time. It swept her hair from her face. Light kisses graced her eyelids, and a delicate flutter tickled her cheek. Kiri jerked awake and stared into a pair of foxy gray eyes.

"Do you know what this is?" Henry asked with a sly smile.

"A daisy. A yellow one."

He smoothed the quilt and patted a spot next to her. "May I?" At her nod, he sat on top of it beside the clearly bewildered woman. "Do you know what 'daisy' means?" he asked, twisting the flower in his fingers in front of her nose. " 'Daisy' means 'day's eye' because, just like your eyes, the blossoms close at night and open again at each new dawn."

Her kittenish smile invited more.

"You told me once that you wanted to paint in daisy yellow. I thought you should understand exactly what that means before you choose the colors for each new day in front of you. I predict you will find a fresh daisy each morning to remind you that every day is a gift to be opened and treasured."

"Very clever, Mr. Callaghan."

"Cunning is a specialty of mine." He handed her the flower. "Imagine what gift is in store for you today while I bring a second surprise."

"There's more?"

"This morning and every morning. Don't move." He flashed a second sly smile and left.

Kiri could not lie still. The sudden appearance of Henry at her bedside, happy and playful, caught her off guard. If/when they confronted one another again, she expected a solemn conversation laden with 'I'm sorry,' 'please forgive,' and 'how do we move on?' He apparently favored a bolder, brighter approach to reconciliation. She tingled with unfamiliar pleasure and did move. She sat up, plumped pillows and ran her fingers through her hair. She tucked the daisy over her left ear and smoothed the quilt beside her.

Henry entered with a breakfast bed tray for two—eggs, toast, American potatoes, juice and tea and one small piece of chocolate. He sat next to her on top of the quilt and invited her to begin their shared meal. "To the first of many," he said, raising his juice glass. Then he stared deeply into the eyes with dancing hazel flecks. "I cannot allow you to wake up without someone who loves you sitting here beside you."

Overcome with emotion, Kiri stammered through an incoherent reply.

He put a finger to her lips to hush her gibberish. "It's time for you to live your name—Aurora, the dawn. My terms? We welcome our days together and anticipate the delights that will fill them."

Kiri made a second attempt. "I was afraid I'd lost you for good, but your text, 'We *all* love you,' gave me the courage to face you one more time."

"We never say what we should when we should," he replied with a hint of guilt that quickly vanished. He raised her hand to his lips and kissed her bare ring finger. "My expectation? That you find enough joy in your life... with me... to paint in daisy yellow again."

*　　*　　*

From that day forward, Kiri and Henry welcomed every morning together. He became a master of timing. With sunrise charts in hand, he awoke Kiri with a kiss in the dusky predawn and presented her with a fresh daisy. Then he sat beside her to watch the sun peek through her bedroom window. Given Dublin's proclivity for inclement weather, they were surprised that even on the darkest, wettest mornings at least one bright ray managed to fight its way through to shine on them, often accompanied by a blackbird's morning song.

The couple traded positive expectations for the day ahead before Henry left to put the finishing touches on a breakfast bed tray for two. Each offering was unique—a combination of the usual and the unusual—and each came with a treat one might expect at an intimate dinner—a chocolate, caramel, spoonful of nuts, fortune cookie, dish of ice cream or champagne. As hard as she tried, Kiri could never predict what delight would be set before her.

She could foretell that Henry would come with more than food for her body. He challenged her mind as well. "Important at our ages to stay sharp upstairs," he explained. They might work on a crossword together or compete with copies of the same one to see who finished first. They read alternate passages from a book, sometimes in a foreign language whose pronunciation was best guess, leaving them both in stitches. They traded word banks from which to create poems, and solved complex word problems—no calculators allowed.

One morning he presented her with a thick Sunday newspaper "to read together like folks used to."

"Where did you find this? Who still prints a newspaper?"

He did not answer. They snuggled against one another and perused stories of troubles in the Middle East, epidemics, drought, starvation, border conflicts, the economy and op eds for and against the government.

"Why do these stories sound familiar? I thought McNealey was dead."

Henry shrugged with that sly look in his eye.

She examined the paper carefully and focused on the dateline—the day's date for sure, but a quarter-century earlier! She wadded the paper up and shoved it against his chest.

"I wondered how long it would take you to realize you were reading ancient history," he chuckled. "I found the paper in our archives and thought it might be good for a laugh." He paused. "But it's a sad commentary on the current state of the world that the news is still much the same."

Kiri nodded. "Everywhere but in our private world. I feel so blessed that you want to share this time and space with me."

They agreed that spending every daylight hour together was selfish. They both had family and civic obligations. A balanced life included devoting time to those pursuits as well. Neither wanted to give up greeting the dawn and sharing breakfast, and given their ages, neither had much vim past mid-evening. The hours in between were the only ones available for individual activities.

They fell into a comfortable routine. Before Henry left at ten for the museum, he drew Kiri a hot bath with his choice of oils and scents to frame her day—orange ginger for energy, grapefruit for rejuvenation, or lemongrass for tranquility. After a long soak, Kiri practiced yoga and sat with another cup of tea. She cleaned up the kitchen. She insisted. Henry could do the wash-up when she cooked. She looked over personal accounts and her business for the day, and she stepped through her door at noon—not a minute before. Henry let it be known throughout the neighborhood that Kiri was not to be disturbed by phone, text, email, knock or holler over the fence before noon, or the perpetrator would answer to him. Productive and exhilarating afternoons made coming together again later in the day—or for a stolen day trip—even sweeter for the senior couple.

Kiri and Henry enjoyed long walks in the moonlight and treks to unfamiliar sights. They alternated laughter with companionable silence. They snuggled in front of fires and went for long drives. They complimented each other and traded expressions of thanks. She discovered a spontaneous and playful man; he uncovered a witty and fun-loving woman.

The two were comfortable sharing affections such as morning kisses so soft and gentle that their lips barely touched like wisps of passing clouds. They wrapped one another in warm, protracted hugs and cuddles, and held hands as much as their activities allowed. They caressed one another with words of adoration and appreciation rather than touches. And oh, how they danced—morning or evening, whenever the spirit moved them and with no need for Presley to set the mood.

Their unusual relationship was a study in compromise and their physical affection, limited. Henry did not move into her house or spend the night, but Kiri never questioned his devotion to her nor asked for more. Over time, they found the closeness they yearned for without the intimacy that dared their demons to come rear their heads.

Thirty-Sixth Anniversary Year: Rebirth: mine

Marriages: Sara Lamb and Jon finally made it official. He's a cyber security expert who frequently lends his talents to Michael Thomas. Sara and Jon develop technology to keep homes, their occupants and electronic files safe from intrusions. No request is too trivial to smartify or secure. They moved into the apartment below Bitsy who, at forty, still looks her daughter's age.

Kody, in Colorado. He served cold beer at his bachelor party as a jab at the Irish cousins. They adapted.

Deaths: Margaret (70)-Tommy's wife. He wore her out early and saved her too late. Their six daughters and Bitsy were with her when she passed. Quincy Hospice provided care.

Several more neighbors have plantings in the memory garden. Their second and third generations settle into their homes/apartments to take their places. The climate on Quincy Street changes about as quickly as that of the atmosphere.

Meghan and Kurt are still an item and maintain a transatlantic relationship, spending alternate months here and there. Polly's mother with Kendra's father sounds like a revival of the original Koyle/O'Connell drama. The spotlight is no longer on my mother or me. Kurt now plays the villain and revels in the role. What in our blood draws us to these people?

I take my second cup of tea gazing toward the memory garden with the sun at my back, and I whisper "I love you, Mom." For so many years I judged my mother from my own point of view, but I hadn't lived her life. I'm beginning to understand her joy at having a second chance because I feel that euphoria too.

I moved Michael's portrait to the sitting room above the fireplace. About time for him to have a new perspective at the beginning of each day. I have. I don't remember painting a grin as broad as it now appears, and there's almost a wink in his eye. When I returned to straighten up the bedroom, I found a black feather on my pillow. I no longer feel I need his approval for my decisions, but it's reassuring to pretend that I have it.

CHAPTER 38

Kiri and Henry spent their first night together sitting upright in Katie's living room awaiting the birth of her first child. Clay rushed in from the bedroom and paced in front of them, sweat pouring from his face. Kiri motioned for him to sit and calm himself.

"How can I relax with m' little Katie so edgy? M' dear granny never told me how a guy should act when his wife's doing all the work and he feels like a helpless oaf. I've never felt so incompetent in my life."

"Katie is fine. You need to settle down too, so you don't overexcite her. What does the midwife say?"

"Same. That babies have a mind of their own and this won't be the last time we'll wait for the tyke to get a move on."

"Is she doing anything to help Katie?"

The expectant father shook his head. "Not that I can see. She sits in the corner knitting and talks soft and soothing to her."

"Then you need to get back in there with your wife and do the same thing."

"Knit! I'm so nervous I couldn't man a shovel, let alone two sharp needles."

Kiri and Henry snickered. "No. Talk soft and soothing to her. Ask if she feels like a massage. Your granny would tell you to use good sense and a tender touch."

"Would you come with me... to double-check?"

Kiri rolled her eyes behind lowered lids. "Of course." She turned to Henry, also trying to hide a smile. "Save my place?"

She followed her son-in-law for the twentieth time along the path the two of them had worn over the last few hours. Her daughter involved everyone in her drama, alternately calling, "Mom, I need you," and within a few minutes directing her to "Please go away." No wonder Clay was so befuddled and claimed to be of little help. Katie ran everyone in circles.

Kiri checked her smartwatch. Bitsy was due soon with her magical music, and Kendra and Polly too. The triplets still did not do anything important without one another on hand to share the excitement. Katie witnessed dozens of births around the globe and at Seamróg House. She assumed she was prepared for her own baby's, but partway into the process, she realized that just as each child is unique, so is its entry into this world. At her command, Kiri returned to the living room with Clay close on her heels. "Your turn now," she nodded to Henry. "Katie wants to see you... alone."

He seemed surprised and rose to straighten his tweed jacket. He was uncomfortable with the idea of attending a birthing mother, but when Katie called him, he never said no.

"Uncle Henry," Katie smiled and invited him in for a hug. "Sit by me and hold my hand like you used to when I was scared."

He obeyed. "Are you frightened?"

She nodded. "A little. And excited and anxious too, but you always calm me down."

He held her hand in his and stroked it with his other while he reminded her of the times she faced challenges and upsets and landed on her feet with a smile. "You've always been one for an adventure. Motherhood will be the greatest of your life."

She suddenly grabbed for his lapel with the strength of an ironman. "Tell me you will hold my baby tonight."

Startled by a tenacity he had not witnessed since she was a child, he gave in. "Of course I'll stay here with your mother if you want me too."

"I mean hold, really hold my baby through the night like you did for my brother and for me and for Sara Lamb. Something inside me knows that's how we should do it in our family... how we stay connected. Pleeease."

Who could resist the appeal of the impish redhead? "With Clay's approval, I am honored to cradle your baby when you are ready. And I won't be hurt if you change your mind." He brushed aside her father's curl to kiss her forehead. "Feel better?"

She smiled and nodded at her handsomely mature, silver-haired Prince Charming. "Much, thanks, now that I know you will stay." She called after him just before he reached the door. "If it's past your bedtime, you could take a little nap now so you'll be fresh when my baby comes to you."

"Dear Henry," Kiri said when he returned to the living room. "You look quite overcome with emotion. Go home for the night."

He shook his head. "I can't. I've drawn first night duty again." He leaned against her shoulder. "But I will take a little nap right here next to you."

His nap did not last long. Kean arrived with Kendra and Polly, and Michael Thomas showed up not long after with Bitsy. Clay wandered back after being shoved out of the bedroom by the triplets. Everyone visibly relaxed once the harpist's soothing strains wafted through the hallways where the triplets first tried out their independence three doors up the road from Kiri's.

"How you doing, Bro? Big night." Kean gave Clay a hearty handshake.

Michael Thomas greeted him with a signature O'Connell bear hug. "I've always told you that you're my best security adv... coworker... and have a much better field eye than I have, but I wouldn't give two sticks for you now. You look terrible."

"You just wait 'til 'tis your turn," a nervous Clay replied. "You won't think yourself so smart then."

"I'm waiting for that perfect gal to walk through the door. Say, does my sister let you keep any of the good stuff around?"

Clay nodded. "Be my guest, but I don't dare touch a drop tonight or 'twill be death by drowning at Katie's hand before I ever set eyes on m' newborn." He led the other two young men to the kitchen. Good-natured ribbing and laughter competed with Bitsy's soft sounds.

Kendra ran in. "Hey, Clay. Where are you?" He appeared instantly. "Time for you to get wet, big guy. Katie says she's ready for the birthing pool."

Color drained from his ruddy face, and his burly body went limp. "Becoming a dad is scarier than an air drop into the Black Sea…"

Michael Thomas and Henry shot him a cautionary look.

"…would be for a camel that can't swim." He let out a deep breath. "I'm not ready."

"No choice," Kean said. "Don't worry. You'll be a pro by the time the fifth one comes along." He kissed his wife and waved goodbye to the other expectant relatives.

"Get down there, Clay," Kendra urged. "Katie's waiting. Once Bitsy's music starts, a body just loosens up so you hardly know it's preparing for new life to slip into your hands."

Henry and Kiri watched the young man hurry down the hall, nearly tripping over his own feet.

"You're next, Aunt Kiri. I'll let you know when," Kendra giggled and hurried off to witness the main event.

"I can't believe it, Henry. A grandchild. It seems only yesterday that Katie and I were locked in our first battle… to drag her into this world. Now she's peopling it with children of her own."

"I remember that night very well… one of the… best." His head slumped as he fell into a shallow sleep.

Sharp, high-pitched cries brought Henry to life. He sat up and stretched, wondering where everyone had gone. The house turned silent except for Bitsy's music. Shortly, Kendra and Polly tiptoed past and out the door without a word. Kiri followed soon after, sat beside him and took his hand.

"I cannot describe the beauty of the moment that redheaded Clayton Michael Moriarty entered this world."

Henry smiled. "A boy. No surprise that he's a redhead. He didn't have a choice, with his parents. Tell me, please, about that moment."

"I can't… because I was not there. No one was. And that, in itself, is the beauty." She leaned back with the dreamiest look in her eyes.

Henry thought that Kiri was the one who needed a nap. Her babble made no sense.

"We were all gathered around the pool trying to stay calm and coach Katie through every contraction, but she was fighting them. Ditsy said, 'Too much bother!' At her words, Clay rose from the water like a colossus... like the man I saw the first day I met him. He knew what he wanted and he was going after it. He did not want us there, despite the shock in Katie's eyes.

Henry chuckled.

"Clay reached deep inside for his 'take charge' persona—firm but tender, commanding but kind, ready to confront the unexpected in an 'outside the box' kind of way. He towered over us and pointed to the door. 'Out!' he said. 'Everyone outside until I invite you in. This baby is *ours*, and we'll bring it into this world *our* way.' He added a kindly and controlled 'Please.' We left and waited just outside the door where we could hear, but we couldn't see. That's why I cannot describe the beauty of the moment."

"That I understand, and I'm not one bit surprised at his turnaround. Clay is one fine man."

"Gentleness oozed out of him. Listening to his voice, his soothing encouragement and instruction, gave me the shivers, as if he knew my little girl more intimately than she knew herself. Guided by some invisible spirit, he coached her with such perfection that even the midwife was speechless. We were all spellbound and could have given birth ourselves right then and there in the hallway. The amazement, the love, the whispers Clay and Katie exchanged at the moment of birth are their secrets."

"He did let you in...."

Kiri nodded. "In his own good time and only for a couple of very quiet minutes, except for the music of course. I get a second chance when they are ready to part with the little guy... when they hand him off to you."

Henry jostled Kiri awake when he spotted Clay approach with a small bundle wrapped up in a wildflower blanket. Curly red fuzz peeking above its edge indicated which end was which. Clay's proud smile signaled that his swift step into fatherhood agreed with him.

"Meet Clayton Michael Moriarty, named after his two grandfathers. That's how 'tis done in my family. We'll call him Mike since there's already a boatload of Clays in the Moriarty clan."

"Pleased to meet you, Mike," Henry said as he carefully negotiated the handoff. "Your father looks much better than the last time I saw him."

Clay reclaimed his color and blushed from head to toe. His eyes rolled to the ceiling. "All those women.... Pardon, Mrs. O, but Mike was not coming out of hiding until all you women were gone. Bitsy made that clear. Then the voice of my dear, touched granny whispered in m' ear. 'Clayton! You put that baby in there. You get him out! If you aren't man enough to coax one stubborn, wee infant into this world, how the devil you ever gonna guide him through it?' That's when I knew we were havin' a boy. 'I told you, if you wanna job done well and good, you get in there and do it yerse'f.' No one dares argue with m' granny." He gently stroked his baby's head and gazed at Kiri. "Guess that's who you are to this little one. 'Tis your job to watch over Mike like m' granny did me. Good luck, Granny O," he said as he walked down the hallway. "This one's gonna be a bruiser."

Before Henry put the sleeping baby to his shoulder, Kiri opened his blanket and reached into her bag to retrieve a soft cloth and what appeared to be a bottle of brew. She opened the bottle and soaked the cloth with some of its odorless contents. She tickled the baby's nose until he opened his mouth to receive a drop of spirit water. She put her lips to his tiny ones and blew a slight soul breath into his lungs. Then she began to swab his soft baby skin with the damp cloth.

At Henry's confused look, she said by way of explanation, "His grandfather's gift—an indelible protective covering on the first night of his life." She kissed baby Mike's precious head. "Wear this shield in safety and good health, little warrior." She swaddled him again and helped situate the bundle on Henry's shoulder. "You know, this dawn is the first we've missed looking out my window."

"I say, this little guy is worth it. This moment is the happiest I've been since... since that first dawn we spent together." He kissed her and nudged the wee infant into his preference of place on his shoulder.

CHAPTER 39

Thunderous pounding on the front door brought Kiri at a run. She glanced at her smartwatch. 11:55. She did not open her door before noon, so this incessant banging must signal an emergency. She opened to find her impatient daughter and eleven-month-old grandson. "Is baby Mike ill? Do I need to take you to the doctor?"

Katie shook her head. "I need to borrow your house."

"That doesn't sound like an emergency to me. Couldn't this wait? You know I like to be left alone until noon."

"Guess my watch is smarter than yours. See? Past twelve." She swiped her watch past her mother's nose, flashed a mischievous grin and jostled her way in.

"You need to borrow my house? Whatever for?"

"A dinner party and...."

Kiri's astonishment muffled the tail end of her daughter's bombshell.

"There will be six of us, including you and Uncle Henry. Don't cook anything fancy, and no beef, please. One of our family favorites will do. See you about six?"

"What about my afternoon appointments?"

Katie stepped to the deck door and peered at the garden. "Perfect," she whispered before turning a broad grin toward her mother. "You'll figure it out. You always do." She thrust baby Mike's fuzzy red head near his grandmother's mouth. "Kisses for us both. You're the greatest. See you about six."

Her daughter's inconvenient demands and hasty departure left Kiri to rethink the priorities in her new, carefree life.

Michael Thomas was first to arrive. "I hear you're throwing a party," he added to his hug. "What's the occasion?"

"I have no idea. Something Katie has up her sleeve. I only found out this afternoon."

"Hmm. That's odd. She's had me booked for a week. 'Canceling is not an option,' she said. So here I am. Why all the secrecy?"

"Ask your sister. I'm merely her servant today," Kiri said and headed to the kitchen for appetizers.

Henry arrived, equally as puzzled. "What are we celebrating tonight? I haven't forgotten a birthday or anniversary, have I?"

Michael Thomas shrugged. "Beats me. Katie probably wants our help for yet another one of her 'projects.'"

That 'project' walked through the door in the company of her two young hosts. Tall, slender, honey-skinned Sala Mishra extended her right hand displaying a henna tattoo inside her wrist. "You must be Uncle

Henry," she said, white teeth glistening from her smile. "And you, the elusive brother Michael Thomas." Her alluring dark eyes locked onto his and reeled him in. "This is indeed a pleasure to finally meet you both. I feel as if we've known one another for years. Katie is not shy in sharing her admiration for you."

Her gazelle-like stride carried her toward Kiri, equally as awed by the graceful figure. "A hug for you, Mrs. O, for catering to your daughter's last-minute wishes." She bent slightly to surround the older hostess with her arms. When she swirled her head back toward the others, her long, straight black hair fanned out like a bird's wing and settled over her shoulder. "I see by your looks that you all are as embarrassed as I by Katie's contrived surprise, so I suggest we pretend that I'm a distant cousin dropped in for a friendly family evening. What's for dinner?" she smiled with a wink.

A scarlet Katie introduced her friend. "Sala Mishra and I first met on internships with the UN seven years ago. She is now their relief agency coordinator who disburses donated funds to organizations they sponsor... like me!" She motioned to the sofas. "Appetizers, first, while Clay and I set up the table." To avoid the accusing scowls of her family, she grabbed her husband by the hand and led him to the dining area that needed no setting up. Her mother laid a charming table in preparation for a family home-cooked meal—no frills. But Katie insisted they rotate it 90° and closer to the deck window, the better to stage the garden and the person framed by its flowers.

An uneasy situation turned amiable quickly as Sala shared details of her background. Born in a small, global village near Puducherry in former French India in the south, she and her family were part of an ongoing experiment in creating a balanced, just and harmonious ideal society. Early efforts to turn acres of red sand into lush green forests of banyan, groves of fig and cashew trees, and sustainable agricultural ground were very successful. The place was at the forefront of energy research—particularly solar energy. "Father became an expert in that field. Mother worked to promote goods produced by the community—especially handmade paper items and incense. But she was Hindu first and a believer in an ideal spiritual community second."

At the behest of her mother, the family moved to London in Sala's early school years. Her father brought his expertise to a university and her mother supported their former village by marketing the community's products abroad. One brother and two sisters still resided in London. She was based in Geneva, a city she did not care for. "Too crowded and sterile. Big city life is not for me. I prefer village life—like your area here—part of a vibrant whole but not so busy and impersonal. People still watch out for one another, and all necessary services are within walking distance."

The beguiling young woman turned her attention to Henry and Kiri. "Perhaps you've heard of my village—Auroville, the City of Dawn, where the entire small population celebrates sunrises together on specific anniversary dates."

They returned her secretive smile with a flicker of upraised eyebrows.

"My name Aurora means dawn," Katie chirped and invited her guest to sit.

"Many are the gifts given with a name, and many are the gifts that spring from the one who wears it—your attribute that first piqued my interest." Sala lowered her cryptic eyes and placed her napkin in her lap.

Chicken lasagna and all the trimmings—the family favorite—appeared on the table. Michael Thomas began to salivate the minute he entered the house and its aroma hit him. Despite his enthusiasm for his plate, however, he could not take his eyes off the captivating woman across from him. They discovered they spoke languages in common: English, French, Spanish and German. She was fluent in Hindi, of course, as well as several African dialects. His specialty was Gaelic as well as Slavic and Middle Eastern tongues. They babbled at one another in several of them.

"You two could travel the whole world and never have to ask for directions," Clay said, sparking laughter around the table. The two principals added nervous smiles and continued their conversation in English while the others listened quietly.

He inquired about her job. She traveled frequently to certify the legitimacy of projects the UN sponsored. "That's why I'm in Dublin now, to see if Katie's project is as good as she makes it out to be and the model her international programs should follow. It is, judging by my tours of the girls' and boys' houses this afternoon."

Katie blushed.

"My day-to-day responsibilities can be done from a hut in the desert, as long as there's a wireless signal close by. And there's always the annual conference. I watched your presentation in Geneva a couple of years ago, Mrs. O, and was very impressed by your ease, given the situation as understudy following Katie's wedding."

Kiri mirrored her daughter's blush. "Sala is a lovely name," she said. "Does it have a particular meaning?"

Her smile sparkled. "My name refers to the sacred sala tree, revered by both Hindus and Buddhists."

"I'm a tree too!" Katie blurted out. "My dad named me after his special tree Aurora." She pointed toward the fir tree in the garden. "I *knew* we had a connection the first time we met."

In an effort to provide some relief for the guest of honor, Henry involved Clay in conversation while Michael Thomas and Sala stared at each other and Katie stared at them with a smug look on her face.

After dessert, Kiri led a tour of the views from her windows, pointing out the memory garden, Michael Thomas' house next door, and Henry's next to it. Katie and Clay lived three doors up the road, she reminded their guest, while cousin Kendra, the counselor, lived two roads south and Polly, one road north.

"How charming. Your extended family is together but separate—in a rectangular pattern instead of a circle—like in my home village. All modern families should be so lucky."

"I wouldn't dream of living anywhere else," Michael Thomas said, and the look in his eyes confirmed his statement.

Sala's deep brown ones got the message. "Your home is so warm and welcoming with gardens outside both front and back. They remind me of my childhood home. I haven't spent time there for many years and miss it very much."

"Let's walk the path in the memory garden, then," Katie suggested. "An octagon is almost a circle like your town, and every planting there has a story."

"You young people enjoy yourselves as long as you like. It's past my bedtime, so I'll say goodnight." Kiri begged off and took their guest's hands in her own. "Despite Katie's tactics, I'm delighted that she introduced such a pleasant surprise into our lives. Please come again... soon."

The entrancing visitor nodded. "In spite of our awkward meeting, I've enjoyed myself too. You are very gracious. Thank you for the lovely meal and for letting me stay in your guestroom tonight."

Kiri tried to recover from yet another shock. She glanced at Henry and saw perplexity in his eyes too. An interruption to their morning ritual was not welcome, but what could she say? "We call it Celtic hospitality on this island. You are very welcome."

The two young couples meandered the marble path from the doorway and across the road into the memory garden. Before he followed them out, Henry kissed Kiri a hasty goodnight.

She climbed the stairs disheartened and, for the second time that day, rethought the priorities in her new, carefree life.

*   *   *

Kiri's breathing stopped in mid-slumber from a hand pressing against her mouth. Soft kisses persuaded her eyes to open to find Henry with a finger hushing her lips. His whisper found its way to her ear. "Get dressed. Something warm. Meet me at the door in five minutes." Then his vision disappeared.

Uncertain what just transpired, she rolled toward the clock. Not even 4 a.m. A glow from the kitchen window onto the fir tree told her that Henry did appear at her bedside and that she lost a minute questioning her fuzzy memory. She hustled into sweats and fuzzies, grabbed a stocking cap and coat, and tiptoed down the stairs like a teenager sneaking out with mischief on her mind.

Henry met her at the door and closed it quietly behind them. "We're having breakfast out this morning," he grinned. "We seniors must learn to adapt to unforeseen obstacles."

They jogged to his car, packed and ready for an outing. He headed south toward Kilcoole and the coast. Along the way he explained their flight through the night. "I left breakfast for two on the table by the deck. Clay will phone Sala to wake her up. Michael Thomas will share the morning meal with her, and the two can fight over who takes her to the airport for her noon flight to Geneva. Done."

He set up a deckchair for two near the end of the pier. They snuggled together under a warm blanket and peered through a shimmering veil of fog toward the east, awaiting the first streaks of dawn on the water. He presented her with a yellow daisy and kissed her good morning. "All this takes is a group of men with similar interests and a dash of creativity."

The sun did find a thin pathway to their feet, their laps and then their faces. They shared hot tea, cold breakfast of bread and meat, cheese and fruit, and champagne to top it off. They expressed positive expectations for the day and laughed at Katie for trapping her brother so skillfully. They absorbed quiet moments in the sun.

Henry spoke first. "I have a secret to share. I always imagined I'd buy this land, build a white cottage on that grassy knoll, and we'd spend weekends here with the children." He turned to face her with a hint of regret in his eyes. "But time got away from us."

Kiri nestled closely against him again. "We have nothing but time in front of us now. Can you still swing a hammer?" She flung the daisy beyond the pier's end where its soft, yellow petals became paddles furiously churning the surf while it decided whether to choose the easy path of catching a current to the sea or to fight to return to its roots on the land.

*   *   *

Sala Mishra did not arrive in Geneva as scheduled. Michael Thomas did not report to work as scheduled. Clay claimed to know nothing but expressed no surprise at learning that the two were AWOL. Katie's excitement carried her three inches off the ground from work to daily chores as she exclaimed, "I knew I could do it! I knew Sala was perfect for my brother from the day I met her!" Kiri worried that her son had inherited the O'Connell men's propensity for acting before thinking. And Henry? Henry purchased the land surrounding the pier and dreamed of spending weekends there with grandchildren.

Ten days later, Michael Thomas found his mother and Henry sitting beneath the evergreen tree examining sketches for a small seaside cottage. "Glad I found you two together," he said.

Surprised at hearing the voice that no one had since Katie's dinner party, the two jumped up to greet him. "Thank goodness you are safe. You know how I worry when you're away."

"I didn't," Henry said. "I knew you would find us when you had something to report."

"That I do." He smiled broadly and waited for the elder couple to reseat themselves. He pulled up a chair in front of them and held one hand of each in each one of his. "You are the first to know. I asked Sala's father for her hand in marriage and he gave us his blessing." He felt his mother's grip tighten in his. "I hope you are happy for me," he said, inviting her approval.

"Of course. If you are happy, then I am happy," her monotone replied.

"Have you begun to talk wedding? When and where?" Henry asked.

Michael Thomas nodded and broke into a second huge grin. "In two weeks and three days... here."

Kiri gasped. "Here? Two weeks? That's impossible."

"Soon, I know. Sala's grandmother calculated 'auspicious' marriage dates to assure our happiness according to sun, moon and star charts and our birthdays. If we don't slide into this narrow window, we'll have to wait another three or four months... and we won't. We dare not marry during a prohibited period, or 'destruction and adversity will rain down on our family,'" he added dramatically but with a nervous smile.

Henry grasped the implication immediately and, to divert attention from the forewarning, he grabbed the young man's hand and shook it zealously. "Congratulations! What can we do to help?"

"Nothing for the moment. Sit back, relax, and enjoy. Sala's family will prepare a list of key rituals they would like to incorporate, and as soon as I break the news to my sister, Katie will have the Irish contingent lined up to help. There is no question that the ceremony will combine elements from each religion and may encompass two or three days. We only have four to work with and Tuesdays are 'not auspicious,' so that leaves Wednesday through Friday—the plus three days." He tried to gauge his mother's emotion from her eyes, but she did not betray any. Instead, her jaw clenched nearly tight enough to bend her teeth.

"With such large families involved, we agreed that it will be safer... more convenient... to stage the ceremonies here. Something about a groom's house, a bride's house and a central place for a fire. Their home in London is not well situated for that kind of celebration and, well, we have everything necessary in our neighborhood. Bright colors and music will be involved."

313

Kiri stumbled up from her seat. Henry grabbed her wrist, but she jerked it away and stepped to the fence as if pulled to the pool by an invisible force. *Go to water in stress.*

"Mom, please don't. Please don't dive into the water to escape."

She leaned against the fence to catch her breath. *I will not be a Thomas, throwing obstacles in my son's way.* "I won't. I'm calculating how many the pool will hold. If your sister plays any part in the festivities, there'll be a pool party for sure." She turned back to face her son and envelop him in a hug. "*Beannacht Dé ort.* God's blessings on you," she said with a loving smile. She patted her kindly companion's shoulder. "Pack a bag, Henry. It's time we fly to London to meet the new 'rellies.'"

Katie jumped into high gear the minute Clay and Michael Thomas peeled her ecstatic little body off the ceiling. With a list of Sala's requests for a "simple celebration"—use of the gardens, simple finger foods and reservations for lodging her relatives nearby—she crossed out the "simple" and enlisted the cousins, second generation neighbors and houses of boys and girls to mount a multidenominational extravaganza.

She appointed Breeda and neighbors in charge of food, Erin to plan music that incorporated Bitsy with her harp, other cousins to construct a circular dais with a fireproof plate-sized bowl in the center, and the boys and girls to come up with a solution to the lodging problem. She asked Sara Lamb to create the perfect atmosphere given the multicultural nature of the festivities. "You know, like the Irish village for my New Year's party and the mangrove swamp in the pool."

Michael Thomas approached Henry with a request—would he canvass the old team for a brother or cousin who was a priest amenable to officiating at multidenominational marriage rites. Doyle answered the call. He had a cousin—a brother to the sheep man—and both were available and anxious to be included—"God bless." Frank offered his culinary expertise to Breeda—"Exotic spices are my specialty." Devin connected with Sara Lamb—"I know exactly what Katie means. I helped develop those illusions." Gus volunteered to provide beverages—"Some of the mild stuff and some that will knock your socks off!"

"Did you save a job for me?" Henry asked.

"The most difficult one. Keep Mom calm and out of our hair. She has trained the family well to rise to any occasion. Since I'm the last O'Connell to wed, we've had plenty of practice. Let my generation do the work this time."

Two weeks passed with secrets whispered up and down the road and to the far corners of the island. "Plus three" day arrived with a quorum of cousins and their teenage offspring to set the dais in the memory garden centered exactly over Michael's shamrocks. They erected supports for a canopy that could be rolled out from above Kiri's door and over the garden in case the weather turned "Irish," and they placed smaller, hand-held portable ones at all the other houses involved.

Sala and her family arrived—from London, Geneva and southern India. They were met by vans and drivers, compliments of Ronan, and representatives of Katie's current crop of boys and girls who accompanied them to their Quincy Street accommodations. Lon Dubh and Tuar Ceatha Houses crowded all current occupants, except the host couples, into the upper floors to leave two floors empty and available for the bride's family at each location. Henry and Frank made space in their building for overflow and team members. Other neighbors offered their spare rooms as well. Dublin's O'Connell cousins hosted their own cousins' families who lived beyond one hour away. "Chock-a-block full" took on new meaning along the road.

Young females lined up outside Seamróg House for "plus two" day, *mehndi* day. When word got out that Sala's sisters arrived with several cone-shaped tubes of henna paste for her tattoos, dainty maidens brought permission slips to exchange for simple, temporary designs appropriate to their ages, painted on wrists or ankles. One of the sisters obliged while the other and Sala's aunt applied elaborate traditional decorations to the bride's hands and feet, symbolizing love and strength in her marriage. Her palms would bear a symbol of the sun to awaken her inner light, and the darker the reddish-brown pigment, the artists explained, the deeper the intensity of her love.

"Age-old tradition holds that the bride's and groom's names be hidden in the design I'm creating and that the wedding night may not begin until the groom has found them," the aunt said, arching her eyebrows.

"You better hope that Michael Thomas is as smart as he is handsome, or you'll have to wait months until the next 'auspicious period' for your 'first night,'" Sala's sister laughed.

Katie made a final pass through the aquacenter during the transition from full use of the facilities by adults in the morning to kids in the afternoon. "Too many overgrown boys need to play off their nervous energy—my brother included!" Her well-trained staff entertained teens and under for the afternoon—boys in the pool and girls in the yoga studio. Their turn to swim would come later, after their designs had time to set and darken, she told them. A few downward dogs would help them keep a close eye on the changes.

Kiri protested when Katie arrived at her door to pull her along to Seamróg House. "I'm too old. I do not need a tattoo."

"Of course you do. Aunt Meghan is going to get one. Aunt Emily, too. Aunt Anne won't, of course. She'll stand on the sidelines and pout. Don't be an Aunt Anne!"

That remark irked Kiri. She did not intend to be difficult. She was staying out of the way like she was ordered to do.

Katie pulled out her ace. "Grandma would get a tattoo if she were here. She'd get lots. Grandfather Thomas would tell her 'no' and scold her until she undressed at night and he discovered the ones he hadn't seen before."

"Aurora Kathryn! What a thing to say!"

"You know it's true. Grandma would love these festivities and be right in the middle of all the activity. I couldn't organize this event by myself. She's helping. Don't you feel her spirit everywhere?"

Kiri had to admit that, one: she had not thought about Paula's influence on her children for some time and two: that her mother would love this multicultural event. Her sandaled feet would flip-flop up and down the road as she danced with bangles and bells on.

"I do," Katie answered herself. I know she's watching. And tomorrow when the music starts, her columbines will swing and sway liveliest of all."

Kiri sat patiently while Sala's sister applied a design appropriate for the groom's mother... in a place that Henry could admire too.

Henry awakened Kiri on "plus one day"—wedding day—with a daisy and a kiss, as usual. They greeted dawn together and agreed that a joint expectation for the occasion was for the marriage celebration to be everything the bride and groom wished. They enjoyed a leisurely breakfast, and Henry drew Kiri's bath. "Sandalwood for serenity today," he said. "You'll understand later. Do not open the door before noon, and don't be one minute late or you'll miss the parade."

"What parade?"

"You'll see," he smiled. "I'm on my way to lay a calming hand on Michael Thomas' shoulder and make sure he eats something. Brendan and Clay are trying their best to work him into a frenzy."

At noon, Kiri stepped outside her door. At mere seconds past, she heard the strains of penny whistles and fiddles at the top of the road. A small procession gathered followers as it made its way toward her. One of the boys pushed an ancient handcart bearing Bitsy playing music for happiness on her harp. The growing band of revelers stopped at Kiri's for Henry to escort her behind the cart as it continued to the groom's house.

Michael Thomas appeared in a white suit and Irish linen sash embroidered with shamrocks. Brendan and Clay attended him. The three slipped into place in front of Kiri and Henry. As the procession continued to the bottom of the road and the bride's house, more and more neighbors and relatives filtered in wearing bright colors as requested.

The bride stunned the gathering crowd when she stepped through the door in a red silk sari, intricately embroidered in gold thread and draped over a fancy white blouse. The pattern in the veil covering her hair and shoulders was the reverse of her gown, as was the sash at her waist. The music stopped for ritual introductions of the bridal couple's families to one another. The bride and groom exchanged garlands of orchids, hibiscus, jasmine and shamrocks. Her father placed Sala's hand in Michael Thomas' to give away the bride, and a hymn to love was pronounced to signal the beginning of the ceremony.

"A *red* wedding gown?" Anne whispered to Meghan. "I've never seen such an abomination!"

"Polly told me that white is for purity and red symbolizes fertility."

"Judging from the lightening speed of this wedding, those barriers have already been crossed."

"Anne!"

Music makers from Sala's family, armed with a small sitar, tabla drum, murali bamboo flutes, bells and tambourines, took their places next to the Irish band. The blend of East and West found harmony as the swelling entourage headed back up the road to Kiri's house and turned in at her gate. Only immediate family members were allowed through due to limited space in her garden. The remainder witnessed the Christian rites on a huge screen set up in front of Lon Dubh House for the occasion.

Doyle's cousin, Sala and Michael Thomas took their places under an arch of sparse branches on the wounded side of the evergreen tree Aurora, now grown tall and strong. The priest conducted abbreviated rites including "Wilt thou" but concluding before "I do" and the exchange of rings. The bridal party then made its way through the house to emerge on the steps facing the memory garden.

Oohs and aahs thundered when Sara Lamb activated holographic magic to transform the garden into a tropical Indian paradise. At its far end facing the couple and just beyond Paula's columbine, a massive sala tree—the revered tree of enlightenment—spread its flowering canopy of yellowish-orange and purple. A meter-high, semicircular waterfall spilled from behind it into a stream flowing in both directions along the perimeter of the neighborhood garden. Banyan and cashew trees lined its banks down the side fences. Thickets of ferns, magnolia, and tulip trees added a rainbow of color and scent to the scene. Bright green parakeets, yellow iora and multicolored broadbills flitted among them as accents, and peacocks strutted throughout the Irish garden's plantings.

Children broke from their parents to run and stick their toes between the lotus and water lilies floating on the water that was not there and to grasp the peacocks' greenish-feathered fans that disappeared in their hands. The bride and groom followed the marble pathway in octagonal circuits until they reached the dais. Their families followed and crowded into the garden with the overflow filling the road and steps of homes nearby. Sala's grandmother was so overcome by the illusion that a real chair was produced for her comfort. When the bridal couple ascended the dais, all music and awed chatter hushed.

The Catholic priest invited them to exchange traditional Hindu marriage vows. Opposite his bride, Michael Thomas lit a fire in the earthen bowl and sprinkled crushed sandalwood and herbs onto it. Sala placed her hands in Michael's and together they recited a mantra of their responsibilities to one another. They tied the ends of their sashes together as a symbol of their eternal bond and began their seven vows. After each one, the couple made a clockwise circuit of the fire glowing above Michael Killian O'Connell's profuse flowering shamrocks.

Kiri listened carefully and was struck by the similarity of her son's Hindu vows to the simple Celtic wedding vows she and Michael shared on their anniversaries beneath the fir tree. Complete one another vs. love and honor; prosper in our wealth vs. everything I own; share food and nourishment vs. first bite of meat and sip from my cup; highest kind of friendship vs. anam ċara; mine forever vs. forevermore. All faiths found strength in common pledges, she realized. Even though they claimed them for their own, they all wished the same blessings on their homes, families and generations to follow.

Tears filled her eyes and cascaded down her cheeks when her son and his bride spoke of their eternal bond. *Is it possible that vows are forever with no time limit on them?*

Henry worked his handkerchief into her hand and gripped her shoulders from behind. "You're allowed," he whispered. "Go ahead and cry."

"I'm happy," she sputtered, trying to mop up her flood. "Really, I am. It's just... I can't help thinking about...."

"I know, and you are entitled to a griefburst just now. Don't fight it. No one will judge you, especially those of us who are closest to you." He wiped her cheeks. "Cry all you want. I have two more handkerchiefs ready just in case."

The priest stepped onto the dais with the couple and led them both through, "Do you" to "I do" and the exchange of rings. "I now pronounce you husband and wife."

Katie's squeal of delight pierced the air, and joyous music took up her call. She swirled to hug her mother and beamed. "Thanks, Mom."

"For what?"

"For making this wedding possible. I tried to bring those two together for years—London, Geneva—but the time and place had to be perfect. Your house, your food, your garden. I knew that before my brother would consider marriage, he had to see that the life he had at home—with all of us—wouldn't change drastically. The old Irish 'tied to the land' thing. I've always had a feeling inside that finding family was my mission in life."

"Where did that silly idea come from?"

"I don't know. Let's say, a fairy whispered in my ear." Katie patted her tummy. "And this next baby is a part of the puzzle too."

"So soon?"

"Don't ask, Mom. Just go with it and be happy!" She pulled her mother into the throng of guests dancing their way across the road to a lavish buffet set up in an illusory palatial courtyard in the aquacenter's party room. Gorilla-man Gus, dressed in a colorful sarong, led the pack surrounded by giggling little girls trying to mimic his jig.

Anne and Emily trailed near the end. "Imagine! An O'Connell marrying a non-Catholic in a highly unorthodox ceremony. Father would turn in his grave!"

"Others of us married outside the Church."

"How did that turn out for you, Emily? Abuse. Divorce."

"I have three beautiful children, ten grandchildren, and I am grateful every day that we are close as a family. Can you say the same?"

Anne did not say anything.

Near dusk, the newlyweds wandered from guest to guest to offer their thanks and say their goodbyes. Michael Thomas cornered his mother dancing with Henry. "Imagine, Mom. Making marriage vows not once, but twice! We're stuck with each other forever, for sure. I don't know anyone else who has married the same person twice. Do you?"

Kiri just smiled and hugged the exuberant couple. *You're holding one now… and the reason you exist to celebrate this joyous day.*

A hastily assembled group escorted the young couple to the groom's house across the road. At the door, Michael Thomas reminded his family that ten years previous he handed the keys of O'Connell House to Brendan "to simplify my life. Now I hand the keys of my humble home to Sala to complicate my life in the most beautiful way."

Cheers, jeers and a cacophony of whistles and bells dogged them through the door. Brendan's cries rose above the rest. "If you run out of time on the hunt, I'll be right here to help!"

The happy couple escaped to the tranquility of their bed to pleasure-search for their names before dark fully descended on their auspicious marriage day.

Thirty-Seventh Anniversary Year: The chosen son is married.

CHAPTER 40

Kiri and Henry spent their second night together sitting upright in Katie's living room awaiting the birth of her second child. The atmosphere was completely different from the first—no people, no noise, no nerves. They sat quietly, held hands and traded smiles but no words. At the sound of sharp, high-pitched cries, they shared a kiss and waited... and waited... for what seemed hours. Finally, footsteps.

"Don't get up. 'Tis only the herald come to announce the flawless birth of a healthy child. As m' dear granny would giggle, 'we're born with the same instincts as the birds and the beasts to take care of our own... with a well-timed nudge from the fairies.' I'm to see that you are awake and ready for the hours ahead while Katie and I take some rest together."

"At the ready," Henry confirmed. "Whatever you want, we'll do."

"As the little mother says, 'the usual, of course!'"

That diminutive person padded up the hallway and planted herself directly in front of Henry. She bent toward him and smiled broadly. "Henry Callaghan, meet Henry Killian. We'll call him 'Harry.' The Henry is for you, of course, and Killian is for Bitsy and all the other Killians in our line." The brightness in Katie's eyes burned into his soul like the flash of a lightening bolt. "Guard your godson well." She kissed the astounded elder on his forehead.

Overwhelmed with emotion, he nearly dropped the baby before the wee one reached his arms. His namesake. He never thought there would be another Henry Killian to carry his name... and his blood—an unbroken thread to eternity. What man could be more blessed? "I am a Killian too!" he wanted to shout.

Katie turned to her mother who anxiously awaited her turn to hold the dark-haired baby boy. "I told you about my mission. I've always had a feeling that I'm supposed to find my family and bring it together. This baby is one more piece. Don't ask me how he fits into the puzzle. I don't understand that yet. But I've worked my whole life to bring you and Uncle Henry together for this moment. And *you* didn't help," she said with an affectionate glare, "by running off to New Zealand like a rebellious teenager! If you hadn't come back, your son would still be single." She shook her limp copper curls. "I'm exhausted. I'm going to bed!"

*   *   *

Kiri and Henry spent their third night together sitting upright in Kiri's living room with Sala's parents awaiting the birth of their daughter's first child, an acceptable fifteen months following the gala marriage festivities. Katie and Clay sat on the stoop of the little house across the road and one door down in case of emergency, but mostly to bar the door from intruders.

Katie burst into her mother's house and shouted, "The baby is here!" Then she hushed herself. "I'll come again when he's ready to be introduced."

The grandparents exchanged excited glances. A boy! When finally summoned, they gathered in the living room across the road for holding and cooing time with Orion Mishra-O'Connell.

"'Orion' with a long 'O' means 'son of fire' in Hindi," Michael Thomas explained. "We made our vows over the ritual fire above my father's memory to symbolize our commitment to each other... and this beautiful little guy is living proof."

Henry was last to hold and lingered the longest over the honey-skinned babe with a mop of black hair. With their houseguests settled back at Kiri's, the two of them sneaked out for dawn and breakfast within the framework of their cottage at the seaside.

At the little boy's christening with some of his grandfather's spirit water surreptitiously swirled in with the rest, Great Aunt Anne's audible whisper reached Grandmother Kiri's ears. "I never thought I'd see the day that a hyphenated, quarter-breed Irishman would head the distinguished O'Connell family. What is this world coming to?"

"Together, Mother," Grace replied. "Together."

* * *

Kiri and Henry spent their fourth night together sitting upright in Katie's living room awaiting the birth of her third child. The evening proceeded much like their second one, but they alternated nodding off due to the silence, the long hours, and their advancing ages. When Katie arrived with a redheaded bundle of baby in her arms, she presented it to her mother. "Meet Daniel Koyle Moriarty, named for his grandmothers. 'Daniel' is common in Clay's mother's family, and 'Koyle' is for yours." When Kiri seemed confused, she explained, "The American part of me is important too."

Kiri hurried to replace her amazement with a smile. Koyles of Colorado had not crossed her mind for years. In all the decades she fought so hard to secure *Michael's* line, she forgot that she perpetuated her own at the same time.

* * *

The race was on between the Moriarty family and the O'Connells to produce the first granddaughter who would be named for her grandmother. The sisters-in-law engaged in friendly battle over 'Aurora.' Katie felt her desire took precedence because that was her name too. Sala contended that with an Aurora already in the Moriarty family, it was only logical to add one to the O'Connell family.

They compromised. Katie's fourth child was christened Dawn Kirin Moriarty and Sala's second, Oditi Mishra-O'Connell. "Oditi," she explained, "is a Hindu name meaning 'dawn.'"

The two namesakes were born within months of each other. As the cousins grew, they became as close as blood sisters. As soon as they could toddle, they sought each other out—day or night—and gravitated to the green marble pathway to link up. Sometimes, they followed the sparkly stone walk to their grandmother's front stoop and waited in morning's chill, their dimpled knees and chubby toes pressed together against the nippy air, until Henry nearly tripped over them on his way out. He found time to invite them in for a quick and quiet breakfast and shooed them away on his second exit.

Their parents frequently found Dawn and 'Diti hiding under bushes or playing among the flowers in the memory garden. Whoever spied the imps scooped them up together and deposited them at one house or the other to be cleaned, clothed or fed. Once their feet touched ground again, they were off hand-in-hand on another expedition. When Kiri found them squirreled away in some corner of her house giggling, she recalled the triplets whose alliance remained strong. "Must be in the blood," she sighed.

Their two families acted as one. When Michael Thomas left "on business," his family was watched over by Clay and his brood. When Clay was sent "on business," Michael Thomas took in the Moriarty contingent—all of them. When the mothers traveled abroad together once a year, their husbands coincidentally had "business" together in the same locale. All their children were left in the capable hands of the boys and girls that the parents mentored and under the watchful eyes of Kiri, Henry and the dragonflies.

*   *   *

Weeks and months turned to years. Kiri and Henry watched their family and village grow and their own cottage take shape, bit by bit and board by board. With each trip to create that reality, they traded secrets and inched toward baring their deepest truths.

"I planted Michael's earwig in your sitting room until your son was born."

"The first time you kissed me when I went crazy before Michael Thomas was born... I was too shocked to enjoy it, but I hoped you would try again some day."

"I placed guards at both ends of Quincy Street when Patrick came to town. If he lingered too long at the shops, I sent Paddy to chase him off."

"On swim test day when I was pregnant with Katie, you put your hand on my tummy to calm us. I felt so safe… and I liked it."

"I installed a camera on Paddy's binoculars to keep track of the children when he walked them home from school. From morning to night, any activity that worried him, worried me too."

"I was jealous of my own daughter and your attentions to her."

"I surveilled Katie and Michael Thomas every minute they were abroad."

"After I spotted you at lunch with Anne, I stalked the café."

"When my mother assumed you and I were married and Michael Thomas and Katie were her grandchildren, I did not tell her the truth. I made your story, our story. I never lied to her, but I never told her the whole truth. I couldn't allow her to go to her grave feeling her life and sacrifices for me had been for naught."

"I took you for granted when I should have taken you in… long ago. You've always been family, even without a certificate to show for it. How dedicated we are to one another counts for more than technicalities. Not only do you have children, you have nine grandchildren and a namesake. Your mother would be very proud of the life her son has lived, and Katie will keep her memory alive."

Technicalities expose the truth. I am Henry Killian, and my blood runs in your children's veins. But I cannot yet summon the courage to reveal how it got there and how I know. He smiled kindly, but the smoky gray of his eyes indicated that he still had a secret hidden behind them.

*   *   *

After fifteen years together on a daily basis, Henry could read Kiri's moods as easily as a first level primer. He sensed her agitation when either of her children or their spouses left Dublin. He shared her joys at her grandchildren's milestone moments, and he accepted that for one day out of every year—autumn, early October, to be exact—she lived in another world but returned to him on the following day—Michael Thomas' birthday.

He never questioned that anomaly in her biorhythm. When he greeted her for daybreak together and recognized that faraway look in her eyes, he served her breakfast for one, drew her bath and left, claiming "business" that would occupy him all day. He promised to resume the regular routine on the morrow. On his way out, he disengaged her communications systems and posted a note on her door to ward off any intruders until the following afternoon.

Kiri was grateful for Henry's sensitivity to her need to spend her anniversary days with Michael. She pecked at the light breakfast left for her, soaked for a while, whispered "I love you, Mom" to Paula's columbine and took her tea outside under the evergreen tree Aurora. Sounds of splashing and youthful laughter from the aquacenter added vitality to the sunny day. She looked up through the branches, then sighed and began her conversation with the barest bits of spirit that might remain after all these years.

"Michael, father of two, grandfather of nine and savior of many, do you know what anniversary this is? Do men keep track without being reminded? Today, 2059, is our 50th wedding anniversary. On this day five decades ago, we could not possibly imagine what course our lives would take, but I have survived and your memory is as strong as ever in our little corner of the world. Your children, nieces and nephews have seen to that, and your grandchildren carry parts of your brilliance, energy and enthusiasm wherever they go. You have much to be proud of. I'll do my best to bring you up to date, though I have a feeling you know it all already and in fact, much before it happens."

She opened her journal and could not believe that she had not written since her son's wedding. Where had the time gone? And her memory with it?

Fiftieth Anniversary Year: Births: Katie and Clayton Moriarty have seven children, all boxy redheads except Harry who is lanky, black-haired and gray-eyed like the man whose name he bears. Oldest to youngest they are: Clayton Michael, Henry Killian, Daniel Koyle, Dawn Kirin, Seán Thomas, Moya Kathryn, and Máire Paula. Stairsteps, like the O'Connells. When I inquire discreetly about the growing size of her family, Katie tells me that the most sublime moments she and Clay share are when they welcome new life into the world together. "Why should we deny ourselves such bliss if we can provide?"

Michael Thomas and Sala Mishra O'Connell have two children, Orion Mishra-O'Connell and Oditi Mishra-O'Connell. Both are honey-skinned, black-haired and brown-eyed—quite a contrast to their carrot-topped, blue-eyed cousins, but the only one who seems to notice or care is Anne.

Sara and Jon have two boys. Henry seemed particularly delighted with their births and counts them as grandchildren too. They are best buddies with the rest of the boys in the clan.

Marriages: Michael Thomas' was the last I will report—the last in his generation. His cousins' children are taking that step now, and I can't keep track of them.

Deaths: Our family has come to accept death as a part of life. Medical advances may postpone, but cannot eliminate, the inevitable. Current focus is on long, healthy life ending in quick, relatively comfortable death. Of all the enterprises I oversee, Quincy Healthcare and Hospice are most in demand. If Bitsy were an enterprise, her name would top the list. Despite middle age, her energy and compassion are limitless. No matter how long the night, she never tires.

Emily (72) spent her final days in her mother's bedroom in O'Connell House. Brendan's family adjusted to accommodate her. Her children and Bitsy were with her. Quincy Hospice provided her care.

Meghan (76) died at home with her children, Bitsy and Kurt at her side. Quincy Hospice provided her care. My brother Kurt sat with her around the clock for several days, stayed for the funeral, then left. He did not set foot in Ireland again. Kendra and her family visited the States as often as they could.

Kurt (78) died in Mom's house at the top of the hill. He called one day and asked if he could request a "symbolic gesture." He promised he would not ask for a special favor again. I said, "Of course" and nearly dropped the phone when he asked that I come to Colorado for a short, but indefinite, period of time and bring Bitsy. He also wanted me to be with Kendra when he called her. Done. No questions asked.

Kendra left immediately. I arrived a few days later with Bitsy and two of our own nurses. All the cousins flew over in twos and threes to thank him for the good times he hosted at Yellowstone and the buffalo ranch and, as Brendan said, "for the eight years of happiness he gave my mother—a rare commodity these days." They all returned for Kurt's funeral in support of their American cousins Kendra and Kody, and they shot off a few firecrackers in their uncle's honor.

Anne and I are the only family from our generation who survive.

Michael would be so proud of the adults his children have become. They both married well—mates perfect for them, but if Katie's fairy whispers are to be believed, her father had a hand in their choosing.

Both are in their mid-forties and have well-established careers. Katie runs two girls' houses and two boys' houses on Quincy Street. Breac (Trout) House joined the other three. Nine more programs in major cities of Ireland are government approved and authorized to use her model and name, as well as three in the north. NGOs sponsor eight of her projects in Asia and Africa, and she is on track to cut the ribbon on a new one every other year. She and Sala travel abroad together once a year for a biennial conference or to inspect funded programs and establish Katie's. Calm follows Sala wherever she goes, and Katie is quite the opposite. She stirs up dust devils the minute she springs out of bed. But together they are a mighty force for good.

Clay asserts his influence on Katie's enterprise too. He suggested that our partnership build a second pool and add staff to maintain quality programs for the general population as well as the underserved "without having the lights on 'til midnight every night!" Aurora Aquatics continues to provide adaptive water therapy for all ages, disabilities both mental and physical, and special needs such as caregivers—and for the young people and babies in its charge "when the sunshine dares come out."

The Moriarty family moved one house west so indoor facilities next to the aquacenter could be expanded too. "We need more bedrooms and the young people, more classrooms." The triplets all work half-time since their children are still young. Sala added her expertise to the program, offering yoga as a tool to heal emotional wounds from trauma—vital to most of our clientele.

Michael Thomas and Clay work together well. You'd think that they see enough of each other at the network, but they enjoy off-times too and seem to find more and more of them as the years go by. The world must be a safer place than when my boots were on the ground.

Both men are terrific role models for Katie's girls and boys. Their field trips that involve boats and water are favorites for young people who've never had that experience. And they express their thanks by helping out with family outings. As extra hand-holders, the boys are often paired with the daughters. Clay stares them down. "You don't imagine you'll father only same sex children, do you? I didn't." I have no idea how many youth the brothers-in-law have helped, but I do know that when it comes time to leave after an average of eighteen months, the young people are reluctant to go.

Paddy's binoculars are still in place on the memory garden fence despite changes in the neighborhood population. The businesses around Quincy Street prosper and grow, but they do not expand. They start branches in other neighborhoods nearby to try to replicate the intimate feeling of ours here. They always have a job or apprenticeship for a boy or girl when their time is up in the program. Then our young people filter into the city or nearby villages and make lives there, spreading the O'Connell/Moriarty mantra of kindness and inclusiveness towards all.

The little I know about Michael Thomas' current work, I glean from eavesdropping on his conversations with Henry. Recently they talked "dragonflies." Henry said, "I don't see swarms of dragonflies much anymore. Climate change, I suppose."

"In keeping with our mission to operate quiet and on the sly and seemingly within the law, we are forced to stay one step ahead of local and international regulations with our technology, meaning even smaller and nearly invisible," Michael Thomas replied with a sly grin. " I do notice that morning's dew comes earlier, stays later and is thicker than usual."

Sudden comprehension lit up Henry's face.

"Small but mighty," my son continued. "You might check the water content sometime."

Henry burst into laughter. They use a secret code. I'm not included.

My son did alert me when he split the team from the network. "We are most effective when we are independent. Ties to a government-funded entity make that impossible when that government insists that we share with its military." As an independent contractor, he picks and chooses "projects" that align with his goals and spread his influence further. "We were not allowed to act as third-party negotiators within the profession. Now we can effect change whenever and wherever, for any government or NGO, as crisis demands anywhere in the world."

He leases the basement facility from the network and gives it preferential treatment. That floor is now impenetrable. "No one has broken through our cement walls or cyber defenses yet!"

When my eyes dizzy with details, he says the usual. "Someday you'll understand the big picture." My son/son-in-law partnership is surely a gift from the fairies. The two complement each other perfectly. MT is the visionary, seeking futuristic solutions to age-old problems. With his gifted eye for detail, Clay transforms the mental image into practicable reality.

I think back to Thomas and what he taught my children and expected of them. He would be pleased, but surprised, to see them today. Michael Thomas can recite any given passage from the Bible in any of three languages, sings or speaks regularly at church functions, and imparts doctrinal counsel when his cousins ask, but he rarely practices his religion outside his interspiritual home. Katie, who spent more time making faces at the people behind her than the priest in front, has her brood lined up and out the door on time every Sunday morning, including the O'Connell two, Sara's sons, and any boys/girls interested. On the home front, she practices the gospel daily in the midst of merry mayhem.

I realize now that Michael's aspirations were too lofty for one man. His grand plan required two children—one with a world view toward bringing truth into the discussion for peaceful solutions and the other, to mother his home village. I liken the feathers that come my way to breadcrumbs along life's path, guiding our core family toward salvation or the witch's oven. I'm not sure which, but I'm leaning toward the positive.

Henry revels in a second childhood, perhaps because he never had a first one. All the grandchildren refer to him as "Poppy," and he wears the moniker like a favorite blanket snuggled around his shoulders. He throws his head back in laughter when little girls with perky noses and downy curls dance on top of his feet. Then he uses those same feet to teach the boys the latest football techniques. He's very good, even at his age. He grows thinner and moves more slowly, but he can still aim a shot and guard a goal. Originality in morning surprises hasn't waned, but best of all, we've perfected the art of the platonic cuddle. When I stopped chasing after happiness so frantically, it caught up to me.

As I read over the last few paragraphs, I realize that sublime happiness doesn't make a very good story. Conflict, and how characters resolve it, color a drama. I'm blessed that for the last several years I've felt free to paint in daisy yellow. But a nagging question underlies my joy: How long will our happiness last?

When dusk crept in, a black feather floated down, dodged branches, and lodged between the pages of her journal like a treasured bookmark.

CHAPTER 41

Kiri's phone sounded. 2 a.m. The nieces and nephews had not called at such a ridiculous hour since they outgrew being stranded after an evening out. Katie and Sala taught their children to get sick either well before their grandmother's bedtime or past noon, or they were on their own for her hugs and comfort. She could not imagine what other crisis warranted her attention in the middle of the night. The phone sounded again, and she fumbled to answer.

"Yes? What's the problem?"

"I've run out of daisies," came the muffled reply.

"Henry?"

"I forgot until late, and the shops were closed." His words were garbled. "I can't come to you without a daisy."

"Of course you can, anytime you want."

"And I need to come to you now more than ever."

A worm of dread inched its way into her nerve center. This was so unlike Henry. He would have thought of an alternative… a surprise. "Then let me come to you. You wouldn't expect me to arrive bearing a daisy, would you?"

"I cannot ask…."

"You're not asking. I'm offering. Give me five."

Apprehension triggered her bolt out of bed. She pulled on sweats and grabbed her keys. Something was sadly wrong. Henry could barely get his words out. They needed a drive. They needed a safe place. They needed each other.

During the drive to their cottage on the coast with Kiri at the wheel, not a word passed between them. Henry's ghostly pallor and tense demeanor distressed her. He was cool to her touch but his forehead and hands were moist as if from fever. When they arrived, she headed straight for the kitchenette to brew a pot of tea. The kettle whistled, and she turned to Henry with as bright an expression as she could muster. "Ready!" she said, but Henry was nowhere to be seen.

The cottage consisted of one sleeping room for napping grandchildren, a bathroom, kitchenette and great room, so she realized immediately that he had not followed her in. She grabbed her jacket and a torch and ran out toward the sound of surf. Dense fog shot the bright beams of light back at her. She called. No answer. She ran further and further toward the sea. They had never been at the cottage so early—the midnight black of the wee hours—so she became disoriented by the dark mist and the distance. The tide was out. She stepped cautiously once she felt the sog of wet sand beneath her shoes. She cut the torch and stared

329

through the blinding fog, calling. Then she spotted Henry's tall form beyond her with white fingers of sea foam curling around his ankles.

When he sensed her approach, he reached out for her hand and gripped it so tightly her knuckles crunched. "You know," he said staring straight ahead, "there were times in my young life that I wanted to die... I prayed to die. But I didn't. Even later when Michael met such a brutal end, I ached to trade places with him. But I couldn't. Now, with such great happiness in my life, I don't want it to end. But that's impossible."

Kiri felt that familiar boulder drop into the pit of her stomach, but for Henry's sake she struggled to remain strong. "How long?" she asked, noting that his face was covered in moisture. Whether from sea spray or sobs, she could not tell.

He continued to stare into the blanket of nothingness. "I'm conflicted. Part of me wants to keep walking forward until the sea takes me like a pebble. The other part of me wants to savor every moment I have left, but I love you too much to subject you to that torture again." He finally turned for his gaze to meet hers. "This secret can't be kept. Weeks. A month or two, at most."

"Don't be selfish, then, and deprive me of the greatest gift I have to give—showing you how much I care for you... by caring for you." Their hands traded places, hers on the outside gripping his with all the courage she could summon as they slogged to shore. "Let's go home."

They shared a final cup of tea on the porch of the tiny cottage they built together and waited for an intense ray of sun to cut through the fog, signaling an end to one chapter of their lives and the beginning of the last.

The drive back to Dublin was another silent one, not because they could not say all the unsaid, but because Henry fell asleep immediately. With one blanket tucked around his damp feet and the other across the rest of him, he lapsed quickly into deep, regular breathing. After a full twenty-four hours awake with his nerves set on hyper, he finally succumbed to acceptance of the fate he had no power to change.

Kiri took this as a good sign. Henry needed to rest... to conserve his energy... to eke out as many days as possible. She kept one ear tuned to his steady sound. The other heard only the creak of rusty gears as her brain buzzed with all the microdetails she needed to address in the days ahead. She and her businesses excelled at managing end-of-life issues. They supported every neighbor, friend, and relative—young and old alike—who came to them for service and comfort. But Henry? Her professional self knew exactly what to do—stay focused. Her personal self wanted to hold him, protect him, will him to live.

Her professional self won out—at least until Henry awoke. She checked the time and called her son.

"What's up, Mom? Near seven on a Saturday is early, even for you."

"Please gather a small group of guys to do some heavy lifting."

330

"What's the occasion?"

"Henry is moving in with me."

"Great! It's about time!" His voice conveyed both joy and surprise.

"Please assemble the following and install them as quickly as possible and with as little fuss as possible."

When he heard the list, including hospital bed, stairlift, and upstairs bathroom modification, Michael Thomas' tone noticeably changed. "Not Uncle Henry! How long?"

"Not long enough." She sniffed back tears. "Do not. Repeat. Do not tell your sister! I will myself... when we get home... within the hour." She wiped her eyes with her sleeve. "And can you work some magic to make morning's first light shine through Katie's old bedroom window?"

For the remainder of that hour, the tragedies in her life coursed through Kiri's mind: Michael, so alive one minute and dead in her arms only moments later with no forewarning. In truth, he suffered very little, but she bore the brunt of it for years. Paula hastened her own death because she could not face life. And now Henry knew of the limited time left for him. If she had to choose for her loved ones—or for herself—what would it be? Sudden? Intentional? Or lingering in a debilitated state? By the time they arrived in Dublin, no ideal answer came to her. Only the truth—that death comes in its own time and in its own way, the only variable being how one chooses to meet it.

She turned down Quincy Street and noticed a small gathering in front of Michael Thomas' house. She patted her passenger on the shoulder. "Wake up, Henry," she tried to smile. "We're home."

*   *   *

Within a couple of days, Kiri had Henry on a strict regimen, despite his protests. "You may be dying, Henry, but you will not experience a miserable death while on my watch," she said. "You will go peacefully in my home in your sleep with very little pain and surrounded by people who love you. Your body will tell you when it's time. And I'm putting myself in charge of keeping that body strong and vibrant for as long as possible."

Henry did not have the strength to argue... and he did not want to. Together they greeted the dawn through Katie's window, took his vitals and touched base with his doctor through video appointments, and ate several small, nutritious meals throughout the day. Short doses of aqua yoga were prescribed to keep his muscles and organs toned. He took frequent naps, frequent walks, and socialized with a never-ending stream of friends, neighbors and family expressing their love and concern. Kiri allowed him brief visits to his apartment to see to "business" as long as a boy, girl or grandchild waited on his stoop in case he expressed a sudden need for help. That freedom lasted for a couple of weeks until he lost interest and strength.

The old team gathered on one of Henry's "good days" and escorted him to Ryan's Pub for a final toast to good times, good friends, good fortune and a good life. Young Harry accompanied Poppy to the museum for a last look-around and goodbyes. The grandchildren, now ranging in age from five to fifteen, kept their grandmother's house running in tip-top order. The neighbors made sure that a hot teapot was always ready and that the cupboards and fridge were freshly stocked even though Henry and Kiri ate little.

Sala perfected preparing meals for a dozen since Katie was on sabbatical next to Henry's side as much as possible. Clay managed to get seven young ones ready and out the door to school every day and was exhausted at the end of it. He shuddered to watch his bubbly Katie dissolve before his eyes when she clenched Henry's shirt collar with her baby fist.

Michael Thomas noticed young Harry cling to Poppy's every word as well as his hand. He recalled his own response during Grandfather Thomas' final illness—trying to absorb every life lesson the dying man had to share in only a few days. His main concern was for his mother. She needed to take care of herself, he tried to tell her, and insisted she take advantage of the caregiver's lane in the swimming pool. "You need the same therapy you give your patients. I'll keep watch if Katie has to go home. We won't leave Uncle Henry alone."

Kiri knew her son was right, even though she resented the time others, especially Katie, spent with Henry—that creeping feeling that her daughter was coming between them again. She tried to brush it off and wondered if Paula felt the same way about those who rallied around Thomas, Kiri included, and intruded on her mother's limited time with him. Then she remembered that her mother held Thomas through every night. If Kiri could not have Henry to herself every day, at least he was hers every night.

Henry, the least likely of the family to seek attention, learned in his last days to appreciate and even revel in it. The nieces and nephews brought smiles to his drawn face; the grandchildren, tears to his clouded eyes. He drew strength from hours spent with young Harry holding one hand and Katie, the other, while she gripped his shirt to keep him from disappearing. He looked forward to sinking into relaxed evenings when Bitsy played for him while Kiri administered circular massages.

Best of all were the nights when Kiri came to him. After a few days of settling in, and after he became accustomed to music and massage, she appeared at his bedside in her nightclothes with a blanket in hand. She pulled the covers up to his chin and stretched out on top of them, throwing the blanket over herself. She pulled him close and held him as tightly as she dared, whispering, "I will not allow you to wake up in the night without someone who loves you lying here beside you."

Alone. Henry had always been alone at night, except for his few dalliances with women when he was a young man, and none of those lasted from dark to dawn. With Kiri beside him now, folding love and comfort around him, he dared his demons to break through. When a sudden stab of pain woke him in the night and he touched her shoulder or pressed his face against her back, she adjusted his medication and massaged him until his wave of discomfort passed. As his ninety-year-old body wasted away, he roused regularly in the night, afraid that those feverish moments were his last. Kiri calmed him with soft touches and soothing whispers. "Breathe through it. I won't let you go. We'll live one more day together."

Haunted by the unfinished business of his secrets, he tried to get her to listen. "I haven't finished telling you everything."

"Some secrets are best left unknown," she said.

"When you discover them, promise you won't think less of me."

"I can only think good about the man who has always had my best interests at heart."

Once Henry was confined to his bed, Kiri made a special effort to customize his surroundings. Michael Thomas' configuration of rotating mirrors captured the sunlight and cast it through the window all day long. She bordered that window with paper-sized portraits of the grandchildren she had painted when they started school, meant for their eighteenth birthdays as graduation remembrances. "These won't be a surprise now, but maybe they'll be more appreciated knowing how much you enjoyed them." She added ones of Katie and Michael Thomas, created in spare moments when Henry napped, to the one he brought with him when he first moved in—the one of his hand that invited her to paint in daisy yellow. Kiri surprised him with a new one she painted while he attended to "business." It featured the two of them sitting in front of their cottage with a mound of daisies at their feet. They looked out to sea while a bevy of curly-headed children played along the beach. "A happy, happy memory for us both," she said.

Visiting hours were reduced and limited to family only. Katie spent most of her days sitting next to Henry's bed, reading to him, and Harry showed up right after school for "private chats" with Poppy. Michael Thomas stopped by for short visits morning and evening. Foremost on his mentor's mind was Kiri's physical and mental condition. "Watch for a delayed reaction. You mother is the strongest woman I've ever known... until she isn't."

One afternoon, Henry interrupted Katie's reading with a deep, agonizing sigh. When he caught his breath he asked, "Do you mind if we stop for today? Tell your mother I need her... and Bitsy."

Katie flew down the stairs to her mother, tears spilling everywhere. The look on her face told the story.

Kiri shot up the stairs in double-time, assessed Henry's condition and met Katie on the landing. The look in her eyes confirmed Katie's worst fear.

"Is he dying now?"

Kiri encompassed her daughter in her arms, trying to be strong for them both. "Yes, dear. He is. I doubt he'll make it through the night. Kiss him goodbye and tell him how much you love him."

"I feel as if I'm losing the only father I've ever really known," she sobbed.

"Tell him that and thank him. Call your brother and Bitsy. Bring Harry to say goodbye as soon as he's home from school. Then go, and check on us at noon tomorrow."

Katie shook her head. "But I want to stay with you... with him."

"I'm sorry. He's asked that we spend his final moments alone together. Honor his wish, and make the time you have now count."

When Bitsy returned for the second time prepared to play through the night, Kiri read in the harpist's eyes that of all the deaths she had attended, Henry's was the first she feared. With her sublime music floating in from the landing, the elderly couple eased into their last night together.

Kiri climbed onto the bed and lay beside him with one arm cradling his head and the other hand grasping his and placing it over her heart "so I can pass some of my energy to you."

"I wish...."

"No regrets, Henry."

"I wish... I had been able to love you... in every way."

She smiled. "Oh, but you did... every time you looked at me... and it was wonderful!"

"Fifty years...."

She nodded. "We've spent nearly a half century together, have history and made memories. Now, Shhh. Save your breath."

"Family...."

"Yes, we raised a family together. Your love and mine helped them to grow into the fine adults they are today."

He shook his head. "Bitsy... Katie... me... family... secret."

"You've always been family. That's no secret. Shhh."

"Thank you... for gift...."

"Thank *you* for the gift of every day we've shared."

He shook his head again. "Blessing... to die... in arms... of woman... I love most."

Kiri stared at the vacant glow in the eyes of the man who passionately but chastely adored her. "I am blessed to have had you in my life." She kissed him tenderly. "Breathe deeply and sense our hearts beat together. With each breath we're going to remember a wonderful time we've shared."

Henry blinked his assent.

"Breathe. Our first year as close friends, you were the only one who came for me... twice... and forced me to choose a full life. Michael Thomas was born our second year. You cradled him through his first night. Katie was born in our fourth year. She imprinted on you immediately and has never let you go. I had to pry her away this evening. You were her greatest love. Another deep breath... yours and mine... together."

Somewhere between Katie's traditional wedding and Michael Thomas' festive nuptials, Kiri heard the gurgling sounds of dying and watched life slowly drain out of her beloved companion, powerless to stanch the flow. By the time she finished the retelling of building their cottage, sun peeked through the window. She felt his hand go limp and his breathing stop. "We made it, Henry, together. One more dawn. Thank you." Kiri gave him a final kiss and cradled him as tightly as she could, well past Bitsy's departure.

CHAPTER 42

When faced with more than you can bear, call for help, Kiri remembered from Michael's story at Glendalough. She gazed on the man who appeared distinguished even in death, dressed in his silver-gray suit and lilac tie and surrounded by the acrylic faces of all the children he nurtured. *But who do I call now that Henry is gone?*

She startled at a light-knuckled knocking at the front door. The time: 10:00 a.m. She was certain that Katie spread the word—no visitors until noon—but the jarring sound continued and became more insistent with each rap. Reluctantly, she opened the door just a crack, determined to be polite but firm.

Harry's adolescent face stared back at her. "I'm here to see Poppy."

Kiri opened the door to the very serious fourteen-year-old dressed up in his Sunday best but with an open shirt collar and no tie. She could not refuse him, so pulled him in for a sorrowful hug. "I'm so glad you're here," she said. "Poppy passed early this morning, and I'm feeling very sad right now."

"Me too, Granny." This time, he pulled her in for a hug and held on tight, sniffling against her shoulder. He fumbled in his pocket. "But I need to see him. I told him I would come first thing."

"I'm sorry, Harry, but I cannot let you go upstairs without your mother's consent."

"That's okay. I'll wait. Mom will come as soon as she discovers that I'm not in my room with a stomachache."

Kiri stifled a laugh.

"Poppy said that when he died, I would be head of his family, and my first job was to take care of you. After we said goodbye yesterday afternoon, I made my first decision—to stay home today and do as he asked." He displayed a nervous confidence. "Is there anything I can do for you now... before Mother comes?"

Kiri regarded her earnest grandson, Katie's number two and Henry's namesake. "You could sit with me on the sofa for a few minutes and hold my hand," she smiled.

They did not have long to wait. A tentative rap on the door accompanied by a mournful wail announced Katie's arrival. She rushed into her mother's arms, toppling them both onto the stairs. "Uncle Henry?"

Kiri shook her head. "Early this morning."

"Oh, Mom," she cried and lapsed into her run-on babble made even less intelligible by overwhelming sorrow. Still numb from the events of the last days, Kiri grasped only snatches of Katie's distress. Her daughter could not imagine life without Henry in it. She had not slept in days and was a physical and emotional wreck. Her husband did not recognize her.

The kids misbehaved as if they had never been taught manners, and she had not hugged them in weeks. Another wail broke through her tear-streaked face. "I'm a horrible mom and so upset that I've... I've misplaced one of my children!"

"Calm down," Kiri said, and turned her daughter away from the sofa. While comforting the distraught lump of adult child, she put a finger to her lips to warn Harry not to show himself just yet. "Your family is grieving too. Children don't have the tools yet to make sense of this dramatic change in their lives. Their instinct is to make you feel better, but they don't know how to do that."

She rocked her daughter gently as she recalled her own experience. "When your dad was killed, your Grandmother Paula was the only one who realized that all your cousins—about the same ages as your own children now—needed to participate in the family's mourning. Mom found activities for them to show that it is okay for adults to be sad and cry and for children too, and that there are ways they can help to make each other feel better. Even little Máire is capable of peeling a banana and buttering toast for her mother's breakfast or opening a fresh box of tissues." She felt Katie give in to a chuckle.

"So, after we've had a good cry together here, you go home and find ways your children can help you feel better. And tonight, you invite Clay to show you all the ways he can comfort and protect you. All the children... except for the one Uncle Henry designated to help me here." Kiri gave her grandson thumbs up.

Katie turned to find her son approach nervously for a hug. "Harry Moriarty!" She roared. "What are you doing here?"

"Poppy told me to come as early as possible this morning. I had a little trouble sneaking out, but I got here as soon as I could."

"We were about to go upstairs for a final goodbye, but both Harry and I are sad and a little frightened. Maybe you can help."

Katie wiped her face, blew her nose, and wrapped her arms around the first of her children to grow a hair taller than his mother. They clasped hands and climbed the stairs together, pausing at her old bedroom's doorway for as long as possible to avoid the inescapable reality that lay there. Their beloved Henry was gone.

Harry approached the bed bathed in sunlight and studied the form that now lay so still. He massaged Poppy's cold hand as tears fell and his shoulders shook with sobs. After a few minutes he straightened to full height, walked to his mother's old dresser, wiped his face with a handkerchief... and put on a tie. When he turned toward his mother and grandmother, he assumed the air of an almost grown young man with his uncle Michael Thomas' demeanor, his great uncle Kurt's lanky build, and the black wavy hair and gray eyes reminiscent of Henry.

"I'll go make some tea now. Then I have to call Groton's and Poppy's solicitor. And ask Mom to call Uncle Michael. You shouldn't have to phone anybody, Granny." He hugged them both and left for the kitchen.

After the shock of her son's transformation wore off, Katie held Henry's hand. "He looks so peaceful. You didn't prepare him all by yourself?"

"I couldn't send him out to strangers. Henry would have been mortified to leave the house without his bath and a shave and wearing nothing but his pajamas!" The two mournful women shared a giggle that turned to tears.

"Mom, how can you be so calm?" Katie asked, dabbing her eyes.

"I've had more practice, but don't be fooled by what you see. This is not calm. This is heartache buried under exhaustion. I can't afford to let down even for a minute or I won't make it through the next few days." She sighed. "I think Harry and I are meant to help each other through them. Actually, the distraction is good for me." She sighed again. "I'll leave you alone with Henry for a few minutes. I believe I have a cup of tea waiting."

The sound of Harry's voice on the phone drifted to her ears as she reached the kitchen. "I'm calling to report the death of Henry Callaghan early this morning." Hearing those words made Henry's death a reality. Soon Kiri would see them in print and on the news—his life reduced to a few sentences.

"Granny, the solicitor wants to speak with you." Harry handed over his phone.

"Sorry for your loss. Mr. Callaghan left an envelope for you, and I have his will as well. Might I stop by later this afternoon?"

Rankled by his canned condolence, she replied, "No rush. We'll be busy here for the next couple of days."

"But this envelope may contain instructions for the disposition of his body."

"The family has those affairs in hand. You may give me the envelope when we meet to go over his will."

She handed Harry's phone back and slid into the nook. A steaming cup of lemongrass tea, a soft-boiled egg and a slice of toast were set before her, beside a limp daisy drooping over the rim of a glass.

"I guess I stuffed it in my pocket too hard," Harry said apologetically. "Poppy wanted you to have one if he didn't die until this morning."

*   *   *

A soft pat on her shoulder roused Kiri from a fitful snooze in the living room recliner. "Granny, wake up. Groton's called about the burial location. I have a taxi ordered. Poppy said you're not to drive for several days—until you've rested and feel better. He said you would be very tired and weren't to be bothered by people or details."

"You're very efficient," she yawned.

"He gave me this mobile-pay phone with lists of what I need to do, phone numbers and an account with enough virtual cash to cover your expenses. All I have to do is access the business, verify the amount and use the phone's fingerprint scanner, and zip, it's done."

That's so like Henry, Kiri thought, to oversee the details of her life even in his death.

Harry sat beside his grandmother in the taxi and took her hand. "Granny, I'm scared. I miss Poppy already. I want to do everything he expects me to, but I don't know how."

"I miss him too, but if Poppy chose you to watch over me, there must be a good reason. Guess we'll have to figure out what that is together. But I am grateful for your help now." She squeezed his fingers. She was hesitant too and did not make a habit of visiting the cemetery often. She preferred the memory garden across her road for commiserating with the departed.

The odd couple meandered between ancient headstones to the O'Connell family section. Kiri reviewed the details of interment again and decided on the soils she would cast into Henry's grave—some from under his mother's lilac, pebbly sand from their cottage, and a fresh daisy, of course. Then, she forced a marker into the ground. "We'll bury Poppy here, near your Grandfather Michael and me."

Angry shoes slapped the gravel pathway behind them, and a familiar voice cried out. "That man will *not* be buried in *my* family's plot!" Anne rooted herself in front of Kiri.

"You are wrong," Kiri shot back. "Henry will be buried right here where I'm standing."

"At your feet like the lap dog he was?" Anne sneered.

"No, I'll be on the shoulders of the giant that he was."

"I never saw that man enter a church except to give away your daughter and bury my brother. It's sacrilege to place him in sanctified ground. Not a priest alive will perform burial rites for a man with no faith."

"Doyle's cousin offered his services as soon as he learned of Henry's condition. He will be buried with *my* family."

"That joke of a clergyman. I won't allow it!"

The two women stepped forward, noses nearly touching, brows bunched and teeth bared like a pair of angry jackals. "I swore I would never say this to any of you O'Connells, but I say this to you now, Anne. Until my last breath, *I* am the head of this family. *My... will... be... done!* If you don't want to be buried in the same ground as the most righteous man I've ever known—your father included—then go somewhere else!"

When Harry noticed his great aunt open her palm and raise it, and his grandmother clench her fist, he quickly stepped between them. "May I escort you to your car, Aunt Anne? It's time for you to leave... please."

*　　*　　*

The task of tallying the monetary worth of a man took place in Kiri's living room on the morning following Henry's graveside service with Anne the only O'Connell noticeably absent. The solicitor asked that Kiri, Michael Thomas and Sala, Katie and Clayton, and their son Henry Killian be present for the reading of the Will. He made great ceremony of spreading out numerous documents on the coffee table, then began with an air of importance.

"Mr. Callaghan wrote this document himself. I came to his apartment a few weeks ago to assure that it met all legal requirements and to witness his signature." He cleared his throat three times, and his voice took on a solemn tone.

"Herewith is my Last Will and Testament, written by me, the man known to you as Henry Callaghan."

The assembled family members traded confused looks. Was Henry ever known by any other name? Michael Thomas shrugged his shoulders.

"I hereby name the following as my immediate family, related to me in the most basic and intimate of ways: Kirin Aurora O'Connell, her children Michael Thomas O'Connell and Aurora Kathryn O'Connell Moriarty, their children, and Kathryn Elizabeth Killian (Bitsy), Sara Lamb Killian, and her children. All references to my family are to them. None other has any claim on my estate."

Basic and intimate? What did that mean? The children stared at their mother. She shrugged. Harry slouched in his seat, bored with formalities.

"In Irish families, much honor and responsibility traditionally falls on the firstborn (son), while the strengths and wisdom of the secondborn are often overlooked. Given that my family is untraditional, my intention is to follow an untraditional path and designate my namesake, Henry Killian Moriarty, secondborn of Katie, as head of my family."

Gasps!

"Did Poppy talk to you about this?" Clay asked his son who was suddenly erect and at attention.

Harry nodded. "Just to take care of Granny. He was real worried about her. He didn't say who else was in his family besides her."

"I place the bulk of my estate into Harry's capable hands for management and disbursal. I appoint his Grandmother Kirin as Executor of this Will and Trustee of my Estate until Henry Killian attains the age of twenty-one. When his cousin, Oditi O'Connell, secondborn of Michael Thomas, attains the age of twenty-one, she shall serve equally with him in all respects, the only limitation to their joint actions being what they deem as in the best interest of my family."

All eyes turned toward Harry again, who sank into the sofa to avoid their glances.

"Did Poppy ever talk to you about a Trust?" his father asked.

The adolescent shook his head. "I don't even know what a trust is."

"What *did* you two discuss during your afternoons together?"

"Poppy explained that because of experiences that happen in their early lives, some kids grow up faster than their friends—like the girls and boys that Mother helps. Then he said that maybe they have to have a job. How would I feel if that happened to me? I told him that school should always come first, but if it meant taking care of Granny or keeping my brothers and sisters safe or making sure they had food or went to school, I wouldn't mind. A guy has to take care of his family."

"Anything else?"

"We talked about the kinds of information you share with other people and what is privileged and meant for only a few people you trust. I'm guessing that this stuff qualifies."

"Moving on," the solicitor said and turned his attention back to the Will. "The only outright gifts I make are the following." He reached for an envelope and handed it to the teenager as he read. "To Harry, the first pound note I ever earned. You may use it to buy an ice cream or to build an empire. Our legacy—yours and mine—is in your hands now."

Inside, Harry found a rumpled Irish pound note from the 20th century before the Euro was adopted, ancient scrip in the young boy's eyes.

Next, a file of documents was passed to his uncle. "To Michael Thomas, loan forgiveness and the deed, free and clear, to his home at 243 on Quincy Street, the house in which I was raised as a child."

Shock did not begin to describe the family's reaction. Katie squealed, "You mean Henry grew up in this neighborhood and he never told us? I *knew* he and his mother were connected to the family somehow. I just didn't know how." Still shaking her head, she accepted the file handed to her.

"To Aurora Kathryn, loan forgiveness and the deed, free and clear, to the house at the bottom of the road known as Seamróg House."

Kiri sighed. "I knew Henry was behind that deal."

"Well, I didn't!" Katie stated firmly.

The solicitor continued. "To Kirin, the keys to unlock my deepest secrets. Please do not think me a coward for holding onto them for so long." The man handed her a ring with three keys on it. She recognized the one to the cottage. The other two were a mystery, and she looked to him for further explanation. He shook his head, implying there was none.

"The balance of my estate is held in trust and enumerated in an attachment, including an endowment for the historical museum located at O'Connell House," he concluded and placed the Will on the coffee table. "That's it. Short and to the point."

He passed fat folders across the table, one to Clay and Katie, one to Michael Thomas and Sala, one to Kiri and the last to Harry. "I'll leave these for you to go over in your own time. You have my number in case you have questions. Note that there are two special provisions on the properties: a life estate in the seaside cottage for Kirin and the same for an apartment in the Georgian home for someone named Frank." He packed up what was left of his papers and stated very solemnly, "Mr. Callaghan did not seek my advice. If he had, I would have counseled otherwise. His very sizable estate is a heady responsibility for such a young lad." He scowled at Harry, dropped the envelope of Henry's final requests in Kiri's lap and left.

The folders contained descriptions of properties—lots of them—all around the neighborhood, every one on Quincy Street that Kiri did not already own and more up to two roads beyond. An extensive investment portfolio seemed secondary. Clay and Michael Thomas exchanged glances that acknowledged the enormity of the responsibility Henry had placed on their children's generation—and the opportunity. Then their attention turned to Harry whose eyes welled up and whose lower lip quivered.

"I don't know how to begin. This job is way too big for me."

Clay squeezed his son to him. His cobalt eyes locked on Harry's gray ones, and he spoke as if they were the only two in the room. "Let me tell you about this family you were born into without any choice. When we buried Poppy yesterday, lots of folks were there. How many do you think?"

"Maybe 100 or 150."

"More, and by my count, all but a handful were O'Connells. We came back to the aquacenter to share a fine meal—all those folks, from wee kiddies to newly retired, laughing and crying, pushing and shoving. Then there was a near scuffle over who got to plant the daisies in the memory garden. I'm asking, who'd want to be responsible for that lot? Who was wise enough and strong enough to keep them all in line?"

Harry looked across the table at his uncle.

"That man over there? One day, maybe, but not yet. Did you know, 'tis Granny who's head of *that* family?"

Harry shook his head. "When she and Aunt Anne fought at the cemetery, and she said she was head of the family, I thought she meant just us here and the rest of the grandkids."

Kiri quickly hid behind a tissue to wipe her nose, but Katie caught her. "Mom? You and Aunt Anne? Why didn't you tell us?"

"My battle. Not yours."

"I stopped them before they hit each other and told Aunt Anne it was time for her to go. I tried to be polite." Harry sat taller.

Clay hid a smile, delighted that his mother-in-law had not lost her spunk. "When Great Grandfather Thomas gave her the good news—that he named her the head of his family—your Granny O said that she didn't want that job, but Poppy encouraged her. 'Just like a puzzle,' he said. 'Gather the pieces and place them one by one.' She divided that huge job into parts and tackled one piece at a time and in the process, she trained that rowdy family how to take care of themselves and each other.

"Who do you think arranged for cars at the funeral, places for out-of-towners to sleep, all that food on the table and all the helping hands to hang onto the little ones? 'Twasn't your granny. She was with you. 'Twasn't your mother. She was busy helping your brothers and sisters understand the goings on. 'Twasn't your uncle. He was with his family. Someone, or many, stepped up because that is what they were trained to do. Poppy asked you to take care of Granny to give you a head start, so when it comes your time, you'll be trained.

"O'Connells are spread all over this island in every trade, business, and profession you could name. In this room alone, there's one who keeps everyone safe no matter where in the world they are. Sala keeps everyone calm, and your mother keeps everyone moving at high speed, with one project after another to advance the disadvantaged. She has a second job, too. Family historian. She knows everyone in this family and how each is related to the others over many generations. She claims her mission is to find family and that *you* play a special part in that search."

Harry studied his mother, uncertain whether to believe his father's story. Then he sized up the man. "What do you do?"

Clay tugged on his earlobe to find the right answer. "I'm the bearer of *my* granny's ancient wisdom. Let me tell you a secret. *My* granny told me that *your* granny is a snoop." He raised his peaked eyebrows and nodded. "My dear granny said that every family and neighborhood should have one, and I suspect she was one herself."

Harry cut in. "That's not a very nice thing to say about someone sitting right here."

Katie scowled at her husband.

"Oh, no. Not the meddling, gossipy kind. The secret detective kind who has a knack for noticing when there is a need and finding a way to meet it. Your Granny O trained her family so well that you don't see her doing her job. In our business, 'tis called 'flying under the radar.' We all do it—our jobs—without tooting our horns. She can teach you how to do that, too—train your charges so well that they don't realize they're doing it for you, and then yours won't seem like a job a'tall. 'Twill be a joy. And if it ever seems too big a burden, do you know what you can do?"

The teen who grew up that morning shook his head.

"Well, you holler for help. That's what family is for."

Kiri nodded at the familiar refrain and turned her thoughts to the men in her life who had come to her aid. Michael, Henry, her son and her son-in-law lived under the radar—did their jobs so discretely that only the impact of their labors was evident. Her grandson was soon to become one of them, with or without her approval.

Fifty-First Anniversary Year
  I didn't think it possible to experience such profound grief twice in a lifetime. And now there's no Henry to console me. Who do I turn to?

CHAPTER 43

Kiri's children expected their mother to plunge into deep depression at some point. Frank warned Michael Thomas about her reaction to his father's death, but they could not imagine what the precipitating factor might be this time. She managed the confrontation with Anne at the graveyard. She survived Henry's funeral. She listened to the solicitor lay out Poppy's plan for her grandchildren's security. Then she awoke to sun streaming in her window and no Henry beside her. And burst into tears. *Go to water in stress.*

Harry spent the two weeks following Poppy's death sleeping over at his grandmother's house—"in case she wakes in the night and needs help." He set his watch to sound every two hours to check on her and always found her upstairs in the sitting room resting in the recliner with her face toward the memory garden. She was not ready to return to her bedroom, she said. Harry countered that he would not sleep in his own house until she did. So, she gave it a try one night. The young boy kept his regular checks on her, and at 6:00 a.m. was shocked to find her bed empty.

His agitated voice shouted into his phone. "Dad! I've lost Granny!"

"Wha...?" a flustered one answered.

"I can't find Granny anywhere. At four she was in her bed, and at six she was gone. Help!"

Help came in sweats, deck shoes and half-opened eyelids. "Have you checked all over the house?"

"Everywhere, including the garage. Both cars still have boots on. I don't know whether to go up or down the road. Should we split up?"

"Let's check one more place." Clay put his finger to his lips to quiet his son. They left through the kitchen door and walked quietly toward the fence. In the glow of early morning they spotted Kiri's arms—one after the other—break water and slide smoothly back in, pulling her forward. Her head barely broke the surface, and her nightgown billowed up from her back with her movements.

Harry bolted for the gate. "Granny's drowning!"

"No, son." Clay held him back. "She's grieving. She held her sadness in for so long that 'tis finally spilling out—enough tears to fill the pool and more."

"We have to help her... pull her out. Do something!"

Clay shook his head. "We need to leave her be to work out her sorrow in her own way. At eighty-two, your granny is still a stronger swimmer than most women of twenty-eight. She'll be fine. You run home and tell your mum that the dam finally burst. She better move today's patients to the other pool. Then you get ready and head for school. I'll keep watch."

Once Harry was gone, Clay went to work. He turned up the heat in the pool and on its deck and turned the towel warmer on before he activated the tea brewer. He grabbed a couple of bottles of water and a towel and settled in a deck chair for the duration. He had not disclosed the whole truth to his son—that Kiri had the power and the will to swim herself to exhaustion. He dared not close his eyes for even a few minutes.

Those minutes ticked into hours—at least four, by his watch. When Kiri's strokes became jerky, he sat up straight. At irregular, he perched on the edge of the pool. When her left arm—the scarred and weaker one— stopped altogether, he eased himself in and floated beside her. When her right arm followed suit and she let herself sink in the deep, he treaded water over her. When bubbles ceased to rise from her exhausted lungs, he pulled her up and onto his chest to float back to the shallow.

He swaddled her in toasty blankets and forced warm tea down her throat. He pulled her onto his lap, held her and rocked her.

"Michael?" she whispered. "Henry…."

"No, ma'am. You're not going anywhere yet. My boy needs his granny. He hangs on your every word. You're not going to topple over the edge today and leave him dangling, believing he failed his first job. What kind of example would that be for a lad who has a long, tough road ahead? You rest… and cry." When she finally lapsed into a disturbed sleep, Clay carried her to her house and tucked her in bed.

Kiri awoke in the near dusk to the strains of harp music and the sight of Sala's soft brown eyes and Harry's worried gray ones.

Harry prepared to stay awake from 4:00 a.m. on in case his grandmother tried another early morning swim. She surprised him. She padded from her room and out to the pool in the dark of predawn. She inhaled deeply, slipped into the water and, with her head turned to the side every eighth strong, steady stroke, she began her marathon.

Her grandson watched for any alteration in her movements. Change came as the sky began to take on morning hues. She no longer turned her head but remained face down, her jaw and lips contorting to the side to strain for the next breath. This continued until the sun was well up.

Harry called his father. "She did it again, but she seems okay. Not as frantic as yesterday."

"I'll be right there. You come home and get ready for school." Clay appeared moments later, ready to wait her out—another three hours or so. When she ran out of energy, he rolled her up, waited until she fell asleep, and carried her to bed.

The following morning proceeded as the previous two, with one exception. Gray, weeping skies obscured the sun. When Kiri realized that not a ray of bright light broke through, she rolled onto her back to float and flung her arms wide, laughed and lapped at the life-sustaining raindrops with her tongue.

When Harry failed to call home, his father appeared with worry furrows above his eyes to find his son asleep in a deck chair, soaking wet. He jostled the boy and wrapped him in a cozy towel. He picked up the lanky fourteen-year-old and pulled him onto his lap, rubbing him roughly to stimulate his circulation. "We need to warm you up before time to leave for school."

Harry shook his head. "Not going."

"You're not sick yet! When you get home, we'll have a talk about not spending the night here anymore. You are not getting the sleep a growing lad needs."

Harry shook his head again. "It's Saturday. I can stay as long as Granny's in the pool."

Clay laughed and held his son tighter. "Of course you can. We'll watch over her together. But we will have that talk. We've got to find a way to keep your grandmother from wandering in the night and swimming to exhaustion every day. Should we put a lock on the gate? Change her doors' key codes? Ask the doc to prescribe something for her?"

Harry shook his head against his father's chest and tilted upward to find his eyes. "We shouldn't stop her from doing what seems to help her. We should help her do it safely. Something about morning bothers Granny. We need to find out what that is and figure a way to change it."

Clay considered his son's observation. "Where did that clever thought come from?"

"I don't know. It just popped into my head."

Kiri awoke mid afternoon to find Harry sitting at the edge of her wildflower quilt, staring at her. She accepted the cup of tea he offered. "Shouldn't you be in school?"

He rolled his eyes. "It's Saturday. Why am I the only one who knows what day it is?"

"Then shouldn't you be with your friends instead of watching me breathe in and out?"

"I don't mind, but I'd feel better if I knew why you get your days and nights mixed up. Most folks sleep at night and are active during the day. You're all turned around." He bit his lip and asked outright. "Granny, why don't you like mornings?"

Taken aback by his bluntness, Kiri fumbled for an answer and decided on an honest one. "Poppy and I... our favorite times together were when dawn broke and filled this room with sun. My body senses when the light is about to change, and I wake up feeling sad because I can't stop it. I feel so empty inside that I want it to be dark all the time."

"I hate to break it to you, Granny, but that won't happen. No one's figured out how to turn off the sun." He watched a smile creep across her elderly face, more wrinkled than he remembered. "If you could sleep until the middle of the morning, would that help?"

"It might. I usually enjoyed alone time by the middle of the mornings, but I don't know how to skip over daybreak. When I stick my head in the water, I don't notice it so much. Swimming helps me to feel safe and tires me so I can sleep." She stared at her grandson trying so hard to do his job. "Are you advising me to change my habits?"

He lowered his eyes and replied shyly, "You'd be healthier, and father and I would get more sleep." He glimpsed another smile creep across his grandmother's face.

"Well, then, when you come up with an idea, I might give it a try."

Harry left in a hurry without a kiss or a goodbye hug and returned a couple of hours later to find his grandmother still in bed. His older brother Mike followed him in, his arms loaded with a roll of black paper. The two boys measured long strips, cut to fit, to cover the bedroom windows. They nattered and poked criticism like typical teenagers, but in the end when they closed the door, the bedroom darkened significantly.

"Not the prettiest curtains, but they might do the job," Harry said.

The third smile of the afternoon tickled Kiri's face. "We'll hope so. Tell me, how did you come up with such a simple solution?"

Harry shrugged his shoulders. "The idea just popped into my head." He reached into his pocket and pulled out a sleeping mask. "Try this too. I've set your alarm for ten tomorrow morning. Don't get out of bed until I'm home from church. Then we'll swim together."

Both boys leaned over for kisses and goodbye hugs from their grandmother and left, carrying their mess with them. Kiri regarded them carefully, one strong and stocky like his grandfather and the other, lithe and lanky like Poppy—her guardian angels in running shoes trying out their wings. Yes, she thought. For their sakes, I can make an effort.

*   *   *.

Michael Thomas did his best to attend to Henry's affairs until his mother was back on her feet. He separated the mail into piles—Now and Someday—and included young Harry in organizing them for his mother to authorize payments as executor.

"How did you learn to do this?" Harry asked one evening, overwhelmed by the stack of responsibilities he was to deliver to his grandmother.

"Mom trained me early when she set up a committee with some of my cousins to help run Great Grandfather Thomas' trust. I was barely older than you when she took over. She decided a member of each family should have some say in its affairs. Once we got the hang of it, she left it to us. Now, she only asks for an annual report and signs the checks. When I become head of the trust after she dies, I plan to do the same. Her system has worked well." He caught the sober look on his nephew's face. "The first major project the trust took on was creating the museum."

The boy's eyes brightened at the memory of Poppy's enthusiasm for the tunneled attraction. "Really? Could I do that? Build something terrific and ask others to help me?"

"Of course, if you trust them. But I'd probably wait until they reach twenty-one. Legal liability, you know. Have anyone in mind?"

"My older brother Mike. He's pretty smart. 'Diti, of course. And 'Rion makes sense—the two oldest from each family, so the other kids don't feel left out. And maybe Cousin Sara Lamb to keep the accounts. That's her business, and I hear she's really good at it."

"Sounds like a wise decision for your first as the head of a family you didn't realize you had. See what your grandmother has to say when she feels better."

Kiri took her time feeling better once she returned to a normal routine, but one issue could not be avoided. All the properties in Henry's estate had been assessed but one—the one containing his apartment and its contents. Frank and the other renters allowed access to their premises and the loft, but Henry's remained locked. Kiri, apparently, held the key.

Reluctantly she agreed to use it late one afternoon, with her children, Harry and a bank officer waiting for her on the stoop of the house. She realized, at that moment, that she had never been invited to enter Henry's living quarters before and to do so now seemed a betrayal. Unsure what to expect, she turned the key to his apartment, opened the door and was shocked by what she saw... or did not see.

The living room—what appeared to be his living room—was bare, containing only a table and chair, a wall of books—many of which she recognized from Thomas' collection—and an overstuffed easy chair with a sweater hanging over one arm and positioned toward the window from which Kiri could see her own home. There was nothing—not a throw pillow, not a photo, not an ancient keepsake passed down through generations—to lend color, personality or a clue to the identity of the person who lived there. A wave of melancholy engulfed Kiri as she realized how lonely Henry must have been for so many years and how vitally he depended on her family to give his life meaning.

"Did you ever enter this apartment when you lived in the loft and worked here?" Kiri asked her son.

He shook his head, embarrassed. "He never asked for help and never gave any of us a key."

"I've never been here either." A quizzical eyebrow from this grandmother provoked Harry's quick response. "We always did our business at your house."

Kiri shuddered to think what they would find in Henry's bedroom—a straw mattress and candle, maybe. That door was locked too. The only key left on the ring of three was a small one, older with a tattered lilac ribbon attached to it, obviously not a fit. She tried the apartment key again, felt the lock give, and pushed the door open slowly.

If the living room were a symbol of life as it was for Henry, then his bedroom was the opposite—life as he imagined it to be. Colorful framed photos covered every inch of wall space except for one bare spot, just the size of the hand painting. The room fairly giggled with happy faces and silly ones, hugs and kisses, swirling dresses and Sunday suits on special occasions, early proofs of life, and a grand tour of the Irish isle through time and locale. The center of attention, surrounding his dressing table, was a series of a young and happy Henry with women: one in pigtails singing; one in a spotted blouse, dripping wet at the shore; one with a team of four more young burly guys near the network building; and one short haired sprite in a canoe on a lake.

"Uncle Henry had a girlfriend!" Katie squealed. Then her eyes jumped out at a photo of him, dressed to the nines and in an ornately decorated ballroom, dancing with a beautiful young woman in a blue ball gown—the one that hung in the back of her mother's closet. "Mom! That's you!" She turned toward the blushing woman standing in the doorway. "Uncle Henry loved you since… since *forever!*"

Michael Thomas and Harry pushed their way into the room and stood amazed at the pictorial history staring back at them—every major and many minor events in the lives of the three O'Connells, the spouses of the younger two, and their offspring. Katie joined in to identify and recount some of the joyful scenes. Kiri recalled a similar discovery some thirty years earlier when her children unearthed a photo box of their father's generation following Thomas' death. Now they had their own stories to share with the next.

"Can we remove these and take them home with us?" Katie asked.

"Uncle Henry would love that, but only if you can divide them without fighting." Kiri turned her attention to the dressing table, the home of the keepsakes she expected to see in the other room: a woman's formal glove—the one she lost at the ball; a framed, pressed lilac; a transparent plastic cube filled with green paint chips; and a small, smooth pebble among them. An empty frame leaning against the mirror caught her eye. She could not remember where she had seen it before, so she asked. "Does anyone recognize this?"

Harry answered. "Poppy brought it from the museum the last time he took me there."

"I recognize it too—the empty one at the end of the Troubles exhibit. He must have found the picture he was looking for but didn't have time to frame it," Michael Thomas added.

"Speaking of missing pictures, I can't find one here of Harry's christening. I can't imagine Uncle Henry forgetting *that* major event. He and his namesake were the stars of the show," Katie harrumphed.

"I'm sure he has one tucked away in a special place. We'll find it eventually," Kiri assured the disappointed teenager standing at her elbow.

His eyes fell onto an old tin box sitting in front of the frame. "Maybe it's in there. Should we look?"

Kiri did not want to look—yet—afraid of what she might find. "I'll take a quick peek, but if I don't spy it on top, you'll have to give me time to sort through the box later." She knew the old key with the ribbon would fit, tried it, and opened the lid a bare inch, just enough for Harry to see that it was filled with papers. "Don't worry. Your photo will be our treasure hunt."

The bank officer entered to find a mess of photos on Henry's bed, other memorabilia and the old tin box. "Not much of value in here, except maybe the clothes and furniture." His eyes settled on the box. "Anything in there?"

"Just old papers," Harry answered in a dispirited voice.

The officer turned his attention to Kiri. "Can you approximate its worth for the inventory?"

"Its contents are invaluable," she said, placing the box under an arm and leaving the apartment in a hurry, before she embarrassed herself by bursting into uncontrollable tears. She crossed the road, entered her own home and climbed the stairs with less energy than usual. She reached her bedroom and placed the tin box on top of the unopened letter the solicitor gave her. Both now rested on Michael's nightstand—the one that held her feather collection. She did not open the box. She did not have the strength to rifle through its contents—Henry's secrets.

CHAPTER 44

Sixteen-year-old Harry left his grandmother's house after a short accounting lesson. Once a month during the past two years, she held a work session for him. His other visits were for fun, since he no longer monitored her daily activities to keep her from "toppling over the edge" as his father would say. This day, on his way out, he nearly flattened a nicely dressed, older woman who stood nervously on the walk. Morning dew still clung to her jacket. "Sorry, ma'am. You looking for Granny?" At her nod, he showed her into the house and called up the stairs, "Granny. A woman is here to see you," and he left more carefully the second time.

The neatly coifed woman scanned the homey surroundings, the shifting green hues of the walls, colorful gardens out front and rear windows, comfy sofas and pillows, and the litter of little people scattered about. She was drawn, however, to its focal point—the merlot wall displaying the For Better, For Worse and Forever photos. Welling inside her threatened to seep through her leopard-spotted and wrinkled skin when she recognized the bottom one as Michael's last breath.

"How may I help you?" Kiri asked kindly as she stepped lightly down the stairs. Her look turned to horror as she came face to face with her visitor. "Alice Richardson! What are you doing in my home? Get…." She stopped herself. Her grandson invited the woman in, an act of hospitality. She stuffed her hands deep into her pocket scarf and cleared her throat. "Why are you here?"

Alice delayed her answer. "Lovely home you have, so warm and inviting. Your children and grandchildren must be happy here," she said forlornly.

"Yes. They do all manage to fit in when we come together," Kiri said, removing a book from the sofa and motioning her visitor to sit. "But I expect you know what an uproar teenagers can create."

Alice shook her head and dropped her eyes. "We never had children. I envy you the happiness they bring."

For a moment, Kiri felt sorry for her old rival.

"I'm sorry you and Jack didn't find happiness together too." The moment she uttered his name, Alice realized the mistake. She had come to Kiri for a favor and could see by the look in her eyes that she had jeopardized her chance. The entirety of the last time she saw him flashed through her mind in a second.

When she and Patrick arrived at Jack MacKenzie's home in the highlands of New Zealand's sheep country for a belated family dinner, they found him in his living room on a bender. A packed overnight bag sat by the door awaiting his guests' departure. The minute he said goodbye to his first wife's second cousin and her husband, he planned to fly to the woman who walked away from him the previous day and bring her back. He invited Patrick to join him while his girls put the finishing touches on the meal.

Jack went on and on about the woman—the second love of his life— and the future he imagined with her until she told him that she could not marry him. She could not face separation from her family half a world away, she claimed. "She fled back to Ireland—Dublin, it was," he said with tears streaming over his cheeks.

"Dublin," Patrick said, trying his best to catch up to his host's inebriated state. "Who is she? I still know a few folks in my homeland."

"The name's O'Connell. Kirin O'Connell. And a foine specimen of a woman she is."

In Patrick's burst of surprise, he spurted his drink onto everyone within four feet. "I know Kiri well. Tried to capture her for myself once, but she spurned me. I got back at her, though. Served her up a dead husband in the Syrian desert." The liquor chased words out of his mouth to spill into the laps of the shocked MacKenzie family, Alice included. By the time he laid out all the details of his bungled assassination attempt, Jack stood over him with a flush as red as a matador's *muleta* and parried his shotgun like a sword in Patrick's astonished face.

"Geet out! Geet out of my house and off my land! Off my oisland! Don't you ever speak the name of that good woman or brag about your despicable act to anyone again or so help me, I will shear your skin from your bones and castrate you myself. It's you who drove Kiri away from me. Your picture. Your name. And I'll never forgive you for that. Now, geet out!"

Alice remembered racing along the narrow roads at high speed with one of Jack's guys on their tail. The chase lasted through the night. Jack's holdings were so vast that it was morning when they reached neutral territory. No one from his family spoke to them again. Jack MacKenzie believed until his dying day, Alice had heard, that his cousin-by-marriage had not only cost an innocent man his life, but Jack, his second chance at happiness. Now Patrick wanted a favor.

"How do *you* know about Jack?"

The phrasing of her hostess' question gave Alice the slightest hope that Kiri had not discovered the family connection. "Word gets around. Can't keep a secret in a closed society like ours, remember."

Kiri did not know whether to believe Alice or not. "You still haven't told me why you are here."

"I presented my case to Henry some years ago, but he refused my request. I approached your son yesterday. He said that our exile order remained in force while you and your immediate descendants were alive. You are the only person with the power to change it, and for the sake of my husband, I make that request now."

Kiri could not hide her resentment. "Are the Falklands suddenly no longer to your liking?"

Alice lowered a tissue from her red-rimmed eyes and worked its fibers with nervous fingers. "Patrick is dying. If you do not grant our request now, we won't return to Ireland. He won't tolerate another long journey. He wants desperately to die near what's left of his family and to be buried in Irish soil next to his ancestors."

"*My* husband was denied that opportunity."

"I'm not asking you to forgive Patrick. I can't. But as his wife, I'm bound to seek your concession. I appeal to your better side, the one that Michael fell in love with. If the situation were reversed and he were mourning your loss, would he seek retribution or would he find it in his heart to grant a dying Irishman his last wish?"

Powerful words, and so unfair to invoke Michael's name, but Alice did hit the heart of the matter and the man, Kiri admitted. She dedicated her entire life to fulfilling Michael's dying wishes. How could she question that he would not do the same for a fellow countryman? She rose, walked to the hall console table and fumbled in its one drawer. When she returned to face Alice again, the woman appeared twenty years older than when she entered—withered, bitter and beaten.

"I will grant your request to rescind Patrick's exile order on these conditions. I want your promise… your word… that you will abide by the boundaries originally set by the order to stay away from our neighborhood and that you will not go near my husband's grave. If I see one bouquet… one flower… one stem… one leaf… or one petal that I did not place there myself, I'll have your husband's traitorous body exhumed and I will take great pleasure in casting his bones into the Irish Sea myself."

Alice did not doubt the widow's power to follow through and nodded a tearful assent.

Kiri placed a card in her palm. "If you find need of hospice services, this business will point you toward appropriate providers. You may use my name as a reference if you wish, but *I* never want to hear the names Patrick Murphy or Alice Richardson again." She opened the door and ushered her visitor out.

Katie encountered a woman lingering at the bottom of her mother's stoop moments after the door closed. "You must be Mom's mysterious visitor," she said. "My son told me I might meet up with you. I'm Mrs. O'Connell's daughter, Katie." She extended her hand with a smile. "And you are…?"

Alice regarded the pleasant-looking woman in her mid-forties who displayed a familiar stature, familiar features and unmistakable blue eyes with an errant curl dancing above the right one. "No one," she said, and turned her back on the life that might have been.

Michael Thomas did not monitor the inside of his mother's house unless someone unusual or unknown entered the neighborhood and stopped at her door. That afternoon, at his system's alert, he placed his eyes and ears on Alice's jacket and witnessed the two rivals' confrontation, confidently predicting its outcome. With pride, he made a note to establish a permanent blanket of "dew" around the O'Connell sector of the cemetery.

As soon as she shut the door firmly, Kiri leaned against it, gasping. She accepted that some skirmish with Alice and/or Patrick was inevitable but as the years passed, the fear found a resting place deep in the back of her mind. Then her grandson opened the door and invited it front and center. She had practiced numerous scenarios but never imagined that the detested couple would play the "dying wish" card. She was caught off guard and could not find her "get off my property or I'll have you arrested" response fast enough. What would Michael say? Was giving in to his enemy a betrayal of his memory?

She staggered back into the living room, swept a black feather from the sofa and collapsed.

CHAPTER 45

With his leaving certificate from school in his hand and acceptance to Trinity for the fall term in his pocket, eighteen-year-old Harry arrived for his every Monday tea-at-four date with his grandmother. She promised to present him with his youthful portrait for graduation. As a typical teen, he did not want to wait for his party; he wanted that picture now!

Kiri did not disappoint, but she held his early likeness behind her back until he stood straight and dignified for her inspection. He was tallest of the grandchildren, now, taller than all O'Connells except for her son, and he still had a few year's growth in front of him. He was slender and athletic, all arms and legs. Irish football was his game and goalie, his claim to fame. There was much to admire in the amiable young man, but her favorite feature was his gray eyes.

"Let me see your marks," she teased and pretended to study them. "They'll do," she smiled and handed his portrait over. They sat, and she poured. "How is your team doing?"

Harry helped himself to two biscuits for starters and sipped the hot beverage politely. "Grand, thanks. The guys don't get after me any more. They used to ask, with a wink, where I got my height and my long arms and legs. I told them, from a long lost cousin and they better be glad for him or our record would be the flip side of what it is."

Kiri smiled at his quirky path to a bull's-eye. "Have you decided on your course of study?"

"Father advises international business, but I love history. I'm fascinated with the Celtic age and its legends, but I don't know what work I'd find other than teaching. What can I do with history?"

"Try not to repeat it," she replied with a sly grin.

"Very funny, Granny. At least I can count on *you* for a laugh."

"Troubles with the sibs?"

"Not really. But you can't expect four teenagers and three wannabes in one house to get along all the time. And Dawn's a girl! Add 'Diti and their friends, and there's not a quiet corner in the place for a guy to hide. Their latest pastime is 'find Harry and giggle.'"

Kiri refilled the plate of biscuits and placed it in front of him. "What's the attraction?"

"I hear their friends whisper that they are in love with me." He rolled his eyes. "But I think that's because I'm the oddball in the family."

"Does that bother you?"

"Not really. Now that I'm so tall, all the cousins show more respect for me, like I'm important or something."

Kiri's eyebrows arched. "Do you give them cause?"

He threw up his hands in defense. "Not on your life. My place in the family is my secret and yours. But I do listen to what they talk about more carefully now—their ideas about what's right and wrong with the neighborhood or school."

"Anything interesting?"

" 'Diti's latest idea about therapy animals. She's lobbying for a pet, but the idea is a sound one. She says there are lots of conditions—both mental and physical—that can be helped by association with animals... dogs mostly. I can see the new boys and girls bonding with an animal that gives them unconditional love more easily than with unfamiliar troubled kids... until they feel safe. With the right help, the kids could train dogs for sale or take them to schools and care facilities—more options for volunteer service and prospective jobs."

"That *is* a good idea. I wish I'd thought of it."

"Of course, there's lots of research to be done before we could consider such a project... a starter project, like you say you'll give me some day," he reminded her.

"Do you have time for research this summer?"

"Not really. I work full-time at the museum programming special effects like the swan-children of Lir singing while they swim in the scullery washtub—a real hit with kids when their fingers disappear into the feathers. Then there's football. I guess I could squeeze out a few hours."

"Or...?" Kiri encouraged her grandson.

He ran his fingers through his thick, coal-black hair. "Or...." His lower jaw moved left to right as he thought. "I could ask 'Diti to do it. If she doesn't want to or if she gives up after a week, that's a pretty good indication that she's going through a 'pet' phase. If she follows through, we may have our first project!"

"Congratulations! You're getting a handle on your secret job."

Harry set his cup down roughly. "I don't get why you and father keep talking about my 'job.' That's a horrible sounding word—like what I'm bound to do is a burden or a drudge."

His reaction startled his grandmother. "How do *you* look at the responsibility that fell into your lap?"

"How about... as an honor or an opportunity. Or... as a chance to con someone else to do the hard work for me?"

Kiri burst into laughter. Yes, she thought. Harry is getting the hang of his responsibility. Henry would be proud of him.

"Keep laughing, Granny, and you'll live to be a hundred." When he heard her phone sound, he bussed her on the cheek, grabbed another handful of biscuits and waved on his way out the door.

Kiri did not recognize the number of the caller but took a chance. "Hello," she said, still laughing at her delightful grandson. "Kiri, here."

"Kiri, this is Anne." Pause. "Anne Geary... Thomas' daughter."

Kiri nearly dropped her phone. She could not remember one time that Anne had called her... in over fifty years! She composed herself. "I'm sorry, Anne. I didn't recognize your voice." Be polite, be polite, she told herself. "How can I help you?"

"I called to ask… to invite you to tea tomorrow. Or if that's inconvenient, perhaps the day after."

Tea? She had not been to Anne's to tea since the early days when she had no choice. "Tomorrow will be fine."

"Good. At four?"

"Four it is. See you then."

"Thank you." Anne rang off.

She shook her head in disbelief. Her last encounter with her stepsister at the graveyard was anything but cordial. She wondered what weapon she should tuck in her bag to stave off Anne's catty remarks and slashing criticisms.

Kiri snapped her spine erect the instant she sat down on a sofa in Anne's sitting room, careful not to slosh a drop or scatter a crumb. Stately as ever, the room had not changed since that first Christmas. She felt a pang of remorse for her stepsister who never saw past her crystal chandeliers to learn how to make a house into a home.

"Thank you for coming, Kiri, on such short notice. I've been thinking lately about the two of us—the last O'Connells left in our generation. Soon…" Anne caught her eye to make sure that her stepsister gleaned her meaning. "Soon, you will be the last one."

Kiri tried to hide her shock behind her teacup. The nieces and nephews had not given any warning.

"So many are choosing their time, now, but the land we live in and my religious beliefs limit my options for the when and how of my death. Modern medicine helps to a point. Then, the day comes when you visit your physician and, instead of comparing your current scans to your previous ones, he finally asks, 'are your affairs in order?' And you realize that you aren't prepared."

Kiri tried to stammer a condolence, but Anne pressed on. "Your kindness to Al… a friend of mine… gave me courage to appeal for your help. I don't want to die here. When the time comes, I want Bitsy's music to help me go like my sisters but I'm afraid she won't enter my house. I've never said one kind word to the poor girl—or to you, for that matter."

"But I came when you called."

"I knew you would. You honor your vows. That's why Father put our fates in your hands, I realize now."

"If you will accept our hospice services, we can move you in with any of your children and take care of you for as long as necessary. Where do you want to pass?"

"I don't want to burden or favor one more than the others. None lives near me anymore. Most live north of the Liffey… nearer you." She turned her wrinkle-laced face away from her guest, lowered her eyes and used a handkerchief to muffle her speech. "I envy you... the relationship you have with my children... with all of the family."

Kiri pretended not to hear the admission that Anne let slip. "Then where?"

"I want to spend my last days in a place where all of my children feel safe and loved and have experienced so much happiness... in your home."

Thud! Kiri's heart cratered into her gut again. *How can I allow my foremost adversary to trespass on my sacred space? Was this a ploy by Anne to have the last word... to force* her *will on* me? She felt Thomas' chain tightening around her, a final test of her loyalty to his family. She remained silent and unresponsive for many moments, weighing her options, but she could not rationalize her way out of the only one. "Your brother's Celtic hospitality knew no bounds. Michael would welcome you... and so must I."

"How can I ever thank you?" Anne asked, near tears.

With the slightest gleam in her eyes, Kiri answered. "I have something in mind."

*   *   *

Anne fidgeted with a list in the pocket of her leisure suit. She never wore a leisure suit outside her house, but Kiri told her to wear an especially comfortable one. She checked the time—five minutes before one. Kiri said she would send a car for her at one; she needed the morning to adapt her house to her guest's needs and video-connect with her medical team. The ailing woman eyed the two items next to the door—one bag and one box, the sum of her life's dearest treasures.

Before her stepsister left the previous afternoon, and after a long and awkward pause during which Anne was certain Kiri would change her mind, she penned a list of essentials for Anne to bring with her—favorite nightdress, shawl, rosary and Bible, quilt, photos and keepsakes, music, and anything else that would help her feel comfortable in her new surroundings. A second list—the one she fingered nervously in her pocket—asked for names of those she wished to be present during her final days and hours and anyone Anne specifically did *not* want to see. Three days earlier, Kiri's name would have been at the top in bright bold letters, but this day that blank was empty.

The other empty blank was for those with whom Anne wished to seek reconciliation or forgiveness. She was humbled and ashamed that she could not write her stepsister's name there. She did not know how to ask her forgiveness after so many years. She tried to remember what started their feud and realized it was the first moment they met—Christmas dinner almost sixty years ago. Her brother Michael stood at her door beaming at the wholesome young woman with an infectious smile and exotic eyes beside him. She knew instantly that her friend Alice Richardson was out of the picture, and Anne erected a wall of ice between them. Now her years of past actions and insults seemed so petty and unfounded, but she did not know how to undo them.

The roar of an engine called her to attention. The predominance of electric cars in her neighborhood made that sound unusual, and Anne pulled back the curtains to investigate. The offending auto—a classic sports car—pulled up in front of her house. Kiri unfolded herself from the driver's seat and waved. She lodged her stepsister's bag and box in the nonexistent rear seat, then returned to the house to help Anne to the auto. "To my recollection, you never took a spin in Michael's beloved speedster. I thought we should do just that in his memory."

Anne could barely find words. "You're not driving us around that horrid racetrack, are you?" she asked curtly and then stopped to bite her tongue.

Kiri brushed off the remark as an old habit hard to break. "No," she smiled. "The safety helmets are uncomfortable. I thought you might enjoy a pleasant drive around the countryside before settling in on Quincy Street."

Anne had to admit that she appreciated her stepsister's casual attitude and a last chance to cement the sights and inhale the fragrances of her country's many greens. She did not become alarmed until they turned off the road to Tara and onto a lonely one that appeared to lead nowhere.

Kiri let the motor idle while she got out and labored to let down the convertible top. "Believe me, we'll want to feel the wind in our faces, feel giddy and free," she said when she buckled herself back in.

A second alarm bell rang when the driver gunned the motor and raced toward a sprawling oak tree ahead. Anne tried to grab the wheel, but Kiri pushed her away. "I see what you're up to," Anne shouted into the wind. "You're going to wrap me around that old tree so you won't have to bother with me. I wondered when you would back out. Stop! Now!"

Kiri threw her head back and laughed... and skirted the tree called "doom," leaving it in a cloud of dust. A mile further up the road, she stopped the car and turned to her rattled stepsister whose relief washed over her blotched cheeks followed by a smile and nervous laughter. "I made peace with that tree long ago," Kiri said and reached beneath her seat for her phone, leaned toward her enemy and snapped... a selfie of two seasoned, squinty-eyed, grinning women whose windblown white hair gave them the look of spent dandelions gone to seed. "This is what I had in mind for your thanks—one honest, positive emotion. Your children will be comforted by finally seeing the two of us smiling in the same place at the same time."

*   *   *

Anne was right about Bitsy. The recalcitrant fifty-eight-year-old harpist balked at attending her aunt's death. She shook her head and held her jaw as tight as one of her treasured instrument's metal strings.

Kiri tried to reason with her. "You played for Gemma's daughter following her terrible accident. The family was certain she held on long enough for you to arrive, and you gave them great peace when you helped that beloved little girl pass. Why not for that child's grandmother?"

"When I play for Aunt Anne, m' music will go away."

Kiri studied the worried eyes of the woman who still looked thirty years younger. "A natural gift doesn't go away, Bitsy. You've attended hundreds of deaths over the years—many for perfect strangers—and you play more beautifully now than ever. Why not for Aunt Anne? She's family."

"You are more important to me."

"Everyone is important in his hour of need, and the entire family needs you now. Please do this for Anne... for me. Your cousins will be eternally grateful."

When the day arrived and all of Anne's children gathered at once, followed by her priest, a shift in the atmosphere signaled to the harpist that her talent was needed. She made her way somberly to the house... the home... where she was allowed to cultivate her gift and develop in her own way. She found Kiri sitting outside on the stoop. She leaned to hug her and whispered, "You're sure?"

Kiri looked into her melancholy blue eyes. "Anne's children deserve your service."

Minutes after Bitsy entered the house, Katie showed up carrying a big box in her arms and noticed her mother's diminishing condition as she fought to accept the intrusion into her home that her stepsister's last illness demanded. "I thought I might find you out here. You know how you always tell us that it's important to have something to do when there's nothing we *can* do if faced with a situation whose outcome can't be changed? Well, I've brought us something to do."

She set down her load and removed sand, candles and handfuls of contorted paper constructed by small Moriarty hands. "Do you know, it's impossible to find little paper sacks these days. I thought we could make luminaries... like were popular when you were a kid." She handed her mother the parts and set her to work. "We'll line the marble path from here across the road and through the memory garden. All who come to pay last respects tonight will find their way over there to whisper a warning to their dear departed that Anne is on her way to join them."

Mother and daughter shared a giggle, then worked in earnest until the twinkling pathway met Katie's specifications. The two sat together on a small bench recently placed for Kiri's comfort between Michael's and Henry's plantings. Katie sighed deeply. "This garden is so beautiful at night. You should take advantage of its serenity."

"I already do... often."

Katie took her mother's hand. "Do you want me to stay with you... until?"

She shook her head. "I'm comfortable and much calmer, here between Henry and your dad. They'll help me through. I'll be fine. You go home and feed your family."

"Try not to be too upset, then. Aunt Anne needs people now, and her people feel at ease in this place—our whole family's touchstone."

Kiri watched her daughter disappear up the road, and then settled in between her two great loves to watch members of Anne's immediate and extended family visit their dying relative. On leaving, they did wander across the road and into the garden to whisper to their departed loved ones, as Katie predicted, and to share a moment with their favorite aunt. Despite her agitation and the nauseating dance in her stomach, Kiri accepted their testimonials graciously and tucked them away to remember on a brighter day—a day she could appreciate them.

Grace, Anne's eldest at sixty-four, was the first to come. She approached tentatively and sat next to her aunt, leaning in for a hug. "The garden is very beautiful tonight. Inside, too. My brothers and sisters so appreciate...." She opened her hand to reveal a small harp carved from green Connemara marble—second largest, second in line from Michael's collection—the one that disappeared after he died. "Mother wanted me to return this. Her way of asking your forgiveness and thanking you. We all thank you."

"I accept, and return the sentiment. A feud takes two, you know, and we both used up too many years learning that."

Emily's eldest Meggie, now fifty-eight, followed shortly after. She handed her aunt a box of tissues, just in case and because she was very good at anticipating what a person needed when upset. She sat with her for a moment before strolling through the garden. "I remember how relieved Mother was to pass in a place she felt love all around her. She chose her mother's bedroom in O'Connell House—a place that held an emotional connection for her. It's sad that Aunt Anne never had a sanctuary during her life, but her children are thankful that you found it in your heart to provide one for her at her death."

Sometime later, after communing at the spot dedicated to her parents Tommy and Margaret, their eldest daughter Caitlín wrapped a shawl around her aunt's shoulders and paused for a sit. "When mother was so ill, you taught us that the power of touch and the gift of music given by ones who care yield benefits beyond the scope of modern medicine. They gave her peace then and eased her transition later when her time finally came. I can see in Aunt Anne's face that she is experiencing that same peace."

Clay wandered through to check up on his children's granny. " 'Tis quite an atmosphere you two girls created. Softens some of the fear of the inevitable for both the living and the dying. In our profession we often say that the more dangerous a situation is, the more its story needs to be told.

My granny would say that the harder a job is, the more important it matters. So buckle up and get on with it, and take stock later." He held Kiri's hand and patted it. "You're a fine woman, oh mother of m' wife, and 'tis a hard job but an important one that you've taken on. Many rewards will be heaped on you, for sure, and my granny will be there to welcome you and lead the applause. You'll recognize her by this same hug." He enfolded her in his two mighty arms and whispered into her ear. "But not anytime soon. 'Tis late and getting chill. Come home with me, hmm?"

Kiri whispered back, "My home—my sanctuary—is across the road. My soul wanders within its walls. I'll watch over it tonight as I would any loved one in distress. Thanks anyway."

"Very well, then." He wrapped the shawl tightly around her aging body and tucked it behind her back. "I gathered as much, so I brought this in case." He pulled a kid's stocking cap from his pocket and pulled it over her head and ears. "My granny would agree with you. 'There's whispers in the walls from all who've lived within them,' she'd say. 'Listen careful to what they tell you.'" Clay kissed her on the forehead and disappeared up the road where word was passed from house to house that Kiri would not leave the garden. Do not even try to make her.

Sala appeared from the little house next door with a blanket for her mother-in-law's legs and feet and a thermos filled with an herbal tea blend "to warm the part of you that aches tonight." She poured them both a cup, and they sipped together.

"In India, we honor, respect, and take care of our mothers. We will help you through this difficult time, but you must welcome us in to do that. We Hindus would say that you live a karmic life, allowing your kind deeds to speak for you. For your children and grandchildren, you embody the virtue sought by followers of all religions. But maintaining that path is a struggle and this event in your life, an obstacle in your way. We also say that our darkest nights are followed by our brightest days, if we open our eyes to them. Move back to your center. Inhale the fragrance of this tea deeply. Exhale forcefully. Release the thoughts that cloud your destiny, and let me capture them and carry them away."

The two women practiced a sitting *pranayama* together, breathing deeply and intentionally for several moments. Then Sala put the cups away, tucked Kiri's hands back under her shawl and left.

Katie returned and found her mother still breathing deeply but alternating each breath with a mutter. "Why me? Why did this task fall to me?"

"Why you?" She snuggled against her mother. "Do you remember Grandfather Thomas' last illness when my chore was cleaning his bathroom? I complained about having to do it, but I did sign up for the job. When you asked me why, I said, 'So none of my cousins would be stuck with the grubbiest job.' This—tonight—is what you've done to spare our cousins as much heartache as possible—volunteered to clean the grubby bathroom."

Kiri snorted a laugh into her tissue.

"If you refused to help Aunt Anne, word would get back to the cousins somehow and who would that hurt? Not you two ancient, feuding, white-haired women. No. You didn't dare risk a rift in the family for *our* sakes. My brother and I, and our children, are grateful."

Brendan, Meghan's eldest son, was beginning to show gray at the temples. "Here we are again, Aunt Kiri, gathered together, for better, for worse. You have a knack for making the worst times better." He made his way to the other side of the garden to take some private time with his mother and stepfather... and then, with his favorite Uncle Michael. As he passed near her, he stopped again. "Thanks, Aunt Kiri. You've affirmed for the whole family that we're always welcome to gather here—no matter when, no matter why."

When Michael Thomas appeared at the entrance to the garden, the oldest grandson of Thomas grasped the chosen one in the family's signature bear hug. "O'Connells stand together forever," he said and left.

"I hear you're being stubborn tonight, Mom," Michael Thomas said as he took a seat beside her, "but that doesn't mean that you must go without your bedtime story."

Kiri gazed on her son who, at fifty, displayed the Koyle look of her brother, the distinctive manner of his grandfather, but few of the attributes of the man who sired him.

"Do you remember Dad's buffalo tale? The one Connor always tells when the whole family gets together?" Michael Thomas repeated the lengthy legend word for word, emphasizing the phrases most meaningful to him while the luminary candles flickered like scattered campfires in the distance.

Long ago, in Paula's ancestral land, there lived a people and a way of life on the point of extinction... Many tribes fought one another... Until you learn to keep peace among you... you will continue to suffer... Your good fortune depends on your good will... Pass the love of peace onto the next generation.

"That's exactly what you have done with your life, Mom. This is no time to dwell on the negative. You have so much to be proud of, but these last few weeks top the list."

Kiri's eyes darted from Michael's shamrocks, to Thomas' lily to her mother's columbine and back to the Connemara paving stone beneath her feet. "To your grandfather, *dilseacht*—loyalty—was everything. 'Family is loyal,' he said. 'Family shows up and stands together in good times and in bad—not as tokens or spoilers, but as participants.' Thomas challenged me... dared me... to hold the O'Connell family together."

She gazed at her son with an intensity he had not seen from her before, and the determination in her voice unsettled him. "*I will not* be the one who rips the family apart, thread by delicate thread, over something so inconsequential as a fairytale's 'wicked stepsister' spending a few days in my house. I came into this family with nothing. I will leave with only my legacy—that I hand the O'Connell family over to you in one solid piece. What has been a chain for me, I pray will not be so for you!"

Michael Thomas was shocked by her frank admission. If his mother truly harbored resentment for the burden of family that Grandfather Thomas placed on her, she never let it show. "I'm in a good place, Mom. The family is in a good place. And I hope against hope that you will rejoin us here soon." He gave her a final hug and left.

After a call from her brother, Katie returned for another check on her mother. "Sitting here in the dark and the damp is not healthy. Come away now. You've completed your mission. The family is intact. You've helped almost every member of the family, and its enemies, to pass where and how they wished."

"For me, this is one way to honor your dad who wasn't granted that choice."

"I know, Mom. Tonight is tough for you and not just because you gave up your home for Aunt Anne. Every death brings back memories and feelings you try to keep stuffed deep inside. But you can't let the ghosts win. You have to stay strong and healthy to outwit them for as long as possible—long enough for them to lose interest and fade away."

Kiri chuckled at her daughter's matter-of-fact take on the situation.

Katie wove her hand beneath her mother's shawl until she found her fingers to play with. "You've accommodated the wishes of so many over the last several years, but you've never said what you want when your time comes."

Misty-eyed, Kiri gazed at the daughter who mirrored the look of her father and answered with a gentle smile. "What I want... is impossible."

Katie accepted her mother's statement without question but pondered its meaning as she returned home.

Sent by his mother as the one who understood his granny's temperament best, Harry recognized in her eyes that she was near an emotional breaking point. He gazed at the dark sky, sniffed the air and held up a wet finger to gauge the breeze. "Tonight is a grand night for a swim. Let's break a few rules and go! Swim and swim until dawn. What do you say?" He attempted to pull her up.

She looked into the gray eyes she recognized so well. "Not until Anne is gone."

Contrary to his usual amiable, gung ho disposition, her grandson sat nearly in her lap, looped his arms around her shoulders and tilted his head to touch hers—like Henry used to do—and remained stone silent, leaving Kiri to her private thoughts. As others sought the comfort of the garden throughout the night, they regarded the two figures as new statuary strategically placed to enhance the solemnity of the occasion.

Bitsy finally emerged from the house, signaling that Anne Geary, first daughter of Thomas O'Connell and the last of his five children to pass, had joined him. The reluctant musician's harp was not clutched to her chest as usual but carried loosely in her hand. She stopped before her aunt and dropped her instrument onto the ground near Michael's shamrocks. "All the harps are home now. My work here is done." She gripped Kiri in a hug beyond her strength like a child moving away from home for the first time—that hug to last a lifetime. "I love you, Aunt Kiri," she murmured, and left.

When Bitsy's slight form disappeared in the darkness, Kiri noticed that her harp still lay on the ground. "She must be more distraught than I realized. She never lets her harp out of her sight."

Harry grabbed the instrument and jogged up the road. "I'll catch up to her and be right back for that midnight swim. Don't jump in without me!"

*   *   *

Her children expected their mother to have an emotional reaction following Anne's burial. Michael Thomas studied her carefully for signs. Katie tiptoed and kept her children on good behavior. And Harry stowed an old swimsuit in the mudroom in case a sudden water rescue was called for. But none of them anticipated what occurred. Kiri cleaned house.

She searched her drawers for grubbies and a kerchief, rolled up her sleeves, and threw herself with a frenzy into scouring, mopping, polishing, shampooing carpets and furniture, and opening the windows and doors wide to the scents and colors of spring. She had restricted the activities surrounding Anne's care to the first floor, so she concentrated her efforts there, anxious to remove reminders of the ordeal. She had reserved the second floor for herself since that was where the body of her emotions rested, and she left that spruce-up for last.

"My dear little house," she said to the walls. "We'll both feel better after a good scrubbing." Her final act to overcome the negative with the positive was to place the marble carving of the harp back in line on the shelf running along the muraled mountains on Michael's side of the bedroom. "All the harps are home now." She smiled and bent to pick up a black feather that rested at her feet.

CHAPTER 46

Kiri maintained her cheerful outlook for some months until her phone sounded in the dark of night. She checked the time. "Who phones an eighty-eight-year-old woman at two in the morning? I thought those days were over," she said into her pillow.

"Aunt Kiri? It's Sara Lamb. Mother is ill. Really ill. Can you come, please?"

Kiri was at the young woman's door even before she rang off. What she saw was more than disturbing. It was haunting. Six months earlier, Bitsy appeared as a youthful thirty-year old. Within three months she had aged a decade for each one. Now, as Kiri looked on the tiny, curled figure lying in her bed, she had aged to a gaunt and wasted ninety—merely a shell of the ethereal creature who appeared from nowhere to minister to her family through music.

Diagnosis—pneumonia. Bitsy was below the recommended age for vaccination so had never received one. This bout hit with speed and virulence. The most Quincy Hospice could do was try to make her comfortable. Without the music of her harp, she failed fast. Michael Thomas had the best suggestion: use a recording of her playing, like they did when Sara was born.

Frantic calls went out to churches, hospitals, and family across the island to search wedding, christening and party videos with Bitsy playing her harp. None. In settings where she should have appeared, there was nothing. Michael Thomas searched network archives with similar results.

Kiri was infuriated. "Do you mean to tell me that in this age of super surveillance when everyone's movements are tracked by someone somewhere, there is not one record of Bitsy playing? What about the original one you made for her?"

"Long gone," her son replied. "I tore that pad apart when I was a kid to see how it worked."

"Well, find it, glue it back together, and get it over here!"

An invisible force seemed to guide Michael Thomas' fingers as he struggled with the ancient electronic gadget and resurrected the harp's melodious vibrations. Kiri kept vigil over the mystical little being day and night. She remained by Bitsy's bedside, stroked her body gently to avoid cracking her bones now as thin and brittle as dried twigs, and watched the layers of her life slough off. She played the heavenly music over and over until the wizened creature shed her grizzled appearance for a mask of peace and allowed her own sounds to guide her soul to heaven.

"I always believed that my mother was sent from another world. She's happier where she is now," a tearful Sara said as she slumped into her aunt's arms.

After the funeral, Kiri returned to Bitsy's apartment to retrieve the electronic pad for use when her own time came, but the strains of harp music had disappeared. Distraught, then angered, she set her jaw, cranked her creaky knees into motion, and marched home and up the stairs to her sitting room for a showdown with the portrait above the fireplace. Her entire body and voice trembled.

"Oh Saint Michael, guardian of soldiers and souls, is this how our story plays out? You've fulfilled your saintly calling to carry souls to heaven—souls linked with your line, that is. You've confirmed for me once more that *your* family is paramount... that *you* sent Bitsy to assure the peaceful passage of *O'Connells*. I'm hurt and I feel foolish... again. I thought that the black feathers were meant for me. What more can you possibly ask me to do? Sing my own anthem? Dig my own grave? Who will play for *me*, Michael? Who!"

Fifty-Seventh Anniversary Year: Birth: Mobs of babies. I continue to add a few drops of Michael's spirit water to the baptismal font at christenings.

Marriage: Must be several. Those babes didn't sprout on their own.

Death: My blackbird dress is almost in tatters now. Just as I think there is no room in my heart for more sorrow, another plant crowds its way into the garden and adds color and vivacity to the memories there. Mom must be very busy tending all of them.

Anne O'Connell Geary (91), second child of Thomas O'Connell and Kathryn Killian O'Connell, but the last to pass.

Kathryn Elizabeth Killian (Bitsy), Michael's cousin. Her harp fell silent at 62. I now empathize with Thomas' loss of a child when Michael died, for that's what Bitsy was to me. Categorizing one death as worse than another is not possible. Each is devastating in its own way.

The quiet and on the sly guys: Doyle, Devin, Gus and Frank all succumbed during the last six years. They watched over us faithfully from the beginning. Frank never married and was the last to go. When we emptied his apartment in Henry's building, Harry suggested that the Callaghan Trust memorialize all four of the guys by providing scholarships for their grandchildren, or in Frank's case, for some whom he mentored from Lon Dubh and Breac Houses. As he explained, "Those good men gave much of their lives to our family and to the job they shared with my grandfather, but they never received much in return." I quickly signed off on Harry's first major financial allocation.

Sara Lamb came to me with a question. She didn't mean to offend, she said, but did I know anything about her father? I was surprised that it took her so many years to ask. Bitsy never did. I questioned why she wanted the information, and she laughed. "I'm not going to go harm him, if that's what you think. Mostly for medical record reasons. For my children's sake. And I'm curious, too."

She told me that she grew up thinking that lots of kids didn't have fathers—like MT and Katie—but at some point she realized that yes, they did. The guy just might not be around. "Mother never did make that connection between the sexual act and a birth weeks or months later. On the farm, she saw dogs and sheep 'do it,' but the later arrival of puppies and lambs sprang from their mothers. I honestly don't believe she was traumatized by the assault. Some teenager came along and the two of them did what was natural for all animals, in her eyes."

I was shocked by Sara's remark that the greatest trauma in Bitsy's life was being banished by her father from the farm that she loved for a reason she did not understand.

"We had a wonderful life here on Quincy Street. We grew up together. My mother found her gift, and I hear her music inside me every day. If that guy hadn't come along, I wouldn't be here. I wouldn't be surrounded by this wonderful family. And I cannot accept that the world would be a better place without me or my mother's music in it."

So true. The value of Bitsy's service to countless souls cannot be calculated. I held Sara while she wrestled with an inner turmoil. When she resolved it, she grew calm again and said, "I can't be bitter. I must forgive. Never knowing what a beautiful person my mother became, what a great kid he fathered, and that he has two grandsons he will never see is punishment enough for an old man, don't you think?"

I went to the safe—it took me a long time to open it because I haven't for so long and I'm not as strong as I used to be—and found the letters Brendan gave me at Bitsy and Sara's dual birthday party. I explained to her that he did the research as a project for a Records Search class and he intended for her to read it someday because "everyone has a right to know where he came from."

She opened it immediately and shared the info with me, unaware that I had a copy I had never opened. She was so grateful to have a head start on what she assumed would be an impossible search. Sometime later, I asked Michael Thomas to see if he could run down the man. He came over a couple of days later to say that he traced him to a modest senior living/assisted living/ long term care facility near Kanturk. Recently installed there by account number only. No name. Would I know something about that? I told him I might, but nothing I could share at the moment. I've said nothing to Sara. I feel a little guilty for intruding, but I knew she would do something good with the information.

I still keep my eyes on the business enterprises that were established at the top of the road over the years, and I continue to patronize them, but I've turned their accounting over to Sara Lamb and their oversight to Michael Thomas.

Quincy Hospice is held in high regard throughout our environs as an example of a health service that specializes in end-of-life care, with its primary objective being to enhance one's priorities in life for as long as possible, i.e. to provide a "good life all the way to the end." Our aging population demands dignity and some measure of control.

Harry and 'Diti's first project—training service and therapy dogs—is very successful and has expanded to include those for whom a "good life" incorporates the companionship of a cuddly critter during their last weeks.

Harry kicked his brother Mike out and moved into the loft in Henry's building to exert his independence. But he shows up for dinner with me frequently. I think he takes his responsibility to watch over me too seriously. He contends that a quiet meal with me is preferable to eating alone or showing up at his mother's where he always has to count plates on the table and wonder who the extra three or four stragglers will be to use them.

I never could stay angry with Michael for long. My life is mine to live, and I'm grateful for its blessings. But having someone listen to my frustrations helps me accept my current state of being. I try not to dwell on the fact that I am truly alone and, without Bitsy's music, must find the strength to pass on my own. My contemporaries have all left this earth. Once again, I have no one to share old memories with—no one to understand the dimensions of my story.

Looking back, I find it difficult to categorize myself. I see my life's work as a transition specialist for all phases, needs and ages. In an unacknowledged partnership with Bitsy, I've been the practical expert in maneuvering through life's obstacle course and she, the ethereal orchestrator of life's final moments.

CHAPTER 47

Katie helped her mother from her walker onto a bench outside Michael Thomas' house on Quincy Street. "I'm a great aunt. I can't believe it. I'm only fifty-two! This is way too exciting, don't you think, Mom?" She did not wait for a reply before running off in search of refreshments.

Kiri smiled. She was all "replied" out. She did not have much to say these days, especially in social gatherings. Thoughts ran at a faster pace than words could escape her mouth. Michael Thomas deciphered her few comments easily. Harry always coaxed a response from her. Katie never seemed to notice; she just babbled on as usual. But in crowded situations, Kiri found that a smile and a nod were adequate.

Her loquacious daughter returned with cups of tea and tiny fairy cakes trimmed in blue. "What's with O'Connell men, anyway? We've seen the instant spark of love ignited in each generation. That must have been what brought Grandfather Thomas and Grandma together again so late in life. Dad was no better. From the tales his team told, he was a lost cause the instant he met you. My brother was smitten as soon as Sala walked in your door, as I knew he would be. And now his son Orion has followed in his father's footsteps... in all of their footsteps. Graduated from Trinity, hopped on a plane for India to 'find his roots' and found enchanting Mei Li from Hong Kong instead. They married secretly and didn't announce to either family until this little guy was on the way—Kai Michael Li-Mishra-O'Connell."

Kiri tilted a corner of her mouth and nodded when Katie paused to take a sip of tea.

"I'll bet this is a first for the prestigious O'Connell family, though—a baptism for the product of a secret marriage. Can you believe it? A *secret* marriage!"

She tilted the other corner to match. Orion's was not the first. She remembered her own secret marriage to his grandfather as if it were yesterday.

"The world needs diversity but if our family keeps contributing, our grandchildren and beyond will never get to travel. Their full legal names won't fit on their passports!"

She emitted a chuckle to accompany the slight curve of her lips.

"I don't know how you managed to add that snifter of bleach to the holy water without one of us helping you to the font."

Kiri's guilt shone through her eyes.

"Don't pretend you didn't. I've watched you for years. What are you trying to do—disinfect the water?"

An eye-crinkling grin crossed her face. Michael's spirit water had lasted to christen his first great grandson, and the O'Connell name lived on. "You're welcome, Thomas," she mouthed. Startled at first when she discovered that the never-ending supply was down to the last bottle, she was relieved to find just enough to do the job with a few drops left for her upcoming anniversary.

The little man of the hour arrived at his reception in the arms of his twenty-two-year-old godfather. "I get it now, Granny. The part you neglected to tell me," Harry said. "A guy makes an innocent vow to watch over his generation, and the next minute he's handed a little tyke like this one and realizes that his responsibility never ends. He's chained to his family until... beyond forever!" He sat next to his grandmother to give her a closer look at the cause for the day's celebration.

Proud grandfather Michael Thomas took Harry's place next to the new great-grandmother. "Four generations under one roof, Mom."

"Not enough room" she managed to say with a chuckle.

Her son laughed. "You don't see what we have here because your only vantage point is from ground level. From a drone's-eye view, we live in one sprawling home with open-air corridors where we get wet from rain when we scamper from room to room. The influence of our style of neighborhood living oozes beyond our invisible borders along Quincy Street. Like the American Indian villages in Dad's story about the white buffalo, we're all related in some way and look out for one another. Cradle to grave is pretty rare these days with such a mobile population. We are blessed here in our little corner of the world and can only pray that will continue for many generations."

"Four is pretty good start," Kiri said as she gazed on her son, soon to be sole tribal chief.

*   *   *

Four generations under one roof. Not even Thomas O'Connell managed three in the same neighborhood, Kiri thought with a smile. *I'll bet he didn't expect his grandson's immigrant regent to accomplish that feat!*

She had seen it in others nearing their end—a sudden flurry, a surge of energy, then a calm, and finally the tranquility that comes with knowing what the future holds. Kiri's active frenzy before the long glide into unconsciousness took the form of sorting, discarding, and rearranging to make room for her house's new occupants. In her sitting room, she took down the portrait of Michael to return it to her bedroom. A sudden tingle inside—an urge to hold a paintbrush one more time—caused her to spend an afternoon mixing bright colors. She added two small figures to the lower right corner of the portrait: her handsome stud with no hair dressed uncomfortably in a tux and beside him, a young woman with flowers piled high in her curls to mimic a horn. The damsel wore a compass necklace and a blue gown with the tail of a lion extending beneath the hem to loop around her escort's ankle. She gave a hearty laugh. *I wonder if anyone will notice the prince and his unicorn?*

She rehung it in her bedroom above the fireplace—its proper place—a place she would spend more time in days to come. She moved her painting of Henry at their cottage to the sitting room for the kids and grandkids to see when they came to visit. She set the small one of his hand on the windowsill above her desk and admired how naturally it blended with the flowers that bloomed across the road.

Kiri's physical decline was not as swift or dramatic as Bitsy's, but it was noticeable and required accommodations. Thomas' hover chair was pressed back into service to carry her across uneven ground to and through the two gardens she visited often, weather permitting. She managed the staircase with Henry's stairlift and moved around the house in slow deliberate steps rather than a shuffle, using a walker sparingly to maintain mobility as long as possible.

She tired easily, napped daily, and went to bed early but never slept well. Clay's granny was right. The walls whispered in voices she never thought she would hear again with snips and snatches of phrases that made no sense: Thomas' *our DNA*; Paula's *you returned our son to him*; midwife Maeve's *Men are so proud to pass along their names, but we women know it's the mothers and grandmothers who make that possible*; Michael's *We are all connected. Discover your history and find your place in this family*; and Henry's *the man known to you as Henry Callaghan*. Words and voices swirled in her mind, trembled through her body, then clashed together like angry clouds in a Colorado thunderstorm.

Depression descended. Mornings, she did not want to get out of bed, afraid that voices lurking in the next room waited to envelop her and suck her breath away. When she finally did roll out, she left the bed unmade. She could not see the point. When she dodged exercising in the pool, someone came to fetch her. She skipped regular mealtimes. Harry supped with her a few times a week. He offered to bring food in, but Kiri declined. She could still get a proper meal on the table—when she felt the impulse.

Then euphoria barged in with one grandchild or another looking for company—but never before noon. Their bright happy faces and active minds tickled her sensibilities and drew her into their social tragedy of the day—usually guys for girls and girls for the guys. As in the early days, she offered a shoulder, an ear and a tissue.

Dark returned and whispers with it. *Our child. Our son would not turn his mother to ash. I entrust the lives of those I love most to you, Henry. She doesn't understand the thin space between us. Related in the most basic and intimate of ways. We're all family.* Her mind conjured up images of those she believed were communicating with her, but the voices were a hodgepodge. Did she hear Michael and then Henry, or the other way around, or both, or was she going crazy, trapped in one of her son's illusions? These frantic hallucinations always ended with echoes of *unlock secrets, finish the puzzle* as the voices faded away, leaving her exhausted and drenched with sweat by morning.

The day neared for each generation's transition into a new world. The family decided together to exchange living quarters on the same day. Harry was slated to vacate the loft for brother Danny's benefit and take up residence in Henry's old apartment—digs large enough for a single adult with a monstrous load of responsibilities. He referred to his décor as "vintage granny's attic." The young man began his tenure as head of Henry's little tribe by refurbishing the old house to accommodate retired independent journalists who had toiled as first person witnesses to history to expose the truth of fellow man's condition throughout the world—an idea that just "popped into" his head.

Michael Thomas and Sala prepared to move across the road to the main floor of Kiri's—"O'Connell House, Quincy Annex" he called it—to be closer to his mother and to build a micro-apartment beyond the back garden for Sala's parents. Orion, Mei and Kai would take over the little house—a good place to start a family under the protective wing of the new grandfather. The date for transitions: Michael Thomas' fifty-fourth birthday—the day after his parents' anniversary.

* * *

Kiri rode the hover chair to her place beneath the evergreen tree for her customary anniversary contemplative session and journal writing. With the hubbub across the road, she thought she would be spared interruptions.

Fifty-Ninth Anniversary Year, 2068: The time has come for a final self-assessment.

I've learned that most important events that happened to me are the ones I did not fully understand. That lesson came from Michael Thomas. When frustrated with my inability to grasp what he tried to explain to me, he often said, "Don't bother yourself now. Someday you'll understand."

Katie taught me that we are all living and dying at the same time but living is preferable, so to make the most of the time we have by gathering those we do love and those we should love as close to us as possible because "we are all related... somehow."

Thomas stressed loyalty to family—responsibility—and that sometimes it comes at a price, but reaps tenfold in return.

Paula reminded me never to part from someone I care for without an expression of love.

My days with Henry showed me that patience and perseverance will be rewarded and that love manifests itself in many forms.

I still believe that Michael guides me through this world even though he does not show himself. From him, I learned to accept and make peace with the life given to me. I've been very fortunate.

Harry appeared with baby Kai in tow. "My turn to keep this little guy occupied. His parents and grandparents are reshuffling and packing for tomorrow. I have my gear ready by the door and could have it stowed away by now, but you know Mom. Tomorrow is an 'event.' No sneaking in before the starter bell after the birthday lunch."

Kiri tickled her black-haired, almond-eyed, honey-skinned and dimpled great-grandson who inherited a slight cleft in his chin like four generations of fathers before him. "Babbles in Cantonese."

Her grandson chuckled. "The family will soon speak more languages than Quincy School." When he noticed her brighten, he remarked. "Granny, your eyes are different today."

"Really? Haven't changed them last couple months." The two shared a good laugh. The old granny was back for the moment.

"How's the road with reins of Trust in your hands?"

"I haven't spent that first Irish pound on ice cream yet."

Kiri grinned at the confident young man with a rakish gleam in his gray eyes.

"My flock has grown to thirteen now, counting you, me and this little tyke. Maybe that's why Poppy never married. With the responsibility of *our* families, he had no time for his own."

The root lies far deeper than that, Kiri thought. *Henry's secrets weighed on him much more than the unexpected demands of her children.* "Wee one in arms suits you. Found special someone yet?" she asked with a hint of a smile.

"Marriage? At the moment I can't see beyond the waves of cousins I'm responsible for to pick out that perfect gal. So you'll have to be patient. I'm counting on *you* to walk *me* down the aisle."

"In hover chair?"

They shared a laugh to last a lifetime.

Kiri returned to her journal to catalogue her place and purpose in the family.

My charge from Thomas was to hold his family together no matter what. I brought two children into this world to ensure his legacy. Quincy Street became like a parish community, but the bond that held it together was based on mutual consideration rather than religion. I surrounded all of his grandchildren with a safe, joyful and loving environment to guide them toward self-sufficiency. Their influence spreads far beyond the boundaries of our city, our island and throughout the world and will have greater impact than either of us. I aided his own children through a compassionate "good death" at home and a peaceful passing.

So, how have I done, Thomas? Have I met your expectations? Have I met my own? Michael would say that my purpose was to fulfill my promises to him. Have I?

Michael Thomas took a break and brought a salad for his mother's lunch. "Are you sure you don't want to picnic with the rest of us?"

Kiri shook her head. "Enjoy private time. Not miss much with rumpus across road." She noticed how well her son wore his middle age despite his burden of family and work. Housing was not the only major decision facing him. "Thomas, your dad, me… all proud of you. But once settled in house, resolve question of Grandchildren's Trust. Continue or disband."

"I'm not anxious for that job, so take care of yourself." He pretended a laugh. "As you know, families are complicated. I have a sense of how the Trust Committee feels, but I'm waiting for a fairy to whisper in my ear," he grinned and reached for her hand. "I'm not the only one who has decisions to make, Mom. We can't avoid the subject much longer. We must have *that* talk."

His mother nodded. "We will. After grand-family settled and you back in home here."

"Sounds good. You must tell us what *you* want. If you leave it to Katie and me, you're likely to have a parade up and down the road. Brightly painted elephants might be involved."

Kiri chuckled at the thought and summoned a well-formed response. "What I want is *impossible*. Not even Katie could manage it."

After her son left, she tackled the loves of her life.

Is it possible to have more than one great love in life? More than one anam čara? I feel I was blessed with two: Michael and Henry. The question is not who was my greater love, for they were very different. In my memory, Michael remains as he was when we married—young, burly, vibrant. Would he accept me as I am now? On the other hand, I spent more than half my life with Henry—kind, gentle, supportive Henry. Our lives were as closely intertwined as a normal family's—like the knots on my Celtic circle—and we grew old together.

The real question is, if there is a God who preordains our paths, was His plan for my life partner Michael or Henry? If I had not been thrown together with Michael, would I ever have met Henry? That leads me to question whether Michael was a conduit to finding Henry or was Michael channeling his will through Henry? Either way, I feel the presence… and the absence… of both men every day.

How does Jack fit into the picture? Surely neither man drove me to him. I did love him in a way. He played an important role as my wake-up call. He reminded me that we are all entitled to happiness but to select carefully that which is right for us. I discovered that happiness was within my reach all the time.

Henry once told me that "happily ever after" comes after the Ball. In a way, he was right.

Midafternoon, Katie came to check on her mother and invite her to dinner before the big day. "The whole moving crew is coming. We'll have a jolly time."

"Fine here. Tomorrow, no more eating alone."

"Dawn and 'Diti are putting the final touches on my brother's cake for his celebration. Then the grand move. I can't wait. But we won't bring Box One until noon, I promise. Imagine, everyone's starting a new life!" She glanced at the journal Kiri held closed on her knees. "At it again, I see. What good is that old book, anyway? I bet you remember every word you've written."

"Something to thumb in *your* old age when bothered. Everyone makes too much fuss." She reached out to give her daughter a hearty hug and whispered, "I love you more than anything, Aurora Kathryn."

Katie was surprised by her mother's clarity. "Whoa. Where did that come from?"

"From my heart."

At Katie's departure, Kiri concluded her final journal entry.

Did I fulfill my promises to Michael? Did I make his dreams—our dreams—a reality? I tried to live up to my name. Kirin—the unicorn—solitary sentinel ready to guide and protect, faithful and chaste to the end. Aurora—the dawn—welcoming each new day with brightness. I tended our village and helped it grow. I bore Michael's children and raised them as we envisioned in the Ireland that he loved. I circled my arms around our family, nieces and nephews included, and nurtured them; folded good friends into the family; and most difficult of all, reconciled with those hostile to me. Yes. To the best of my ability, I fulfilled my promises to Michael. But one question lingers. Does one's vow of unconditional commitment last forever… or am I finally free?

Kiri leafed through the pages of her journal and determined that her words were a fair representation of her thoughts at each stage of her life—a tome to entertain her daughter in old age. She planned when to pass it on, and recalled Paula's handing over her own journal. Kiri had never opened it. The memory of receiving the treasured diary when Paula was so ill made her reluctant, but her mother's words returned to her. "Children have a right to their history. When you're ready." Was she ready now?

Where had she stowed Paula's journal? She tried to remember as she labored back to the house to retrieve it. She hovered to the kitchen door, took slow deliberate steps to the stairlift and from the top, to her bedroom. She found the small book with 1968 embossed on the cover underneath assorted memorabilia in her nightstand, and she slipped it into her pocket scarf.

Before opening a conversation with her mother, she entered her octagonal kitchen—the site of so many memorable events—and collected a thermos of tea, a cup, the last of the spirit water, a candle and lighter and tucked them into the carrier on the hover chair. What used to take five minutes now became a half-hour journey over a bumpy path. "Let the energy expended on one trip satisfy two goals," she sighed.

Settled back under the evergreen tree, she decided to forgo a snooze for a cup of aromatic tea and a relaxing, good read. In the script she knew so well, the writings consisted largely of impressions of foreign places. *Alone! Hitchhiked! Mother!* Kiri never knew that side of Paula. In Ireland that carefree young woman met some unnamed guy. "He was a really good ride," her mother wrote. They met up later in Rome in September of 1968. Then she added nothing more about him until Feb 3, 1969. "It was a boy." Inserted notes began when Kiri's children entered the family. "MT born—*our* DNA." "Katie born—*our* DNA." "Thomas believes that *our* lost son returned to us as MT. His eyes are the color of the sea." "His flowers bloom as if our son welcomes us with a smile whenever we are at home in Colorado." A handful of similar notes followed.

Memories of Thomas' interactions with her children flooded back to Kiri, especially his inviting them to plant new flowers on their Colorado hillside when the occasion arose, "so we'll never forget those who have left us." The one unexplained was a mystery no longer. Thomas and Paula conceived... and then lost... a child! *He* was the missing piece—the thread that drew the couple back together and held them.

The old patriarch's words to Kiri now made sense. "You hold the delicate thread of my family in your hands." A thread he never intended to reveal. Paula's disclosures explained why it was so important that Michael Thomas and Katie were not separated from their grandfather, why he chained Kiri to Ireland and his entire family. Her children were not just Thomas' legacy, but Thomas *and Paula's* legacy—the true embodiments of their summer love!

Discovery of the DNA connection sent Kiri into a second frenzy. Was Paula's revelation the missing piece? The secret? Or were there more? Determined to follow through with the anniversary ritual, she pushed those questions aside for later. She withdrew the ceremonial articles from the hover chair and lit the candle before evening's foggy chill descended. She ripped a scrap of paper from one of Paula's notes to write down her pledge—*I will love you for as long as I have memory*—and to hold it to the candle's flame. She watched its smoke curl up through the tree and beyond. A whisper followed its path downward through the branches to her ear. *'Tis good of you to come. I was afraid you might give up on us this year.*

Kiri brushed the sound aside as just another mysterious voice playing in her mind. She poured the last drops of spirit water into her cup before reciting her vows that on their fifty-ninth repetition had not dulled the significance of her anniversary ritual. "My love… sip from my cup… cry your name… honor you…."

The temptation of Jack MacKenzie nearly scuttled that one for us came from nowhere.

She sipped the last of their water from her cup, allowing her lips and tongue to play with each precious drop before it slithered down her throat. "Our love is never-ending like a Celtic Circle." The last phrase took on greater meaning now. "We will remain, forevermore… in our marriage."

You see, 'tis simple. We made a vow not bounded by "till death do us part." We married in the Church twice, 'tis true, but we exchanged vows a third time… our first time… when you pledged that I would be the first, last and only man you would ever give your full and complete love to. Bless you for believing in us and honoring that vow.

Kiri's fingers quaked like aspen leaves in a breeze, and the muscles in her throat seized. Were those her words or Michael's? She was too confused to be certain, but she summoned the strength to conclude the ritual as always, now hearing two voices recite in unison. *"Grá anois agus go deo… love now and forever… mo anam ċara."*

With a response to the last line of her journal now clear in her mind, Kiri turned toward the house with an overwhelming urgency to pass on to her daughter the truths she discovered about herself and her mother.

CHAPTER 48

Kiri crawled onto the wildflower quilt worn down to its batting, but why would she discard it? Why change anything in her life now? She stretched out with paper and pen and began. "Dear Katie. One hundred years ago, a young Paula Koyle stood on the side of the road to Valencia Island in the pouring rain with her thumb out begging for a ride. A young Irishman rescued her in his blue sports car, and *your* story began."

She detailed facts, clues and suppositions, pausing to ponder deeper implications. How many other stories were just like her mother's—a series of chance meetings and choices made one hundred… two hundred years ago and over how many generations before that? What choices became turning points in anyone's life? How did a person know which choices were the defining ones and which merely colored the life he was destined to live? When finished, she dropped the pages to her side and fell back, all energy wrung from her weakened body. "So weary. Can't hold up our nest much longer. A short snooze…."

She closed her eyes, but the old voices resumed their refrain. *Unlock secrets. Finish the puzzle.*

Was she going crazy? Was there more? What was unfinished? Surely Thomas and Paula's lost love child was the last piece.

But the voices persisted. *Unlock secrets. Finish the puzzle.*

"I don't have any more pieces!" she shouted. In a sudden burst of energy, she jerked Michael's drawer from his nightstand and upturned it onto the bed, scattering feathers everywhere. "All that's left are these. How can these be pieces? They all look the same."

She studied them carefully and engaged the long-neglected strategizing part of her brain. "The feathers may appear the same, but they represent events. Arrange the events," she said. She cleared a space on the bottom half of the quilt and sorted them into three piles—Paula, Kiri and Katie. Time stood still as she tucked the small pinions here and there, and a pattern emerged like the complex interlocked design on her Celtic circle. She rustled in her drawer for the ancient ornament and arranged it in the center. "This must be the missing piece." She placed her mother's journal on Paula's vertex. Her own diary on her own, and the connection story on her daughter's. Exhausted beyond measure, she lay back. "I'm tired. So tired. But now I am finished."

Voices returned. *Unlock secrets. Finish the puzzle.*

"I have! Don't you see?" She slid down from the bed and spread her arms wide to showcase her creation.

Unlock secrets. Finish the puzzle. Eons of ancestors.

That was a new one. What did it mean? *Ancestors.* She rallied to reach for the thin tissue surrounding the ornament and read in Michael's letter, *Circle… the connection of one generation to the next from grandmother to mother to daughter... until generation layered on generation continues around the circle.* When she set his words aside to study the design again, she spied two errant feathers that had not been placed. *Finish.* She racked her brain for their significant events. Why did she not make a list as they dropped to her like grains of sand to fill her life's hourglass?

Years flashed before her eyes for the second time that night. Bingo! Bitsy and Henry's mother. She climbed back onto the bed to place Bitsy with Katie, but where did Henry's mother belong? She reread Michael's words. *A father may pass his name to his descendants, but mothers provide a seamless passage to complete and continue a circle.* But that did not help her place the feather. How was Henry's mother connected?

Muintir... Bitsy... Katie... me... family... secret. Unlock secrets.

Her eyes darted around the room and settled on the tin box atop Henry's final letter. She had never opened it nor investigated the contents of the box. Like setting Paula's journal aside because her death was so painful, she had done the same with Henry's final wishes and the last secrets he did not have a chance—or the courage—to share. Her hands trembled as she opened the letter first. She was right. Final instructions. "If you can find it in your heart, please bury me somewhere near you so the same sunlight will shine on both of us. The happiest moments of my life were with you." Affirmation. She fulfilled his last wish.

She reached into the back of her drawer and found the keys he left for her "to unlock all secrets." She turned the tiny one hanging from a lilac ribbon. As she remembered when assessing his possessions, the box contained mostly documents. A slip of paper topped all in writing she did not recognize—definitely not Henry's. "A child is entitled to his history." Paula said much the same, and Brendan too when he handed her the search for Sara's father. The puzzle became more complicated, not less. She pressed her fingers to her eyes. How do these pieces fit in?

First—a baptismal certificate for Henry Callaghan. "Take that, Anne. Henry had every right to the same hallowed ground as you and I!" Next, the missing photo of Harry's christening with Katie, Clay, Michael Thomas and Sala standing behind a seated Kiri and Henry. He held little Harry. She turned the photo over and read, "Henry Killian Devane, born 1970, called 'Harry.' Henry Killian Moriarty, born 2046, called 'Harry.' My Dear Family."

How strange. A myriad of possibilities roiled up in her mind. The man known to them as Henry Callaghan was obviously the one in the photo. Why did he call himself Henry Killian Devane? Next, an old photo of a baby with parents—a duplicate of the one on the museum wall—the family whose story Henry used to describe the Troubles with an empty frame next to it for a final portrait of living family members. Next, two birth certificates intimating name change for mother Kathryn Killian and her young son Henry from Killian to Callaghan. Killian! But why? And then a news clipping from a 1973 IRA bombing. Why, Henry? Why didn't you tell us? Surely sons do not really pay for their father's sins. Or was there something deeper… something she suspected for several years? Perhaps a shame born of Sins of Fathers?

Then, a family tree, now so thin and worn that the words were barely visible—Henry's family tree with Fergus Killian as oldest known relative. She had seen that name before—when Bitsy came, dragging the family connection with her. Finally, she unfolded the medical records for her two children, Michael, Bitsy and Henry—DNA so well mixed that its contributory elements could only be distinguished in a lab. Proof positive of their blood relationship!

How he came by such privileged information never crossed her mind. Hard salt tears like mini-hailstones dropped into the creviced wrinkles of her cheeks and fell onto the delicate thread of family she held in her hands. "You've always been one of us, Henry. *Really* one of us," she cried. "And Katie sensed it. You two bonded in a special way from the night she was born. She could always tell that you were related to us… *in the most basic and intimate of ways*… somehow. Now she has that proof."

Kiri crawled across her bed to reach down between Michael's nightstand and the wall to find Henry's frame and to fix the christening photo in it. She tucked the last feather into the circle, placed the framed photo on top of Katie's point, and scooted the tale of Paula and Thomas by its side. Let her daughter decide which to investigate first.

Satisfied that she had solved the mystery of her Celtic circle, she gazed on her creation with a deep sigh, and another thought came to mind. What about a Killian circle with Katie, Bitsy and Henry's mother? "We're all part of more than one bloodline," she murmured. Katie could form a Killian circle and rotate backwards to find more common ancestors for how many generations? Not eons, probably, but with DNA tracking, lots for sure. The possibilities were endless for every child. What a wonderful puzzle for Katie to work on now that her children were beginning to leave her nest.

"I've done it, Michael. Solved the puzzle! I uncovered the connection that Michael Thomas with all his technological expertise could never flesh out, one that Katie will be ecstatic to follow backwards and forwards until she collects everyone who is 'family' into her world."

She flopped across the bed so as not to disturb her feathery creation. "Exhausted. So tired. Need sleep. Energy for tomorrow." She planned when and how to reveal her discovery to her daughter. Noon. Lunch and cake to celebrate her son's birth and Thomas' legacy with all immediate family present. Then steal Katie away and bring her upstairs to explain the circle and Henry's thread to eternity—her daughter's son Harry. Squeals of surprise were sure to bring the others on a run. "What fun! This old dame has a spark left in her yet!" She laughed as she gazed upward through the octagonal skylight into night's blackness.

Out of that inky void dropped a coil, like a spring on a string. A line of beings, then humans, then forebears marched along that spiral strand carrying genetic code as old as life itself. By choice, chance or divine intervention, they followed the path out of darkness—or branched onto a new one—leaving broken threads along the way. Rebels, rogues and the righteous evaded the ravages of famine, plague and plunder to survive long enough to pass their genetic code to offspring.

Kiri watched the parade of ancestors as it wended its way in helixed cobweb fashion to all corners of her room—her world. Even a spider's intricate creation begins at one point, she remembered. "Point" brought her attention to her vertex on the circle. Layers and layers of generations were represented by that point, Michael wrote. If she picked the circle up at her point, the layers would descend in the same spiral pattern—her DNA strand—representing decades, centuries, millennia, maybe eons of ancestors—who knew for sure? If any of her ancestors had died before sharing their love, then she would not exist. Nor would her children or new baby Kai.

She tried to pick them out of the moving maze—emigrants from the Old World, natives of the new, revolutionaries and the salt of the earth, Great-grandfather Schultz the farmer, and Great-grandfather Koyle the academician. As keenly as she scrutinized for familiarity, she could not pick them out; she had never seen their faces. She only knew them by name. She searched frantically for Michael, for Henry, for her mother, for Thomas or his Aunt Moira whose flight to the western coast of Ireland brought Thomas there for a visit and his chance meeting with bohemian Paula Koyle.

Her child's... every child's... history lay on a similar twisted ladder. On her way to this world, Katie reached out and grabbed Henry's broken filament to twist it around her cherubic finger and weave him back into the Killian thread through the buttonhole in his shirt, fixing him forever to her family.

Kiri's mind tingled like a sleeping foot awakened. The prickles turned into throbs and then thunderous crashes of surf on a stormy beach sweeping everything away in its wake. She pressed her palms to her temples to stop the deafening pain. When she removed them, the room was empty and dark again; her memory, the same. All that remained was an echo, *know them by name*. How could she recall the last inspired moments? *Know them by name*. The clue... the connector... must be a name. But what name? Her name? Surely not Kirin the unicorn or Aurora the dawn. They did not evoke any emotional reaction. Koyle. The delicate, coiled thread that held her family together. She felt a flash of recognition. That was it!

Her excitement brought on a sudden surge of adrenaline throughout her body. "How naïve to believe my life was about me. Today is 'someday,' Michael Thomas. Today I understand. And when she sees my circle... I can't wait to see Katie's face!"

Me too.

A familiar voice—Michael's voice—intruded on her happy moment. "Now you speak. After all my years of begging. Are you coming to our party?"

No. For you, love. We'll watch together.

She was too weak to lift her head to search for the voice's source. Terrified that her mind would crack, she cried out for a spark of clarity, a glimmer of consciousness. She shivered and struggled to shake off her trepidation. "Not now. Not before I tell Michael Thomas and Katie. Please...."

Children may have a right to their histories, but discovering them on their own is part of the puzzle. You don't want to deny our daughter that thrill, do you?

"But I have so much left to do... to tell the children. I'm not ready."

No one is. The time we're given is never enough, no matter how long it lasts. But in the dimension beyond the thin space between us... in that time, the life you lived has transpired in the blink of an eyelash.

"Where's Henry?"

Close by, wearing a smile as broad as the sea, now that his secrets are free.

"Tell him that I could never think less of him. Only more."

He knows.

She struggled to move, to breathe. "I'm frightened."

Mustn't be. I'm with you. Take my hand and place it over your heart. We'll breathe together for as long as you have breath. Now, close your eyes.

"But my soul... restless... yearning... Who will play for me?"

Feel my touch. Don't let go while I tell you a story. 'Tis a tale of a unicorn, a warrior and a blackbird—the blackbird that guarded the beast after the brave hero passed to the Otherworld.

Do you know why 'twas so important for St. Kevin to guard the blackbird's eggs until they hatched? To perpetuate the gifts they encompassed. Celtic myth holds that blackbirds are heavenly messengers and symbols for the human soul flying from this world to the next. Our unicorn shoved that thought away when she left her anam ċara by the still water of the medicinal spring on the plains of Meath. For days she wandered the forest at the edge of Tara in despair. Her head hung so low that her horn carved a trail into the ground. All the lessons she passed to her soul-friend when he fought to return to a life of meaning were dead to her because her life no longer held any meaning. She could not sense the nearness of his soul.

A blackbird flitted through the forest to find her. It perched on her head and whispered in her ear to live her name in honor of her fallen warrior and to have faith that someday he would return for her. After many proddings, the elegant beast changed course and followed her own chiseled trail back to the spring, there to lie night after night in the place where his scent still lingered.

Through time, she marked her territory and guarded all within it from afar. Together the unicorn and the blackbird foraged in a sunwise circuit along the fringe of the forest surrounding the spring. When her boundaries and the creatures within them were threatened, the beast stepped from the shadows to confront and defend her turf, blackbird riding on the tip of her spiraled horn like a herald. Alabaster and onyx together, they triumphed against all challenges but one.

Blackbird retold the fury of that day through its song of how the animal fought a chain so deftly slipped 'round her neck. She sprang high into the air and landed, stiff-legged, with a jolt so intense that the bird was thrown from its outlook and nearly trampled by her deer-like hooves. "'Twas all I could do to grasp the end of her leonine tail as it whipped through the air, showering my feathers everywhere and leaving me near bare."

The crafty antagonist disappeared beyond the forest, leaving his chain to drag the ground that the animal walked as a reminder of his power. The noble beast bucked, tossed her head frantically, and plunged into the spring in a desperate attempt to float the shackle from 'round her neck. Try as she might, the unicorn never could lose it, but over time it loosened, and she learned to bear it with grace.

The might of a mystical beast rarely diminishes with time. This one's did. The day came when her sunwise circuits lasted longer, the length of her painful steps grew shorter, and the wait for her soul mate's return dimmed to an impossible dream. She staggered to the spring, snuffled, and pawed at the soil beside it to turn up a scent, a speck, the barest hint of her anam čara's soul. Then she dropped to her knees, rolled to her side, and lay in the very spot she left him.

Unable to force her body onto its feet, blackbird invaded her mind, whispering of the gifts it gave and the omens it cast her way throughout their days together. Since the Celts believed that blackbirds were their connection with nature and natural spirits, their link between heaven and earth, folk were mindful of their winged friends' habits. The birds passed their gift of camouflage for family protection on to their fledglings. And understanding their connection to all things, they imbued their young with a like sensitivity.

As for omens, a nest near one's home was a good one. Dreaming of a blackbird in flight carried good fortune too, but the creature might steal your innermost secrets, both good and bad, from under your pillow on its way. Two of these feathery creations seen at the same time also brought good luck in one's day-to-day. But the grandest of all? Folks longed for the rare sight of three together at the end of their days, for they... well... 'tis said that a trio of three that sit and sing will lull you into a deep sleep and carry you on their song through a peaceful passage to the Otherworld. Not many are so blessed.

As the unicorn lost strength and purpose, blackbird stroked her neck with an outstretched wing and pecked at the rusted chain to break a link and free her. Alas, the task was too great for one, so it called on another and then a third. The heavenly song of three together split the chain and released the unicorn's soul to fly with her gallant warrior through the thin space between them and into the Otherworld.

The room fell as still and frosty as the woods after a snowfall. A weak, halting whisper hung in the air like an icy flake contemplating its landing.

"Morning... yet? Henry... always comes... in morning."

Hush, now. Three blackbirds are perched on your pillow. Listen to their song. Hold to me and don't be afraid. Soon 'twill always be light.

CHAPTER 49

Noon. Moving day. The O'Connell and Moriarty contingents lined up at Kiri's door—both sets of parents, their nine offspring with the youngest just turned thirteen, and baby Kai. At the stroke of twelve, Katie rapped on the door. "Mom. Let's get this party started!"

No answer.

Michael Thomas tried the intercom by the door. "Mom. We're here. Stop whatever you're doing and let this rowdy bunch in for my celebration."

No answer.

Clay produced a worried flush. "We'd better go in. She might have fallen in the bath and can't get to the 'com." His worried eyes darted over the group as he imagined carrying Granny out on a stretcher when her grandchildren anticipated a party.

Sala took his cue. "I'll stay with the kids. You three go." She turned toward their expectant faces. "Your granny likely lay down for a short nap and lost track of the time. The whole lot of us barging in might frighten her, so we'll stay right here while the others wake her up gently."

Michael Thomas placed his face up to the sensor, and the door opened. "I'll check down here and the service stairs. Katie, take Mom's bedroom and Clay, the kitchen and then upstairs."

The three scattered at lightening speed. Katie was the first to squeal in surprise.

"Mom?" her brother shouted back.

"No. A mess! There's crap all over her bed. Hundreds of feathers everywhere, but no Mom!"

The two men were by her side in a cybersecond and gazed with amazement at Kiri's bed. Michael Thomas recognized immediately that the disorder was not random. "This isn't a mess. It's a pattern. She must have had trouble sleeping and passed the time by creating a... a design. But where is she?"

Clay darted into the bathroom and returned, shaking his head. "No Granny. Just a wet bathtub and two damp towels draped over its edge."

"Look! Out there!" Katie ran to the upper floor's deck door and opened it wide. A sudden rush of air swooped in and swirled feathers and papers in tornadic fashion throughout the octagonal bedroom like thousands of dried leaves scattered in tangled heaps. Only the framed photo of Henry's "dear family" remained in place on the wildflower quilt.

The two men flanked her as she leaned over the railing and pointed beneath the evergreen tree. A woman dressed in a midnight blue ball gown and a compass necklace lay peacefully beneath its branches, her head suspended above the ground as if resting in the lap of someone who was not there.

Clay reached for his wife's hand and shook his head. "I'd say that your dad scooped your mom onto his wing and carried her to a special place where they shared their deepest love and devotion." He shrugged. "But… 'tis impossible."

Michael Thomas twined his arm around Katie's shoulders to enfold her in an empathetic embrace. Brother and sister from the same Koyle/O'Connell threads—but unique shades of green—smiled tearfully at one another and chorused, "Exactly!"

AWARD WINNING AUTHOR SHERRY SCHUBERT, named 2012 Writer of the Year by Idaho Writer's League and a recipient of an Editors' Choice award from Idaho Author Awards, is a graduate of the University of California at Berkeley, Class of 1967. Subsequently, she spent two years hitchhiking abroad, gathering grist for stories and a packful of dreams. "Life" called her back to her home state of Idaho where she raised a family and taught teenagers to solve quadratic equations.

Ms. Schubert's yen to write fiction during retirement is precipitated by her daughter's observation, "I have no idea who you were before you were Mom." The author specializes in fiction appealing to contemporary women from Baby Boomers to Thirty-Somethings.

Puffin Island relates how the historical events and social issues of the Sixties shaped the author and still reverberate in her children's lives today. *Celtic Compass, Part 1,* applies her experience in a "blended family" of the Sixties—before that term was coined—to present-day realities. *Celtic Compass, Part II,* explores the challenge of divided loyalties faced by members of a blended family in a time of crisis. *Celtic Circle~for Better, for Worse* examines how antagonistic members of a blended family channel their bitterness and grief. In *Celtic Circle~Forever*, hostile members of a blended family seek pathways to reconciliation following tragedy.

In addition to her five novels, Ms. Schubert is a contributing author to short story anthologies, *Hauntings from the Snake River Plain* and *Family Recipes from the Snake River Plain*. All of her works are available as ebooks or paperbacks from www.amazon.com or www.sunwaypress.com.

Sherry continues to live and write on the family farm. For the record, she did shake the hand of President Kennedy, and she did play the guitar… badly.

www.ingramcontent.com/pod-product-compliance
Lightning Source LLC
Chambersburg PA
CBHW061301170626
46817CB00001B/4